Dripping Blood II

Norma Linenberger

PublishAmerica
Baltimore

Hardcover 978-1-4512-0160-4
Softcover 978-1-4489-4425-5
PUBLISHED BY PUBLISHAMERICA, LLLP
www.publishamerica.com
Baltimore

Printed in the United States of America

Dedication

This book is dedicated to my husband Leo and family, Cheryl, Elva, Deborah, James, Valerie, Jacqueline and Jeff. Grandchildren Milah, Morgan, Dayton and Cayden.

Special Thanks to:

Trent Rose and his staff in the technology department at the Salina Public Library, Salina, Kansas for their help in the formation of my new novel, "Dripping Blood II." It was greatly appreciated.

Table of Contents

Introduction

Once again another mass killer is on the loose in the bludgeoning, carving, horrendous deaths of numerous victims known as "The Notorious Serial Killer of St. Louis, Missouri. Mystery sprinkled with murder and suspense infiltrates the mind in the following pages as the characters come to life. For your reading pleasure the following chapters are incorporated with a wide variety of unique and uncommon settings encompassing the inscrutable deaths of a variety of characters.

As a new author of my third book "The Final Floor Zombies II," I hope you will enjoy the introduction of a new cast of characters, setting and plot that is involved in the writing of this book. It was a fulfilling experience and "thank you" for reading "The Final Floor Zombies II."

Chapter 1
Lights Out
2003

Jane Linton's sleepless nights on her cot in the privacy of her cell are filled with the same self pity, remorse and self loathing at what unfolded the past eight years in Rockwood, Illinois. A mixed bag of emotions courses through her veins as she relives every dastardly deed she performed while living as a resident of the Rockwood Apartment Complex 1995-2003. Twelve tombstones in the Rockwood Cemetery account for the lives that were snatched at the hands of the Notorious Serial Killer from Rockwood, Illinois, Jane Linton. She lies in the dark night reliving her evil acts of violence as she preyed on her innocent victims till their last breath. No, she's not alone in her thoughts tonight because she hears a cough, a soft crying whimper, occasionally words spoken to one's self in anguish.

As the seemingly long night stretches endlessly ahead of Jane she recounts the twelve murders as if they occurred yesterday. She asks herself, "Why did she kill Fern Taylor? What had Fern ever done to her? We had barely spoken to each other in the past. She really was a nice, older woman and I'm sorry I did that. After all, I am older now and wouldn't want that done to me, even though tonight I lie on a prison cot for the rest of my life.

Then there's Bob Cain, such a nice, older gentleman. Bob and Ella always acknowledged her in the hall with a cheery greeting plus a little conversation. Bob was always making a witty remark, a joke of course. Bob didn't deserve to die from the venom of a snake in his heart and blood stream. Why did she kill Bob? Now Ella lives alone and is very fearful! Am I jealous of Ella because Ella had a husband and I didn't? Oh! That's absurd!" Jane began to cry softly as these killings go through her mind one by one. "Also, let's not forget George Sloan. Good old George a devoted, wonderful husband, father of two children and his wife, Mary. Neither did George deserve to have his life snuffed out" Once again Jane wept silently as her thoughts kept coming in spite of the hard shell she encased herself in. "Mary Blane! Yes, she remembers Mary Blane. Not only could she cry when she thinks of her, Jane feels like killing her own self for allowing Mary to endure such an agonizing, untimely death. Poor Charles! He and his family suffered tremendously at her hands. She deprived Charles and his family of a mother, mother in law and grandmother. Why did she bring the pit bull into the elevator to kill Mary Blane? Mary had never crossed her at any time and neither had Charles and his family. Then why are all these killings taking place? What's happening? What went wrong? Will this killing desire ever decrease?" Jane says a prayer out loud to our Lord while the other prisoners are sleeping soundly, oblivious of the turmoil that's going on in Jane's mind.

Then there's Rich, his wife Lila and Pearl. Jane asks herself, "Why did I kill them with seeping gas in the elevator? I know they didn't always answer me when I tried to initiate a conversation with them. Somehow, they knew of my past history in a mental institution for killing three women three years ago and they didn't want anything to do with me. I'm sure they were scared of me and they had every right to be. It doesn't really bother me that I killed them because of the way they treated me. Even Rich would look the other way when he saw me coming into a room.

Yes, I know the elevator crash was the worst killings of all of them because of the amount of people's lives that I took. I guess my killing instincts were really bad then. I wished I wouldn't have killed those five people because I enjoyed their company and actually played cards with them sometimes. Sue and I ate at the pot luck suppers across the table from them and we also visited with them in the recreation parlor. They didn't ignore us like Rich, Lila and Pearl.

Now, when I think back to years ago I remember what my problem was. Guess what? I hated my own mother for years when I killed those three women. I remember what I said when I killed Fern Taylor. I hate old people like you and I'll never get old because I'll see to that. You won't get out of this elevator alive and she didn't. But things didn't quite work out that way. I'm seventy four years old, still living and I'm in this women's prison for life. I guess I'm what you call a lifer. I'm not getting much sleep tonight because of everything that's going through my mind and will continue to do so as long as I live."

An assessment was made when Jane was admitted to St. Louis Prison for Women. She is confined in a maximum security cell and is isolated in the prison yard where the inmates spend an hour outside exercising, playing ball etc....

Jane says, "When you're in prison for life things aren't easy on a typical day. I arise at five o'clock in the morning, shower, eat breakfast with my fellow inmates and go to work in the prison laundry until it's time for my lunch break. After that I resume working until four o'clock, eat supper and spend an hour in the prison yard. After that I come inside with the other prison inmates and read or watch television for an hour or two and then it's Lights Out at ten o'clock pm. Doesn't sound too interesting, does it? Well, it isn't!Oh by the way, my cell number is 15 if you ever want to come and visit me. I don't get any company because Sue's too far away in Rockwood, Illinois although she does come to see me occasionally."

As soon as Jane stretches and yawns a female prison warden strolls up and down past the cell blocks yelling, "It's five o'clock! Time to get up! Get up, everybody," as she bangs her club against the cell bars. "Breakfast is at 6:00 AM and you're to report for work at 7:00 AM in your department. Let's get moving! Linton!" I said, "Get Up! What is your problem?" Jane said "I don't have a problem. I'm just tired. I didn't get much sleep last night." The prison warden said, "Oh," and continued to scream out orders. "Girls, it's time to get up, shower, dress and walk single file down to the dining room. That's more like it!"

Jane lined up with the other women prisoners as they picked up their trays and proceeded down the cafeteria line. Jane was very tired with a decrease in appetite as she forced her weary body through twelve, long, grueling hours of labor in the prison laundry. Jane has made a few friends since she's in prison but not while she's been working because they keep them too busy. When Jane is on a lunch break she exchanges a few words with her friends and then continues to work. Her new found friends are Alice Bell 65, Sharon Mayer 70 and Molly Levins 59. Alice has been in prison for seven years for the murder of her brother in law. She has a three year prison sentence left to serve because of her ten year conviction. Alice is originally from East St. Louis, Illinois, a secretary by trade and never been married. Sharon also has a life sentence the same as Jane for the murder of a family of five people. A mother, father and three children were shot to death execution style by Sharon five years ago in the basement of their home. Sharon was working for the family at the time of the killings. To this day Sharon Mayer has no remorse for the killings because of the inhuman treatment she received at the hands of the Pelton family. One evening after supper Sharon recalled to her friends an account of the shootings:

She was infuriated at the Pelton family and their children for the verbal abuse they had exposed her to. The night before Sharon bought herself a revolver at the local hardware store and went back to their residence. When she entered the house the father screamed at her and the whole family chimed in. She was completely innocent of the accusation and she vowed to get even with them. When they were relaxing in their recreation parlor in the basement, sitting on the sofa with their backs to the door, Sharon approached them saying, "You've treated me shabbily for the last time. I want every one of you to kneel in front of me or I'll shoot you just as you are setting there right now." Everybody including the father started screaming and crying as they said, "Please don't shoot us, please. We'll treat you better. We didn't mean anything by it." The mother was beside herself with fear for her family as she cried and started praying. "Lord, please help us, please." Sharon continued on her rampage calling them one by one to kneel in front of her. "Dave, kneel in front of me execution style," Sharon said, "I held the gun to Dave's head and pulled the trigger. Bang! His head exploded as his brains shot out onto his wife's face and his children as he slumped to the floor." Blood poured forth uncontrollably and ran onto the floor in a stream. By now his head was dangling by some muscles and tendons off his neck. His wife Angela and children Tom, Mark and Cindy were screaming as she ordered them forward one by one.

Sharon continued to recall the events to her three friends: "I said, Angela, kneel in front of me execution style. As she did I placed the gun to her throat and pulled the trigger. Bang! Her head fell to the floor with volumes of blood gushing out of her neck. By now half the carpet in the room was drenched with blood, brains and bodily fluid." Sharon said, "Who wants to be next?" She laughed as she called twelve year old Tom forward saying, "Tom, kneel in front of me execution style. I held the gun to Tom's head just like I did to Daddy's and blew his damn brains up to the ceiling as his body hit the floor. This added even more blood, brains and bodily fluid to what was already on the floor. Actually, I could feel Tom's brains dripping off the ceiling onto my head."

Sharon then said, "Mark, It's your turn to kneel in front of me execution style. I held the gun pointing face down to the top of his head and pulled the trigger and Bang! Mark's head split four ways exposing the complete inside of his head and skull cavity. Both eyes were blown out of their sockets as were others lying on the floor."

Sharon said laughingly, "One more to go. Sandy, it's your turn now. Kneel in front of me execution style. I pointed the gun to Sandy's throat as she pleaded. I pulled the trigger just like I did Mommies and her head fell onto the floor and split into three sections bleeding profusely." Sharon laughed to herself as she recalled, "After the last execution we felt like we were swimming in a sea of blood."

One by one Alice, Sharon and Molly recounted the reasons for their prison confinement. Molly gave an account of what brought her to prison. Molly Levins, 59, is from Plattsville, Indiana as she recalls: "Like they say, I'm also a lifer. I'll be in prison for the rest of my life because of the ten older people I killed while working as a registered nurse in Plattsville Community Hospital years ago. In a way I'm not really sorry for what I did because all they did was whine and complain about their aches and pains. The only control I had over that was to inject them with pain medication, namely Morphine. I simply got tired of listening to that crap so gradually I injected one a month the double amount of Morphine they were accustomed to and within an hour they died. I thought possibly I could get by with this but it didn't work out that way. After it continued month after month I was finally apprehended, taken to court, found guilty and given a life sentence." Jane asked her, "How long have you been in prison?" Molly said. "Twelve years."

Is Jane going to recount why she's serving a life sentence in the St. Louis Women's Prison? Let's see.

All of a sudden Alice, Sharon and Molly all chimed in unison and asked Jane, "What brought you here to the St. Louis Prison for Women? You don't look like the type like the rest of us." Jane said, "It's a long story but I will tell you. Gather around."

Jane gave this account to the small group of inmates: "Many years ago I was convicted of killing three women whom I personally couldn't relate to. I recall at the time I had a deep seated hatred for women much older than myself. So I conveniently eliminated every one of them from the picture with a gunshot to the heart. I was institutionalized for ten years, heavily medicated and doing very well. After I served ten years I was released to my family and started a new life with them in another city. As the years progressed I became busy with my job and negligent with my medication. There were days I literally forgot to take any of my medicine, yet other days I would take it religiously. Not only that, my medication was getting very expensive and I could hardly afford to purchase it. Yes, I know I could've tried to get a cheaper version of the pill but I failed to do that. So consequently, given all these facts, my mind reversed and I acquired my old killing tendencies again. My first killing was in 1995, an 85 year old woman in the Rockwood Apartment Complex where my daughter Sue and I lived in Rockwood, Illinois. Sue is my only daughter and my husband, Bob, passed away before the first killing in 1995. I stabbed Fern Taylor in the heart numerous times in the elevator until she slumped to the floor in death. She tried to beat me with her cane several times but I overpowered her." Alice asked Jane, "What time of the day did this happen?" Jane answered, "This killing happened at 6:00 am across the street from Dan's Diner. I knew that Fern went for coffee and a bite to eat every morning around this time at the diner so I kept an eye on Fern for several mornings to make sure this was her normal routine, following the same pattern every day. The police were unable to trace the killing to me and I kept quiet about what I did. This is how I got by eluding the police many times.

The second killing was a man by the name of George Sloan, 82 years old, also residing at the Rockwood Apartment Complex. I knew George and his wife were going to a pot luck supper that night in the recreation Parlor. I disguised myself, voice and all, and asked George for all the money he had. I remember he didn't have much money with him and that irritated me so I shot him execution style facing Mary with Mary crying, screaming and pleading. I remember blood and brains seeping down the wall in tiny rivulets like a little stream. I'm sure he was dead instantly as I fled the elevator and out of the complex. The police had no clues or leads to George Sloan's murder either so I went undetected as usual.

The victim of the third killing was Bob Cain an 86 year old retired school teacher. Bob went downstairs on the elevator every night at the same time to get his mail. This time I decided to use the rattlesnake technique. One of my friends in the city of Rockwood harbored a 6 ft. long Arizona rattlesnake and I had access to him. Before Bob got on the elevator I quickly pulled a box into the elevator with the snake in it and watched it crawl out. I dashed out of the elevator knowing that Bob would be coming in shortly. When Bob entered the elevator the rattlesnake attacked him immediately puncturing his chest and heart. Bob died in the ambulance on the way to the Rockwood Hospital. The police had no clues or leads as to Bob Cains death so I went scot free. Nobody was the wiser.

The fourth killing was very unusual, unique and different. The victim Jean Blane, 81, was the mother of the Chief of Police, Charles Blane. Yeah, I kind of took a chance there, didn't I?

One evening I happened to know that she was going on the elevator to play Bridge with some of her lady friends so I pulled one of my friends' pit bulls into the elevator before Jean Blane entered and I dashed out. The pit bull was raving mad and snarling the whole time. When Jean Blane stepped into the elevator he literally tore her to pieces. Some of her body parts were actually lying on the floor like her eyes and a large chunk of her cheek and hair. They said he bit her in the jugular vein in her neck and a pool of blood had settled on the floor and ceiling. Jean Blane must've passed away instantly. The police department was never able to figure that killing out either.

They went to great lengths but to no avail.

The next murders are multiple killings. I "gassed," yes, I said "gassed" three people, a man and two women in an elevator headed to a Bingo game. I knew they were going to take the elevator so the night before they got in I hurriedly opened a small trap door outside the elevator and poured some gas into a small glass jar that was labeled "for gas only" and shut the door. Once the elevator started humming the gas came seeping through a vent inside the elevator. They were gassed in about five or ten minutes. The police had no clue or leads to this murder either. No one knew who engineered this killing except me.

The last five killings were done all at one time. This time it was the cable technique. One evening I overheard a conversation in the Recreation Parlor about five people that were going to meet on the elevator to go to the Recreation Parlor to play Bingo. The day before they got killed I opened the trap door looked in, saw the cables and decided to splice them with the cable cutter I bought at the hardware store. It worked! The next night when they got into the elevator around 6:30 PM I stood on a bench where I couldn't be seen. When they pushed the start button I immediately spliced the cables and the elevator went crashing to the basement floor. It left a gaping black hole in the floor because everyone in the complex went to look at the scene including my daughter and I. There were three men and two women that got killed. They were worse than killed. Their heads were dismembered from their bodies, their eyes were lying on the floor and rats were gnawing on their neck and feet. Heads, feet and legs were rolling around in blood on the basement floor. The odor that permeated the air was unbearable so the police had to wear gas masks to control the odor. We could even smell the stench in our apartments.

Yes, I know your all wondering how I was apprehended. Well, get this! One evening I knew my own daughter, Sue, was in the elevator with some other tenants so I stepped in completely disguised with the intention of robbing my daughter, Sue, and the others. At this point I was the worst I'd ever been mentally. I approached Sue with a revolver and asked her to hand over her money. Guess what happened? The elevator made a grinding noise, a shaky jerk and my revolver fell to the floor. Sue quickly reached down, picked it up, pointed it at me and said, "Remove your mask or I'll remove it for you. I reached for my mask pulling it down and revealing my identity. If Sue wouldn't have grabbed the revolver there's a good possibility I would've shot all of them."

Sue and the other tenants were shocked beyond belief. Sue said, "Mother, it's you! How could you do this! Kill twelve people! Mother, that's awful! No wonder you were always conveniently gone at the time of a murder. I always thought that was strange. I'm going to do one of the hardest things I've ever done in my entire life and that's call the police on my own mother. And that's exactly what she did! Even though I told her I did it for a joke pretending I was the assailant but the joke backfired on me. Right?

The police came to the complex, asked me some questions, handcuffed me and took me to the police station. I was in jail for awhile and then taken to St. Louis District Court for a trial. I was found guilty and sentenced for life in the St. Louis Prison for Women.

Well, that concludes my story and as you can see this chain of events that I related to you are what led me to where I am now."

Alice, Sharon and Molly all agreed it was quite a story and asked her, "Jane, did you ever consider writing a non-fiction book or autobiography about your life?" Jane said, "No, that never crossed my mind but now that you mention it that's something to think about. It would give me something to do in the evenings besides watch television."

By this time Molly, Alice, Sharon and Jane are through eating their lunch as they had recalled all the events that led them to prison. They proceeded back to the prison laundry where they filled the commercial machines to wash and dry the clothes plus a machine to mangle the bedding and everything else that is required in a laundry from 6:00AM till 3:00PM. At 3:00PM the inmates are free to do whatever they want. From 4:00PM to 5:00PM they go out into the prison yard, even in winter as is the case, to play ball, exercise, or just visit with each other. From 5:30PM to 7:00PM they eat supper and from 7:00PM till 10:00PM they can go to the prison lounge to watch television, play cards, have a cup of coffee, whatever they want. At 10:00PM all the inmates have to be in their cell blocks for the night. A female prison warden walks up and down the wide hall and yells, "Lights Out! It's 10:00 o'clock! Lights Out!"

Morning comes early in prison especially at 5:00AM in the winter. The inmates get up, shower and get dressed to meet the day. They all walk to the cafeteria line as a group picking up their breakfast and then back to the laundry, supper and free time until Lights Out at 10:00PM.

Some prisons, like the St. Louis Prison for Women, offer a course in leather crafts which the women inmates work at and sell to the public at various events in St. Louis. On Sunday mornings there are non-denominational church services and religion classes for those that want to attend. There is also an auditorium with a stage and movie screen for plays, performances and movies once a month for the inmates. Jane has attended several movies and plays with Molly, Alice and Sharon since she's been at the prison for something to do.

Sharon, Molly, Alice and Jane are taking a course in leather crafts every Tuesday evening at 7:30PM. Their instructor, Mrs. Cloves walks from table to table giving assistance wherever needed. The women inmates are allowed to keep the small leather articles they make but the larger articles are sold within the city. Quite a few of the inmates are enrolled in the leather craft class and Mrs. Cloves, the instructor, is in need of an assistant to help her so Jane volunteered. Jane and her friends enjoy their class very much and look forward to the classes every Tuesday evening at 7:30PM.

When the inmates received their mail this morning Jane received a letter from Sue asking how she was. Sue sounded deeply despondent and was tired of her dull, boring job at the Murphy Finance Company because it's her only source of income. Sue said, "Mother, I'd like to come up to see you but I can't drive, don't have a car and I will not come with Marcus Reil that's for sure. I don't like him anymore or his slimy friends he hangs around with at the Rockwood Apartment Complex. They are so disgusting! When I can afford it, maybe in spring, I will take the bus to St. Louis, Missouri for a couple of days and stay at the same motel that I stayed at the last time. Remember? It was a cheap motel but that was okay as long as it was nice and reasonably clean which it was, I'll stay there again." Jane was glad to hear from Sue once again, because she hadn't received a letter from her for quite awhile. Immediately, that evening after supper during her free time, she sat down and wrote Sue a letter. Jane once again described different aspects of prison life to Sue, which she had done numerous times before, but each time with a little bit different news. This time Jane told Sue, "I have a new volunteer job as a leather crafts assistant in class every Tuesday evening at 7:30PM. Our instructor is Mrs. Cloves and I like her very much. We get along great together and the inmates are allowed to keep the small leather projects they make free of charge. The larger projects are sold at different functions and events within the city of St. Louis.

Jane also told Sue, "It was very cold and snowing the other day and we were required by the state authorities to go out in the prison yard for twenty minutes for fresh air and then come back in." Jane asked Sue, "How's the weather been in Rockwood? Cold and snowy? Anything new at the apartment complex? Well, I guess I'll close this letter for tonight. I want to watch a little television and then it's Lights Out at 10:00PM. Please answer my letter soon." Mother

In the meantime, Sue is very despondent and depressed about her mother's confinement in prison for life, her hatred for Marcus, her dull, uninteresting job at the Murphy Finance Company, her insecurity and suicidal tendencies. If only those tendencies wouldn't invade her mind so often. She slashed her wrists once! What if she did it again? She didn't trust herself to be alone anymore because there's no telling what she'd do.

Her suicidal tendencies scare her the most! Sue remembers when she slashed her wrists that time and had to be taken to Rockwood Hospital for several days to recuperate. After that episode she lost volumes of blood but that doesn't explain her hatred for Marcus. The doctors thought her loss of blood might've caused her brain to malfunction. She doesn't know! But the fear is there, nonetheless. Maybe she should move to St. Louis, Missouri closer to her mother and then she could see her every week? She's thought about it, but she hasn't mentioned anything to her mother yet. She knows her mother would be extremely happy. After all, what has her seventy four year old mother got to live for? In prison for the rest of her life? She might as well be close to her mother and spend the rest of their days together, since that's the only close, living relative she has. She hasn't committed herself to anything, only psychologically.

Then again, Sue thinks she could squeeze a trip on the bus to St. Louis out of her paycheck the next time around. She would like to apply for a job at different finance companies after checking the "Want Ads" in the St. Louis newspaper. She'll pick up the St. Louis newspaper on her way to work tomorrow.

The next evening on the way home from work, Sue stopped in Joe's Convenience Store, purchased the St Louis Herald, slipped it under her arm and continued her walk back to the bus stop. After her supper she thumbed through the newspaper until she came upon the "Want Ads." She searched through the business ads until she found some that would apply to her. She also looked at the apartments for rent and found a lot of them that were reasonably priced and close to the downtown business area. This got Sue's adrenalin going. Now she was anxious to make the bus trip to St. Louis, see her mother and check the apartments and jobs. She called the bus terminal to check what time the Greyhound bus left for St. Louis and they said "everyday at 8:00AM and 12:30PM." She checked with her office the next day and was told she could take several days of vacation time off with pay. Sue agreed to that and was on her way to St. Louis on Tuesday morning at 8:00AM, bright and early. The bus stopped at Whitesville, Illinois for dinner and then continued on to St. Louis,

Missouri arriving around 8:00PM. Sue took a taxi to the St. Louis Motel she stayed at two months ago. Like Sue said, "It's inexpensive, nice and clean and not far from the women's prison. Actually, on a nice day a person could walk over there."

When she arrived at the motel she unpacked her suitcase, scanned the apartments for rent and the business ads for a job, watched television for awhile and went to bed.

The next morning Sue got up extra early, showered, dressed and took a taxi to downtown St. Louis where the business offices were that required help. She put her application in at all of them and was told, "We will call you back if we are interested in hiring you." Sue said, "Thank you" and left.

She ate lunch in a local diner and immediately took a taxi to an area where there were a group of apartment houses, plus more down the street and across. Sue went with the landlady, Mrs. Styles, to look at the apartments and told her, "My name is Sue Benson and I'm from Rockwood, Illinois. My mother is confined to the St. Louis Women's Prison for life and the only way I can be near to my mother, Jane, is to move up here. I've been thinking about this for some time now and I still haven't made a definite decision. After viewing the apartments Sue said, "The apartments are nice, clean and spacious, which is what I like."

Sue took Mrs. Styles' name, address and telephone number in case she would mail her first month's rent. Sue told her, "I need time to think about this whole undertaking, a new job, a different place to live in and a different city. It isn't easy to re-locate, especially to a big city like St. Louis, Missouri." The landlady, Mrs. Styles, said, "That's fine, whatever your comfortable with. I'll go along with that."

Sue ate supper early and went to see her mother, Jane, at the prison on Sunday. Jane was so glad to see Sue she almost cried because she never gets any company. Since Jane is in maximum security there can be no physical contact between Sue and Jane. They each pick up a phone and carry on with their conversation, a glass screen between them. This room is reserved for phone visitation only.

Sue told Jane of her intentions of moving to St. Louis and Jane was overcome with joy that she was practically speechless. Jane said, "Sue, that's a wonderful idea. I'm so happy for both of us, because this way we can see each other often, instead of just a couple of times a year. When are you planning on moving up here?" Sue said, "As soon as I get my refund from the Rockwood Apartment Complex, pack all my belongings and rent a moving truck to have everything hauled up here. I have to notify my boss that I'm quitting my job, say goodbye to Pastor Hale and all my friends at the apartment complex and otherwise. I'm sure everybody will be real surprised, especially because I'm leaving on such short notice." Today their visitation time was short so Sue and Jane said their goodbyes with Sue saying," Mother, I'll be back soon." Jane said, "Okay" and was almost in tears saying, "I'll be waiting." Jane looked after Sue with a tearful, sad look on her face till Sue exited the room. Sue called a taxi at the front entrance of the prison for a ride to the motel.

In the meantime the next morning Sue called the landlady, Mrs. Styles, and told her, "I made a quick decision to re-locate to St. Louis, Missouri, mainly because of my mother, Jane." She also told her, "I will be sending you a check for the first months' rent when I get back to Rockwood." Mrs. Styles was delighted that Sue was moving in.

Before Sue left St. Louis she notified Grove's Financial Company and told them she would be at the St. Louis Motel. She received a call from them this morning asking her if she wants to fill the position as secretary and she said, "Yes." Before she left for Rockwood she went to the Groves Financial Company where she would be working for last minute details. Sue arrived back in Rockwood at 11:30PM in the evening and took a taxi to the apartment complex. When she walked in she encountered Marcus in the hallway. He said, "Hi, Sue, how are you?" Sue came up close to him, looked him straight in the face without blinking an eye and said, "I'd still like to kill you!" Marcus didn't say anything and quickly walked away.

Chapter 2
Life in the Big City

For the next several weeks Sue's cloud of depression seemed to lift considerably because of her anticipation to move to St. Louis, Missouri. She has everything packed except a few, last minute articles. Sue went to the office on the main floor and asked for the refund coming back to her as she is planning on leaving throughout the next week. She took her goodbyes from her personal friends, acquaintances and relatives at the apartment complex plus the Murphy Finance Co, Pastor Hale and other different businesses.

Her relationship with Marcus has come to a complete standstill. When she passes him in the hall and the occasion does arise because you can't live in an apartment complex without encountering Marcus sometime or other she either snubs him or glares at him and walks on by. Strange? What's Sue's problem? Why does she dislike Marcus? He's always befriended her, taking her to see her mother in jail and in prison, plus taking Sue to downtown St. Louis to hunt for her mother when she escaped the St. Louis Prison for Women. There are numerous other times he's come to her assistance and furnished transportation for her. What happened?

Secretly Marcus is glad when Sue moves out of her apartment. He's glad to see her go because she's threatened to kill him several times and he doesn't trust her. Actually, he's scared of her. Wouldn't you be? She might have inherited her mother's killing tendencies. Why is he the only one in the apartment complex that gets treated this way? Marcus doesn't ride the elevator anymore but takes the back stairs for fear he might encounter Sue on the elevator.

This evening he spent a few quiet hours in his apartment watching television and eating a snack before retiring to his bedroom. At exactly 7:00PM the phone rang and Marcus answered, "Hello… Hello….Hello… Who is this? May I ask who's calling, please?" No answer so Marcus hung up figuring someone had the wrong number. He continued to watch the movie which was holding his interest in spite of the disruption. Once again at exactly 8:00PM the phone rang and Marcus answered saying, "Hello….Hello…Hello….Who is this? Who's calling?" No answer but all of a sudden Marcus heard a heavy, labored breathing into the phone. He asked again, "Who is this? This is the second time you've called. What do you want? Why don't you speak?" All he heard was a continuous, labored, heavy, breathing but no voice. By this time Marcus was disgusted and screamed into the phone saying, "Get off the phone and if you persist in calling again I'm going to call the police" and hung up. He went back to watching the movie but couldn't concentrate after this last telephone interruption. He got up and checked his apartment door which was locked securely. So he sat back on the recliner and continued to watch television but his mind was not at ease. At this point he had forgotten the plot of the movie and was so mad he thought about discontinuing watching the movie and retiring for the evening. All of a sudden the phone rang again at 9:00PM and Marcus picked up the phone and said, "Hello….Hello…Hello…, Who in the hell is this? Get off the damn phone and quit calling me or I'll call the police department." Not only after the first call but after the second and third, the calls are always blocked so there's no way of tracing the call. Marcus called the police and Officer Boyle who was new to the police department came out and asked

Marcus some questions, namely, did Marcus have any idea who was making the calls to him? Marcus said "Yes, I think its Sue Benson and she lives upstairs. Officer, her mother, Jane, is the person that killed twelve people here in the Rockwood Apartment Complex from 1995—2003." Officer Boyle made the remark, "I remember hearing about that but I forgot where it happened. So, this was the place?" Marcus said, "Yes, and her daughter, Sue Benson, is acting very strange when she passes me in the hallway, either snubbing me or coming up to me and threatening to kill me. Officer Boyle, asked Marcus, "Where is her mother now?" Marcus replied," She's in the St. Louis Women's Prison for life." Officer Boyle asked, "Did you do anything to upset her?" Marcus said, "No, in fact we were very good friends until this happened with her mother and she turned on me like an animal. I furnished the transportation for Sue when her mother was in jail, the trial in St. Louis and numerous other times. When she really started acting weird was after she became despondent, slashed her wrists and was admitted to Rockwood Hospital for observation. She lost volumes of blood according to the doctor so maybe that affected her mind. I don't know. I don't understand this because I'm the only person here in the complex that she treats this way. Why?" Officer Boyle said, "I don't know, Marcus. I don't doubt for one minute that you're telling the truth and I also know for a fact that you are the assistant deputy at the police department." Marcus said, "Yes, that's right Officer Boyle, so you know I wouldn't be making everything up." Officer Boyle said," No, I know you're not. Well, I guess I'll go up to her apartment and see if I can have a talk with her. Thank you for the information, Marcus, and hopefully we can clarify this matter for you. I will also check the roster at the police department for minor offenders that might be into harassing people by phone etc…. I'll get back to you, Marcus, but it might take a couple of days. Goodbye!" Marcus said, "Goodbye, Officer Boyle."

Marcus could hear Officer Boyle take the elevator up to the next floor. Since there was no reason to stay up any longer he decided to go on to bed. He thinks the telephone calls are over for the night especially since Officer Boyle was talking to her this evening. Officer Boyle knocked on her door several times and Sue answered immediately. She said, "Hello Officer, is something wrong?" He said, "Yes, there is. I came up here this evening in response to a complaint from one of the tenants here at the complex. This person received three, consecutive, harassing telephone calls with no speaking only heavy breathing. He thinks the telephone calls are coming from your apartment. Is that correct, Sue?" Sue said, "No Officer, I just returned from the restaurant downtown where I ate supper and then went shopping for awhile being careful to get back before dark." Officer Boyle made the remark, "This tenant said that when you pass him in the hall you either snub him or walk up to him and threaten to kill him."Sue said, "Officer, I don't even know what you're talking about. I've never done anything like that in my life. I'm moving to St. Louis next weekend and don't have time for trivial jokes of that nature. Can you tell me the tenant's name that's accusing me of doing this?" Officer Boyle said, "No Sue, I'm sorry I can't because of the Confidentiality Clause." Sue continued defending her accusation vehemently saying, "I'm sorry officer, but I can't help you any further. Did you have any other questions? If not, I'm going to bed for the night" Officer Boyle said, "No, that will be all. Sorry, I hope I didn't inconvenience you. Thank you." Sue said, "Thank you" and closed the door behind him. Sue is thinking. "Was that Marcus that called the police? How dare he do such a thing? If it was Marcus, even though I'm moving next week, he might be sorry. The nerve!"

Towards morning, at exactly 3:00AM, Marcus was awakened from a sound sleep with an incessant banging on his apartment door. At first he thought he was dreaming but the longer he listened and looked at the time he knew it was for real. Someone was actually banging on his door! He decided to get up and see what was going on and confront the person. As soon as he opened the door the banging stopped and Marcus stood there dumbfounded and slightly embarrassed. He closed the door knowing full well that he couldn't go back to sleep so he made some coffee, watched television for awhile wondering who would be up during the night banging on tenants doors. Could it have been Sue again up to her scary tactics? What was wrong with her and why always him? Isn't that strange? He didn't want to call the police during the night so what should he do? Wait till the next day, I guess. So he went back to bed since it was now after 4:00AM in the morning. Besides this evening he would be conducting their monthly meeting in the Recreation Parlor in regards to different issues that have surfaced since the last meeting plus the incident last night in regards to him.

The complex tenants filed into the Recreation Parlor for their monthly meeting that night but not Sue. She won't be found anywhere near Marcus. Tonight he is conducting the monthly meeting in regards to discussions about a variety of issues concerning the Rockwood Apartment Complex. After everything had been discussed at length Marcus brought up the issue of the three anonymous telephone calls plus the banging on his door at 3:00AM in the morning.

Marcus asked the tenants, "Have any of you received three anonymous telephone calls an hour apart with no talking just a heavy, labored breathing? My calls came last night at exactly 7:00PM, 8:00PM and 9:00PM. This morning at 3:00AM I woke up from a sound sleep to an incessant banging. I got up and answered the door with no one there. Have any of you experienced anything of this nature this past week? Don't be afraid to speak up tonight. Because if you have please come forward and talk about it because it could be a potentially dangerous situation." Everybody in the Recreation Parlor was silent as Marcus waited for someone to raise their hand or to speak up. Nobody came forward so Marcus said, "Very well, that answers my question. I guess I'm the only tenant that received the telephone calls and had their apartment door banged on. I have an idea who's behind all this but I'm not at liberty to say until I'm completely positive. Incidentally after the last telephone call at 9:00PM that night I called the police department and they sent an officer to my apartment to talk to me. I told the officer whom I thought was behind all this and he went to the tenant's apartment and questioned them. All he got was a denial about the telephone calls so I guess we're stumped on this situation also. This concludes the meeting for tonight but let me remind you, if you experience anything of this nature in the future like we have discussed this evening please report to me as I am still an Assistant Deputy of the Rockwood Police Department. Okay?" All the tenants nodded their heads and departed.

On the way back to Marcus' apartment he encountered Sue in the hall coming towards him. She quickly stepped up to him screeching, "Marcus, you'd better quit accusing me of calling you and sending the police to my door. I did not place those calls." And with that she spit in Marcus' face and walked off. Marcus yelled back, "You ugly bitch, I know it was you. How can you deny it?" Sue just kept on walking. When Marcus got back to his apartment he remembered he needed to call Officer Boyle at the police department to report the incident of the banging on his apartment door the other night. Officer Boyle came out and talked to Marcus and decided to take Sue in to the police department for questioning. When he knocked on Sue's apartment door and explained the nature of his visit Sue was very belligerent and refused to go along to the police department. Officer Boyle said, "Sue, if you refuse to go to the police department I will have no alternative but to arrest you and call a backup policeman to take you by force. Then we will impose a large fine on you for resisting arrest and refusing to co-operate with an officer in the line of duty. You have your choice." Naturally, she chose to comply with Officer Boyle's orders. When they got to the police station Sue was booked in jail for the night. The next morning she was connected to a lie detector test and asked numerous questions which she failed. The lie detector test proved she was lying through the whole interrogation process. Police Chief James gave her a fine plus a two week jail sentence in spite of her moving to St. Louis, Missouri. Sue finally told the police the truth how she hated Marcus and called him on the phone three times and banged on his door at 3:00AM the next morning to scare him. The police asked Sue, "Why do you despise Marcus so much? What has he ever done to you?" Sue answered, "I don't know why but I've always had a deep seated hatred for him and I'd rather not talk about it. That's all!"

Sue spent two weeks in jail with Marcus not even going near her cell. Marcus was literally scared of her and didn't want to be in her presence. He will be glad when she moves to St. Louis, Missouri and so will Sue. Marcus often thought to himself, "I can't believe that I took her to St. Louis, Missouri to see her mother plus drive around and hunt her up when she escaped from prison. Also, the trips I made when Jane was on trial and imposing on my brother Adam and his family for lodging the length of time we were there. There were other times I took her to see Jane when she was in the hospital and in prison. That just makes me sick! Good riddance! Bad rubbish! Sue was released from jail several days ago, packed her belongings, rented a U-Haul and moved to St. Louis, Missouri. Marcus called a short meeting last night with all the tenants attending and discussed several issues, further announcing that Sue Benson was released from jail for harassing him and has now moved on to St. Louis. All the tenants breathed a sigh of relief and made remarks saying, "I'm glad she's gone because I felt uncomfortable around her." Another tenant said, "There was something about Sue, kind of eerie, scary. I can't describe it." And yet another person said, "There was something about her, she was different. There was something sinister in her personality." Of course, all the tenants knew how she harassed Marcus in spite of the way he helped her. Marcus expressed his dismay at the way he was treated by Sue and was happy she was leaving the apartment complex hoping their paths would never cross again. Everybody agreed.

St. Louis, Missouri

As soon as Sue was settled in the eight story Styles Apartment Complex she went to visit Jane at the prison on a Sunday. They went to the visitation room and picked up the phones and immediately started visiting. Jane asked, "Sue, Why did it take you two weeks longer to move up here than you thought it would?" Sue said, "Well, I might as well tell you the truth, I was in jail for two weeks. Jane said, "In jail, what on earth for? What did you do Sue to be confined to jail for two weeks? I hope it wasn't anything real bad?"

"Well, like I mentioned awhile back, I don't like Marcus and consequently don't want anything to do with him and he knows it by the way I act. One night I decided to scare him so I called him on the telephone at exactly 7:00PM, an hour later at 8:00PM and then at 9:00PM but never talking, just a lot of heavy, labored breathing. The next day towards morning I decided to bang on his apartment door and give him a good scare. Officer Boyle came by one night to talk to me about scaring Marcus and I told him that I didn't do anything like that. Later Marcus reported the banging on the door incident and I denied that also. I denied everything, mother. Later Officer Boyle came to my apartment again and decided to take me along to the police station for questioning. I got angry, refused and he said he would call another policeman and force me to go so I went along. They connected a lie detector to me noticing that when they were interrogating me I lied about everything. So they gave me a fine which I paid besides staying in jail for two weeks. That's why I was late two weeks coming to St. Louis, but I'm here now, mother, and things are fine.

How have you been besides waiting for me to come?" Jane said, "It's the same old story every day, day in and day out. Get up, go to work and go to bed. It's a repetition of this nonstop for the remainder of my life. I can hardly stand it anymore. If I wouldn't have committed any of those twelve murders I wouldn't be sitting in this women's prison today. I would be like you, out, free, doing what I want. No matter how the people were they still didn't deserve to die those horrendous deaths. I'm very, very sorry for what I did. If I would have to do it over I would not be doing those things. Everything's too late now. I should've thought of all this sooner! Sue, don't ever follow in my footsteps and wind up like me. You see what happened to me, don't you?" Sue said, "I agree with you, mother, that everything is too late and you'll just have to make the best of it from here on out. Myself I'm truly sorry it happened and I don't want that to happen to me. I guess it's time to go, mother." They hung up their phones and Sue walked out of the Visitation Room and into a waiting taxi while Jane watched with tears welling up in her eyes. Don't you suppose Jane should've thought twice before all this happened?

Sue's New Life

After Sue got back to the Styles Apartment Complex she decided to go to bed soon because she wanted to be at work extra early the next day and make a good impression for her new boss, Mr. Groves. He's so nice, after all he didn't have to hire her. He needed a person right at the moment and Sue filled the qualifications. She would be Mr. Grove's personal secretary taking care of all his personal bills, reports, appointments even to the point of buying his wife her Mother's Day or birthday gift as lots of women in a secretarial position are expected to do. Just standard procedure.

Sue awoke bright and early the next morning and got ready for her first day on her new job. She left her apartment on the third floor and took the elevator to the main lobby leaving the Styles Apartment Complex to meet the city bus on Filbin St. It was a fifteen minute ride from the Styles Apartment Complex to Grove's Financial Services in downtown St. Louis. Throughout the day Sue paid bills for Mr. Groves, filed reports, scheduled appointments, plus various office work that is required of a secretary. Sue took the evening city bus back at 5:15PM from a corner downtown. By 6:15PM in the evening she was in her apartment and getting ready to fix supper for herself. After supper she usually watched television till 10:00PM and then went to bed.

Everything is working out well for Sue, in fact she's even started her own personal checking and savings account at the Union State Bank in St. Louis. She tries to visit her mother, Jane, at least once a month. Jane is always anxious to visit with Sue about her new job, apartment, etc.... and always gets misty eyed when she leaves. Jane knows that what Sue has now in regards to her life she could've had also but she chose a different life behind bars for the remainder of her days on earth. How sad! Think about it!

Mrs. Styles, the landlord, posted a notice on the bulletin board in the community room announcing the monthly meeting the next night at 7:00PM. Sue decided to go since she had never been to any of their monthly meetings. She arrived a little earlier the next night and sat in the front row next to her neighbor, Mrs. Lands. A large group of tenants filed in and took a seat as the meeting had just started. Mrs. Styles said, "We are discussing the usual issues confronting an apartment complex of this size, 125 tenants in both buildings A and B combined. She also mentioned the issue of the rent and utilities. Everybody's rent will be increased and they will be expected to pay the water bill for this apartment." She also said, "Those of you that are paying $350.00 a month will be paying $450.00 a month plus the water bill. The reason for this increase is because our taxes on the apartment complex increased double and Mr. Styles and I discussed this and decided this is the only way to keep the complex open. If this fails we will be forced to close the buildings." The tenants were whispering among themselves and shaking their heads. Sue was utterly shocked and dismayed at the idea of moving out of her apartment she had just gotten settled in and wasn't far from the bus stop on Filbin St. Her neighbor, Mrs. Lands, seated next to her said, "I'm not moving out of here. I'd rather pay the extra $100.00 a month plus the water bill then hunt all over St. Louis for another apartment. How about you, Sue? What are you going to do? Are you moving out?" Sue said, "I'm not sure. I'm going to have to give it some thought." Mrs. Lands said, "The rent increase and water payment will go into effect next month already and that's April." Sue said, "I know."

When Sue got back to her apartment that night she sat down at the kitchen table with a pen, paper and her bankbook, doing some thinking and figuring. "There's no way I could afford to pay $450.00 a month for rent plus the water bill. I can barely afford my anti-depressant pills. And my mother, Jane, can't afford to help me so there's no one else to ask. What am I going to do? That's enough to make me sick with worry." After Sue was done figuring she went on to bed but couldn't sleep a wink for fear she might have to look for another apartment again. She was awake every hour on the hour.

The next morning as Sue was riding the bus to Grove's Financial Services she was thinking, "I don't dare mention a raise because I've only been working there about two months. Not only that, to matters worse, I don't even have enough money for my anti-depressant pills that I take faithfully. My bank account just keeps going down until it's almost depleted. I knew it was coming on but I don't know what to do about it." Should she look for another job at night? It's hard enough working during the day much less at night and she needs her sleep. Sue doesn't know what kind of action to take. Is she going to stay in her apartment or look for a cheaper place to live? She doesn't particularly want a night job but what if she has no choice? Sue's been doing a lot of thinking since Mrs. Styles made the announcement. So far she hasn't come up with a solution. Have you?

Sue decided she definitely doesn't want to get a night job because it would be too hard on her and like she said, "I need my sleep. I can't do without that." She also decided that she didn't want to resort to her mother's "way of life."

Tonight was the monthly pot luck supper and Sue was tired because she had a busy day at the office and therefore didn't feel like going. She fixed her own supper and sat in front of the television to eat.

About 6:30PM everybody was startled in their apartments when a couple of tenants were screaming and yelling saying," We've been robbed! We've been robbed! Call the police someone, please! That was all the money I had left and now I'm broke until my next paycheck. What will my wife say?"Sue came running out of her apartment saying, "What's the matter? What happened? Are you hurt?" Mr. Buhler said, "No, I'm not hurt but I just got robbed of the last $100.00 I had and I know my wife won't be very happy. What am I to do?" Sue said, "Explain to us what happened, Mr. Buhler." Mr. Buhler proceeded to say, "Mr. Jones and I were on our way down to the pot luck supper to meet our wives who had gone down earlier to take the salad down to the table. We decided to come down later and were in the elevator at this time. All of a sudden the side door to the elevator opened quickly and a disguised stranger stepped in and said, "I want both of you men to hand over your money or I will be forced to shoot you. Don't make me do that because I will if I have to. Don't tempt me." Sue said, "Did you get a good look at the stranger?" Mr. Jones said, "No, we couldn't get a very good look at him because he was dressed very slovenly and most definitely wore a hairpiece." He also wore a very ugly, hideous mask which reminded me of Halloween. His voice was almost light like a woman's yet he could reverse it to a low, masculine tone which he did. Mr. Jones remarked, "No, we didn't recognize him as anybody we knew or had previously encountered. Yeah, we were scared because we didn't know whether we were going to get shot or not. How would you feel?" Mr. Jones said, "Mr. Buhler gave him $100.00 and he turned his pockets inside out to show the stranger that he didn't have any more money on him. It was a very scary situation wouldn't you say?" Sue said," Yes, I would most certainly say so. "

In the meantime one of the tenants called the police and they interviewed Mr. Buhler and Mr. Jones. They asked for a description of the robber, his height, weight etc... They took this description to the police station to see if they could connect him with the repeat offenders. Officer Brown and Officer Smith would be in contact with Mr. Buhler and Mr. Jones within a couple of days. Several days later the police department contacted Mr. Jones and Mr. Buhler telling them the description and type of offense they had experienced in the elevator didn't match anything they had on file. So the police department reached a dead end.

An Emergency Meeting

An important meeting was posted on the bulletin board yesterday and will be held at 7:00PM this evening in the Community Room. Mrs. Styles will be conducting the meeting in regards to the robbery in the elevator. There was a good attendance in spite of people having to take the elevator instead of the back stairs.

Mrs. Styles made the comment, "I called this meeting this evening to bring to your attention the recent robbery of Sam Buhler and Horace Jones in the elevator last week. Sam was robbed of $100.00 and Horace didn't have any money with him. The disguised stranger was unidentifiable by Horace, Sam or the police department. In the near future please refrain from carrying more than $10.00 with you when leaving the apartment to take the elevator. A similar situation occurred in Rockwood, Illinois several months ago only worse with twelve people losing their lives at the Rockwood Apartment Complex. How many of you recall that?" Almost everybody raised their hand and started talking among themselves. Mrs. Styles said, "I repeat, when you enter the elevator please don't have any more than $10.00 on your person. Thank You! Now on to the next issue at hand which is the problem of your rent and water payment. There are a number of you that are in arrears in your payments which have to be brought up to date. Please make it a point to be paid up by the last day of this month or you will be evicted. Please bear in mind that we cannot tolerate late payments because of our expenses, taxes and the upkeep of the apartments. Your promptness will be appreciated in this matter. Are there any questions? Please feel free to address them to the assembly. No questions? Very well then. Thank you. This meeting is adjourned." Everybody got up to leave mumbling and grumbling to themselves saying, "I think I'm going to move out of here and find myself a cheaper place to live because it's getting too expensive in here, yet I hate to go through all that trouble." Another person said, "I'm scared that these robberies will escalate into actual shootings and murders and I don't want to be around to witness that like the tenants at the Rockwood Apartment Complex in Rockwood, Illinois." And yet another resident made the remark, "My name is Joan Brier and I'm going to start looking for a different apartment tomorrow morning. I can't afford to pay more rent plus the water payment so my daughter and I are going to check out the apartments for rent and see what we can find. Something I hope! How about the rest of you?" A large crowd of people were discussing the issue at hand and also threatening to leave if the situation did not improve one hundred percent. What do think? Would you want to live under these circumstances? I wouldn't!"

Sue's bank account at Union State Bank is slowly depleting and her finances are looking very dim like everybody else's because of the increase in the rent and water payment. She can't afford her antidepressants which she now does without and is not holding up too good. Sue is having a hard time getting up in the mornings for work in spite of going to bed early the night before. Her work performance is not up to par, being reprimanded by her boss Mr. Grove on certain occasions. Mr. Grove was saying, "Sue, if your quality of work doesn't improve considerably I will be forced to terminate you permanently. I'm sorry," Sue said, "I'm sorry too, Mr. Grove, I've had some personal issues which I must address and therefore I'm very depressed." Mr. Grove said, "I didn't realize that"

Once again Sue is not eating and constantly in bed trying to sleep to avoid all her problems. Her quality of work is poor, she has lost all interest in everything and withdrawn from the public. She has the classic symptoms of depression. She can also be seen various times in private weeping to herself. Maybe Sue needs to get another part time job in the evening for the time being until she gets back on her feet. Then she can always quit her second job when she gets caught up. Right?

Her mother, Jane, can't be of any help because she doesn't have any money herself at the prison. One evening on an impulse she searched through the want ads and found an advertisement for a nanny for four hours a night and transportation to and from work. The children were ages two, four and seven years old. She applied for the job with Mrs. Rigsby and was hired. The parents of the children picked her up, took her to the house and briefed her on what they expected of her. Sue would prepare a meal for the children, help them with their baths and get them to bed for $10.00 an hour. Sue accepted the job and went to work the next evening. She fixed the evening meal which they refused to eat because they wanted to eat sweets. They wouldn't take their baths or go to bed because they were very unruly and undisciplined. As soon as their parents came home from work Sue told them what had happened and said," I'm sorry, but I won't be back anymore and you'll have to find yourself another nanny." They paid Sue for one day's work and took her home. The next morning she could hardly get out of bed she was so tired but she managed somehow and went on to work. She didn't sleep much because the three children had stressed her out plus her depression. Sue vowed that she would never look for a second job again unless one just fell into her lap. And that probably wasn't going to happen. She would have to continue on as best she could. Maybe she could get some antidepressants from a medical company free of charge?

Chapter 3
Looking for a Job

One Sunday afternoon Sue depressed as she was decided to visit her mother in the St. Louis Prison. Maybe this would lift her spirits and her cloud of depression she hoped. Jane and Sue went to the Visitation Room to talk by phone and immediately Jane noticed a marked change in Sue's personality, attitude and conversation with her. Jane was saying, "Sue, what's wrong? Are you ill? You look like you don't feel well, dear. Can I get you something?" Sue started crying and said, "Mother, I have a severe depression now and I can hardly conduct my life in an orderly fashion anymore. I have no appetite so consequently I hardly eat anything and most of the time I am sleeping. I have lost interest in everything and I don't mingle with the other tenants at the Styles Apartment Complex. My job performance leaves a lot to be desired and my boss, Mr. Grove told me I am in danger of being terminated permanently. I don't know what to do or where to turn. Not only that, the other night we had a meeting in the Community Room and we were notified that everybody's rent went up $100.00 a month plus we have to pay our monthly water bill. My paycheck at Grove's Financial Company doesn't cover my expenses plus I had to discontinue my anti-depressants and I'm sure that's why I'm in this situation. Mother, is there any way at all that you can help me financially?"

Jane thought for a minute and said, "No Sue, I'm sorry I can't help you because I don't have any money to speak of myself. If there's any way I can help you I would. The only thing I can do Sue is pray for you that you will find a way out of this predicament you're in. Once again I'm truly sorry" Sue said, "That's okay mother, I know you would if you were able to. Thank you anyway. I just thought I'd ask."

Jane asked, "Sue, is there any way you can borrow money from the bank you do business with to carry you through until you can get back on your feet again?" Sue said, "No, I tried that mother and it didn't work because I don't have anything to put up for collateral until everything's paid off. I can't borrow any money anywhere."

Sue said, "Oh mother, I forgot to tell you. I had a job for one day as a nanny taking care of three small children for a couple but it didn't work out. The children wouldn't eat what I cooked, they didn't want to take their baths and they were unruly and undisciplined. I was miserable struggling with the stress, depression and constantly screaming at them. When their parents came home I told them I wouldn't be coming back. They didn't have much to say but still gave me a ride home. I was glad to get out of that situation."

Jane made the remark, "Sue, have you ever thought about looking for a different evening job besides being a nanny?" Sue said, "I've thought of it, mother, but I don't think I could manage to work at night, getting to bed much later and then getting up early again the next morning just like before."

Jane said, "I have a suggestion, Sue. Why don't you get yourself an evening job, try it for awhile and see how it works out for you. If you can't handle that, Sue, you always have the option to quit. How does that sound to you?" Sue said, "Yes, I think I'll try that approach again but not as a nanny and see what happens. Thank you, mother, for your advice." Jane said, "Keep me posted, Sue, and let me know how things are progressing." Sue said, "I will, mother and now I think I'd better be going since it's almost 4:00PM and the city bus will be coming by soon to me pick up." With that she bid her mother farewell and left the prison with Jane's eyes following her misted with tears as usual.

Sue arrived at the Styles Apartment Complex, went into her apartment, kicked off her shoes and flopped into her recliner thinking of her mother's suggestion. She decided to try to get another job again and see what happens. With that decision made she went into the kitchen to fix herself a bite to eat and watch television for the evening. After a few hours of television she decided to go to bed early for the night. The next day she would be pounding the pavement looking for another job.

Sue bought a newspaper after work the next day and checked the want ads for a job that she would be qualified for. What appealed to her was a light housekeeping job while the childless couple was at work. She would be required to come in twice a week to straighten things up and do little dusting. She called the number listed in the newspaper and they said, "Please come over for an interview" which she did. When she got off the city bus and walked to the correct house number on Blumen St. she noticed that the lawn bushes were neatly manicured and the flowers were arranged in clusters according to variety, height and color. So Sue assumed the inside of the house was likewise. She was in for a big, big surprise! As soon as the man of the house opened the door Sue was nearly barreled over by two dogs and four cats. They all ran past her barking, yelping and meowing with the cats scratching the dogs and the dogs biting the cats in return. They headed down the sidewalk and were soon out of sight.

Mr. Beller invited Sue into the house saying, "Sue, come in, my wife Elizabeth and I have been waiting for you. My name is Louis and we are glad to meet you. Sit down, please. Tell us a little about yourself. Are you from the St. Louis area?" Sue said, "No, I'm from Rockwood, Illinois and my mother and I moved up here about four months ago since my father passed away several years back. I'm divorced and have two children in different states. During the day I work for Groves Financial Services as a personal secretary to Mr. Groves, the manager. I enjoy my job, Mr. Beller, but it looks like I'm going to need an extra job because my landlady raised the rent on everybody at the Styles Apartment Complex where I live plus we each have to pay our own water bill. My paycheck at the Grove's Financial Services will not cover my living expenses therefore I'm forced to get an extra source of income. No, it isn't to my liking but I have no choice." Mr. and Mrs. Beller sympathized with her and also agreed. Louis explained, "We both have night jobs from 6:30PM until 12:00AM working at a local restaurant, "The Flower Tree." We have been cooking there for almost ten years." Mrs. Beller said, "Sue, I'd like to take you around the house a bit and show you what will be required of you. Come along."

Sue got up from her chair and followed Mrs. Beller down the hallway noticing a pungent animal odor coming out of each room she was in. Every room was filthy, with clothes strewn all over the floor, dishes piled high in the sink and the beds unmade. The bathroom was equally as bad. The front room had dog and cat feces in the corner plus damp spots on the carpet which could've been animal urine. The longer Sue was in the house the worse the odor seemed. Finally, she had to excuse herself saying, "It's getting late and I need to be going before I miss the last city bus. Thank you for your time and I'll be getting back to you within the next couple of days" She almost felt sick from the odor when she left and vowed she would never return. And she didn't. Sue called Mr. Beller several days later and told him, "No, she didn't think she was interested in the job. Sorry and thank you."

The smelly situation threw Sue into a severe state of depression again because she thought it might've been a job that would've suited her. But in this case it didn't. Her work performance was gradually getting worse until Mr. Grove called her into his office one day and said, "Sue, I'm sorry to have to tell you this but I'm going to terminate you because your workmanship is not up to par and intolerable so I'm relieving you of your duties. Thank you and goodbye." Sue got up with tears in her eyes and said, "Thank you, Mr. Grove and I'm sorry it had to end this way. I wish it would've been different. Goodbye." Now what's Sue going to do? What would you do?

By this time Sue was beside herself with her depression, no job, consequently no money, very little food and no medication. Like we said earlier Sue has no collateral so she can't borrow any money from the bank.

Well, tomorrow's another day. Right? Sue will check the want ads and maybe she'll find something that will interest her. Indeed! The next day she applied for a secretarial position with Wells Financial Company in downtown St. Louis for twice the amount of money she was getting before. She was hired and would start immediately the next day at 8:00AM. That evening as Sue ate supper setting in front of the television set she reminded herself she had to get to bed earlier because of her new job.

Sue was engrossed in a very interesting movie on television and lost track of the time. Pretty soon she looked at her watch and it was already 11:30PM longer than she had intended to stay up. She was approaching the end of the movie and naturally wanted to see what would happen so she continued to watch. The movie ended at midnight and Sue didn't get to bed until 12:45AM, having to get up at 6:00AM for her first day on the job.

The next morning Sue overslept because she forgot to set her alarm clock so consequently she got up too late to be at work at 8:00AM. She hurriedly got ready, took the last city bus for the morning and walked into the office at 9:00AM. Sue apologized, "I'm sorry for being late but I overslept." She immediately started working and nothing was said.

The next night Sue was watching a movie on television again and she was thinking, "I wouldn't miss this movie for anything especially with all my favorite actors. She went to the kitchen for a snack, came back and resumed watching the movie until 12:30AM the next morning. She went to bed around 1:15AM and as she lay there before falling asleep she knew there was something else she had to do but couldn't remember so she fell asleep. The next morning Sue awoke at 8:00AM because she forgot to set the alarm again (that was the other thing she forgot to do) and walked into the office at 9:30AM, excused herself and started working. Nothing was said again. Strange, isn't it? After work she took the city bus back to the apartment complex, ate supper and proceeded to watch television again. The next several mornings she came to work on time but the following Monday morning she was late again. After the office closed Sue's boss, Mr. Wells, approached her and said, "Sue, I understand you were late for work three times with no report to my office as to the reason. I'm sorry, but I have no other alternative but to dismiss you from your position permanently. Your dismissal is effective immediately and your paycheck is forthcoming. Once again, I'm sorry." Sue said, "Thank you." She emptied her desk of her supplies and walked out. Now, after this dismissal Sue was more depressed than ever. She was practically in tears as she boarded the city bus for her return trip to her apartment. When she walked into her bedroom she flung herself on the bed and cried for hours not knowing what to do. Should she try and look for another job? She already tried three different jobs and they didn't work out. Should she ask her mother's advice at the prison this Sunday afternoon? She hasn't visited her mother for several weeks.

Sunday afternoon Sue took the city bus to the prison to visit Jane. Her mother was delighted to see her once again as they went into the visitation room to use the phones for visitors only and discuss various issues. Jane talked about the craft class that she is assisting the instructor in and the different items the inmates make and sell. On the other hand Sue brought up the subject of her dismissal at her office job and the other jobs that she didn't continue with. As she was speaking she broke into tears with Jane trying to console her again. Jane said, "Sue, maybe you'll have to start looking for another job again and try to stay with your job when you find one. Don't forget to set your alarm clock when you go to bed at night. Also, maybe you can use your paycheck to buy yourself some anti-depressant pills. They will help you feel better, Sue. I know because I'm speaking from experience. I'm on anti-depressant pills myself from the prison doctor." Sue said, "Well, I'll try and see what I can do, mother. I'm not going to guarantee anything. I'll try my best." Before she left Sue promised to come for a visit a little sooner than three weeks. They hung up their phones with Sue walking down the hall and Jane watching her leave the prison crossing the street to a waiting taxi. She briefly wiped the tears from her eyes as she walked back to her cell in time for supper.

The next morning Sue got up extra early to take the first city bus downtown for a newspaper she would read in her favorite coffee shop on River St. Today there was nothing in the want ads so she finished her coffee and strolled around downtown for awhile before she took the city bus back to her apartment.

In the evening Sue went to a meeting at 7:00PM in the Community Room conducted by Mrs. Styles, the landlady. It was reported that there are no new leads on the robbery in the elevator two months ago. If anybody sees anything unusual please report your findings to the office immediately. Also on the agenda Mrs. Styles announced, "Once again the new rental and water fees are due on the first of every month and no later. Certain exceptions can be made only in extreme cases. Is this understood?" The tenants smiled and nodded their heads in agreement in spite of possibly thinking otherwise? Mrs. Styles also had other issues that she discussed with the tenants such as the upkeep of their apartments, the noise level etc... As far as activities are concerned, there's never been anything like the activities at the Rockwood Apartment Complex in Rockwood, Illinois. Mrs. Style also announced, "We will have our regular Thursday night Bingo game here in the Community room at 7:00PM. If anyone wishes to volunteer as a Bingo caller please be here at 6:30PM. Refreshments will be served. Thank you. The meeting is adjourned." Sue went back to her apartment taking the elevator to the third floor. She was due for some rest and relaxation in front of the television set for an hour or two and after the ten o'clock news she would go to bed.

Sue slept till 9:00AM the next morning not bothering to set her alarm because she barely had enough change for the city bus, so she decided not to go downtown for the day but to spend more time in her apartment cleaning and picking up after herself. Besides she couldn't always afford to eat downtown at the prices these days. She made her bed, washed the dishes and vacuumed her apartment. By this time it was close to dinner so she made lunch and proceeded to eat. After dinner she took a short nap and watched television until supper. She ate supper and decided to volunteer as Bingo caller for the evening. Sue walked into the Community room at 6:30PM and said, "I'm willing to give it a try. I've never called Bingo before but I'm sure it can't be that hard."

They assured her it wasn't and briefed her on the particulars to which Sue complied. Prizes consisted of dollar gifts and the charge was $2.00 to play. A lot of the tenants participated in the game for something to do in the evening. After Bingo was over everybody got up and left for their apartments including Sue.

When Sue got back to her apartment she was tired even though it was only nine o'clock so she decided to go to bed early. Around midnight she got up for a drink of water and noticed police cars and ambulance lights flashing in her window. By this time she heard shrieks of fear and screaming in the hallway so she decided to open the door. She noticed the police coming up the stairs and the paramedics pushing a gurney weaving in and out through the crowd of people congregated in the hall and toward the elevator. Sue quickly slipped her housecoat on and stepped over to the elevator to get a quick glimpse inside as she let out a blood curdling scream that would wake the dead. Inside the elevator one of the tenants, Mr. Cole 80, was suspended from the ceiling with a bed sheet wrapped around his neck which choked him immediately. The killer had a large, round gadget that was magnetized onto the ceiling that held the weight of a human body. From there Mr. Cole was robbed, knocked unconscious with a sharp blow to the head and left to die. His eyes were open with a strange glaze and his tongue was black and hanging out of his mouth. His skin had turned dark in the process and void of any color. When his body was released it was as rigid as a corpse that had been hanging there for weeks. What a sight! Someone notified Mrs. Cole but they wouldn't bring her to the elevator because of the grisly picture. The paramedics released Mr. Cole's body from the bed sheet and transported him to William's Mortuary for final preparations. They will bring Mrs. Cole to the mortuary later for a private viewing. Someone was asking, "Who did this? How did this happen? I just saw Mr. and Mrs. Cole at the Bingo game because they were sitting in front of me. In fact, I remember they even won Bingo. What a shame to be hung in an elevator! I've never heard of such a thing, have you?" Everybody shook their head emphatically and said, "No." And they hope they never see it again. After awhile everybody dispersed and went back to their apartments including Sue. At this point it was 2:00AM Wednesday morning and I'm sure no one slept a wink the rest of the night. Is there a killer in the apartment complex? What's happening here? Nothing's ever taken place like this before! I'm sure these questions are running rampant through the tenants' minds. What do you think? Keep reading!

The elevator was inoperable for a day or so until a crew could clean, disinfect and deodorize the elevator for further use. The tenants were resigned to the fact they had to take the back stairs for the time being.

Most of the tenants including Sue attended the funeral service at William's Mortuary several days later. Mrs. Cole and her family sat in mourner's row amidst soft whispers and constant weeping. Pastor Brown said some prayers, gave a eulogy and Bob Cole reminisced about the life of his father which was very touching. Everybody followed the funeral procession to the cemetery with the black hearse leading the way. An open grave was dug and the casket was set on top with a vault below. Family members, friends and relatives gathered around as Pastor Brown conducted the service. After everything was over Pastor Brown announced there would be a free luncheon for everyone in the basement of the Living Christ Baptist Church on 4th and Oliver St. Sue attended the luncheon with several other tenants, joined in some light conversation and went back to her apartment to rest.

She got up early the next morning to take the city bus to downtown St. Louis, scraping some extra change out of her dresser drawer for a newspaper. As she looked through the Want Ads she noticed a secretarial job opening at Beeler's Insurance Office right across the street from the coffee shop where she was sitting. Sue immediately went across the street and applied for the job to which they replied, "We will contact you by Monday either way. Thank you." Sue left and took the next city bus back to her apartment. When she arrived back she went through her mail receiving her last check from Wells Financial Company. Also a note was included stating, "We're sorry but your job has been terminated. Thank you." Sue already knew that.

A loud knock on the door broke Sue's train of thought as she went to answer. A detective and policeman were standing there so Sue invited them in. The policeman said, "We're canvassing the whole apartment complex to see who was home the night of Mr. Cole's hanging in the elevator. Did anybody see any unusual characters loitering around or anything questionable taking place? Sue, how about you?" Sue said, "No, I didn't. I had called Bingo that night, came back to my apartment and went to bed only to be awakened after midnight by a terrible noise in the hallway. That's when I came out of my apartment to see what the commotion was about. I soon found out. It was awful! I never expected anything like that to happen here." The policeman and detective agreed and said, "Thank you. We'll be on our way now and in the near future if you see or hear anything unusual please don't hesitate to call the St. Louis Police Department without further delay. We hope we didn't inconvenience you." Sue said, "That's all right officer, I wasn't doing anything of importance anyway." She watched a few hours of television and retired for the evening.

Sue didn't accomplish much over the weekend except volunteering for Bingo Saturday night. Sunday she cleaned her apartment and did a little extra cooking for the coming week. She was anxious for Monday to come because Beeler Insurance Company would be calling her about the job.

Sue woke up bright and early Monday morning dressed, ate breakfast and washed the dishes. At 9:00AM the phone rang and it was the Beeler Insurance Company to tell her, "You have been accepted for the job and can you start the next day." Sue replied, "Yes, that would be fine and she would be there at 8:00AM the next day." Sue was glad she was accepted for the job and she vowed to herself that she would not forget to see her alarm nor be late for her job like her previous encounter with the work force. The next morning Sue was up at 6:00AM, showered, dressed, ate breakfast and was headed for the bus stop. She arrived at the Beeler Insurance Company at 7:45AM, ready to start work ahead of schedule, although she didn't really start until 8:00AM. Her job was a repetition of filing insurance claims, filling out forms, etc… nothing out of the ordinary. She had an hour off for lunch so she ate a salad at the deli next door and then browsed in Pickle's Department Store across the street. At one o'clock she was back at work again until five o'clock taking the five thirty bus back to her apartment. She ate supper, visited with Mrs. Lands next door and then went back to her apartment to get ready for bed.

The next evening Mrs. Styles called a meeting to order with Officer Bob Wilton scheduled to give a speech in regards to the hanging of Mr. Cole in the elevator five weeks ago. Officer Wilton announced, "Sleazy, unfavorable characters have been loitering inside and outside of the apartment complex so caution should be exercised. The officers transported the unfavorable characters to the police department, questioned and finger printed them, releasing them because of their negativity. Officer Wilton asked, "Are there any unanswered questions tonight? I'll try to answer them if I can. Yes, ma'am? What is your question?" Mrs. Shale asked, "Officer, have you gotten any farther with your investigation about the robbery and hanging in the elevator?" Officer Wilton said, "Frankly, no we haven't. We're at a dead end right now because there are no new leads or clues for us to follow. The person that did the robbery and killing has eluded the police completely. It's just like they vanished into thin air. Neither hide nor hair of them. They completely disappeared. Like we keep telling everybody at the complex if you see anything unusual please report it to the St. Louis Police Department and we'll gladly check it out. Anymore questions? Yes, Mr. Lane? What is your question?" Mr. Lane asked, "Officer, are we going to have extra security inside and outside the building in the near future?" Officer Wilton remarked, "Yes, this has been discussed at the police meetings and we are planning to post policemen inside and outside of the apartment complex and also by the elevator for quite some time."Officer Wilton asked, "Does anybody have a question they'd like answered? I'll be glad to oblige." Mr. Wagner raised his hand and Officer Wilton said, "What is your question, Mr. Wagner?" Mr. Wagner asked, "At this point, is it dangerous to use the elevator at any time day or night?" Officer Wilton said, "No, I don't think so but I would not get in the elevator with a totally strange person that you don't even recognize. But, if you decide to ride the elevator please glance around inside and outside to make sure there is nothing unusual to draw your attention. Anymore questions?" After there were no more questions Mrs. Styles said, "That concludes our meeting for this evening and I want to thank all of you for coming. We had a good representation of tenants tonight." Everybody arose and went back to their apartments with the exception of a few that went into the Community Room to play billiards and watch the local news together. While a few of the tenants were playing billiards the remainder of them were watching the St. Louis channel KIBX. Immediately after a few minutes of television viewing the tenants were startled as the reporter broke into the main program to announce a robbery at the St. Louis National Bank happening a few minutes ago. A picture of the bank at the corner of 12th and Hall St. was flashed across the screen. Two masked men clutching money bags jumped into a getaway car and sped down the street in a heavy downpour obscuring the vision of their car in the darkness. As soon as the breaking news was over the tenants discussed the bank robbery for a few minutes and then went back to their regular viewing channel.

About a half an hour had lapsed as the time edged closer to 9:00PM with the tenants still playing billiards and watching television. All of a sudden the front door of the apartment complex opened and two men entered the foyer drenched to the bone. The tenants welcomed them to the Community Room saying, "Good evening. Welcome to the Styles Apartment Complex. It looks like your sopping wet. Stay awhile and dry off because it is pretty wet out there. Why don't you warm up with some coffee?" The two strange men helped themselves to some coffee and cookies continuing to visit with the local tenants at random. They said, "Oh we're just passing through St. Louis headed farther east and it started raining heavy. We were just in the neighborhood so we decided to stop here at the complex to use the restroom, dry off and be on our way again. Thank you for the hospitality. We will resume our travels in a little bit."

At this point everybody was continuing to watch the St. Louis television station KIBX as they flashed the scene of the bank robbery at the St. Louis National Bank. The two male suspects were watching television and they soon noticed they were being flashed across the screen as the two biggest bank robbers in the state of Missouri. They immediately turned their heads the other way so they wouldn't be recognized by the apartment tenants. Fortunately Mr. Wagner recognized both of the robbers, quickly went to his apartment and called the police telling them to send a policeman to the complex immediately because the robbers would be leaving soon. Mr. Wagner no sooner got off the phone than the St. Louis Police Department came into the Styles Apartment Complex, guns straddling their hips, knowing full well that the two strange men were the bank robbers of the St. Louis National Bank about an hour ago. They were arrested, handcuffed, escorted out of the building and into a waiting police car for the ride to the police station. On the way out one of the bank robbers said to the other one, "Well, we didn't get too far, did we?" The other bank robber said in reply, "No, we didn't. Remember, I told you we shouldn't stop at the apartment complex because of getting recognized on television, but you wouldn't listen to me. That ruined everything." The other bank robber just shrugged and said, "Whatever! It probably wasn't meant to be." They were taken to the police station for finger printing and questioned about the hanging of Mr. Cole using the lie detector technique. Everything was negative but they were kept in jail for the bank robbery to be tried at a later date.

The next morning after word got around about the two bank robbers dropping in the apartment complex, a lot of the tenants including Sue came down to the Community Room to hear about the action and get all the details. Mr. Wagner, the spokesman for the group, fully explained in detail what transpired till the police arrested them and led them away. There was a full page article and picture on the front page of the local newspaper, the St. Louis Gazette, the next morning for the benefit of those that missed it on television the night before. Isn't it strange that the two bank robbers just happened to stop at the Styles Apartment Complex of all the apartment complexes in St. Louis? They didn't have anything to do with Mr. Cole's murder. What was the reason? Read on! A month later they were tried and given a prison sentence of three years each in an out of state prison.

Constant surveillance is being enforced by the St. Louis Police Department twenty four hours a day and a policeman is posted at the entrance to the elevator day and night. Any unsavory characters loitering around will be politely escorted out of the building. Also any undesirable people caught on the outside of the complex causing problems will be taken into custody for the remainder of the day and night at the St. Louis Police Department. Also, at this point the tenants have no fear or problems calling the police if they encounter any strange or unusual circumstances not to their liking.

Chapter 4
Prison Breakout
March–2004

This evening as Sue was watching the 10:00 o'clock news on KIBX television channel the screen went dark with no sound for a minute. All of a sudden the sound and color came back on and a breaking news flash came across the screen indicating a prison breakout at the Women's Prison in St. Louis, Missouri. Twelve women inmates are still at large as they read the names including Jane Linton. Sue was beside herself with a barrage of mixed emotions not knowing what to think. She was outraged, disgusted, fearful, compassionate and scared for her mother because she has no money on her person nor means to get around. Sue hopes her 75 year old mother isn't thinking about hitchhiking because of the danger involved. Sue is thinking to herself, "Is she sitting in the diner all night? Where will she sleep? Why did she go along with this idea? It seems like she's in game for anything that comes around. Maybe she'll stay up later in case her mother comes to the door during the night for a place to sleep and stay." Periodically, while Sue is watching television pictures are flashed across the screen of the breakout in the prison yard. They scaled the fence to the other side and scattered to the four winds. Evidently Jane took off by herself not knowing where to go. Sue thought, "Why did she do this? This is the second time this happened and she needs to stop this. When they get back they will wind up in solitary confinement. Is this better? No!"

It's almost eleven o'clock and Jane hasn't come to Sue's apartment yet so Sue has decided to go to bed because she has to get up early for work the next morning. She slept soundly, woke up early, got ready and took the city bus to the office downtown. When Sue went to eat dinner at the local diner next door she was also reading the paper between forkfuls of food. When she looked up there stood Jane bedraggled and forlorn staring at Sue. Sue exclaimed "Mother, where have you been since last night? What happened to you after the prison inmates staged a breakout? Have you eaten anything since yesterday? Whose idea was this anyway?" Jane answered, "Sue, I'm getting tired of that place and I'd like to get out of there permanently. I'm sorry for what I did to most of my victims except a few, but I guess it's too late to dwell on that now. What do you think? Sue said, "Yes mother, I agree. There's not much you can do about that now. It's a little too late for that anymore." Jane and Sue visited long into the night and then went to bed.

Sue got up early for work the next morning and Jane continued to sleep. While Sue was at work Jane showered, ate breakfast and stayed in the apartment for fear of getting recognized. She watched television all day because the prison breakout was the main topic of the news on KIBX. Five inmates were still at large including Jane. Jane was thinking, "When Sue comes home from work this evening they will decide what to do about her. She doesn't want to go back to prison but what choice does she have?" What do you think? Would you send her back? Remember, it's her mother. Keep reading!

Sue came home at six fifteen and Jane had fixed supper. They visited over supper about everything but the prison breakout. Finally Sue said, "Mother, we have to reach some conclusion about your going back to prison." Jane immediately started crying and saying, "Sue, I don't ever want to go back to prison again but maybe I have no choice. I guess you don't want me here." Sue got up, came over and put her arms around Jane's shoulders saying, "That isn't it, mother. You could probably stay but I don't know if that's the correct thing to do since that would be harboring a criminal which is wrong. Actually, I could get in trouble with the law. My suggestion is to return to prison and make the best of it." As soon as Sue mentioned going back to prison Jane started crying again, lamenting the early morning rising, twelve hours of grueling laundry work and no real friends to confide in during times of sadness, loneliness and depression. But she knows she has no choice but to go back to the women's prison for the rest of her life. In the morning Sue will make arrangements with the prison officials to have Jane picked up at the apartment while she is at work and transport her to the St. Louis Women's Prison on the edge of town.

Sue left for work at 7:30 this morning giving her mother a last minute hug telling her, "Prison security will be here to pick you up shortly, mother. I'll see you in a few weeks. Goodbye." Jane said, "Goodbye Sue" amidst sniffles and tears. At 8:45AM a prison van pulled up and two prison guards came to the door to escort Jane to the van and back to prison. They told her four inmates were still at large but they were glad she was back. They said, "It's a dangerous world out there with no money, job, food or a place to live. It can be mighty scary." Jane said, "Yes, I'm well aware of that. I escaped the first time I was transferred here so I know what you mean."

Back to the Slave Mine

Jane is back in the women's prison again in spite of a frivolous flirt with the outside world. She arises at 5:00 o'clock in the morning, eats three square meals a day, works at her twelve hour laundry job and is in bed at 10:00 PM. Everyday is the same, the same, the same, nothing different. Except one evening a week Jane is the assistant leader to the head crafts leader in the crafts department making different items for personal gratification and sales. But other than that the prison is one, dull, boring, routine way of life. She should've thought twice…three times before she killed twelve people those fateful days and nights. She'll be in prison until her dying day. Can you imagine a life like that? What will happen next? Read on!

The St. Louis Women's Prison always has four or five women on death row. This morning an acquaintance of Jane's, Patty Muldeen, will be executed by way of the electric chair in Room 7 at 9:00AM. Jane got a glimpse of Patty as she passed by the laundry room at 8:45AM escorted by two security guards. Patty was asked if she had anything to say before the execution and she said emphatically, "No!" Patty was strapped into the electric chair ay 9:00AM as shock wave after shock wave of electricity coursed through her body and brain. Her body jerked because of the electrical impulse as her head slumped to one side and her limbs became rigid like bands of steel. Again her frame twisted and heaved once more and then collapsed in a limp position in the electric chair. Death was pronounced at 9:28AM. Notification will be pending upon the next of kin and burial will be in the prison cemetery or the cemetery of the family's choice. The body was placed on a gurney covered with a black shroud and transported to the prison morgue. Jane observed a few minutes of silence while she was working, out of respect for Patty Muldeen and her family which must be grieving at this time. Patty was probably someone's wife, sister, mother, aunt etc… She was forty five years old and had been on death row for ten years. She was a native of Columbia, Missouri.

After supper that evening Jane and the other inmates have access to the prison yard for a sports game, exercise or otherwise. Since Jane is in maximum security she doesn't participate in anything and just chooses to lean against one of the buildings by herself wrapped up in her own thoughts until it's time to go inside for the evening for a few hours of television and then to bed. Jane's friend Sharon remarked, "It's too bad about Patty Muldeen dying in the electric chair this morning. Does anybody know what she was serving time for especially on death row?"Somebody said, "She deliberately asphyxiated twenty three people in a retirement center years ago. I don't know why. Too bad! She's probably better off than we are."By this time the yard warden said, "Everybody inside, please. It's time to go inside. Move along." The prison inmates went inside to watch a movie and then "Lights Out" by 10:00PM.

The next evening, Friday, Jane worked in the Craft Room as assistant leader, helping the inmates master the art of crafts as a hobby, sales and intermingling with the other inmates. She became acquainted with a variety of inmates, some of them "lifers" like herself.

Saturday came and went with Jane looking forward to Sunday because Sue would be visiting her in the afternoon. Early Sunday morning Jane rose for church services in a non-denominational chapel in the prison as she has every Sunday since she's been there. After services she ate an early dinner with the rest of the inmates and went to her prison cell to await the arrival of Sue. Visiting hours were from 2:00PM-2:40PM by phone which is the only way to converse with Jane since she is in maximum security. Jane was lying on her cot in her cell and accidentally fell asleep. When she awoke she noticed it was 3:15PM and still no Sue. That's strange! Something must've happened. Jane hoped Sue was okay and not sick or anything.

The maximum security inmates are not allowed to make calls at anytime from the prison to outlying areas. About this time a warden was patrolling the cells and Jane told him about the situation. He told her to check with the main office because they should be able to give her the information she so desperately needed. Jane immediately checked at the main office and asked about the restrictions on the use of the telephone. They told Jane, "If it's an emergency a prison official has to make the telephone call, since you're not allowed to make outside calls." Jane said, "Thank you" and hung up. Jane and her fellow inmates had restrictions themselves. If they disobeyed in any way, shape or form they would be subject to trouble with the prison officials.

About 10:00PM Mr. Clyde Biggs, Sue's neighbor, called Mrs. Styles apartment saying, "I heard a loud blast coming out of Sue's apartment and I've been scared ever since." Mrs. Styles reassured him, "We'll be sending the police immediately to check your story out. In the meantime don't try to enter the apartment by any way or means. It is not advisable." As soon as Mr. Biggs hung up the phone he saw the police coming down the hall, pushing the gurney, kicking the door open and entering the apartment. What they discovered brought tears to their eyes. Sue was sprawled on the bed, a loaded gun still in her hand, moaning and groaning as her mutilated body was gushing volumes of blood infiltrating the carpet and other objects likewise. A gunshot blast caused an opening the size of a small marble in the center of her chest with blood flowing freely. Her eyes were closed and a scrawled suicide note was clutched in her other hand stating, "My finances were low therefore I couldn't afford my anti-depressant medication so for myself this was the only way out. Please explain this to my mother who is incarcerated at the St. Louis Prison for Women at 1-694-728-2672. Bury me beside my father, Bob Linton, in the Rockwood Cemetery in Rockwood, Illinois. Thank you." Sue. The police immediately transferred Sue to the St. Louis Regional Hospital without delay because she was still alive with a shallow, labored breathing and ashen pallor in her face. When they brought her into the emergency room they connected her to oxygen and intra-venous feedings, administered to her needs and re-located her to the intensive care unit. Her eyes have yet to open as she lies motionless balancing between life and death. Do you think she'll continue to live? I don't know for sure. Read on! The hospital staff kept a close vigil on Sue the remainder of the night and reported any unusual activity on her person. She was basically quiet the rest of the evening with her eyes remaining closed. No visitors were allowed at this time because Sue was a very sick woman. Towards morning the next day, Wednesday, Sue's eyelids began to flutter a little and she asked, "Where am I at" and said, "I'm hungry." She also asked, "What happened?" The staff told her, "We will explain everything later on and someone will be bringing you something to eat soon."

Sue spent two more weeks in the hospital until she was released back to her apartment. She hasn't been able to go to work and has had to explain the whole situation to Mrs. Styles. She will have to make back payments on the rent and water bills plus put up with a second job even if she doesn't like it. Sue is using her leave of absence and has no vacation time since she hasn't been at this job long enough so there isn't much money involved.

Sue is slowly improving every day. She is going to have to start looking for an evening job again as soon as she can get a hold of the local paper in the lobby when you enter the building. She went down to the lobby immediately and started pouring through the want ads looking for a job. Today there weren't any interesting jobs in the paper that suited her. Yet she can't be too choosy if she wants to make some extra money.

A New Job Again

Sue applied for a nanny job again and she got hired a couple of miles across town on Bailey Street. Her employers, Joe and Ann Strove, will pick her up from her day job at the Beeler Insurance Company and take her to their home for the night job so they can go to work in the evening. The children are a seven year old boy, Mark, and a four year old girl, Mary. The requirements of Sue are that she prepares their evening meal, see that they take their baths and do their homework, one hour of television and off to bed. The children are well behaved, mannerly and took a liking to Sue immediately, likewise. Joe and Ann both work at the Grafton Chemical Plant on the edge of St. Louis, Missouri until 11:30 in the evening. They will return home and one of them will drive Sue back to her apartment. After Mark and Mary are in bed Sue usually washes the dishes, cleans up after the children which is not required of her and then watches television until Joe and Ann come home. It is usually midnight when Sue walks into her apartment and almost one o'clock in the morning until she gets to sleep. Sue sets her alarm for six o'clock the next morning so she only gets about five hours of sleep a night which is not enough. No wonder she can barely make it to work and be able to function the next day. I'm sure that's why her work performance was poor on her last job.

Actually, Sue likes her job as a nanny and also the family itself but the lack of sleep is taking its toll on her to the point where she is always tired, cranky and crabby with Mark and Mary. The children are beginning to cry often when she gets angry at them for no reason and they are getting scared of her. Mark related the story to his parents one night and Ann confronted Sue when she took her home saying, "Sue, there's something I'd like to discuss with you in regards to the care of the children. Mark has told my husband and I repeatedly about the times your voice was in anger when they've done nothing to provoke or upset you. Is that correct, Sue? Can you comment on that?" Sue made the remark, "That's correct, Ann. The reason these angry episodes occur is because of lack of sleep. I only get about five hours of sleep a night going to bed at one o'clock in the morning and getting up at six o'clock. I need about eight hours of sleep at night. I'm sorry about the whole situation and I don't know what to do."

Ann said, "Sue, I'll give you another chance because otherwise you are a good nanny and the children seem to like you as well as Joe and I but only under one condition, Sue. You will have to refrain from raising your voice in anger so as not to frighten the children. Okay?" Sue said, "Okay I'll try, Ann. Thank you."

Sue continues to go to her nanny job every night except Saturday and Sunday. She has improved her disposition greatly and managed to keep her anger under control. Things went smoothly for several months with no problems until Sue started running low on her anti-depressant pills and no money to refill them. Her depression seemed to worsen every day for lack of sleep and a generalized feeling of weakness over her whole body. The last time Ann took her home she said, "Sue, I'm sorry to have to tell you this but my husband and I decided not to have you back anymore because of your angry episodes again lately. You are creating a bad environment for our children and their mental welfare could be at stake.

I'm sorry." Sue said, "That's okay, Ann. I understand." Ann said, "Here's the remainder of the money that we owe you." Sue said, "Thank you" and got out of the car at her apartment as Ann sped off into the dark of the night. Sue let herself into the apartment, dropped onto the bed and cried herself to sleep. What was she to do? No extra job or money. No anti-depressant pills that she so direly needed. She couldn't go to her mother for help because she didn't have access to any money. At this point she dropped to her knees in prayer to God for help out of this terrible situation. If anybody could help her he could. Since she was still crying prior to falling asleep, she knew she wouldn't be able to go to work the next morning and she would have to call in sick. She'll probably get fired from that job also just like the other office jobs where they dismissed her.

When Sue awoke the next morning she had a splitting headache while calling in sick to the office. An hour later the office manager, Mr. Beeler, called back and said, "Sue, in the past you've called in sick too many times for the company to keep you on the payroll. I'm sorry, but I'm going to have to relieve you of your services as of today. Your check will be in the mail shortly. Thank You." Once more Sue cried bloody tears. Fired two times in eight hours! Ann fired her at midnight last night and Mr. Beeler fired her at eight o'clock this morning. This is terrible! What's happening? How is she supposed to live? How will she pay her bills? What if Mrs. Styles evicts her and she has nowhere to go? After this thought occurred to Sue she immediately decided to call Mrs. Styles to explain her situation over the phone. Mrs. Styles answered on the second ring and Sue said, "Mrs. Styles, this is Sue Benson in Apt. 4G. I decided to call and make you aware of the fact that I lost both of my jobs within eight hours and I don't know how I'm going to pay the rent and water bill next month. Is there any way you can postpone these bills until I can come up with some money? I don't even have enough money to buy food and medicine." Mrs. Styles said, "Well, yes I suppose I can but I don't want you to tell anybody or all the tenants will want their rent postponed for some reason or another." Sue said, "No, Mrs. Styles, I won't repeat this and I'm deeply gratefully to you. Thank You!"

Well, what's Sue to do for money now? Once again no money, no medicine, barely no food, nothing. She's at loose ends and getting looser.

Sue went downstairs to the lobby to look at the daily paper as usual and then came back upstairs for supper and a few hours of television. After several hours of sleep she awoke and went to the kitchen for a drink of water. On the way back to the bedroom she thought she heard voices but she dismissed it from her mind thinking it might have been her imagination. After she got back into bed she heard the same sound and decided to get up and see where it was coming from. She grabbed her robe and opened her apartment door only to be confronted by the police, paramedics, a gurney and other tenants. Sue said, "Oh no! What happened?" She walked over to the elevator looked inside and saw the most grisly sight imaginable. Mr. Platterson, eighty four, was dangling from the ceiling with a rope around his neck stretched to the limit. He was decapitated with his head lying in a corner of the elevator and his eyes gouged out and stuck in his shirt pockets. Blood was pouring immensely out of his neck and covering the floor. He was stabbed repeatedly with a long bladed knife sticking out of his stomach pouring blood. His face had turned a dark color and his tongue had been cut off and lying next to his head on the elevator carpet.

The killer had used the same round mechanism as before, fastened it to the ceiling and hung Mr. Platterson by a rope stabbing him repeatedly. A note was clenched in Mr. Platterson's fist stating, "Will you be the next victim?" The detectives took it to the police station to see if they could match it up with other suspects. The police ripped the mechanism off the ceiling, removed the rope from his neck and lowered the body onto the gurney, laying the head, tongue and eyes on his torso. What a shame! Mr. Platterson's body and head were mutilated beyond recognition. The paramedics took him to the William's Funeral Home where they prepared him for cremation. Mrs. Platterson and her children were notified and they were all beside themselves with grief. Their four children, spouses and families were on their way to St. Louis, Missouri as soon as they became aware of what happened. His remains were cremated several days later and his ashes strewn in an area he often visited in his boyhood outside the city of St. Louis.

The St. Louis Police Department and detectives did numerous investigations into the brutal killing and hanging of Mr. Platterson in the elevator but so far they have come up empty handed. The police have even gone so far as to enlist the help of the Chicago, Illinois Police Department in regards to the strange, untimely death of Mr. Platterson. Did Mr. Platterson have any enemies? Why did he have to suffer and endure such a grisly, morbid ending? Why are all these murders taking place in the Styles Apartment Complex? Why not in another apartment complex across town? Nobody knows! Maybe no one will ever know!

Mr. Platterson's Murder

Incidentally, the night of Mr. Platterson's murder there weren't any policemen posted at the elevator or anywhere in the apartment complex for that matter. The St. Louis Police Department had a one day meeting, luncheon and seminar for local and area wide policemen in St. Louis and outlying counties, so nobody was on duty at the Styles Apartment Complex that day. How did the killer know there would be no policemen there that day? I can't figure that out! Can you?

Later in the week the St. Louis Police Department placed the tenants of the Styles Apartment Complex on a bus and transported them to the police department. There they reviewed a "Suspect Lineup" for possible further identification of characters that have been loitering in and around the apartment complex. As the suspects were brought through the lineup none of the tenants recognized any of them as having seen them at the apartment complex. Later on the detectives from the St. Louis Police Department interviewed Mrs. Platterson asking her, "Mrs. Platterson, did Mr. Platterson have any enemies that you rightly know of inside or outside of the apartment complex?" Mrs. Platterson answered, "No, Mr. Platterson and I didn't have any enemies that I know of." The detectives continued the interview, "Have you had any salesman coming to your apartment door soliciting their goods where you might've refused them?"

Mrs. Platterson said, "No, the only people that came to the apartment door are the people that we have invited personally and we allowed them entrance. On different occasions we have had appointments with tax preparers and insurance salesmen when we experienced inclement weather and couldn't leave. Everything went along just fine." The detectives continued to ask, "Had Mr. Platterson and yourself personally seen any unsavory characters lingering inside or outside the apartment complex after hours?" Mrs. Platterson replied, "No, we hadn't. Actually, we didn't leave the apartment after dark. We were in for the night." The detectives said," Okay, Mrs. Platterson, were sorry to have bothered you. I hope we didn't cause you any inconvenience. We'll be on our way. If we have any further questions we'll be contacting you, thank you" and they left. The detectives stepped into the elevator for one last quick check before they proceeded to leave.

Once again Mrs. Platterson was at a loss for words as she asked, "Who could have taken Mr. Platterson's life? He was robbed and had to give his life for a measly $100.00. Who could have been so cruel as to perform such a dastardly deed?"

After the detectives left Mrs. Platterson immediately prepared for bed as she was tired, anxious and slightly depressed. She fell asleep soon only to be awakened by the jingle of the telephone in the stillness of the night. She got up to answer the telephone in a hurry and nearly tripped over something that fell on the floor. When she picked up the receiver she said, "Hello…Hello….Hello….May I ask who's calling, please?" The anonymous caller said, "Yes, I do mind being asked who's calling because it's none of your damn business. And incidentally there's a strong possibility you might be the next victim. What do you think of that?" Mrs. Platterson started weeping uncontrollably into the phone saying, "Oh please, don't hurt me, please!"It's sad enough that you took my husband's life but please don't take mine also. Have pity on me. I've gone through so much already." The anonymous caller said, "You might be going through a hell of a lot more yet." At this point Mrs. Platterson tried to differentiate between a women's voice or a man's voice but it could've been either one. All of a sudden the anonymous caller gave a snickering, hideous laugh and slammed the receiver down in Mrs. Platterson's ear. She continued crying and pleading on her behalf to leave her alone. Then there was dead silence.

Late as it was Mrs. Platterson called the St. Louis Police Department and they sent two officers out to investigate the matter. They were the same two detectives that had been out earlier. They asked Mrs. Platterson a variety of questions about the telephone call. "Had anyone else in the apartment complex received such a call? What was the nature of the call? Were there any names mentioned?"Mrs. Platterson briefly described everything to the best of her ability not eliminating even the slightest detail. The detectives posted an officer at the entrance to the elevator for the remainder of the night. It was well after midnight when Mrs. Platterson went to bed again only to toss and turn most of the night anxious for morning to arrive. The anonymous caller will be keeping her on edge for a long time from here on out.

Chapter 5
An Organized Search

Mrs. Styles received a firsthand report of the hanging murder of Mr. Leon Platterson, eighty four, and a coinciding report of the anonymous telephone call that Mrs. Platterson had to endure. As we are finding out Mrs. Platterson isn't the only recipient of such harassing telephone calls. Several other apartment dwellers received a similar call in the same time frame. So what are the tenants planning to do?

Mrs. Styles husband, Arthur, is planning to organize a search party for the following Sunday May 14. He will transport a bus load of tenants to a park not far from the Styles Apartment Complex. The tenants will have lunch and spend the day at Lowler's Park getting acquainted and meeting new people. They will also canvass the complete park in search of anything that has been used, a knife, a note, anything of any significance. Anything that can be associated with the murders at the Styles Apartment Complex. The tenants will be divided up accordingly and will have to be back in three hours. Mr. and Mrs. Styles will transport them by bus back to the apartment complex. It is a beautiful spring like day and the weather is very accommodating. If any of the tenants get tired beforehand they can sit in the bus and wait for the rest of the tenants to come back.

Mr. and Mrs. Styles divided them up two by two and sent them in different directions, each with a walking stick to guide them along the way. The tenants were given explicit instructions not to destroy any evidence but to use their cell phones to contact the police in their group.

There's a small fishing pond in the center of Lowler Park where four or five tenants can fish after they've taken their turn canvassing the park looking for anything unusual they can tie in with the murderous hanging of Mr. Leon Platterson. Most of the tenants went along and helped search the park for clues but so far they've had very little luck.

One of the tenants found a knife lying close to a pond but it was clean as a whistle on both sides so he left it that way. While yet another person found a note lying in the grass with no importance connected to it so it was not picked up. At 4:30PM everybody was brought back to the Styles Apartment Complex.

Early Monday morning a meeting was posted on the bulletin board for Tuesday night at 7:00PM with some forthcoming, interesting news for everybody in the complex. Please be sure to attend. When Tuesday evening arrived swarms of residents filed into the Community Room to share in the good news. The meeting started at exactly 7:00PM with a wide array of announcements, comments and questions. Before the tenants were dismissed Mrs. Styles brought up the last issue announcing the remodeling of the large, center room down the main hall. She said, "Mr. Styles and I have discussed this at length and have decided to bring this up at the meeting tonight. How many of you this evening would be interested in eating your meals here in a dining room? We would probably be serving two meals a day, breakfast and dinner." Almost everybody raised their hand. A few shrugged and looked at each other quizzically as if they didn't know what it was all about. Mrs. Styles continued further, "We'll probably be open for meals by August 1. A payment of three dollars a meal will not be added on to your existing bill because there might be days when you would eat your meals in your own apartment. So we will collect the money as you come in to eat. If anybody knows of any good cooks around please report that to our office because we will be hiring three. The tables will accommodate about sixty tenants, so we will have to eat in two shifts. How does that sound to all of you?" Everybody nodded and said, "That sounds good." Mrs. Styles also remarked, "We will be serving meals from 11:30AM till 1:30PM Monday through Friday excluding Saturday and Sunday. This concludes this evenings meeting and thank you all for coming. May the rest of your evening be enjoyable." A few of the tenants lagged behind to ask some more questions while the rest went on ahead.

Sue was surprised at the outcome of this evenings meeting due to the fact that so many people expressed interest. Well, it would be nice for a change to eat somebody else's cooking once in awhile besides your own. Wouldn't you think so? I would!

The tenants that left the meeting went to the Community Room to play billiards, have a cup of coffee, and watch television or just visit. Some were reading the today's paper they had forgotten about. Everybody enjoys the articles, illustrations, advertisements, current movie listings at the theaters in town and a variety of other presentations. It's a paper well read.

One by one the tenants start to go back to their apartments when they are finished playing billiards. The coffee is all and the 10:00PM news is over so there is nothing left to do but retire for the night.

As the weeks passed by the remodeling continued for the dining room at the Styles Apartment Complex on 114 Donley Street. The tenants walked by glancing in to see carpenters, painters and floor repairmen working diligently to provide the necessities for a clean, comfortable eating area. Eventually as August 1 drew near the tenants could see the dining tables, chairs, silverware and napkins positioned into place. Flowers adorned each table with a serving area close to the wall. Lacy curtains covered the dining room windows to give the room a homey, uncluttered atmosphere.

An open house for the Barker Dining Room was posted on the bulletin board with the first meal being served to the tenants on Sunday August 3, 2005. Admission price is $3.00 per person. The noon meal will be served to residents only, no visitors. The menu for the day will be meat loaf, mashed potatoes and gravy, creamed corn, jell-o, coffee or tea and pineapple upside down cake. Sounds good, doesn't it? Yummy!

August 3 dawned bright and early with the noon day sun blazing in the sky. The three cooks that were hired, Mary Black, Catherine Powell and Joe Bleer, were starting to make the meat loaf to bake in the oven. As the morning wore on Joe and Mary peeled a mountain of potatoes and Catherine made several flavors of instant jell-o that would be firm by 11:30AM. The pineapple upside down cake was baked the day before ready to be devoured. As 11:30 rolled around all the tenants that lived at the apartment complex came and lined up to partake of the first meal. Sue and several of her friends attended the meal commenting on the flavorful food being served and the variety.

After the meal was over everybody joined in some free Bingo games with an abundance of prizes. Sue won Bingo five times and walked out with a bag full of surprises. It was hard to hear the Bingo caller because of the whirring of the air conditioner. Sue made the remark, "I guess I'll volunteer my services as a Bingo caller the next time they need one."

At suppertime many of the tenants decided to stay for the evening meal which consisted of the leftovers from dinner. The tenants spent a good part of the day in the Barker Dining Hall for two meals and Bingo acting like they enjoyed every minute of it. After supper everybody broke into groups to play cards for several hours and then retire for the evening.

The head cook, Joe Bleer, has decided to take up residence with his aging mother, Melva 87, in one of the apartments on the first floor. Melva is in poor health and doesn't get out of the apartment much anymore while Joe has worked in various nursing homes, restaurants etc…Mr. Bleer passed away ten years ago and Joe moved in with his mother immediately. He applied for the job at the Styles Apartment Complex and was hired that same day. Joe is a 48 year old confirmed bachelor with no siblings, originating from St Louis, Missouri. Living at the apartment complex is very convenient for Joe because he'll be cooking breakfast and dinner in the kitchen. He'll have to be at work at 6:00AM in the morning until 2:00PM in the afternoon. Melva, his mother, does what she can in the apartment and then awaits anxiously for her son, Joe, to return. Joe is a homebody by nature. He's never gone out with the crowd, dated or such. His cooking profession always required that he went to bed early and arose early to cook at the different locations. He really hasn't had much of a social life to speak of. After he gets out of his kitchen job he eats a bite and watches television. Melva finishes watching a movie, the 10:00PM news and then retires for the evening. Joe is up at 5:00AM while Melva sleeps on.

One evening Lyle, one of the billiard players, came in to the dining room and asked Joe and the others if they would care to play billiards and they said, "Yes, as soon as Joe is finished working." So they waited and brought Joe back to the Community Room with them. They proceeded to play billiards choosing sides, Joe and Lyle on one side, Nick and George on the other.

As they were conversing and playing billiards the conversation turned rather personal. Lyle asked Joe, "Are you originally from St. Louis, Missouri?" Joe said, "Yes, I am." Lyle then proceeded to ask him "Have you been a cook all your life, Joe?" Joe remarked, "No, as a matter of fact I was just released from St. Louis Men's Prison several years ago where I had served ten years. Actually, that's where I learned the art of cooking at the prison. I was assigned to the breakfast shift for awhile and then I was re-assigned to the dinner and supper shift. I just stayed with cooking after that. I've worked in various hotels and restaurants around the area where my mother and I lived at the time." Lyle asked him, "Have you ever been married?" Joe said," "No although I was very close one time before I went to prison but everything fell through the cracks. I guess it wasn't meant to be. Who knows?" Lyle, Nick and George agreed and continued on with the billiard game. They all three explained to Joe how their wives had passed away within the last ten years and each of them had moved into the Styles Apartment Complex after that. Joe sympathized with them and continued playing billiards. By now it was getting close to suppertime and Joe said, "I will have to eat and check on my mother. I can probably be back after supper if you guys will be coming back?"They said, "Yes we'll be back because there's nothing interesting on television this evening." So they all agreed to come back around 7:00PM.

At 7:00PM sharp all the players returned to the Community Room for a couple of hours of billiards before retiring for the night. Once again it was Joe and Lyle on one side, Nick and George on the other, with Joe and Lyle winning every game. They all continued discussing different aspects of their lives until the cuckoo clock on the Community Room wall cuckooed ten times indicating ten o'clock. Also the last cup of coffee was gone so they all went to their apartments.

As Joe walked down the hall towards his apartment he sensed something was wrong. He approached the door and noticed it was ajar so he walked in. He called, "Mother! Mother!" He thought she probably didn't hear him so he went into her bedroom and found her lying on the bed fast asleep. Or so he thought! He edged up closer to the bed and took her pulse but there was none. He checked her heart and it wasn't beating nor was she breathing. His mother had died in her sleep during the time he was playing billiards with the guys. Joe started sobbing because he wished he could've been with her those last moments of her life. To hear her last words she would echo to him. His mother, Melva, was 87 years old and in poor health the last couple of years. She was confined to her apartment most of the time. Joe meditated in silence awhile before he called the ambulance to take her to St. Luke's Hospital in downtown St. Louis to pronounce her dead. The ambulance came immediately and transported her body with Joe following in his car. After Melva was pronounced dead she was taken to Baker's Funeral Home for the autopsy and final burial preparations. The autopsy report the next day indicated Melva had a silent heart attack in her sleep because she did have a history of heart trouble. Her casket would be open for viewing the next night with a church service and burial the next day. All the tenants of the Styles Apartment Complex plus other friends and relatives paid their respects as they filed past the casket for a last look taking a seat for a small service conducted by Pastor Jones. The St. Louis Baptist Church was overcrowded the next day for the memorial service and burial following at the St. Louis Cemetery on the edge of the city.

The Barker Dining Room at the Styles Apartment Complex furnished the lunch after Melva Bleer's funeral for the tenants, friends and relatives. Joe was overwhelmed with gratitude at the acts of kindness bestowed upon him at the death of his mother. Joe will continue to live in his apartment and work in the Barker Dining Room as a cook as long as they can use him.

Joe continues to play billiards in the evenings at 7:00PM when he is finished working for the day. Occasionally he brings a snack of cookies or something he personally baked to share with his billiard friends. Joe has a car but he doesn't drive it much because he doesn't have anywhere to go. Except now he visits Melva's grave once a week to decorate it with fresh flowers and say some prayers. When Joe drives back to the Styles Apartment Complex his car just sits outside at the mercy of the elements.

One day Joe said, "I wasn't raised to go to church on Sundays years ago and neither did my parents so that's why I don't go like the rest of the tenants. I'm thinking pretty strongly about going along with all of you some Sunday." George said, "Would you like to come along this Sunday for the 11:00AM services at the Galilee Baptist Church on Brinkley Street? You can ride along with me and we leave at 10:30AM. Services last about one and a half hours, and then we all go downtown for dinner. You're not working anyway Joe and it'll give you a break from your own cooking and a chance to sample someone else's." Joe said, "That's true and that suits me just fine. I'll be in the lobby waiting at 10:30AM. Thank you!"

When Sunday finally approached Joe was all dressed up in a suit and sitting in the lobby waiting for his ride from George. As the elevator came down into the lobby George made the comment, "The elevator was sure bumpy this morning. At one point I got kind of scared because it acted like it was going to stop between floors but it kept on going. I guess I'll report that to the maintenance man. I think everybody should take the back stairs for the rest of the day. What do you think Joe?" Joe said, "I agree with you. When we come back I'm taking the back stairs rather than have something happen. I never did trust elevators anyway."

The church was packed with people although they still found a place to sit. The pastor had a wonderful sermon about the after life, they offered communion and a variety of hymns. When they came out of church Joe said, "That was a nice service and I thoroughly enjoyed it. I guess you're stuck with me every Sunday from now on." George said, "That's fine Joe. We'll be glad to accommodate you." They all headed downtown to the Border's Restaurant for their Sunday special of baked chicken and the trimmings. They pushed their tables together and sat in a square circle. Everybody enjoyed this arrangement and continued to sit in this position when they came in. They ate their meal in this fashion conducting an informal meeting on various issues pertaining to the complex and otherwise. After they left the Border's Restaurant they were nearly drenched with rain as it came pouring down in sheets. When they arrived at the Styles Apartment Complex it was raining even harder and the tenants all sat and waited till the rain subsided even more. Then they proceeded into the apartment complex. Several ceilings in the apartments were leaking and had to be reported the same day. It rained for several hours and many streets in downtown St. Louis were flooded. The tenants were wet when they got inside so they proceeded to the Community Room where they dried off and had some warm coffee or tea to drink. Some watched television while others continued to drink coffee and visit. Finally as supper time drew near everybody headed back to their apartments. After supper was over some of the tenants went back to the Community Room for several games of cards. Joe decided he would play a game of cards because he hadn't played cards for years. The first game that was dealt was a winning hand for Joe. The second was equally a winning hand for him. Lyle shuffled the cards extra well the third time around and Joe had a winning hand again. Now how could that be? Explain that! A winning hand three times in a row! I can't believe that. Actually no one wanted to play cards with him because he was too lucky and they would probably lose. They told Joe, "Oh well, we'll play some other time. Were getting kind of tired anyway." What would you do? Do you suppose someone was cheating? Was it Lyle? It's good they weren't playing for money. They would've walked out of the Community Room broke.

September 6

A meeting has been posted by Mrs. Styles on the bulletin board for tomorrow night Tuesday at 7:00PM in the Community Room. Problems have been arising regarding certain issues and they have to be addressed. Mrs. Styles conducted the meeting with an opening prayer and then proceeded to tackle the agenda for the evening. Mrs. Styles said, "The tenants have been getting careless with their cards and keys which have been returned to the office. Please carry your cards and keys with you at all times. Also some of the tenants are not bothering to pay their water bill as was previously explained. A new specification will be enforced at the apartment complex.

Namely, if anyone fails to pay their water bill with their rent three times in a row they will be evicted from the premises. I repeat we will definitely enforce this new specification. I think a lot of you know who you are because I see a lot of sheepish looks on some of your faces. Please clear this matter up with me in my office privately. Another issue we have to address tonight is in regard to the wasted food that is left on the plates after you are done eating. It's a shame the amount of food that is being thrown away. If you can't eat all the food you have taken please don't take so much food the next time. Take only what you can eat. This concludes our meeting for this evening. Good night!"Everybody got up to leave angry, muttering to themselves about the food waste, water bill, cards and keys. Everybody could identify with one of the issues. They all went back to their apartments to mutter some more. Little good it's going to do them! If everybody would conduct themselves in a mannerly fashion Mrs. Styles wouldn't have to address these issues.

Anonymous Calls Again

Mrs. Leon Platterson was also at the meeting and had returned to her apartment with the intention of retiring for the night when she received a phone call asking, "Is this Mrs. Leon Platterson?" Mrs. Platterson said, "Yes, this is. Who's calling, please?" The anonymous caller shrieked into the telephone, "What the hell do you care who's calling anyway? Your main worry should be whether you're going to wake up or not tomorrow morning. Remember, I told you awhile back you're going to be my next victim. Have you forgotten that? I'm not that far away from your apartment you know." Mrs. Platterson started weeping and pleading with him again. "Please leave me alone. If you need money I will gladly give you some to save my life but please don't harm me, please. Why did you single out my husband to kill and now me? I'm sure we don't know you." The anonymous caller said, "Never mind why I singled you out. You are my next victim, lady." SLAM! The receiver was slammed into Mrs. Platterson's ear and then there was dead silence. She stood there dazed and dumbfounded with the receiver still in her hand not knowing what to do or say. She decided to call the police department even though it was well after midnight. When they came to the door they could hear her crying from the outside. Officer Brown and Officer Burns knocked on the door and Mrs. Platterson invited them in. She explained the details of the telephone call amidst constant crying, stress and anxiety. The officers asked her a variety of questions such as "Did you recognize the voice? Did it sound like a man or a woman's voice? Have you heard that voice before? If so, where?" Officer Burns said, "Mrs. Platterson, the police department will post a policeman at your door for the next few nights for protection. My suggestion is, If you are fearful of staying by yourself from now on you might consider having someone stay with you at night. After we leave there will be a policeman up shortly. If you have any disturbances from here on please don't hesitate to call the police department. That's what we're here for. Thank you!" When Officer Gray posted himself at the door Mrs. Platterson felt safe enough to go to bed for the night.

Everything was fine for the next several days until Sunday night rolled around. Mrs. Platterson had finished eating supper in her apartment and decided to sit in the Community Room to watch the 7:00PM news. While she was sitting on the divan a grungy, surly type of man with tattered clothes and a pungent, filthy odor sat across from her saying, "Mrs. Platterson, I have a small revolver in my pocket and I won't hesitate to use it if I have to. I want you to get off the divan slowly and quietly, walk to the elevator, go inside and wait for me. Don't talk to anybody. At this point I have the loaded gun pointed right at you. I will be in the elevator after you."

Mrs. Platterson didn't recognize him as anyone she had ever seen in the apartment complex before. His mask was hanging below his chin but when he came into the elevator he had it pulled over his mouth. He demanded all the money Mrs. Platterson had in her purse and she gave it to him. As she was emptying her purse she swung it towards his face as a distraction but he somehow avoided the impact of the purse. He grabbed Mrs. Platterson by the throat yelling, "I hate old people like you because you're a menace to society. If I had my say so I think they ought to line you people up 60 years or older and shoot you one by one. That way we wouldn't be bothered by the likes of you anymore. Maybe that'll happen one of these days." After he loosened his grip on her throat she literally dropped to the elevator floor in a heap crying, begging for mercy and pity pleading, "Leave us all alone and please leave the apartment complex. It seems like I've seen you in here before already. What has anyone ever done to you besides let you warm up, watch television and drink coffee? No one has ever approached you before like you have us."

What Mrs. Platterson said must've angered him immensely because he immediately tied her hands behind her back and stuffed a handkerchief in her mouth as he went from anger into laughter. After he tied Mrs.

Platterson up, he had her sit in the corner of the elevator while he made a fast getaway with her jewelry and money. He ran out of a side door, into an alley and down the street.

Mrs. Platterson sat on the elevator floor all night long since no one rode the elevator after 11:00PM at night anymore. Bob Smith came into the elevator the next morning at 7:00AM to get the mail from the day before and he untied her and asked her what happened. She told Bob she had been bound and gagged, threatened at gunpoint and robbed of her money and jewelry. The masked man also said, "The next time I'll take your life, you old bitch. I'll never get as old as you, I'll see to that. I'll do away with myself before that happens. I won't be a bother to anybody else like you crusty, old bitches!"

Mrs. Platterson called the police department once again and they sent two detectives to the apartment complex to interview her. Detective Jordan and Detective Burns came as soon as they got the call. Mrs. Platterson related the story in detail from the scene in the Community Room to the scene in the elevator. The detectives asked her, "Would you recognize the masked man in a police lineup and she said, "Possibly." So they brought her to the police station and showed her a lineup of suspects for various crimes but none of them looked like the masked man in the elevator. They took her back to the apartment complex and said they'd keep in touch with her. They posted a policeman at her door again for the next several nights.

Bingo Night

A Bingo game is scheduled for this evening Sept. 25 at 7:00PM for a good cause. Proceeds will go to the Harry Clone Foundation for his medical treatment while battling leukemia. Harry and Elizabeth Clone are residents of the Styles Apartment Complex and natives of St. Louis, Missouri. They have three children two sons in St. Louis, Missouri and a daughter in Nashville, Tennessee. They also have seven grandchildren. Bill has three sons, Mark has two sons and Ann has two daughters.

Bingo is $5.00 for the evening with money for prizes and the refreshments are free. Sue Benson is the caller for the night since her voice is loud, clear and can be heard very well. While the residents were playing Bingo the conversation turned to Mrs. Platterson and her experience of being bound and gagged in the elevator by an unknown assailant. Mrs. Platterson used to come to the Bingo games but not anymore. Not even for a fund raiser like this evening. Mrs. Platterson is fearful of getting on the elevator since her past experience two weeks ago. She stays in her apartment day and night only venturing downstairs to get her mail. She takes the back stairs even though it's hard for her to walk them. Anymore Mrs. Platterson is very quiet and subdued living the simple life. I think the stalker has scared her for the remainder of her days.

The proceeds of the Bingo game amounted to $200.00 which will be donated to the Harry Clone Foundation for his leukemia treatments. Everybody left the Bingo game and took the back stairs to their apartments. A few residents went to the Community Room to watch the 10:00 news with their friends, share a cup of coffee and retire for the evening. While the residents were in the Community Room a strange looking man in his forties was stretched out on the blue divan also watching television and drinking coffee oblivious of everybody else. He was of average height and weight with a foul smelling odor about him. The hair he had wasn't combed plus an unshaven face to match his hairstyle. His clothes were tattered and torn and he had a grungy appearance. When the residents tried to engage him in a conversation he grunted and grumbled and kept his eyes focused on the television avoiding their conversation. The residents left a few minutes before he did yet they could see him lurking around the corners kind of sheepishly trying to cover his tracks where he'd been. Finally they saw him head for the front door and leave the apartment complex headed for, "who knows where?" He has been seen by other residents but he doesn't reveal his identity when they ask him nor does he play Bingo. He's just what you'd call a loner. Several people have watched him out of the window and noticed that he keeps walking north closer to the downtown area. They watched him till he was clear out of sight only to return again a couple of days later. Why was he sitting in the Community Room at the Styles Apartment Complex watching television when he should've been in bed? Because he's a homeless person without a job so he doesn't have to get up in the morning and go to work like other people. The residents reported him to the police and by the time they arrived at the Styles Apartment Complex to search for him he had disappeared. That was the last anybody had seen of him for a long time.

The days are getting cooler, jacket weather, with rain occasionally to make it feel even cooler yet. The residents are staying inside in the evenings unless they go in a group on an outing by bus and come back the same way. It's just too dangerous to venture out by oneself at night because of the random killings that have transpired in the elevator in the last nine months. Someone is still out there waiting to take advantage of an innocent victim.

Chapter 6
A Wielding Axe

The residents are anxiously waiting for the posting of the new activities for the month of October. Several ladies are standing at the bulletin board studying the list to see which activities they want to participate in. There are the usual birthday parties, Bingo games, cards and transportation of a group of residents by bus to Whitmer College for plays and something new! A Halloween party! Can you believe that? A Halloween party at an apartment complex for older retired residents? That's right! October 31 at 7:00PM in the Community Room. C'mon, let's go! The residents are urged to dress in costumes befitting the occasion. Let's look for our costumes!

As 7:00PM rolls around the tenants of the Styles Apartment Complex enter the Community Room one by one as ghosts, goblins, skeletons, the walking dead etc.... Some of them are even devils with pitchforks and corpses in coffins. A sign on the front door of the complex reads Trick or Treaters welcome. Please knock. The trick or treaters are already knocking and gaining entrance from the tenants. The tenants have a wide variety of candy to choose from as they pitch it into their Halloween bags."Knock! Knock! Trick or Treat! Give me something good to eat," they yell as they file in and out of the door until 11:00PM. At this point the complex door is locked for the evening and no trick or treaters are allowed in anymore. But the Halloween party goes on for the tenants as usual. Three top prizes were awarded to the best dressed tenants. First prize went to 84 year old Joe Dreven dressed like the devil with a pitchfork. Second prize went to 89 year old Adam Blume dressed like a skeleton with a mask carrying his tombstone under his arm. Third prize went to 75 year old Maggie Minton dressed like the walking dead covered with dirt carrying her tombstone with her. The top three winners were awarded money as their prize. At the refreshment table the tenants ate Halloween cookies shaped like ghosts and goblins drinking orange and black cold drinks. They also nibbled orange and black mints plus a variety of other Halloween sweets. Some of the tenants watched a scary Halloween movie besides a break in on the movie channel depicting vandalism in some of the residential areas of St. Louis because of Halloween. Someone always has to spoil the fun! Right!?

At midnight the first set of tenants decided it was time to go back to their apartments. Mr. and Mrs. John Steel and Mr. and Mrs. Gordon Grebner said their goodnight and walked out of the Community Room. As they headed towards the elevator they noticed that the doors were closed and no amount of prying could get them open. So they pounded on the doors and all of a sudden they miraculously rolled open revealing a sign on the elevator wall that read "Trick or Treat." Suspended from the ceiling in the corner of the elevator hung 82 year old Lewis Brown who had been widowed for five years living on the sixth floor dressed as a skeleton with blood dripping from his face onto the carpet on the floor. He was suspended by the same mechanical device that was used to hang a couple of other residents sometime ago. His heart was cut out of his chest and also his hands and fingers. Everything was lying at his feet in a heap. His chest was gushing volumes of blood onto the walls and floor covering it completely. His eyes were cut out of their sockets and thrown on top of the other body parts in a corner. He had a cigarette between his lips that had been lit and had burned holes through his skin. The Styles

Apartment Complex could've burned down with a lit cigarette! Lewis Brown's legs were both cut off at the thighs and thrown on top of his heart, fingers and hands. What a miserable sight to behold! More blood was flowing from the amputated thighs till the complete elevator floor was one solid mass of blood wall to wall. It was running out of the elevator and down the hallway making it very slippery and dangerous.

Yes, Lewis Brown's body was completely mutilated and totally unrecognizable beyond belief. A foul stench permeated the air to the point of wearing a mask to alleviate the odor.

The Steel's and Grebner's screamed at the top of their lungs as they stood and viewed the horrific, unbelievable sight confronting them in the elevator. By now various tenants in the complex had congregated at the elevator lamenting and crying at the sight of Lewis Brown hanging before them mutilated worse than an animal. Someone hurriedly notified the authorities in regards to what had transpired in the elevator. The police and detectives arrived immediately assessing the sad situation, asking the tenants questions …the usual procedure. Nobody knew anything or saw anything unusual because they were all at the Halloween party.

The paramedics wheeled a gurney to the elevator, collected the torso and body parts going to the Brown Mortuary for the final preparations. The remains of Lewis Brown's body was sealed in a casket and a memorial service was held at the Church of the Nazarene a day later. Burial was at the St. Louis Cemetery following the church service. A luncheon was served in the church basement for the family, relatives and friends of Lewis Brown. Extra detectives will be added to the St. Louis Police Department for the time being in the hope that more heads are better than one theory when it comes to cracking a case such as this one.

Billiards

One evening as Joe, the cook, was sitting in the billiard room watching the 10:00PPM news Detective Sline and Lentfor entered and sat down with Joe. Detective Sline asked him, "What's your name, sir?" To which he replied, "Joe Bleer." He asked, "Where are you from?" Joe said, "My mother, Melva Bleer, just passed away two weeks ago and we've lived all over already. Detective Sline asked him again, "What do you do for a living?" Joe replied, "I'm the head cook here at the Styles Apartment Complex. Is there anything else you'd like to know?" To which they replied, "No, not really. The reason we're asking you these questions is because someone here at the complex called in the other day and gave us your name so we decided to check things out. Joe, would you ride down to the police department with us tonight for some random checking and then we'll bring you right back?" Joe said, "Sure, that's fine. I'm tired of sitting here anyway." Joe asked Detective Sline, "What did the tenant from the complex say about me?" Detective Sline proceeded to say, "Well, they said they've seen you oftener at night around the elevator. By the way, I never did ask you what you're doing around the elevator at night anyway? Can you answer that?" Joe said, "Yes, I can. Sometimes I take the elevator back and forth to the Community Room at night before and after I play billiards with my friends. They've already gone back to their apartments for the evening." Detective Lentfor asked him, "Why were you still sitting back there and all the other tenants are back in their apartments for the evening?" Joe said, "Because I wasn't sleepy yet, so I decided to drink a cup of coffee and watch the 10:00PM news for a change." By this time they were parked in front of the police department so Joe got out of the car and entered the building. They gave him a lie detector test, asked him some more questions and checked him out generally speaking. Everything tested negative for the time being so they took him back to the Styles Apartment Complex. On the random checking they found out that he had gotten out of prison several years ago. Detective Sline said, "We see you've been in prison again. What were you in there for this time?" Joe said, "I shot a man and killed him during an argument in a bar in Piler, Indiana. I was guilty of first degree murder." Detective Sline said, "I see." When they parted they said they'd be checking back on him periodically. Joe said, "That's fine because I'm here to oblige."

Around 3:00AM the next morning, Monday, the tenants were roused from their sleep by the wail of sirens, police cars, etc...., lined up at the Styles Apartment Complex. Someone had broken into the complex office and stolen $3000.00. Everybody came out into the hallway thinking there was another elevator murder but they were wrong. Someone knew the combination to the safe or jimmied it because it opened and $3000.00 was taken. Detective Sline and Lentfor were there again asking questions as usual. The lock wasn't broken nor changed so they had to use their key a certain way. It sounds like it was somebody from the Styles Apartment Complex. Doesn't it? It does to me! How else would they get in without knowing the combination? And they would've used the key that everybody has for the main door. Whoever is doing this, are they stealing now besides killing?

The next morning Joe was up bright and early at 6:00AM to cook breakfast for the residents. Everybody filed in at 7:15 for their helping of bacon, eggs, cinnamon rolls and coffee. While the residents were eating breakfast they were discussing the break in that occurred at 3:00AM that very morning. Someone opened the front door of the complex, entered and cracked the safe. Three thousand dollars was taken and they exited the same way. The thieves made a fast getaway with no clues or fingerprints left behind. It had rained a little bit before morning so there were fresh footprints inside and out which the detectives took care of. They brought everything back to the police department to see if they could match the footprints or anything else with that of the prisoners incarcerated at the time. At this time nothing's been matching up yet. Not even Joe, the cook's footprints, matched anything the detectives brought back. After the residents went back to their apartments the same Detectives, Sline and Lentfor, and two more policemen came to the complex to question them again. The policemen and detectives canvassed the complete complex with a pencil and notepad jotting down anything unusual the residents saw or heard the day before.

They went door to door questioning all the residents in the apartments. When they arrived at Felix and Beth Tabor's apartment they were socially invited in and Beth offered them a cup of coffee which they politely accepted. Detective Lentfor approached the Tabor's with a wide variety of questions such as, "Did you see anybody unusual the day before lurking around the apartment complex? Any anonymous or harassing telephone calls? Has anybody been following you home from downtown the few times you go out at night?" Mr. and Mrs. Tabor answered an emphatic "No" to all the questions. The detectives thanked them for their time, coffee and bid them goodnight. As Detective Sline and Lentfor headed back to the police department, Detective Sline said, "I didn't think we'd get any information from anybody. Sometimes I wonder if some of these people have information they're not releasing because their afraid the police might disclose their name and they might be considered a suspect. "What do you think?" Detective Lentfors said, "That could be."

The next morning, Tuesday, Joe didn't report for work in the kitchen at 6:00AM because of an appointment with Dr. Marlen at 10:00AM for his heart condition which he has had for twenty years. Joe's medication was changed and the doctor warned him, "Joe, you'd better take it easy for the next couple of days because the tests revealed that your heart's been under a lot of stress and it has weakened considerably. This change of medicine should improve it immensely. I want to see you back here in my office in a month." Joe agreed and left Dr. Marlen's office.

That same night after supper instead of resting like Dr. Marlen recommended Joe was in the Community Room playing billiards and drinking too much coffee. He was also missing out on some much needed rest for his body. About 10:30 everybody decided to call it a night and go to their apartments including Joe. He had one more cup of coffee, said goodnight to everybody and proceeded to his first floor apartment to retire for the evening because he had to be in the kitchen at 6:00AM.

Joe's kitchen helpers, Mary Black and Catherine Powell, reported for work at 5:45AM as usual waiting for Joe to show up. Mary said, "I wonder if Joe overslept this morning? I've almost had that happen to me already. Have you ever had that happen, Catherine?"Catherine said, "Yes, I almost overslept one day last week remember? We got home from Bingo late the night before and I forgot to set my alarm clock. I woke up just in time. I didn't hear any roosters crowing though. Ha! Ha! I'll never do that again."

By the time it was 6:15AM Mary and Catherine had started making fresh coffee, bacon, cinnamon rolls and scrambled eggs for the breakfast residents that would be coming down to eat at 7:00AM. It was always close to one hundred residents.

It was now 6:45AM with Joe not showing up for work so Mary and Catherine knew immediately something had happened to him. Mary went to the office and reported Joe's absence to Mrs. Styles which she was unaware of and asked that his room be checked out. Mrs. Styles called for the maintenance man, Norbert, to see if Joe was okay and why he didn't come to work in the kitchen this morning. Norbert went to Joe's first floor apartment and knocked on the door repeatedly but no answer. Norbert also thought it was strange that Joe didn't respond. Norbert started calling Joe's name out loud screaming, "Joe, Joe, are you in there? If so, please answer!" Norbert twisted the door knob but it wouldn't open. It was locked. Joe either was not in the apartment or something had befallen him. Norbert went back to the office and reported his findings to Mrs. Styles who in turn called the St. Louis Police Department for help. As the police department, ambulance and paramedics pulled up in front of the apartment complex the residents gathered in the hallway as the police kicked in the door to Joe's apartment. Since Mrs. Styles allowed pets in the complex Joe's apartment was a terrible mess. Rover, the dog, jumped up on Captain Parks as he led him through the mess into Joe's bedroom where Joe was stretched out on the king sized bed. Everybody had to be careful to avoid walking into dog feces and urine all over the carpet. The odor was unbearable as the police department passed out gas masks to anybody that entered the apartment including Mrs. Styles, the owner. Joe's eyes were wide open with a glaze on them. Vomit was evident with puddles all over the apartment. He was moaning and groaning clutching his chest as if in pain from a heart attack. His face was ashen gray and covered with sweat. He was trying to point at something and mouth the words but no one could understand what Joe meant. He was placed on a gurney and transported to St. Luke's Memorial Hospital in St. Louis for medical treatment. Since Joe has no parents nor siblings and relatives unknown there was no one to accommodate him to the hospital. He was taken immediately to the emergency room, treated and transferred to intensive care where he was hooked up to a life support system. There was no one to speak for Joe except a few friends at the apartment complex. They stayed with him until it got dark and then they headed back to their apartment. Before they left the hospital they gave an attendant the number they could be reached at just in case.

During the morning hours, around 2:00AM, Lyle received a call from the hospital intensive care unit telling him Joe Bleer had suffered a massive heart attack and died at 1:22AM. During breakfast it was announced over the intercom as everybody was shocked and dismayed at Joe Bleer's sudden heart attack and death. Joe followed his mother, Melva, exactly five weeks to the day. His casket was open for viewing at Brown's Mortuary with all of the residents and staff attending. The next day was a memorial service for Joe at the mortuary with burial at the St. Louis Cemetery beside his mother in a pauper's grave because of his financial status. His funeral and burial were well attended with a free lunch following at the Styles Apartment Complex.

The next day Mr. and Mrs. Styles started to clean Joe's apartment. The carpet had to be thoroughly cleaned and fumigated before the apartment was rented out again. All of Joe's personal belongings will be donated to the St. Louis Salvation Army. Any money that he had on his person or in his apartment will be donated to the Galilee Baptist Church on Brinkley St. where he had been attending services.

Mr. and Mrs. Styles had a stack of Joe's personal belongings piled outside his apartment door until...you'll never believe what they uncovered clear back in the corner of the bedroom closet? $3000.00 in a cloth bag that Mrs. Styles had placed in the safe for safe keeping. Imagine that! The police department had given Joe a lie detector test and finger printed him which all turned out negative. Mrs. Styles immediately called the police department, with them coming over right away to check everything out. They agreed that Joe had taken the money from the office safe two weeks ago and denied it to the police. Mrs. Styles took the bag of money and transferred it back to the safe. What a denial! No wonder he was in prison at one time!

Mr. and Mrs. Styles worked on the apartment for several days concluding on a Wednesday. By Thursday morning it was in the St. Louis Chronicle newspaper for rent.

The St. Louis Police Department reported back to Mr. and Mrs. Styles that their lie detector equipment was not working properly and therefore didn't register the correct answers Joe Bleer gave. The finger printing equipment was working just fine so they assumed it was the lie detector equipment because it was defective.

Well, that's one problem solved, but that still doesn't tell us who's responsible for the hangings and mutilations taking place in the elevator periodically.

A new job opening for a breakfast and dinner cook has been posted in the apartment complex and the St. Louis Chronicle newspaper. Men and women alike are being interviewed for the job as one leaves and another goes in. Mrs. Styles is kept busy all day long finding the best suitable person for the job. Finally she reaches her decision and once again it's a male cook. Thirty nine year old Mark Beale from St. Louis, Missouri, married to June with two children. They live approximately two miles across town on Juniper St. At present Mark is unemployed and June is a nurse at St. Luke's Medical Center. Their two daughters are six and eight years old. Mark has been a head cook at hospitals, infirmaries, restaurants, schools etc. There is never a great demand for head cooks because they usually promote the next cook in line. You just automatically go up the ladder. Mark was very happy he landed the job by his sheer expression of delight as he exited the interviewing office yesterday.

The next morning Mark reported for work at 6:00AM, flanked by assistant cooks Mary Black and Catherine Powell on either side cooking breakfast with him. By the end of the dinner shift Mary and Catherine had resigned themselves to the fact that they enjoyed Mark's company, labor and looked forward to working with him in the future. And we're sure the feeling is mutual.

Monthly Meeting

A monthly meeting is scheduled for this evening plus the regular Bingo game for the night. Mrs. Styles is conducting the meeting at 7:00PM to address several issues forthcoming. She immediately passed an extra memorial basket up and down the aisles in memory of Joe Bleer in spite of the $3000.00 robbery that Joe was guilty of. Several residents dropped money into the basket but the majority of them passed it right on by.

Mrs. Styles welcomed and formally introduced the new head cook, Mr. Beale. Mrs. Styles said, "Mark, would you care to say a few words to the residents?" Mark said, "Yes, I would like to thank Mrs. Styles for the offer. It is my pleasure to be working here at the Styles Apartment Complex. I hope my employment will bring new friendships and new relations among us." Everybody clapped including Mark's wife, June, and children, Anne and Sarah. Mark also said, "I hope you enjoy your meals. Thank you!" The residents clapped and nodded their heads in agreement.

Sue Benson called BINGO for the evening with $1.00 prizes as gifts. Bingo is $5.00 for the evening and the proceeds tonight will be added to Joe Bleer's Memorial Fund. As 10:00PM drew near, the residents filed out to return to their apartments. The cleanup crew came in and took over after the last resident left.

Mr. and Mrs. Styles are on the elevator headed for their 6th floor apartment for the evening, only to have Mrs. Styles come back down to the office because of something she forgot. When she stepped back into the elevator for the second time she was confronted by a scary, animal type, person growling, grumbling and muttering. He was saying "Argh! Argh!" like a beast with his eyes glazed. Mrs. Styles screamed with no one to hear her because the elevator doors were closed and it was sound proof. The beast like person was swinging an axe at Mrs. Styles and with every chop a chunk of her body was gone. Pieces of Mrs. Styles were lying all over the elevator floor. Her head was chopped to pieces as were all the other body parts. The beast man kicked the parts on a pile in a corner of the elevator and laughed to himself muttering, "The Final Floor" and pointing to the pile of flesh in the corner. The ceiling and walls in the elevator were dripping with blood. The beast man was sitting on the elevator floor sucking the sticky blood off of Mrs. Styles gouged out eyes and stroking the hair on her chopped up head. All of a sudden he jumped up letting out a yell, pressing the control panel as the elevator door opened up and he ran off into the night. He left behind a miserable mess of decapitation, amputation and a wielding axe.

Has someone reported a beastly looking man running down a public street? Why are the police cars with their sirens on chasing someone? What's going on? What happened? Let's get back to the apartment complex. Poor Mrs. Styles! She didn't deserve to die like that! I wonder if her husband, Arthur, is aware of what happened to his wife, Grace Styles? Let's go inside!

As they stepped into the main lobby of the complex the police, detectives, paramedics and residents are milling around, crying, whispering to each other and shaking their heads.

Mrs. Styles body parts have been taken to the Williams Funeral Home for cremation because of the type of death she endured. There will be a closed casket with her framed photograph on a small table. The service will be at 2:00PM at the Williams Funeral Home and burial at the St. Louis Cemetery following. A free lunch will be served at the Styles Apartment Complex for all those attending the funeral. Poor Arthur Styles! He looked so sad, depressed and broken hearted. He'll probably have to go to a nursing home now. He can't be alone. Who's going to take care of him?

After everything was over some residents went into the Community Room for coffee, television and visiting including Sue Benson. She made the remark that, "I"m scared to ride the elevator and live in the apartment. Or were they going to sell the Styles Apartment Complex? That's a possibility! Who knows?

Come Monday Morning

The residents were awakened this morning by a hammering outside of the Styles Apartment Complex. When they looked out at the still, dark sky they caught a glimpse of a real estate agent hammering a "For Sale" sign into the ground in front of the complex. When everybody came into the dining room this morning for breakfast, the room was abuzz with the "For Sale" sign issue. The residents were chattering, wondering what the outcome would be if the complex were to be sold? Would the new proprietor continue to keep it open as an apartment complex in spite of the horrendous killings that have transpired or would they have it torn down and a new building erected in its place? It seems like the old complex has a curse on it, doesn't it? After breakfast everybody left the dining room only to be confronted by the maintenance man's wife, Laura Mack, posting an emergency meeting on the bulletin board for this Monday night at 7:00PM encouraging everyone to attend. This evening everybody at the complex was there by 7:00PM for the meeting. Mrs. Mack conducted the meeting with information given to her by the Arthur Styles family. She said, "At this point the residents can continue to live in the apartments paying their monthly rent plus the water bill. If a new proprietor will not come forward to take over the ownership of the complex we will be forced to close and the tenants will have to take up residence elsewhere. We will inform you well in advance of this matter so you will have sufficient time to conduct yourself in an appropriate manner. Thank you."

The tenants listened quietly immersed in their thoughts about where to go and what to do about the situation. Mrs. Mack asked, "Any questions, anybody? That's what I was appointed for by the Styles family this evening." Mrs. Ruth Logan raised her hand, "Yes Ruth, what is your question?" Ruth asked, "Is it all right if we move out before our possible, appointed time? I'm getting too fearful and so are some of my friends about living here. It's just too dangerous. We're in danger of getting killed every time we step into the elevator. We're anxious to move. I already have an apartment spoken for. Can you comment on this?"Mrs. Mack said, "Of course, Ruth. You are free to move any time you want as long as your apartment and water bill are paid up. In other words no outstanding bills. Any other questions? Now's the time." Mrs. Flint raised her hand and Mrs. Mack said, "Mrs. Flint, what is your question?" Mrs. Flint asked, "Why are the hallways always dark in the evenings and during the night? That's dangerous in itself. It never used to be like that. I've just been noticing this lately." Mrs. Mack commented, "Thank you for bringing this matter to our attention, Mrs. Flint, because we weren't aware of this. We'll have Norbert check the electrical status of the complex and see what could've caused an electrical interruption. Anymore questions, anybody?" Mrs. Joan Appleton raised her hand, "Yes Joan, what is your question?" Joan asked, "What are these loud, unexplainable, noises and voices that I hear outside the complex during the evening and towards morning around 2:00 or 3:00AM? I've been to the office and complained about this before but nothing was done about it. Why not? Mrs. Styles never had an explanation." Mrs. Mack said, "We'll look into the matter for an explanation. Thank you." Mrs. Mack asked once again, "Anymore questions?" No one raised their hand anymore so Mrs. Mack said, "This concludes the meeting for this evening and if there are any further questions they can be directed to the main office as I will be occupying it as time allows." Everybody got up and left, most residents not too happy at the thought of packing and looking for a new apartment in today's world. It's always such a hassle!

At present Sue is barely hanging on to her checking account. She made arrangements with Mrs. Styles before she was murdered to pay for two months rent at one time, which she will do, but then she definitely has to take any job that's offered to her. She cannot be particular about anything. Monday morning she will have to start checking the want ads again for a job somewhere in the St. Louis area, especially if she might be moving to a more expensive apartment. No one knows for sure whether the Styles Apartment Complex will be sold or not. Everybody is in a tizzy about this. Mrs. Ruth Logan has already spoken for her apartment on Napier Street, about a mile north of the Styles Apartment Complex. Two other residents have also spoken for apartments close to where they are now. Mrs. Flint is also thinking about leaving because her eyesight is poor and the hallways are just too dark, dim and dingy. Mrs. Appleton is moving to another apartment regardless of whether they close the complex up or not. She is getting tired of being woke up during the night because of voices, noise and not being able to go back to sleep. No one else has complained about that. Have you?

Well, this past week at different times several men were seen sitting in the complex office discussing something with Mr. Arthur Styles' daughter, Sharon, at length. I'm sure it was about the fate of the Styles Apartment Complex. Arthur Styles has been admitted to the Forbes Nursing Home across town. Arthur was still qualified as an assistant manager but the loss of his wife, Grace, took care of that fast. His depression and broken hearted attitude has gotten the best of him.

Chapter 7
Who Killed Marcus Reil?

Sue got up early Monday morning to take the street bus downtown because there were several want ads that she wanted to apply for. She was glad she'd saved a little money in the bank, but by now that was running low and she would have to get a job soon. Her first office job application was at Green Financial Services as a secretary. She filled out a resume of past jobs and was told she would be contacted next week. No, she didn't tell them that she had been fired from several jobs. Well, that's Sue's problem not ours. Right?

She also applied at a vegetable canning factory several blocks from downtown St. Louis as a day worker in the canning department. They also said they would get back to her next week sometime.

Her third application was in Sara's Dress Shop as a sales clerk which she had never done before. She filled out her resume there and was asked, "Have you ever worked in a dress shop before?" To which she replied, "No, I haven't." The clerk said, "That's okay, because a lot of people haven't. We'll contact you in about a week either way."

On her way to the bus stop Sue stopped in for a cup of coffee at Bob's Diner and then went on her way back to the Styles Apartment Complex.

New Owners

On Saturday morning when Sue came down to breakfast the dining room was abuzz with the news that the apartment complex had been sold to the Ben Pickwell family. The "For Sale" sign had been removed from the premises and a name change is evident outside of the complex as they eat breakfast. The name had been changed from the Styles Apartment Complex to the Pickwell Apartment Complex. An introductory meeting at 7:00PM this evening has already been posted on the bulletin board.

At 7:00PM Ben and Joan Pickwell introduced themselves as the new proprietors of the Pickwell Apartment Complex. They are originally from the St. Louis, Missouri area having lived in Jacksonville, Florida for many years but there ties are still in St. Louis, Missouri. They moved back three years ago because Ben, a practicing attorney, secured a position with Grafte and Bell Attorneys and Margie is a registered nurse at St. Luke's Memorial Hospital. They have two children both married and living out of the state. They are both resigning from their jobs to become the managers of the Pickwell Apartment Complex.

Mr. Pickwell announced that the activity schedule would continue as usual. The monthly rent and water payment would be due the first day of each month. If any changes need to be made in the status of your rent and water payment please contact the office at your earliest convenience.

The cooking staff in the Barker Dining Room will retain their jobs as usual. A position is open for a new maintenance man besides Norbert to replace Mr. Styles who was transferred to a nursing home. The two groundskeepers will keep their present positions as will the two janitorial supervisors also be retained. A few other issues were addressed and the meeting was concluded. Mr. Pickwell also announced, "I understand there are those of you that are moving out of the complex because of the ongoing problems with the elevator. Please come to the office and straighten your rent, water bill, etc. before you leave. Thank you and Good evening." Most of the residents went back to their apartments while a few went to the Community Room for the usual visiting session.

A Week Later

Sue received three calls this week from her want ad jobs. Her day job at the vegetable canning factory was already taken and no more jobs were available. The clerk from Sara's Dress Shop called to tell her the position had been filled. The financial supervisor from Green Financial Services called and told her she'd been accepted for the job as secretary. He asked her if she could start tomorrow morning at 8:00AM and she said, "Yes." She thanked him and hung up. Sue also thanked God in the form of a prayer for making it possible for her to get a job. For awhile after supper Sue was watching television when all of a sudden who should appear on the screen but Marcus Reil, big as life itself! Sue recognized him immediately. It had been a year since she'd seen him. What was he doing on television anyway, that freak? Oh, now she knows why he's on television! It's been a year since the murder trial of her mother, Jane Linton. She's labeled the Notorious Serial Killer of Rockwood, Illinois. Remember? How disgusting! All those sordid details! Marcus explained the series of murders as they took place one by one. He is now manager of the Rockwood Apartment Complex and nothing has happened since. Jane Linton has been committed to the St. Louis Women's Prison for life. Marcus ended with Jane Linton's biography of her life as a killer dating back to a young married woman when Sue was just a young girl. Sue was absolutely livid with rage. She was thinking, "How could Marcus embarrass her on national television like that? He's got some nerve! Who does he think he is anyway?" A lot of bad thoughts are going through Sue's mind as she continues to watch the screen till Marcus disappears. For some reason this really gets her mind to thinking. Long after Sue went to bed, she couldn't conceal her distaste and hatred for Marcus and she couldn't get it out of her mind. It seemed like she lay awake for hours smouldering mad. Should she call Marcus on the phone and give him hell or what? Or should she curse at him? What do think she should do? What would you do?

A Month Later

About three weeks later Sue was watching television one night and who should appear on the screen but Marcus Reil, the Rockwood Apartment Complex manager, from Rockwood, Illinois. Marcus was murdered by a knife wound in the heart, twisted and left there after he answered a knock on the door. Marcus let out a loud scream and immediately slumped onto the front room carpet. The unknown assailant dashed out the side door and down the alley, just like old times, knowing his way around. Sue didn't say a word but just continued to watch the screen as the announcer said he was discovered that same night, transported to the hospital and pronounced dead on arrival. It was a huge funeral at the Brown Mortuary with burial following at the Rockwood Cemetery and a large luncheon at the La Bamba Restaurant in downtown Rockwood, Illinois. Marcus was 51 years old and a confirmed bachelor. His killer was never identified because they made a very fast getaway, discarded their disguise and were just another figure blending in with everybody else on the street that night. Marcus' killer will probably never be identified anymore. Chances are slim.

Several people at breakfast the next morning mentioned what they saw about Marcus Reil and asked Sue if she knew him and she said, "Yes, very well." She also said she watched the same program on television and was shocked and saddened by it.

Sue's secretarial job at Green Financial Services is coming along just great, her work performance is above average and Mr. Green, the owner, is very pleased with her. Now that Sue has a steady income she has a better chance to make her rent and water payment on time, enough money for food, change for her bus fare to work and back every day and incidentals.

Sue's depression has also improved since she received a thirty day supply of free sample pills until she can afford to buy her anti-depressants herself. So, Sue's been doing pretty well. She's even going to church services and praying oftener. She's made a few friends at the Pickwell Apartment Complex, maybe three or four. She sits at mealtime eating and visiting with them but not with other people at the table. She more or less picks and chooses her friends. Some people do that, I guess.

Once in awhile Sue goes to the Community Room after Bingo to get caught up on the news she's never heard before. She can't sit there too long because she has to get up early in the morning for work.

Sunday Afternoon

Sue decided to visit her mother, Jane, the Sunday before Thanksgiving which she did. They both went to the Visitation Room to talk by way of the phone with a glass shield between them. She told her mother, "On national television this past week Marcus Reil talked about your being in prison one year already, the beginning of your life sentence. He explained all the sordid details of the twelve murders of the Notorious Serial Killer of Rockwood, Illinois." Jane listened with a saddened face and tearful eyes as Sue told her everything Marcus said about her. Jane didn't say much about Marcus' remarks about her acting as if she didn't even care. She knew everything Marcus said about her was true, so how could she deny any of it? She couldn't! Marcus was telling the truth.

Sue told her mother about her new job at Green Financial Services as a secretary and how she liked her secretarial position. Jane was happy to hear that and asked, "Sue, can you finally make ends meet with your apartment and everything else?" Sue said, "Yes, I can."

By now Sue decided it's time to go back to the apartment complex for supper. After that she promised Mrs. Lands across the hall that she would be over for a visit this evening before she retires.

Thanksgiving Day —2005

Thanksgiving Day is here and so are one hundred and three residents seated in the Barker Dining Room to feast on roasted turkey and the trimmings. Everyone was seated at the table with their special friends as were Sue and her three lady friends. Mark, as usual, was the main cook for the meal plus his counterparts, Mrs. Mary Black and Mrs. Catherine Powell. The one hundred and three residents were seated, silverware in their hands, smiles pasted on their faces, ready to devour Mark's first Thanksgiving meal at the Pickwell Apartment Complex. They did partake of the whole meal but the main focus was on the turkey dressing. Isn't that everybody's focus? It's mine! They put the finishing touches on the meal with a big slice of pumpkin pie topped with whipped cream. It was a scrumptious meal! Sounds good? Yummy!

After everybody was finished eating some residents went to their apartments while others went to the Community Room for billiards, coffee and the 6:00PM news.

During the 6:00PM news Bridget LaGand asked, "Does anyone have a stomach ache or feel like vomiting?" Several residents said they didn't feel well and thought they would retire to their rooms. Some of them started complaining of unusual symptoms and left the Community Room. Still others thought they had the stomach flu because they had the classic symptoms. Neither Sue nor her lady friends were feeling well either. They all went on to their apartments including Sue. Mrs. Greer across the hall called Sue and asked her, "Sue, do you and your lady friends that you ate with feel okay after the Thanksgiving meal? My husband, Don, and I've been vomiting with a stomach ache awhile after we finished our meal. Your neighbors on the other side of you are sick, too. In fact, Mr. Grove took his wife, Ada, to the emergency room a little while ago. My friend called me from the second floor and said the hospital is sending some gurneys to the apartment complex to transport people to the hospital. Sue, quite a few residents got sick after eating Thanksgiving dinner. Do you think its food poisoning? I hope not." Mrs. Greer said, "It could be because everybody got sick about the same time with the same symptoms. Wouldn't that be strange?" Sue said, "Yes, it would be strange." She's going to bed so she'll be all right in the morning to go to work. She needs her rest and that's why she can't ever hold down two jobs like other people can. She's tried and it just doesn't work out! She gets too tired all of a sudden and she has to go and lie down. Actually, she gets so tired she's almost physically sick. Mrs. Greer and Sue both hung up as the ambulance pulled up and the paramedics came hurrying into the complex pushing gurneys to transport people to the hospital. Sue watched from the window as they took three people to the hospital.

At breakfast the next morning everybody was curious how the residents were feeling that were confined to the hospital. Mrs. Pickwell was there early this morning and announced, "The hospital residents are all three doing fine and will be back in their apartments in a day or so. The three people in the hospital were diagnosed with food poisoning so if any of you have the same symptoms that's probably what you have. We're sure the food poisoning came from the turkey which was thawed out too long. In the near future we will have to be more conscientious about these matters." Everybody looked at Mark Beale, Mary Black and Catherine Powell, but they showed no emotion. We know they didn't do this on purpose but they should know that a turkey cannot be thawed out extra long for safety's sake. We all know that! There just lucky no one got really sick and died! Now that would've been terrible! You just can't be careful enough! That same day the left over turkey was discarded but the remainder of the meal was eaten by the residents and tolerated very well. The residents all recuperated from the food poisoning and everything is back to normal.

Snowy Days

The first measurable snowfall was recorded on television last night with two inches in St. Louis proper and one and a half inches in the outlying areas. The temperature has been in the twenties during the night and the fifties and sixties during the day. No wind has been accompanying the cool temperatures for now. Numerous people can be seen Christmas shopping in the evenings in the downtown St. Louis area. Carolers are singing Christmas hymns on the downtown street corners, porches of private homes, etc.…. Sometimes they get invited inside out of the cold for a cup of hot chocolate and a warm, freshly, baked cookie. Sounds yummy, doesn't it?

Retail department stores have their Christmas wares on display plus neat decorations depicting white and green Christmas trees in their picture windows. The buildings in downtown St. Louis are illuminated with Christmas lights both inside and out. Shoppers are smiling and singing as they carry their packages to their cars hoping Santa Claus will be extra good to them this year. Everybody is yelling, "Merry Christmas and Happy New Year!" All the children have gathered for the arrival of Santa Claus at 6:00PM and here he comes! With a light snow falling he has landed his sleigh on a low roof of a store downtown, crawling out with a large bag of goodies while his four reindeer look on. He passes goodies to all the children and then continues into the store with all the children following him. He sets in his big, wooden, Santa Claus chair and one by one each child sets on his knee and tells him what he or she wants for Christmas. Santa Claus says, "I think I can make your toy when I get back to the North Pole, but I'll sure have to hurry," and the children nod their heads in wild glee and anticipation of Christmas Eve. Adults and parents alike are milling around and reminiscing of Christmas' past when they told Santa Claus what they wanted to unwrap on Christmas Eve and he would always oblige them, if possible.

By now the snow is getting heavier and most people are going home for the evening as a newly forecast winter snow storm is predicted with eight inches on the ground by tomorrow morning. Freezing rain will accompany the storm in advance. It's a chilly forecast!

Sue and her two lady friends are also shopping downtown. They split the taxi fare going down and will be doing the same coming back. Sue was shopping for her mother, Jane, for something she could use at the prison and also for a secret name that she drew at the Bingo game the other night. Her friends are doing the same.

Christmas Eve—2005

A Christmas buffet will be set up with the apartment complex furnishing the meat and the residents each bringing a pot luck dish starting at 6:00PM. A Christmas party, a gift exchange and Christmas snacks will be available throughout the evening. Everybody was seated with the exception of Stan, Martha and Lois Shohls. Lois is a sister—in—law to Stan Shohls, being married to Stan's brother for fifty three years. Raymond passed away last year of congestive heart failure at the ripe old age of ninety four. Someone said, "Let's say our communal prayers," but Steve said, "Let's just wait a few more minutes. I'm sure they'll be along shortly."

Sue came walking in late with her pot luck dish and was wondering why they weren't eating yet. Steve asked her, "Did you happen to see Stan, Martha and Lois Shohls anywhere on your way down here?" She said, "No, I didn't even look towards their door when I walked by. Maybe they took a taxi to town, forgot to watch the time and before they realized it was too late to show up. That doesn't sound quite like them though. Does it?" Everybody shook their head emphatically, "No." The residents waited another fifteen minutes, and then decided to partake of the delicious pot luck supper set before them. After they were finished eating, they exchanged Christmas gifts and snacked on goodies while singing some Christmas carols. A few tables played cards while others sat and watched television.

I don't understand this! Where are Stan and Martha Shohls and their sister—in—law Lois Shohls? Why didn't they come down and eat the Christmas buffet with the rest of the residents? Steve's curiosity got the best of him and he volunteered to knock on their door and call them each by name and see if they'll answer. When Steve got to their door and tugged at it, it was locked. He called them each by name but no answer. Mrs. Pickwell just happened to be in her office for a few minutes when Steve reported this. Mrs. Pickwell unlocked their door herself to find no one home and nothing out of place. Do you suppose all three of them decided to spend the night by relatives or friends somewhere without telling anybody? It would really be hard on Lois because of her age. Ninety two? Mrs. Pickwell said she would call the police in the morning and file a Missing Person's Report.

The St. Louis Police Department came out the next morning and asked, "When did you see them last? Did they have a car? How old are they? Do they keep to themselves a lot? Do they ever talk about out of town relatives or friends they have ever stayed with?"

Missing Persons

Within a week the St. Louis Police Department posted a missing persons flyer of Stan, Martha and Lois Shohls. Lois is ninety two years old, Stan is seventy seven years old and Martha is seventy five years old. Lois' husband, Raymond, was ninety four years old when he died. They were all natives of St. Louis, Missouri. The police are circulating the flyers to all the businesses, posting them on windows, doors, posts and car windshields. A missing person's bulletin has been in the St. Louis Chronicle, radio, television and the internet. A few leads have been called in to the police department but when the police checked them out they were all false.

The police questioned everybody at the apartment complex and the few relatives and friends of the Shohls. To no avail! They were of no help whatsoever. What happened to the Shohls? Did somebody kidnap them? Are they still alive? There were no families to involve since neither family had any children.

Someone reported to the St. Louis Police Department that they saw Stan, Martha and Lois Shohls several days before they were reported missing. In fact, the individual that saw them even talked to them for a few minutes. They were their same, old self jovial as usual.

The next morning news circulated around the apartment complex about the organization of a search party for this coming Sunday afternoon. Mr. Pickwell announced, "Anyone that wants to go along is welcome. You should wear good, comfortable walking shoes and also use a walking stick in case you are confronted with any wild animal. While you are walking don't disturb any substantial evidence. If you have a cell phone with you please use it. It could save your life. We will meet back here at four o'clock. Please take your designated partner with you to search the area you were assigned."

One of the men found a woman's purse with no identification inside which they will turn in to the police department. Mrs. Alwan that came along with the search party found a woman's shoe that they will give to the police department for further reference.

The policemen seined Silverstone Creek in the vicinity where the search party was combing the area. Nothing was found in Silverstone Creek, except an old, dead, dog, some turtles and harmless snakes.

The weather was very accommodating today for a search party because the eight inches of snow had melted and the temperature had warmed up nicely, into the sixties. Actually, it was jacket weather and that's what everybody wore. On the way back to the complex the bus driver took the scenic drive through the newer outlying areas of St. Louis instead of the old downtown area.

The St. Louis Police Department is still actively pursuing the three missing person's report from the Pickwell Apartment Complex. They have contacted police departments in larger cities to be conscious of a small group of disconnected, misplaced persons, namely two women and one man. They have knowledge of their whereabouts but will be walking around aimlessly, oblivious of where to go or what to do. They will be very obvious and stand out in a crowd. Reports have been coming in to various large cities about a very small, descriptive group of people fitting the above mentioned. The police have approached these people but it has served no purpose. They are all dead leads.

The St. Louis Police Department also contacted different bus terminals in the bigger cities in hope of them either boarding or coming off a bus. No reports have come back on this issue.

In the last week several different leads have come in from major cities across the United States because of the Shohls picture and information on an All Points Bulletin. These people were killed, plus they fit the description of the Shohls, although it wasn't them.

The major airports in the surrounding cities such as Kansas City, Kansas and Missouri have been contacted. St. Louis, Missouri Airport was contacted the same day they were discovered missing. There have been no major leads to go on. The Amtrak Railway System has been made aware of the situation and they are keeping a watchful eye. None of the reports have materialized into something firm and conclusive. There is nothing left to do but follow every lead that comes in and hope for the best.

Mrs. Pickwell has a chance to rent both apartments to other people, but out of respect to the Shohls she will wait a couple of weeks in hopes they will be found. Several tenants have reported to Mrs. Pickwell that Mr. and Mrs. Shohls telephone keeps ringing constantly all hours of the day and even during the night. Mrs. Pickwell checked the phone while she was checking the room because it started ringing while she was there. She answered, with a "Hello…Hello," but no one spoke and the phone recorded a Blocked Call. Mrs. Pickwell reported it to the police department and they are wondering if the phone calls are related to Mr. and Mrs. Stan Shohls and his sister—in —law Lois Shohls. What do you think? It's a possibility! Right?

Why would someone want to dispose of Stan, Martha and Lois Shohls? They didn't harm anybody! Maybe there's someone here in the Pickwell Apartment Complex that is the villain? I hope not!

Chapter 8
Snakes Alive

A month has passed since the three members of the Shohls family have disappeared. Mrs. Pickwell has traced the church where they worshipped, the St. Louis Baptist Church on 1114 Frontier Street downtown. She visited with Pastor Floyd and he agreed to conduct a funeral service in spite of three missing caskets. They will display a picture of them in their honor. The worship is set for this Sunday at 7:00PM. Everybody is welcome to attend.

When Sunday evening arrived for the worship service it was well attended amidst a light snow falling, just enough to use your windshield wipers. Pastor Floyd said some prayers with a soft choir in the background and gave a befitting eulogy for the three members of the church. A collection was taken up for the benefit of them because they have been missing since Christmas Eve Dec. 24, 2005.

The Shohls apartments have now been rented and the telephone calls have discontinued. The caller is aware that someone else is living in the apartment now. We still don't know if the calls were related to the disappearance of the Shohls or not. We might never know! Especially if they can't ever be found! Correct?

Eventually there will be a tombstone erected in the honor of Stan and Martha Shohls. Lois Shohls name will be inscribed on her husband's tombstone. A private memorial service and recognition of the tombstones will be announced at a later date.

February 15—2006

Recently several of the residents complained to Mrs. Pickwell that they thought they smelled a gas odor coming out of the vents when the furnace came on like a smell of rotten eggs. This is a familiar smell when it is associated with escaping gas. Mrs. Pickwell said they would have an unexpected emergency meeting tonight and check with the other residents to see if they have experienced anything or are aware of this at all.

At promptly 7:00PM that evening the residents filed in and took their seats, curious as to the reason for an emergency meeting in the middle of the week. Mrs. Pickwell addressed the issue immediately saying, "Several of the residents have been complaining about the odor of gas coming out of the vent whenever the furnace comes on like the smell of rotten eggs. Has anyone in here experienced this odor? Please raise your hand because this is very important. Several men raised their hand saying, "Yes, we've smelled this odor but we thought it was just due to the furnace being on for the first several times this winter. We remembered that when we were living in our homes years ago. We didn't think anything of it as far as that was concerned because later on the odor would disappear." Mrs. Pickwell asked, "If anybody else has noticed the unusual, rotten, egg odor would you please come forward?" Several men and women stood up and said, "We don't light any matches anymore for fear of an explosion in the event that it's gas." Since this was the only news to be discussed at this meeting Mrs. Pickwell suggested that everybody try and refrain from running their furnace for one day until the St. Louis Gas Company can inspect it and see if anything is wrong. Everybody got up to leave but you could hear the residents mumbling under their breath, "Does Mrs. Pickwell know how cold it will get in here for one day? She doesn't live here like we do. What's the matter with her anyway? Mrs. Styles didn't treat us like that!" Someone else said, "A number of us have colds already. I guess I'll have to run my little space heater again tonight." Another lady made a remark, "I not only smell something like rotten eggs but something worse than that which I can't describe. Like a foul, fleshy odor! It smells like it's coming out of the furnace room itself."

The next morning Mrs. Pickwell announced on the intercom, "Everybody is to evacuate across the street to Bell's Diner for the duration of the time it takes to inspect the furnace. Please meet in the lobby. We will walk across the street as a group until the inspection is over and we get the results. I'll see you in a few minutes."

After the residents were situated in a private, back room eating their noon meal they started to play cards for something to pass the time, while the gas company was at work determining the cause of the rotten egg odor.

Around 4:00PM a St. Louis Gas Company worker came over to the Bell's Diner and told them everything was under control. Yes, there had been a leak and it's good it had been reported when it was or there could've been some deaths involved. Everything was in working order now.

Everybody walked back across the street to their apartments to prepare their evening meal as supper was not served at the complex. They were all relieved that the gas problem had been alleviated. Now we can all sleep well tonight! Right? No???

A couple of days have passed by and everything seems fine until one morning at breakfast Mrs. Laird asks the other residents at her table if they smelled that foul odor coming out of the vent. They all said no but that she should still report it to Mrs. Pickwell. Mrs. Laird forgot to report the incident to Mrs. Pickwell and was awakened out of her sleep by a strange feeling in her bed. She immediately sensed something was terribly wrong. Fear gripped her body as she snapped on the bed lamp to discover a huge, six foot, boa constrictor snake lying on top of her bed covers making a weird noise. Mrs. Laird let out a blood curdling scream, "Help me! Help me! There's a snake in my room! Someone please help!" She kept on screaming as she ran out into the hall. By this time everybody came out of their apartments screaming. They all had larger snakes infesting their rooms. What a ghastly sight! Where did they come from? The only way they could've infiltrated the apartments is to come up the toilet stool! No one could walk on the floor without stepping on a writhing, slithering snake. When all the snakes were together they made an eerie, humming noise. Also, the odor was unbearable from all these filthy snakes. They were crawling in the kitchen sink, table, bed and anywhere they could manage. They were even crawling up the curtains towards the ceiling. Mr. Flanders screamed, "Call the fire department and the St. Louis Police Department for help. We'll tell them we had to evacuate to Bell's Diner because we couldn't take the chance of getting attacked and bitten from the snakes." They all walked across the street as a group into the Bell Diner telling the proprietor what happened. By this time it was Monday morning 3:00AM and the diner just had a few late night coffee drinkers. The residents were lucky the diner was open all night long or else they wouldn't have had any place else to go.

The St. Louis Police Department pulled up in front of the apartment complex with their sirens going as did the fire department. They immediately killed all the snakes and fumigated the whole Pickwell Apartment Complex so that it was livable again. The police and fire department reported to Mrs. Pickwell that there must be something faulty with the plumbing system in the apartments or else this wouldn't have happened.

The next morning Mrs. Pickwell called the St. Louis Plumbing Company and had them come out and check the plumbing in the basement to see what could've gone wrong. Mrs. Pickwell directed them to the basement and she went back upstairs. As soon as the plumbers were at the bottom of the stairs they smelled the foul, decaying odor that Mrs. Laird was talking about. Back in the corner of the furnace room where the plumbing system, pipes and controls are for the plumbing itself for the Pickwell Apartment Complex came the stench of rotting flesh. The plumbers went back into the corner equipped with heavy drills used for drilling into cement but they didn't need them. The cement floor was cracked and shifted to one side like someone had moved it. The plumbers picked up a hunk of cement and pulled it to one side to uncover cut up body parts, rotting flesh, insects and long snakes eating the body parts. A head was protruding through the gory sight, that of Stan Shohls. The heads of Martha and Lois Shohls could also be seen. So this is where the snakes came from! The chunks of decaying flesh and repugnant order is more than anyone can stand. That's disgusting! A bloody, gory mess!

One of the plumbers went upstairs to call Mr. and Mrs. Pickwell and they came down to the basement to view the carnage. They cried and were overcome with grief at the sight and said, "The Shohls were listed as missing persons. No wonder they couldn't be found. They were hard to find buried under the cement in the basement. Who would've thought of that? Really!

The next morning Mrs. Pickwell posted an emergency meeting again for that evening at 7:00PM. She encouraged everyone to attend which they did. Mrs. Pickwell announced what her husband and herself witnessed in the corner of the basement where the dismembered bodies of Martha, Stan and Lois Shohls were buried under the cement. The appearance of the snakes came from a combination of the toilet stool and under the cement. They were crawling out from under the cement, slithering upstairs and invading the apartments. How disgusting!

Everybody was aghast at Mrs. Pickwell's presentation of the dismembered bodies of the Shohls. Many of the residents cried because they knew them so well. Some ate with them, played Bingo, cards and had a good time. Others watched television and visited with them while Stan played billiards. Sometimes Lois Shohls hosted card parties at her apartment for her friends and Stan and Martha did likewise. They were very likeable and sociable people.

Lois Shohls liked to knit and she would spend her days knitting afghans, shawls, lap covers etc—she would give them away, no money involved. Stan and Martha Shohls always had a wide circle of friends in the St. Louis area, with Stan owning his own insurance company plus a large variety of clients. He sold different forms of insurance, mainly life, health, automobile and homeowners insurance. Martha was a retired superintendant of the St. Louis Public School System for years. Both couples were childless and adoption was never an option for both families. Lois knitted for an extra activity but for years she worked as a librarian at the St. Louis Public Library. Her husband, Raymond, was a public accountant for Weller Grain Company located on the north edge of St. Louis, Missouri.

Now that the body parts have been transferred to Williams Mortuary and Crematory, a memorial service will be held at the Williams Mortuary and Crematory for friends and relatives. To be precise it will be tomorrow morning at 10:00AM with inurement at the St. Louis Cemetery.

Memorial Service

Everybody at the Pickwell Apartment Complex plus friends and relatives attended the memorial service at Williams Mortuary. It was a beautiful day for such a sad occasion. Pastor Fuller gave a befitting eulogy during the service about Stan, Martha and Lois Shohls. He reiterated the different aspects of their lives and what brought them the most joy of which there were many.

A lot of residents from the complex plus relatives and friends went to the St. Louis Cemetery for the inurement and prayers. Their ashes were placed in small, labeled urns and buried by the tombstone like memorial that was erected in honor of them. Another small urn with Lois Shohls ashes was buried at the gravesite she shared with her husband, Raymond. After that they all came to the Pickwell Apartment Complex for a free lunch and visiting.

Everybody made the remark saying, "What a beautiful service and eulogy Pastor Fuller conducted for the mourners. It was so befitting for the occasion."

Later on in the day the relatives and friends of the Shohls went back home and the residents to their apartments. Mary was asking herself and others, "Who do you suppose did such a horrible deed? I can't even begin to imagine." Someone else remarked, "When are these killings going to end? I've been scared in here for some time now. I've also been thinking about moving into a different apartment complex. Several other residents are scared like I am and are also thinking about moving out of here. I know we can find other apartments here in town where killings like this aren't taking place. The rent at the other apartments is the same as this and we can also eat our meals there. So there's really no difference either way. Actually, if a resident wants to have a pet that is even permissible."

The Police at Work

Now that the police know that a killer dismembered three bodies possibly in the elevator, they are taking fingerprints inside and possibly footprints outside of the complex. Even though this actually happened about six to eight weeks ago there's still a chance that the killer could get caught. They checked the basement again for fingerprints and footprints were forthcoming. All the snakes have been fumigated and killed, yet the opening under the cement in the back corner has everybody worried. Consequently, the plumbers have sealed the hole where the body parts were stashed. No snakes are able to push up against the cement and crawl out. The reason they got out before is because someone drilled a hole in the cement to dispose of three bodies and they never bothered to put the cement back into place. As a result of this the snakes crawled out of the cement hole and scurried all over the complex.

The Lie Detector Tests

Remember Joe Bleer, the cook that had a massive heart attack and passed away? The police questioned him and also used a lie detector test on him to confirm whether he was telling the truth about stealing the bag with the $3000.00 in it. The lie detector test confirmed Joe was telling the truth. When Mrs. Styles cleaned his bedroom closet she found the bag with the $3000.00 that Joe had stolen from the safe that night. So the police are in agreement that the lie detector machine is a faulty device that either needs to be repaired or replaced with a new one. The police opted to have it repaired because a new lie detector machine is very expensive.

The St. Louis Police Department is going to start tomorrow morning picking up a police car full of residents, taking them to the police department for a lie detector test and then returning them safely back to the complex. The police are vaguely wondering if any of the one hundred and two people that live at the complex might be guilty of these murders. Why would someone come in off the street, kill the residents in the Pickwell Apartment Complex not being familiar with them, the building, or anything of this nature?

One by one the residents of the Pickwell Apartment Complex marched into the police station to take their lie detector test and then were driven safely home. It took a week till all the residents had their tests completed. The police were happy with the results because they were all negative. But that still doesn't dispel the fact that there's a "killer" loose somewhere in the area. The problem is, "How do you find him or possibly her?" Even the inmates at the St. Louis Jail tested negative on a routine examination.

March 2, 2006

Everything has been going fairly smooth at the complex for a change with no killings, snakes, unsavory characters etc—The Bingo games are well attended with fun prizes and Sue is the Bingo caller. Refreshments are served halfway through the game and then the residents resume playing Bingo. Every couple of weeks a birthday party is held for one of the residents in the Community Room where their meetings take place.

Once a month the StarVue Theater treats the senior citizens to a discounted movie for $3.00. The movies are top rated and the only thing you are required to pay for are your movie attendance and popcorn. What else could you ask for? Right?

About the middle of the month the residents take the senior bus to St. Louis College for a basketball or football game whatever the season. Everybody enjoys going to their games and fun is had by all. On certain days of the week some of the residents take the senior bus downtown to go shopping for several hours. The residents are never lacking for something to do at the complex if they just want to do it.

March 17—St. Patrick's Day

Tonight is the annual St. Patrick's Day Party and Pot Luck Supper whether you're Irish or not as explained at the meeting. Everybody came into the Barker Dining Room with a pot luck dish, a smile on their face and a hunger in their stomach. All the residents that live at the complex attended the Pot Luck Supper and St. Patrick's Day Party except Mabel Siller. Poor little Mabel. She was so tiny and skinny. Someone always had to come to her rescue. Everybody was surprised that Mabel didn't come down to the Community Room because she was of Irish descent. She wasn't in the best of health with her congestive heart failure, so maybe she's not feeling well this evening.

The cabbage rolls, Irish stew and other Irish delicacies emitted an odor in the whole apartment complex tonight. After everybody feasted on the above mentioned and the party was over they went back to their apartments while a few stayed to help with the clean up.

Before Mrs. Laird went to her apartment she knocked on Mabel's door and called her name, "Mabel…Mabel… Are you in there?" There was no answer so Mrs. Laird repeated the question, "Mabel…Mabel… Are you in there?" Still no answer. Mrs. Laird turned the knob which was unlocked and went inside from room to room. Mabel was nowhere to be seen. She left Mabel's apartment and walked into the hall thinking she would see her there but she was nowhere around. What happened to Mabel? Where did she go at this time of the night with snow still on the ground from the last snowfall and bitterly cold? Did she go outside and fall somewhere? Mrs. Laird went downstairs to see if Mrs. Pickwell was still in the dining room which she was. She said, "Mrs. Pickwell, I knocked on Mabel Siller's door to check on her because she didn't come down to the St. Patrick's Day party and no one answered and the door wasn't locked so I went inside and she's nowhere around. Mabel's gone, Mrs. Pickwell. I hope she didn't go outside and fall in the snow."Mrs. Pickwell was also very worried because so many deaths have been occurring at the apartment complex so she immediately called the police department. When the officers pulled up to the apartment complex they started searching the grounds around the building in hopes of finding Mrs. Siller and no indication of foul play. After they were satisfied with the results outside they proceeded into the apartment building to inspect her living quarters and interrogate the residents for further information about Mrs. Siller. Nobody had any worthwhile information to contribute to the interrogation because no one had seen her for about a week because she usually kept to herself in her apartment. The officers went back to the police department for further incoming information telling the residents, "We will be back in several days to do a further check on Mrs. Siller. Thank you! Goodbye!"

Two weeks have now passed since Mabel Siller was reported missing. Nothing's been done to Mabel's apartment in the event that she will be back among us. Mabel could not survive on the streets in the inclement weather. Everybody is very concerned about Mabel since this situation is very unusual where Mabel is concerned.

The next morning, being Monday, brought the usual breakfast residents to the table at 7:00AM. They were all very hungry because they had been up later the night before watching news flashes on Mabel Siller's disappearance. Several people called the St. Louis Police Department thinking they encountered Mabel walking down the street but they were all false alarms. Mabel was nowhere in sight.

While they were waiting for their breakfast which was taking unusually long the conversation turned to Mabel Siller, naturally.

Mark, the head cook, and his helpers Mrs. Powell and Mrs. Black decided to make some breakfast biscuits to compliment the scrambled eggs and bacon this morning. They preheated the oven without opening the oven door and immediately a foul, filthy odor escaped the oven making it almost impossible to breathe. They looked at each other in sheer disgust and shock as Mark said, "What's that decaying odor coming out of the oven? Stand back because I'm going to open the oven door." As he opened the door dried, black blood fell out of the sides of the oven as huge hunks of carved human flesh piled on top of the oven racks were smouldering and being kept warm at 200 degrees heat. Mabel's head was lying in the middle of the oven rack with her eyes staring wide open. She was dismembered at the neck with her body parts scattered around her. Half of her black tongue was hanging out of her mouth and the other half had been cut off. Blood continued to drip in the oven as a foul stench permeated the air. Someone had mercilessly mutilated and carved Mabel to pieces. Mrs. Black and Mrs. Powell ran out of the kitchen to call the police and to report this to Mrs.Pickwell.

The police sirens are going as the police cars pull up to the curb and the officers dash into the complex, guns fully loaded just in case. They carried several boxes of human flesh to the William's Mortuary to be cremated first thing in the morning. A funeral service would be pending till they notified the next of kin. Mabel is survived by two sisters, Anne and May, and one brother, Jacob, still living in the St. Louis area. Her other brother, Peter, lives in Macon, Georgia. She also has several nieces and nephews but no children. Her husband Nick passed away eleven years ago from stomach cancer.

A Small Funeral

Mabel Siller's funeral was Thursday afternoon at 2:00PM at the Stern Funeral Home with one sister, one brother and three nieces attending. Inurement followed at the St. Louis Cemetery. A lunch was held at the Pickwell Apartment Complex for all the residents and a few friends and relatives of Mabel Siller.

The police aren't any closer to catching the mindless killer of these dastardly deeds than the residents are. Who is doing all these killings here at the Pickwell Apartment complex? Why has this apartment building been singled out? I wish I knew don't you? Keep on reading and see what else happens. After the funeral lunch some of the residents went to the Community Room to watch television, drink a cup of coffee and do a little visiting about the day's activities while others were tired and went about their business.

Friday Morning

The next morning came bright and early as the residents filed into the dining room for their morning breakfast of bacon, eggs and fluffy pancakes. This is always the menu for Fridays as the three cooks hurriedly prepared breakfast because they were running a little late. The cooks were very busy and not paying attention to anything in particular, except the work at hand.

Mrs. Black mentioned, "I guess we'll turn the oven on low to keep the bacon and eggs warm while we make the pancakes." The other two cooks said, "That's fine" as they started to heap the bacon and eggs on a platter to keep them warm in the oven. By this time the odor in the kitchen had changed to a pungent, filthy, slimy, smell coming out of the oven which the three cooks noticed. They also noticed a strange humming noise in unison escaping the oven. Mark said, "I also smell the foul odor coming from the new oven, so everybody stand back because I'm going to open the oven door to see what's going on or what's causing this." When Mark opened the door and looked inside they all screamed, including Mark. Inside the oven on the racks lay six, large sized, rattlesnakes all coiled and ready to strike with their rattlers going strong. The humming was louder by now with the oven door open. Their fangs were protruding out of their mouths as they all slithered out of the oven at one time. In the meantime after hearing the screaming in the kitchen, the residents ran back to see what the commotion was all about. Everybody screamed, "Help! Someone call the St. Louis Fire Department. We are being overtaken by a horde of snakes. If they bite us we could die if we don't get help soon enough! Somebody go for help, please!" The rattlesnakes stayed in the kitchen slithering and writhing around until Mrs. Flin was so overcome with fear that she had a heart attack. Mrs. Crider, 84, is a registered nurse living at the complex and she instantly ran to Mrs. Flin's side, checking her pulse on her wrist and neck. There was no pulse indicating Mrs. Flin had passed away.

A few snakes crawled up the kitchen walls while some lay on the kitchen cabinet eating whatever they could find. Some were drinking dirty dish water while others were immersing their scaly, filthy bodies in it. What a horrible sight. Gross!

Mr. Sein quickly went to his apartment and called the St. Louis Fire and Police Department so they could dispose of the snakes effectively. Before Mr. Sein could place the call he had to take a broom and push the snake off the top of the telephone on the desk. The snakes have infiltrated the whole apartment complex, every room. By now it has a foul, nasty odor and will have to be fumigated again just like the last time.

The sirens could be heard coming down the street to a screeching halt in front of the complex. The firemen jumped out and ran inside with their heavy fire hose to either put out a fire, hose down the snakes or otherwise. Some of the snakes were poised, ready to strike with their rattlers very loud, while some of the other snakes slithered away in fear of the firemen and noise. The firemen fumigated and cleaned the apartments to the best of their ability with the help of Mr. and Mrs. Pickwell. The residents were sent back to their clean, sanitized apartments bedding down for the night. During the night Mr. Stone got up to go to the bathroom and he encountered a snake in the toilet stool. He flushed the stool and the snake disappeared for the time being. So the residents still have to be on the lookout for snakes.

Chapter 9
Buried Alive!

Likewise Mrs. Donaldson came running out of her apartment at three o'clock the next morning screaming "Help! Help! I'm tired of this! My apartment is full of snakes again. Please call the fire department and police station. Hurry!" By now there was a whole complex floor full of snakes, hissing and rattling in unison. There were also several rattlesnakes with their fangs protruding, poised to strike at the residents which they did. They were taken to the hospital, sedated, treated medically, and released. They were transported back to the apartment complex for bed rest for several days and then only mild activities. Once again the snakes were seen in the toilet stool, slithering their slimy, scaly bodies in the diseased, filthy water. Occasionally they would stick their heads out of the water and slowly immerse them again.

The Fire Department and the St. Louis Police Department came to a screeching halt as they pulled up alongside the apartment complex. The firemen came running in with their heavy hoses ready to douse every snake in sight.

The residents were taken by bus to the American Motel downtown which was a version of a cheap motel. In the morning they would be picked up as soon as the all clear signal was given by the different departments.

Emergency plumbers have been called to check the plumbing system at the Pickwell Apartment Complex, especially the part where the snakes are coming up through the pipes into the actual toilet stool. How are they getting into the pipes? Where are the snakes coming from? Have you ever had a snake in your toilet stool? No? Neither have I!"

Later on in the morning the plumbers from the St. Louis Plumbing Company reported to Mrs. Pickwell that there were probably millions of snakes living under the city of St. Louis, Missouri. There were also many pipes that developed holes in them throughout the years and had never been repaired. Mrs. Pickwell decided to replace the defective plumbing in the apartment complex immediately. The residents will be living at the American Motel for a week until the plumbing has been repaired.

Later the residents moved back into their apartments and everything is back to normal. No more snakes! Thank God! What a relief! I've never heard of anything like that in my life! Have you? Snakes inhabiting a complete apartment complex? Really!

The next day Mrs. Pickwell posted an information sheet on the bulletin board indicating an urgent meeting for tonight in the all purpose room down the hall at 7:00PM. Everyone is urged to attend and voice their opinion. At 6:45PM the whole apartment complex can be seen filing in to take their seats as the meeting comes to order. Mrs. Pickwell is conducting the meeting making reference to the onslaught of rattlesnakes that had just taken place, how it was overcome and how they could be avoided in the future. A question and answer period followed such as; Will the snakes come back? If so, when? Mrs. Pickwell answered, "No, the snakes shouldn't be coming back because she had the defective plumbing replaced and the pipes that developed holes in them throughout the years had been repaired. There shouldn't be any problems anymore." Another frequently asked question was, "Who should we call in the event that something happens again, the St. Louis Plumbing Company or you, Mrs. Pickwell?" Mrs. Pickwell said, "Both of us!" Someone also asked a question, "Are our apartments fumigated and sanitized enough to be able to be living in them again?" Mrs. Pickwell said, "Yes, I explained everything to the Missouri Health Department and everything has been fumigated and sanitized effectively to allow the residents to move back into the apartments." Mrs. White asked the following question, "If any of us decide to relocate to another apartment complex what kind of a refund will I get back?" Mrs. Pickwell responded by saying, "Your refund will be equivalent to the amount of days inhabited for that month. Do you understand, Mrs. White?" Mrs. White said, "Yes, thank you." Mrs. Pickwell said, "I have time for one more question. Anyone? Mrs. Anderson raised her hand and Mrs. Pickwell said, "Yes, Mrs. Anderson, what is your question?"Mrs. Anderson asked, "In regards to Mrs. White's question, "How soon do we give our notice before we leave?" Mrs. Pickwell said, "At least a week in advance because common courtesy would indicate that. I want to thank everybody for attending the meeting. If you think of any further questions please contact me in my office. Thank you and goodnight." All the residents left the Community Room to go back to their apartments for the night. Some stayed behind for that extra cup of coffee and light conversation with friends they don't ordinarily see every day. Others stay behind because there not tired enough to go to bed and want to watch the news on television. A few of the men like to play a game of billiards before retiring. The Community Room is a popular place at the Pickwell Apartment Complex for food, fun and conversation. Especially on cold, winter nights when the residents don't have anything to do, they come down to the Community Room to mingle with their friends for a couple of hours.

The Bingo room is one of the most popular rooms in the complex. The residents play Bingo every Thursday evening at 7:00PM with refreshments served at intermission. The Bingo room is adjacent to the

Community room on the first floor. Down the hall from the Bingo room is a large Exercise room for the residents to walk around several times to make a mile. They also have various exercise machines for the residents to use day or night as it is open from 7:00AM in the morning until 9:00PM at night. Many times when you come in to exercise on a machine they are all taken up.

At one time there used to be a non—denominational chapel with a minister coming in every morning at 10:30AM for services. Finally the attendance got so low it wasn't even worth it for the minister to make the trip to the chapel for two or three people and keep the lights burning. After all, they have to curtail their expenses. Because of the poor attendance the chapel has been converted into a public restroom.

The dining room is off to the left as you come into the Pickwell Apartment Complex. It seats 110 people with extra space left by the time everybody is seated. The dining room has only been open for a year. The only meals that are served are breakfast and dinner. The residents eat in their own apartments for supper. Holiday meals are also served in the Barlow Dining Room so the residents don't have to go to downtown St. Louis for a holiday meal in inclement weather.

Every Sunday morning after church services at the Fellow Baptist Church at 10:00AM, the residents go to Joe's Restaurant for their noon meal. After their meal the church Bus Line brings them back to the complex. They spend the rest of the day in the Community room or in their apartments eating their meals, watching television, reading, taking a nap, etc....

Springtime

Spring is fast approaching as birds are chirping in the air, children are taking to the streets and couples are going for long walks. The smell of spring is everywhere, except at the Pickwell Apartment Complex. When a person enters the outside doors of the complex a strong, foul, stench greets them similar to that of a corpse. It's been reported but so far nothing's been done about it.

An older couple has been walking by repeatedly noticing the odor permeating the air when they finally decided to stop by and report their findings to Mrs. Pickwell. She answered the door saying, "Yes, may I help you?" They proceeded to say, "Yes, we'd like to report something to the owner of this complex." Mrs. Pickwell said, "Yes, I'm the owner. May I help you?" The couple continued to explain to her about the rancid, fleshly odor that is coming from the grounds of the apartment complex now that it's turning warmer. Mrs. Pickwell said, "Really? I've never noticed anything unusual. Of course, I haven't been outside for any length because of a bad cold. That would account for my not being able to smell anything." The couple remarked, "Is that right? Well we were just passing by again so we thought we'd bring it to your attention."

"Thank you" said Mrs. Pickwell and closed the door. Immediately Mr. Pickwell asked her what the problem was and she related the conversation with the strange couple. Mr. Pickwell remarked, "I'll take care of that right now. After all our tenants shouldn't be exposed to that." Mrs. Pickwell stepped outside to show him the area where the odor was coming from and he immediately started digging. After digging about twenty minutes Mr. Pickwell's shovel couldn't go any farther. He was shocked to the point of disbelief as he unearthed three, dead, slimy rattlesnakes and two, huge rats covered with mounds of dirt. Who would've had the nerve to bury these humongous, filthy, dead rodents in the front yard of the apartment complex? They would've been buried after dark to conceal their identity. Mr. Pickwell disposed of the remains and covered the hole. Several tenants were aware of this but nothing was said openly for fear of arousing the remaining tenants even more so. Well, at least the foul odor was gone. None of the tenants had ever complained about that. Strange?

What happened to Mrs. Bond?
As I said earlier, spring is in the air as children are frolicking to and fro, couples are walking hand in hand and tenants are taking to the streets.

Some of them are going to the theater at night or the restaurants in a group. One of their favorite is the Briner Restaurant within walking distance from the apartment complex. They walk down and come back together before the lights dim.

Everything seems fine except eighty five year old Sylvia Bond hasn't been seen for several days and nobody knows her whereabouts, not even her immediate family. Her daughter, Ann, is beside herself with fear because of her age and fear itself. Tonight she'll call the St. Louis Police Department if her mother doesn't show up. That's not a good sign. Two hours later Officer Hoage and Officer Shelton interviewed Ann about her mother's possible whereabouts.

Her apartment has been cleaned, her best clothing apparel and dress shoes are missing and she had an appointment with her hairdresser to get her styled the same day she was last seen. No one saw her leave during the day but she could have left during the night? After hours? Surely not! Sylvia Bond has no relatives or acquaintances at the complex other than a few lady friends that she visits with at the dinner table. But her family has since become aware of the fact that Mrs. Bond did leave towards evening to meet her friends three days ago. She was confronted at gunpoint and taken to an undisclosed location where she was beaten, tortured and left for dead. The assailant called the St. Louis Police Department and reported the attack leading the police to believe she was possibly not alive. After they picked Mrs. Bond up and transported her to the hospital, the doctor in the emergency room declared her "legally dead." The complex was notified and a service was held in her honor at the Baptist Newfound Church in St. Louis.

Every once in awhile several mourners noticed a thump inside the casket which was closed at the graveside. The mortician opened the casket at the request of the mourners and nothing was amiss, followed by mounds of dirt thrown on the vault for burial. A day or two later several friends were paying their last respects at her graveside. They were sure they heard an audible scratching or clawing from the grave again. After everyone left to go home, the grave diggers decided to exhume the body for medical purposes etc… When they opened the casket they saw that Mrs. Bond was turned over on her side with her eyelids open wide and her mouth drooling. Her fingernails were clutching the inside of the lid on the casket and tearing away at the satin material because SHE HAD BEEN BURIED ALIVE!!! The St. Louis Hospital emergency room doctor was negligent in his medical diagnosis when he declared Mrs. Bond "legally dead." In all reality she was still living with very shallow breathing. She was rushed back to the hospital where she passed away several hours later. Once again she was declared "legally dead," only by a different doctor.

What a sad, panicky, fearful feeling to know that you are buried alive and can't do anything about it? Scary, isn't it? Years down the road insects and rodents will infiltrate the casket until there is nothing left. Her son, George, wife and family from Houston, Texas are beside themselves with grief at the thought of their mother being buried alive for several days scratching, clawing and raking her fingernails on the covering of the inside of the casket. Before they departed they have already discussed among themselves the possibility of a lawsuit against the St. Louis Regional Hospital. George has a personal attorney that will represent them when he arrives back in Houston, Texas. Ann and her family are in total agreement with her brother's proposal to proceed with the $5,000,000 lawsuit.

Where's Sue Benson….April 2006
Sunday

Sue's well aware of what's been going on at the Pickwell Apartment Complex in spite of her misgivings and personal problems. She went to visit her mother, Jane, at the St. Louis Prison yesterday to update her on the news at the complex and anything newsworthy Jane might have to offer. They both walked to the Visitation Room and sat opposite each other with a glass shield between them talking on the phone.

Jane was not well and in a very depressed state of mind. She made the remark, "Sue, I'm not feeling well because of this pain I'm having in my stomach and I've been very depressed lately. I can't seem to get over this depression, so I guess they'll have to change my medication." Sue answered back, "I won't stay too long mother. I just thought I'd drop by and see how you're doing because I haven't been here for several weeks. I didn't know your depression was back again. I'm sorry to hear that mother. I've been doing fairly well considering all that has transpired at the apartment complex. I'm sure you've heard about all the gruesome things that have been going on. Marcus was killed several weeks ago at the complex in Rockwood, Illinois. Three people were chopped up and buried underneath the cement in the basement where I live.

Hordes of snakes infiltrated the complex till we had to move to a low income motel till the filth and infestation were cleaned, fumigated and our habitat was livable once again." Jane said, "Oh my! I guess it's been awful since I talked to you, Sue, because this is all new to me. I've never heard any of this before." Sue said, "Mother, did you hear about Sylvia Bond?" Jane said, "No, what happened?" Sue said, "She left her apartment one evening and was kidnapped, robbed, beaten and tortured and left for dead in a private home. The doctor at St. Louis Regional Hospital declared her legally dead and she was buried. Strange sounds kept coming from the casket at various times and the mortician did some investigating. When they opened the lid she was laying on her side eyes wide open and her mouth drooling. They called an ambulance to the cemetery and had her driven back to the hospital and put on a life support machine for several hours. They called her family again and they stayed until she passed away." Jane didn't know what to say because she was so overcome with grief at the thought of being buried alive and then reburied again. She said, "How could the emergency room staff make such a horrible mistake? I thought they were trained for such things? I've never heard of anything like that! Of course, like you said, Sue, it will go to court and justice will be served. That's good! When you find out when the court trial will be let me know because I will want to follow it in the newspaper." Sue said,

"Anything new here at the prison, mother?"Jane said, "No, except one of the female prisoners was given a death sentence several years ago and she had a lethal injection this past week which ended her life immediately."

Jane and Sue decided to carry the conversation to a lighter side, with Jane saying, "I'm still assistant instructor at the leather craft classes during the week because I enjoy helping other people and it helps to pass the time, especially in the winter evenings. Other than that it's the same old stuff day in and day out. Up at 5:00 o'clock in the morning; work twelve hours in a laundry and back to bed at 10.00 in the evening. A repetition the next day, the day after that and so on. I have a sad, monotonous, dull life Sue and it will stay like that until I close my eyes in death. I brought this misery on myself and now I'm paying for it." Sue said, "That's right mother but things can get better down the road. Hang in there. I'm greatly improved compared to the way I was despondent and all. Remember? I was also at death's door but God wasn't ready for me and he brought me back. I can't thank him enough! Well I guess I'd better be going mother because my transportation will be here shortly and I want to go to bed early this evening so I won't be late for work tomorrow morning." Jane followed Sue's departure with wistful eyes damp with tears as usual. Sue took the evening bus back to her apartment walking in at the stroke of 5:30PM. Just in time to eat a bite, watch a little television and go to bed.

Six o'clock comes bright and early for Sue as she gets ready for work and catches the 7:30AM bus for her downtown office. Everything is the same at the Green Financial Office day in and day out, filing reports, answering the phone visiting with clients, filling out paper work and so forth. She has dinner at a neighboring café and back to the office again till five o'clock, then back to her apartment for the night. But this evening was different because as she was watching television the announcer started broadcasting the news about Sylvia Bond being buried alive last month and a court case will proceed next month with Sylvia's family suing the St. Louis Regional Hospital for burying their mother alive at the St. Louis Cemetery for an undisclosed amount of money. Sue wasn't surprised when she heard the announcement on the St. Louis, Missouri television station KIBX. She continued to watch television for awhile and then went to bed.

Sue reached over to shut off the alarm clock even though she was still groggy from not getting enough sleep the night before. Her nerves are always frazzled in spite of telling her mother she was doing much better. Of course Jane believed this because she didn't have any reason not to. It took all Sue's strength of mind and body to crawl out of bed and drag herself through the morning ritual of showering, breakfast and getting presentable for her job at Green Financial Services. She still had a fifteen minute walk to the bus stop on Barnes Street. While she was walking she could feel a slight drizzle coming down even though it called for a sunny forecast for today. As she neared the corner of the first block she looked up to see a man pointing a gun at her amidst a group of women, children and several other men in the van. The man seated on the passenger side said, "Get in the van or I will be forced to shoot you in broad daylight." Sue refused saying, "No, I'm not getting in the van with you and please leave me alone." He warned her again and she heard the click of the gun knowing he meant business. By this time the van stopped and she was forced to get in, in spite of her misgivings about the whole situation. All the seats were filled except one in the back which she took. Everyone ignored her and the van proceeded on. Sue knew she had been kidnapped as she looked around not recognizing anybody or anything. Why her? What did they want with her? She didn't have that much money with her. Maybe she'll try and escape at the next rest stop.

Sue kept a close watch on the direction they were taking which was west. As suppertime approached sandwiches, potato chips and soda were passed around the van and they continued driving. As nightfall drew nigh the children slept in a reclining position while the men and women sat up all night and slept. The incessant snoring and foul stench of the people surrounding her kept her awake half of the night. By now the drizzle that she experienced earlier turned into a blinding rainstorm creating a deluge on the streets, byways and the main highway they just turned onto. She encountered one rest stop after the next as they continued on their journey west. At daybreak they ate breakfast at Bosselman's Truck Stop in Salina, Kansas and continued on their way.

While they were riding along Sue attempted to strike up a conversation with the lady across the aisle. She said, "How far do we have to go before we reach our destination permanently? Anybody?" Everybody turned around and looked at her as the lady across the aisle said, "As long as we are riding in the van we aren't supposed to speak to anybody, not even to each other." Sue asked, "Why can't you speak to anybody?" The lady said, "I don't know why. I wasn't told." Therefore everybody continued to sit in absolute silence as the van rolled along and the people in it were oblivious of everything and everyone in sight. As the evening wore on they were beginning to nod off to sleep, Sue being the only one awake in the van. The rain had subsided which left a clear, cold night, a little out of the ordinary for the month of June. As she was staring out of the window into the bleak night she suddenly observed a sign along the highway that read, "You Are Entering Colorado." She immediately knew that they had come cross country from Missouri to Colorado in one long sweep.

Searching for Sue

Meanwhile back in St. Louis, Missouri Sue's boss, Mr. Greves, called the Pickwell Apartment Complex inquiring as to why Sue Benson didn't report for work at her appointed time. Mrs. Pickwell answered in her office making the remark, "I was unaware that Sue Benson is missing and didn't report for work today. I will check her apartment immediately if anything is amiss and call you back," which she did. Mrs. Pickwell checked Sue's apartment, found everything in order and decided to call the St. Louis Police Department to report Sue Benson missing. The police issued an APB (All Points Bulletin) on Sue Benson indicating that she's been missing almost two days. The St. Louis Chronicle, one of St. Louis, Missouri's oldest newspaper companies, carried a full picture, explanatory article on Sue Benson from the day she moved to St. Louis, Missouri to her abduction at gunpoint. Anyone having information as to the whereabouts of Sue Benson is to call the St. Louis Police Department at 749—262—1270. Radio station WRBI has been broadcasting the missing person news about Sue Benson all day long but up to now there has been nothing new to report. Several people have called the newspaper office and police department to report sightings of people with the "similarities" of Sue Benson but they were wrong leads.

The St. Louis Police Department has been searching the city of St. Louis but so far nothing of interest has come forth. Neither has a person of interest come forward with any information leading to the recovery of Sue Benson. Sunday Mrs. Pickwell made a trip to the St. Louis Prison for Women to talk to Jane in the Visitation Room by phone with a glass shield between them. Mrs. Pickwell introduced herself saying, "This is Mrs. Pickwell, owner of the Pickwell Apartment Complex, where Sue Benson resides. I thought I'd call and tell you that Sue has been missing for two days now. I wasn't aware of this until Sue's boss, Mr. Green, called me and said Sue didn't report for work this morning. I told Mr. Green that I was unaware that Sue was missing and I would check her apartment, which I did. Everything was fine, yet I decided to call the St. Louis Police Department to report her missing.

Jane is weeping out loud in between Mrs. Pickwell's missing person's report on Sue. Jane said, "Where could she have gone on such short notice? Was she kidnapped? Where is my baby? Oh no! Sob, Sob!" Mrs. Pickwell continued the conversation telling Jane, "The St. Louis Chronicle, one of St. Louis, Missouri's oldest newspaper companies carried a full picture, explanatory article on Sue from the day she moved to St. Louis, Missouri to her abduction at gunpoint. Anyone with any information as to the whereabouts of Sue is to call the St. Louis Police Department at 1—749-262-1270." Mrs. Pickwell also told Jane, "Radio station WRBI has been broadcasting the missing person news about Sue all day long but up to now there has been nothing new to report. Several people have called the newspaper office and police department reporting sightings but they were of no significance."

Jane asked Mrs. Pickwell, "How did the police department know Sue was abducted at gunpoint?" Mrs. Pickwell remarked, "An unknown man approached the van thinking it was a small, city bus and witnessed the whole incident. He was fearful for his own personal safety so he kept a low profile and immediately disappeared. He went to the closest police station and reported the incident license tag and all." By this time Jane was beside herself with grief praying for her daughters safety amidst doubts of what could happen in a van with unknown people in a situation like this. Jane reported her findings to the prison officials and said, "My daughter, Sue, is missing. Please let me know if there is any further information of her whereabouts."

A Nevada Commune

This morning Sue noticed a sign that read, "You Are Entering Nevada" while they were travelling along. She overheard several women whispering that "that they have finally come home." After another hours ride they pulled up in front of a huge building plus a group of adjacent buildings where they all got out of the van.

Everybody was briefed on their job description and the lodging they were assigned to. Sue's job was to help with cooking two meals a day, breakfast and the noon meal to which she must comply. She was allowed outside one hour a day and then back inside for visiting and television. She had to be in bed by 10:00PM and no contact with the outside world. The schedule was the same as her mother's in prison. Sue was ordered to relinquish her cell phone and the money in her purse which would sever her ties with anyone that could help her.

One evening as she was spending her hour outside a friend told her that this was a "commune" type of living for women and children only, managed and directed by several men and women. Everybody plus the children had their own job with no paid wages except their room and board.

Sue's friend, Grace, said, "I was abducted the same way you were, at gunpoint, and brought to this "commune" for physical labor two years ago and have been here ever since. My family has me listed as a "missing person" in Colorado. Several of us have tried to escape but the guards will catch you and transfer you to hard labor. Don't try anything, please, because it could cost you your life." Grace also told Sue, "Don't worry about anybody attacking your person because I talked to someone that's been here since this "commune" opened and there's never been anything happen like that." So that's a comfort for Sue. Personally, Sue still thinks about escaping down the road. Let's see what happens!

One evening after supper as nightfall approached Sue was walking down the hallway to her room when she noticed the door ajar to one of the rooms. She stepped inside and saw in amazement a pile of women and children's purses on a table with no one in sight. Sue stepped forward to claim her purse on the bottom row when a guard carrying a gun confronted her saying, "What are you doing here tonight? This is not your place to be." Sue said, "I was on my way to my room and I saw my purse on the bottom of the pile so I decided to claim it because it belongs to me. Is there something wrong with that?" The guard said, "Yes, there is something wrong with that. Your purse and anything inside your purse does not belong to you anymore. That's why it was brought into this room. Get it? The next time I catch you in this room I will report you to the person in charge of this commune and you will be in solitary confinement." Sue went back to her room in tears thinking, "Help me, Lord! Is there no way out of here? What kind of a place is this and why am I here? I don't understand this. Please help me!"

Sue has been at the "commune" exactly a month and the boring schedule is the same for everybody. They have a community garden where everybody takes their turn in helping reap a plentiful harvest of potatoes, onions, cucumbers, radishes, cauliflower, berries, lettuce and numerous other vegetables. The women and children also tend to the flower garden in front of the main building and to the side. They are eighty five miles north of Las Vegas off the main highway, miles and miles from nowhere. You couldn't escape if someone paid you.

Still Trying to Escape —July, 2006

Sue has been at the "commune" for a total of three months and hates it worse every day. She thinks she has an escape plan devised that will work that she is willing to try in spite of winding up in solitary confinement.

Sue heard the news from her friend Grace that this Sunday afternoon none of the security guards would be guarding the "commune" because they all had to attend a meeting in Reno, Nevada and stay overnight. Sue decided this was her only chance to escape, although it would be very risky. She left the "commune" with a satchel of personal items, her identification, no money but an address of a personal friend that she knows in Las Vegas to help her get back to St. Louis, Missouri. She will stay with her until she has earned enough money at her friend's restaurant to buy a bus ticket to St. Louis, Missouri. Sue is preparing to hitchhike to Las Vegas, Nevada with her thumb pointed south as she is standing by the side of the highway. Soon a couple slowed down and a lady on the passenger side asks Sue, "Do you want a ride?" Sue said, "Yes, how far are you going?"The lady said, "Las Vegas." Sue said, "Fine, that's my destination." The lady said, "Get in, my husband and I will be glad to have the company. Where are you from?"Sue said, "I'm from St. Louis, Missouri." The lady said, "What brought you clear out here?" Sue related the story of the kidnapping, the escape and her plan to stay with her friend until she had enough money earned to buy a bus ticket back to St. Louis, Missouri. The lady was amazed at Sue's strength and courage to fight back such impending doom. By this time they were in Las Vegas bidding Sue farewell, wishing her luck and dropping her off at her friend's restaurant. As soon as Sue entered her friend, Maxine's Restaurant, she experienced that same warm, friendly, welcoming feeling that she gets whenever she is in Maxine's presence. Maxine and Sue have been friends since their high school days in Blueville, Illinois. Maxine got married after high school to a local young man, Nick Spamone, moved to Las Vegas, Nevada, raised a son and daughter plus opening a restaurant business together. The business is booming because of the casino trade that Las Vegas generates all year round.

When Nick and Maxine saw Sue coming in the door they yelled, "Sue!" and were overcome with joy as they came rushing toward her. They threw their arms around each other, hugging one another, laughing and crying at the same time. Maxine said, "Let's go back to the office and I'll order us all a meal and we can visit. It's almost dinner time." After they were seated in the office Maxine said, "Sue, what brought you to Las Vegas? I know you're not a gambler, at least not the last time I saw you, which was about fifteen years ago." Sue said, "Well,Maxine and Nick you're not going to believe this preposterous story. I was kidnapped at gunpoint by a van full of people and driven eighty five miles north of Las Vegas to a "commune" for women and children. For three months I cooked breakfast and dinner every day. The afternoons were spent cleaning various parts of the "commune." We were allowed to spend one hour a day outside, watch television and then go to bed because I had to be up at 5:00AM the next morning. What a horrible life! No, we didn't receive any wages because we got free room and board.

Maxine, I couldn't take this kind of life anymore so I decided to escape yesterday afternoon while all the security guards were at a meeting in Reno, Nevada. I remembered that you and Nick were still here in Las Vegas, so I hitched a ride with a couple that were willing to drop me off at your restaurant on their way to Arizona. I was not allowed to make any telephones calls or mail letters the length of time I was there. The main reason I came by was to ask you if you need any help in the restaurant in the dishwashing or cooking department. I also need a room to stay in while I'm here. As soon as I have enough money saved I will buy a bus ticket to St. Louis, Missouri where I and my mother live. I am willing to pay for my room and board as long as I'm here. Can you help me in any way? I'm so destitute. I have no other way to get back to St. Louis, Missouri. I'm so lucky this couple picked me up while I was hitchhiking and brought me to Las Vegas."

By this time Nick and Maxine were almost in tears not realizing what had befallen Sue since they had last seen her. Maxine said, "Sue, of course you can stay with us as long as you need to. We'll be glad to keep you at our house because we have an extra room that we aren't using. We can always use help in the dishwashing and waitress department. It won't take you long to make the money for a bus ticket to St. Louis, Missouri and we won't charge you for the spare room." Sue thanked them saying, "I'm ever so grateful to you and I'll keep you in my prayers. If I can return the favor please let me know."

When they got to Maxine's home in the evening, Sue made a telephone call to Mrs. Pickwell telling her what happened the past three months. Mrs. Pickwell was a mixed bag of emotions not knowing what to say or do. Her reaction was fear, anxiety, joy, hope, apprehension, jubilation, all rolled into one. Sue said, "Mrs. Pickwell, I should be back in St. Louis in several weeks. I'll call you the day before I leave on the bus from Las Vegas and let you know what time I arrive in St. Louis." Mrs. Pickwell was in agreement with everything saying, "I'll see you when you get back. I'll be going to the prison Sunday to relate the whole story to your mother, Jane, since she can't have any outside contact. Goodbye, Sue."

Chapter 10
A Happy Reunion

As Sue's departure day came closer she was getting very excited about seeing her mother, Jane, her friends at the Pickwell Apartment Complex and her boss and co-workers at Green Financial Services. She bid farewell to Maxine and Nick as she boarded the Greyhound bus on Tuesday at 8:05AM. She will be arriving at the St. Louis Bus Depot at 12:30AM on Wednesday. Her ticket cost $202.00 round trip plus money left over for food etc…

Sue spent a sleepless Monday night thinking about her upcoming trip the next day back to St. Louis. Besides she had to be up at 5:00AM the next morning to eat breakfast and make the necessary preparations for the trip. Well, she can always sleep on the bus. Sue finally fell into a fitful, restless sleep with the alarm ringing at 5:00AM. She slowly arose, ate her breakfast with no appetite and proceeded to get ready for her long trip. Maxine knocked on the door saying, "Sue, are you up already? It's 5:00AM." Sue replied,."Yes, Maxine. I just finished eating breakfast. It won't take me long to get ready." Sue quickly made her bed, got dressed and packed her suitcase. Maxine and Nick took her to the Las Vegas Bus Depot and waited with her until the bus pulled in. Within five minutes the bus was at the front gate, allowing people to board. She hurriedly bid Nick and Maxine goodbye and entered the bus in the hope of finding the best seat for herself only, which she did.

Sue arrived in St. Louis after a safe, comfortable trip besides getting a good night's rest in spite of sleeping on the bus all night. Plus some delicious, nutritional meals enroute to St. Louis.

Mrs. Pickwell was overjoyed at the prospect of having Sue back living at the complex again. She said, "Oh, I'm so glad Sue is back with us once more. I'm sure everyone at the complex will be anxious to see her and visit. I will post a notice on the bulletin board about a welcome back reunion party in her honor this coming Sunday afternoon at 2:00PM in the All Purpose Room. Maybe she will give a talk about her experience while she was gone. We'd all love to hear what happened. I'm so glad I didn't rent her apartment to someone else. Actually, I had a chance to but I always had a feeling she would be coming back because her mother, Jane, still lives here. I will start soliciting help for refreshments and anything else that's needed."

Sue's Back in the Complex

When Sue entered her apartment she found it just as she had left it, untouched except for an occasional cleaning. She was happy to be in her apartment once again among her friends and co—workers etc. It just felt good to be back among everybody. She unpacked her suitcase, ate supper and decided to watch television for the evening. Sue was watching the new St. Louis television Channel 39 that recently came into existence while she was gone. As she was listening nothing was of any importance to her until the announcer mentioned Sue's name. He said, "A missing person's report was just handed to me a few minutes ago about a woman named Sue Benson that escaped from a "commune" eighty five miles north of Las Vegas, Nevada, possibly headed for her home in St. Louis, Missouri. She was last seen in Las Vegas a week ago working at a local restaurant. If anyone knows the whereabouts of Sue Benson, please notify the Nevada Commune at 1-729-464-0174. Your name will remain anonymous. Thank you."

When Sue heard this she was beside herself with fear, thinking someone might report her to the local authorities or the "commune" in Las Vegas. With this thought in mind she decided to go to bed since there's nothing else she can do about it anyway. She doesn't have any enemies at the complex that she knows of but you never know. Do you think Sue has lots of friends at the complex? Hah!

Visiting Mr. Green

Sue decided to take the later 9:00AM bus to downtown St. Louis to Green Financial Services to talk to her boss, Mr. Green. She wants to explain what happened the last three months and make sure she still has her job. She detests waiting at the bus stop because that's how she got abducted at 7:30 in the morning. She decided to go at a later time to avoid any future problems.

Half an hour later she was sitting at Mr. Green's desk relating her three months experience at the Nevada "commune." Mr. Green was shocked and astounded saying, "Why didn't you try and call for help anytime?" Sue said, "I had no phone in my room or on my person. We were not allowed to use any phones that we saw. Not only that, I had a security guard with a gun posted at my door every night I was there. I was too scared to try anything. The only reason I had a chance to escape was because I found out the security guards were all going to a meeting in Reno, Nevada and there wouldn't be any guards around. I decided to take my chances and hitchhike into Las Vegas with an older couple. I stayed with a high school classmate of mine and her husband, working in their restaurant. When I had enough money saved I bought a bus ticket to St. Louis and here I am." Mr. Green said, "I'm sorry this happened to you, Sue. Please be careful from now on, you never know what can happen to a person. Of course, you still have your job anytime you're ready to come back." Sue said, "Well, I was thinking about starting back to work this coming Monday." Mr. Green said, "Fine, I'll see you Monday, Sue." Sue said, "Thank you" and left his office. She stopped for her usual cup of coffee like she used to do and then took the 12:00 noon bus back to the complex.

Upon entering the building she decided to check the bulletin board to see what was on the agenda for the month. She noticed a welcome back reunion party for herself this coming Sunday at 2:00PM in the All Purpose Room. She knows she's expected to give a talk on her three month's absence from the complex. She is willing to do that to keep the same thing from happening to someone else.

Sue is still tired from her long bus trip so she is going back to her apartment a little earlier this evening. In the back of her mind Sue is still fearful someone might report her whereabouts to the St. Louis Police Department or the Nevada "commune."

Sunday morning Sue awakens bright and early to take the bus to town to attend services at the Filmont Baptist Church on Filmont Street at 9:45AM. She knows she needs to pray and thank God for making conditions possible for her to get back to St. Louis. She knows she couldn't have done it on her own. It took a higher power and she was grateful for that.

Sue attended services and came back in time to eat dinner in the Barlow Dining Room with the rest of the residents. After dinner she went to her apartment to prepare her speech that she would be giving at her Welcome Back Reunion Party.

As she entered the All Purpose Room at 2:00PM everybody was seated as Mrs. Pickwell introduced Sue, "We are happy to have Sue Benson back among us this afternoon. Sue will relate her experience to us from the day she was abducted till she came back four days ago by bus." Sue stepped to the microphone as everybody clapped. She said, "Thank you" and proceeded to relate the whole story from beginning to end with a question and answer period following. After she was finished several hands were raised with questions on their minds. Sue asked, "Mrs. Cole, may I have your question, please?" Mrs. Cole asked, "Why did you get in the van to begin with?" Sue said, "I got in the van because I was forced to at gunpoint." Mrs. Jones raised her hand and asked Sue, "Why did you not try to escape sooner?" Sue replied, "I couldn't because the security personnel were guarding us day and night. There was a security guard posted at my door all night long with a gun. Anymore questions, anyone?" Mr. Keller asked Sue, "Did you get paid for the work that you did." Sue answered, "No, we didn't get paid because our room and board was considered our wages."

The party concluded with refreshments and visitation after which everybody went back to their respective apartments. Sue took the elevator back to her apartment to eat supper, watch television and on to bed because tomorrow would be her first day back to work since she came home.

Sue is getting ready to leave her apartment to catch the 7:30AM bus for Green Financial Services. On second thought, Sue just remembered there is another bus stop on Striker Street that arrives at 7:30AM that she can get on. It will be an extra four blocks but it will be worth the effort because of the safety concern.

Sue arrived at Green Financial Services at 8:00AM sharp and started her morning ritual of work. She answered the phone, filed business papers, interviewed prospective clients, etc… everything in a day's work. For dinner she went to her usual eatery and then back to her work. She worked until 5:00PM in the evening, catching the 6:00PM bus back to her apartment. She ate supper, visited with Mrs. Blake in the All Purpose Room and retired.

Like I'm saying, "Sue Benson's life is practically nonexistent. By today's standards Sue's life is dull, boring and monotonous with nothing but bad luck. Look at the embarrassment Sue has had to endure because of her mother, Jane, in prison for life. Can you imagine your mother being "The Notorious Serial Killer of Rockwood, Illinois?" Really!!! And if that isn't bad enough being abducted at gunpoint, transported by a van amongst a herd of women and children to an unknown part of the country to live in a "commune" in no man's land?"

The Slasher—September

The evenings are getting longer and a bit cooler as the residents are flocking to the All Purpose Room for a little recreation. While the men are playing billiards their wives are gathered drinking coffee and sometimes discussing the latest novel they read. By nine o'clock the lights are off in the All Purpose Room and everybody goes back to their apartment. Sue does likewise because she has nothing better to do to pass her time.

Around 3:00AM she is awakened by a blood curdling scream as she wrenches her front door open. She is met by the St. Louis Police Department running past her door with their guns pointed straight ahead, heading for the last room at the end of the hall. Mrs. Rane was screaming, "Help me! Help me! I think my husband, Harold, is dead." The police immediately called 911 thinking Mrs. Rane's wildest fears have come true.

The paramedics entered the room, placed the sections of Mr. Rane's body on a gurney and transported him to the St. Louis Memorial Hospital where he was pronounced dead on arrival at 3:38AM. Mrs. Rane was beside herself with grief as she tried to describe to the police what actually happened but the police were already aware of her story. Mrs. Rane described the evening's events such as: She said, "Harold and I went to bed at 10:00PM and were awakened around 3:00AM with the turning of a doorknob in the front room. The next thing we knew someone dressed all in black and wearing a black mask was slinging a long knife over our heads and screaming, "Get out of bed or I'll slice you in half, all both of you." Mrs. Rane proceeded to jump out of bed but poor Harold was too late. The murderer had already chopped Harold's body into sections but left his head intact to his upper torso. The "Slasher" ran out a side door onto the fire escape and into the dark of night.

The police told Mrs. Rane this wasn't the only case as described because they have witnessed other killings that the so called "Slasher" has performed in the course of a few minutes. A policeman was posted at the front door of the apartment while other residents took Mrs. Rane to their apartment for the night. According to the police these killings have been going on in the St. Louis area for about a month now. Up to this time there have been no "persons of interest" or leads. This is the first murder at the new Pickwell Apartment Complex of this nature to date.

The same morning the cooks Mark, Mrs. Black and Mrs. Powell are awaiting the arrival of the breakfast bunch as usual at 7:30AM. Finally at 8:00AM the residents slowly trickle into the Barlow Dining Room all abuzz about the activity on the third floor earlier in the morning. They were also relating how the "Slasher" escaped by the fire escape on the side of the building. The three cooks were appalled at the events of the night before and were glad when their shift was over. Mark said, "I'll be glad when it's time to go home this afternoon, won't you?" Mrs. Black and

Mrs. Powell agreed vehemently saying, "We can't wait until 3:00PM rolls around." At 3:00PM the three cooks walked out the door debating whether to come back the next morning or not.

Rest assured they'll be back because jobs are too hard to get right now and they know it.

Funeral Service

The funeral service for Mr. Harold Rane will be Tuesday at 2:00PM at the Briar Funeral Home in downtown St. Louis with burial at the St. Louis Cemetery. The casket was closed as the residents entered the funeral parlor to pay their respects to Mrs. Rane and her family seated in mourners row. A large photograph of Harold adorned the table next to the casket, while sprays of flowers decorated the background. After the funeral service ended everybody paid their final respects at the St. Louis Cemetery and then returned to the Barlow Dining Room for a luncheon in honor of Mr. Harold Rane. Mrs. Rane will be leaving the next day to stay with her daughter in Indianapolis, Indiana for several weeks so she won't have to be by herself.

Things are getting too scary and creepy at the complex anymore to encourage
residents to keep living there. I wouldn't want to live there! Would you?

The Slasher is Back…October 2006

September went out with a BANG with Harold Rane's murder. October is starting well with crisp days, cool nights and lots of activity in the Community Room. The residents are anxiously waiting for the ghosts and goblins to come trick or treating on Halloween night. They are ushered into the Community Room for lemonade, Halloween cookies, a little conversation and on their way again.

The next morning at breakfast everybody was accounted for except several women. Mrs. Pickwell said, "Mrs. Lyle is in the hospital with an infection, Mrs. Baker has the flu and is in her apartment in bed and Mrs. Cane didn't come down for breakfast this morning." Mrs. Pickwell went to her apartment calling her name and still no answer. She then proceeded to unlock the door and was aghast at what she encountered. Mrs. Cane lay on her bed in a pool of blood that was running off the bed covers. What really floored Mrs. Pickwell was the fact that Mrs. Cane's legs were severed at the groin and missing. What happened to Mrs. Cane's legs? Mrs. Pickwell came to the dining room crying and Mrs. Powell ran to her and said, "What are you crying for? What happened?" Mrs Pickwell related, "I went to Mrs. Cane's room and found her murdered plus her legs are missing. It seems like the "Slasher" was here again. What I don't understand is what happened to her legs. Why would he take her legs along? I can't understand that, can you?"

Nobody seems to have the answer to that question and it was forgotten for the time being. Many of the residents are seriously thinking about moving out of the complex because of the fear that's been instilled in them with the murders etc....Like they say, "We are living in constant fear of what will happen at nightfall. First it was the elevators and now it's the apartments themselves." Mrs. Pickwell announced, "We are having an emergency meeting tonight at 7:00PM in the Community Room for everybody to attend. I will post a notice on the bulletin board immediately. Please be sure to attend."

As 7:00PM approached all of the residents of the complex filed in except those that were sick. Mrs. Pickwell started the meeting, "Good evening, residents. I quickly set up an emergency meeting because of what's been going on at the complex. It seems like the "Slasher" has visited us twice already. I don't know how he enters the complex except to think he has a key to every room like I do. I don't know how he would have managed that. They are very hard to get or have made.

Incidentally, please don't answer your door if someone knocks unless you know who it is because you could be saving your own life. If someone approaches you in your apartment please call 911 and that should scare him into leaving. By that time help will have arrived. Any questions? What is your question, Mrs. Barkley?" Mrs. Barkley asked, "Is there any way you can post security guards, at least two on every floor, for safety's sake? I and several of my lady friends are exceptionally scared." Mrs. Pickwell remarked, "I will ask the police department if they have extra policemen on patrol they can send out here for several days. Anymore questions?" Sue asked, "I have to get up at 6:00AM in the morning on account of my job. Is there any danger that he could be around that early in the morning?"Mrs. Pickwell said, "According to the pattern that he's adopted I'd say no but that doesn't mean anything. I guess he can come anytime. Right?" Sue said, "I guess so because time doesn't mean anything to some people."

Thanksgiving....2006

A group of residents, including Sue, were gathered at the bulletin board reading the posted notices of upcoming events one day. Sue remarked, "Oh, this is something new! We are having a pot luck supper a week before Thanksgiving, Nov. 18 and a program. We can bring any kind of dish or dessert that we want. That way we can get a larger variety. We'll have to keep that in mind." Among other activities that were posted were Bingo night, free blood pressure check, a speaker for the monthly meeting and a variety of other events.

The pot luck Supper which is scheduled for this evening has the lady residents of the complex cooking and baking all afternoon as the aroma fills the hallways. The hot dishes and desserts should be on the serving table by 5:45PM and the pot luck supper starts at 6:00PM.

At 6:00PM the residents are going through the serving line to partake of the scrumptious dishes and desserts of their choosing. A variety of coffee, tea and soft drinks are also available. The program consists of Mrs. Pickwell's enumeration on several issues at the complex and three local musicians that will put on a performance while everyone is eating their meal.

Sue and her personal friends and residential acquaintances are busy visiting and eating the delicious food besides listening to the musical performance. All of a sudden several women started screaming and vomiting food onto themselves. They were bent over crying in pain and grasping their swollen stomachs in sheer agony. Mrs. Pickwell ran to them saying,"What's the matter, Mrs. Cole? Are you in pain?" Mrs. Cole couldn't answer anymore and Mrs. Peebles sitting next to her had the same reaction. Mrs. Skill at the end of the table was the same as the other two tenants except her breathing was shallow, labored and her facial color was beginning to get a blue tinge. Mrs. Pickwell said, "Quick, someone call the hospital and tell them to send an ambulance here to the complex because we have three ladies that have to be transported to the St. Louis Regional Hospital! Please tell them to hurry!" Several men carried the three women to couches that were vacant in the Community Room. They were followed by paramedics, who took their vital signs and reported their findings to the doctor on call. By this time all three women were barely breathing and CODE BLUE was called for them. Mrs. Cole died at 7:45PM, Mrs. Peebles at 7:58PM and Mrs. Skill lived another forty five minutes. She passed away at 8:45PM. All three women had the same symptoms of raspy breathing, excruciating stomach pain, vomiting etc… Before Mrs. Pickwell and her assistant manager left the hospital they said, "We would like to request an autopsy on all three women to see what could have caused these unusual deaths. Please report your findings to the Pickwell Apartment Complex."

What were these women eating at the same time that made them violently ill and claimed their lives? Did someone bring a poisonous hot dish deliberately? Oh no! Continue reading!

Mrs. Carl, Mrs. Peebles and Mrs. Skills families were all notified and arrived respectively amidst tears and numerous unanswered questions about their mothers. The family members gathered in the All Purpose Room to make arrangements for the funeral services and burial. They all went to the Baptist Memorial Church on Seneca Street and burial will be in the Baptist Memorial Cemetery on Pond Road. Services and burial were set for Thursday morning at 10:00AM with a luncheon to follow at the Barker Dining Room later. All the residents of the Pickwell Apartment Complex attended the funeral and burial at the Baptist Memorial Church amidst floods of tears, bewilderment at the type of death they endured, sadness, just a mixed bag of emotions. The last report indicated 879 people at the funeral services with many coming to the luncheon at the Barlow Dining Room. As the family members were exiting the dining room Mrs. Pickwell told them, "I will be sending each family a report indicating what type of illness your mother had that brought her death on such short notice. Once again I extend my condolences at this sad and sorrowful time. Thank you." The family members said, "Thank you" and we will be taking our mother's personal belongings with us when we leave in a few days."

A laboratory Surprise

When Mrs. Pickwell went through her mountains of mail Monday morning she immediately recognized the white business envelope titled St. Louis Laboratory. She hurriedly tore it open and read the following report: Mrs. Pickwell, we are sorry to inform you that the report we received from the laboratory indicated the following: After the autopsy and the stomach contents were disclosed and examined, the three women had eaten chunks of human flesh, blood and particles cooked together to be concealed in the form of a soupy broth. Their sensitive stomachs could not tolerate this form of ingestion which led to their death." Mrs. Pickwell was shocked at the report that she would have to relate to their family members, plus their friends at the complex. This report would also make other residents skeptical, fearful of eating in the Barlow Dining Room and wanting to relocate to another complex. Oh dear!

The next day Mrs. Pickwell sent the laboratory report to each of the family members of the three deceased women. Within a week all three families threatened a law suit because of the loss of their mother. Their lawyers said, "Our client wishes to engage in a law suit upon the death of their mother." If that arrangement is not satisfactory, an out of court settlement will be required for an undisclosed amount of money. Thank you."

Mrs. Pickwell answered back immediately and said, "There is no proof who cooked the soup and no one will step forward and admit to this, so I will settle this discrepancy out of court for an undisclosed amount of money. Thank you."

A Special Meeting

Tonight at 7:00PM there will be a special meeting regarding the deaths of Mrs. Cole, Mrs. Peebles and Mrs. Skill.

Mrs. Pickwell called the meeting to order and immediately brought up the three deaths. Mrs. Pickwell said, "The laboratory report came back after the autopsy and stomach contents were disclosed that three women had eaten chunks of human flesh, blood and particles cooked together to be concealed in the form of disguised turkey vegetable soup. Their sensitive stomachs could not tolerate this sensitive form of ingestion which led to their deaths." She also said, "Each family's lawyer sent a letter in regards to a law suit but she decided to settle out of court for an undisclosed amount of money." Mrs. Pickwell asked the group, "Does anybody have any idea who might've been behind these deaths or who would've cooked the human flesh that the women ate?" Everybody was quiet, no smiles, no emotions on their face, just a blank stare. Mrs. Pickwell dismissed the meeting because she knew she wouldn't make headways with this discussion, nobody would own up to the killings and besides everyone looked tired and withdrawn including herself. Well, somebody at the meeting tonight knows there the killer, they know who they are. Do you know who the killer is?

Another court issue that needs to be addressed by the family members of Sylvia Bond as Attorney Joe Lorn stated is: The Case of Mrs. Sylvia Bond Buried Alive. This is the result of a wrongful end of life diagnosis by the emergency room staff at St. Louis Memorial Hospital in St. Louis, Missouri. The emergency room staff was incompetent in their medical diagnosis of labeling Mrs. Sylvia Bond "legally dead" thereby releasing her body under this condition.

The court date is set for Jan. 7, 2007 at 10:30AM unless a settlement is made out of court. Signed, Attorney Joe Lorn. Thank you.

When St. Louis Memorial Hospital received the court letter they immediately held an emergency staff meeting and decided not to contest the case but to send the family members five million dollars they requested, their apologies and a closed case.

Police Protection

Mrs. Pickwell called the St Louis Policed Department stating, "I am requesting police protection for my residents at the complex in the event that the "Slasher" tries break into the complex at any given time. Officer Collins said, "We will be glad to accommodate you, Mrs. Pickwell, because we're aware of the fact that you've had a rash of incidents occurring at the complex that require police protection especially at night. How soon do you want us to start putting the police on patrol?" Mrs. Pickwell said, "How about tomorrow night? I would like to have one policeman on every floor and two outside the building for awhile. Is that too many?" Officer Collins said, "No, Mrs. Pickwell, we can spare that many. If it gets to be too many we will let you know." Mrs. Pickwell said, "Fine, I'll be expecting them tomorrow night. Thank you." The next evening eight policemen showed up at the Pickwell apartment Complex to guard the building and its contents for the next couple of weeks. The night policemen changed shifts every four hours so the counterparts could go home and get some much needed rest. During the day no policemen were needed since there was no danger. The second night the policemen were guarding the complex they heard a crash like the sound of a window breaking and they hurried to the south side of the building. They discovered a young, homeless type of man trying to crawl through a first floor window onto the window sill. The policeman said, "Hold on there, buster! What are you trying to do here? What's your name?" The man said, "My name is Elmer Grigsby and what does it look like I'm doing? I'm trying to crawl through this window tonight. I didn't have anything better to do this evening and I can use a few extra dollars," as he was laughing to himself. The policeman said, "Put your hands up against the building and stay there. Are you armed with a gun?" The homeless man said, "No, I don't even own a gun, I'm harmless. I just thought I'd try my luck tonight. Ha! Ha!" By this time the policeman was a little aggravated at the homeless man and he said, "It might not be too funny by the time I get done with you tonight, Elmer. I'm calling a squad car to take you to the police department for questioning and a lie detector test."Fifteen minutes later a squad car transported Elmer Grigsby to the police department for the above mentioned. He was released because he was completely innocent of everything and was a first time offender. When the policeman escorted him to the door they said, "I wouldn't try this stunt the second time if I were you." To which Elmer answered, "Don't worry, I won't. I learned my lesson tonight."

By this time of night the policemen were back patrolling the complex for the rest of the shift. As the weeks went by and there were less problems at t he complex, the police department reduced its policemen. They positioned them across the city where they were in dire need of police protection. They still kept two policemen outside the complex all night changing shifts every four hours. Everything was quiet at the complex except for one night. The same man kept walking past the complex, staring at the building and the police. Officer Bell yelled at him asking, "Are you looking for someone or something at this address since you are always walking past this apartment complex." The man said, "No, I'm just enjoying the fresh air." Officer Bell said, "At 3:00AM in the morning?"The man said, "Yes, I couldn't sleep so I got up and took my dog for a walk. I do this oftener. Sorry if I'm disturbing you."

After their shift had concluded Mrs. Pickwell asked, "Would you please step into my office for a few minutes because I have something I wanted to talk to you about?" They said, "Of course."Mrs. Pickwell proceeded to explain, "As you know we had three deaths here at the complex a couple of weeks ago and it still preys on my mind as to who committed these mindless killings. I scheduled a meeting after it was all over but naturally no one is going to admit killing these three women. I know the residents are fearful of this because they know someone from the complex brought the food to the pot luck supper that killed these women.

Eventually they won't be attending anymore pot luck suppers and probably will be moving to another retirement center where these things aren't going on. There is no way I myself can find out who's doing these killings. I don't know what to do. Do you have any suggestions?" Officer

Bell said, "Yes, as a matter of fact I do. Have you ever thought of having all the residents finger printed and given a lie detector test? I mean all of the residents. Don't leave anybody out. Just because they aren't home the day of the fingerprinting, lie detector test and interrogation, have them make arrangements with the police department to come in another day. They all have to be accounted for." Mrs. Pickwell said, "That's a good idea. Why didn't I think of that? Fingerprinting! They do it all the time. Why not? Can you make arrangements with the police department about starting this procedure?"Officer Bell said, "Sure, we'll report this to the Chief of Police, James Rhine, and someone will get back to you when they want the first group of residents to come down. I know they'll have to have their own transportation as we aren't equipped to transport groups of people to the police department." Mrs. Pickwell said, "That's fine because we have our own personal mini bus that takes residents to different activities in the St. Louis area."

Several days later Mrs. Pickwell received a call from the police department about the fingerprinting procedure. She explained this to all the residents at a meeting saying, "I have made arrangements with the St. Louis Police Department to have every resident fingerprinted for everybody else's safety. I hate to say this but I feel we have an unsavory character among us and I want to get to the bottom of this because I'm scared myself. I happen to know that a lot of you are scared to eat at the pot luck meals and I don't blame you because I don't like the idea myself. I thought fingerprinting, interrogating and a lie detector test might be the way to catch the person or persons responsible for all these killings dating back since they first started. I'm sorry something wasn't done sooner because I always thought this problem would alleviate itself but it hasn't. Does anybody else have any other suggestions or comments?" Everybody was extremely quiet and had a scared, fearful look on their face as if they were ready to break into tears. Mrs. Pickwell said, "Very well then, but remember it's for your future safety. Please keep that in mind. Monday morning the first fifteen people beginning with the last name starting with an A will board the mini bus at 8:15AM in front of the complex. Your appointment is at 9:00AM at the police department for the fingerprinting, interrogation and lie detector test. After everybody is finished you will all come back as a group. I will send a group coordinator with you. Thank you. Any further questions?"

Fingerprinting

All the residents at the complex went to bed extra early in order to get up even earlier than usual for the fingerprinting procedure. They will be eating breakfast at 7:00AM according to Mrs. Pickwell at the last meeting. The fifteen residents were finished with breakfast at 7:45AM and were waiting in the lobby of the complex for the 8:15AM mini bus. Sue saw the mini bus coming down the street and said, "Here comes the mini bus. It's time to go. Hop on everybody!" The doors swung open and the fifteen residents flocked into the bus and took their seat. The St. Louis Police Department is a twenty five minute ride downtown on the southeast corner of Bern Street.

Everybody exited the bus and entered the police department in time for the 9:00AM appointment. After everyone was fingerprinted, interrogated and a lie detector test taken they all boarded the bus for the ride back to the Pickwell Apartment Complex. The results of everything will be sent back to the complex in several days. Mrs. Pickwell asked the group coordinator, Mrs. Rane, how the morning went and she said, "Just fine. No problems." Mrs. Pickwell said, "Wonderful! That's what we like to hear! We'll be looking forward to the test results."

The next morning, Tuesday, fifteen more residents will make the short trip to the police station for testing and then back to the complex. This will continue every day until all of the residents have been tested.

A week later Mrs. Pickwell received a letter from the police department stating, "Our recent test of the residents of Pickwell Apartment Complex indicated three "persons of interest" that needed to be tested again at the earliest convenience. Please call back and set up an appointment. All three women have failed the lie detector test which is the most important. Their names are Germane Lipman, Martha Minton and Sue Benson.

Mrs. Pickwell immediately checked their charts to see if they were all available to go back down to the police station Monday morning at

9:00AM to be retested. They were all available and raring to go to clear their names and avoid the suspicious glares of the residents.

Monday morning Germane Lipman, Martha Minton and Sue Benson boarded the mini bus for their ride down to the police station. This is the second time Sue had to take off work again and the results will manifest itself on her paycheck. Officer McConnel greeted them when they arrived saying, "Good morning, ladies! How are you on this bright, cheery morning?" Martha answered, "We'd all be fine if we wouldn't have had to come down here to be retested. Such a waste of time! Let's get this over with." Germane and Sue agreed saying, "We're ready! Let's go!"

Officer McConnel said, "Very well ladies. Right this way, second door to the left and down the hall. You'll run right into it." Germane, Martha and Sue went through the complete lie detector test plus the interrogation and fingerprinting. After they were finished they took the mini bus back to the complex with Germane saying, "Boy I hope my tests turn out okay because I'm innocent of everything. I brought an apple pie for dessert and kept one at my apartment for myself. I bought them at Boll's Food Store the other day." Martha also said, "I bought a bowl of mashed potatoes and turkey gravy to the pot luck supper which everybody ate and said it was simply delicious." Sue Benson also remarked, "I brought a large plate of baked turkey and dressing fresh out of the oven on my way home from work. Actually, here's my store ticket from my purchase, reaching in her purse and showing the receipt to Germane and Martha. That puts me in the clear, don't you think?" Germane and Martha said, "It most certainly does."

Test results came back on the three residents this afternoon stating that everybody's results turned out fine. The lie detector machine's power was a little low which could've caused the misinterpretation of the tests of Germane, Martha and Sue. Everybody was happy at the results.

Bingo and Meeting

This is a busy week so a meeting and Bingo are scheduled for this evening. Mrs. Pickwell has called the meeting to order addressing different issues that come to mind.

First of all Mrs. Pickwell announced, "Germane Lipman, Martha Minton and Sue Benson have been cleared of any wrongdoing in the case of the deaths of Mrs. June Cole, Mrs. Alice Peebles and Mrs. Eunice Skill. The police department indicated the lie detector machines power was lower than it should have been causing faulty misinterpretation of the tests of Germane, Martha and Sue."Everybody at the meeting was happy about the outcome of the tests.

The next issue on the agenda Mrs. Pickwell talked about was, "For those of you that are still contemplating moving out of the complex, please contact me at your earliest possible convenience. I will make further arrangements about the future rental of your room and any back pay that you might still owe the complex. If I owe you a refund on your apartment it will be taken care of. Any questions regarding this part of the meeting? Please raise your hand." Mrs. Roman raised her hand and Mrs. Pickwell said, "Yes, Mrs. Roman what is your question?" To which Mrs. Roman replied, "I and several other tenants are planning to relocate at the beginning of next month which will be Jan.1." Mrs. Pickwell said, "Very well, step into my office sometime today and I will set up an appointment for you and your friends to straighten your accounts and any refunds due. Thank you, Mrs. Roman. Any further questions? Very well, we will resume our monthly Bingo game. Sue Benson will be your Bingo caller for the evening."

Sue stepped forward working with the Bingo cage awhile before she started calling the numbers for a winner. There were numerous prizes awarded, an half hour intermission

playing Bingo until 10:00PM.

Christmas—December—2006

Christmas is fast approaching as is the weather. Two feet of snow are forecast for the month of December with rain and windy conditions. There will be many streets closed and traffic will be difficult. Don't go out if you don't have to.

The complex itself and the apartments are all decorated up and holly, jolly cheer is spreading throughout the building.

Tonight will be a pot luck supper and gift exchange at 6:00PM. Mrs. Pickwell received a slightly heavy box addressed to her wrapped in

Christmas paper and fastened with a pretty, red, bow, no name or return address, delivered by a postal carrier. She set it under the Christmas tree with everybody else's packages, opening it after the pot luck supper.

After everybody had opened their Christmas exchange gifts they all exclaimed, "Mrs. Pickwell, open your gift. Hurry! We are anxious to see what it is since there's no name or return address." Mrs. Pickwell started to unwrap the gift feeling uncomfortable about the whole situation by now. Before she could open the cardboard flaps covering the gift she could already hear the tick, tick, tick. A BOMB! Oh no! Someone sent an actual explosive to the complex? Get rid of it! Call the police! Some of the tenants were crying while others were leaving the room for their apartments. Mrs. Pickwell called the police department and they came immediately asking lots of questions. Officer Shelton asked, "Mrs. Pickwell, who would send you a bomb on Christmas Eve?" Mrs. Pickwell remarked, "Someone that wants us all dead, I assume."

In the meantime several of the officers hurriedly took the bomb several miles out of town and detonated it in a large, empty field. They came back to town to file a report telling Mrs. Pickwell what had happened. Officer Shelton said, "You'd better be careful of any further packages or even envelopes. If you are scared of any of your mail please call the police department to assist you. Thank you."

Mrs. Pickwell said, "Thank you for your assistance in this matter. If I need your services again I will surely call you. It's nice to know we can rely on the St. Louis Police Department in our time of need. You are greatly appreciated." The policemen said, "Thank you" and went on their way.

Chapter 11
A Long Winter Ahead
Christmas Day–2006

All of the residents including Mrs. Pickwell and her assistants will be boarding several buses to take them to a nondenominational church for Christmas day services at 10:00AM. Several couples with privately owned cars will attend 10:00AM mass at St. Mark's Catholic Church about two miles from the complex. After services and mass everybody will come back to the complex for their Christmas day meal. After the meal is over the residents will attend a Christmas movie in a Community Room setting provided by Mr. and Mrs. Pickwell and the staff as their way of saying "thank you" to the residents for their kindness and goodwill throughout the year. The name of the movie was "A Very Merry Christmas" and it was enjoyed by everyone.

New Years Day was a repetition of Christmas Day with a special meal at noon and Bingo to follow. The festivities were over at 5:00PM and everybody visited among themselves for the remainder of the evening.

It's been a long, cold winter with tons of snow, icicles hanging from the buildings and people bundled up with layers of clothing scurrying through the deep snow anxious to reach their destination. Several residents braved the January weather to take the mini bus downtown at ten degrees above zero to buy items of necessity. They said, "We were mighty happy to get back to the complex and wouldn't attempt that again. With all the snow on the ground we were lucky we didn't fall."

The Walking Dead

In spite of the inclement weather Joe and Marla Hines decided to visit their longtime friends, Bob and Sheila Cover, five miles east of St. Louis. It's a Sunday afternoon with the snow stopping and the sun shining brightly. The only problem is, it's extremely cold, about fifteen degrees above zero, with a slight wind blowing.

They visited Bob and Sheila Cover, ate dinner and played cards all afternoon. Around five o'clock Sheila asked them, "Would you do us the honor of eating supper with us tonight?" Joe said, "I don't think we'd better because it's beginning to snow lightly again. If we stayed for supper, by the time we'd get back into St. Louis it could be much heavier." Marla agreed saying, "I think Joe is correct. I would just as soon leave now especially while there is a little daylight left." When Sheila heard this she immediately brought their coats and bid them farewell.

As they were driving Marla suddenly remarked, "Joe, what are all those people doing over there with no coats or hats on? Who are they? What's the matter with them?" Joe *said, "I'm not sure but I'm going to slow down so I can get a better look". Well, Joe and* Marla saw more than they cared to see. The strange people came walking to the car trying to get in with them. Some of them were carrying baseball bats, clubs and ropes dripping with blood. All of the people are walking with three inch fingernails, barefooted in the snow with chains on their ankles. They do not speak except to say, Arg! Arg! Arg! One of the people took a club and slammed it down on Joe's hood creating a large dent which made Joe furious. He said, "I didn't come all the way out here to get the hood of my car dented up. Bob and Sheila will be very surprised when they hear about this."

When Joe and Marla reached St. Louis they could still see the group of people walking toward the city. They are humpbacked and walk with a limp. Marla said, "They remind me of those pictures we saw of the "walking dead" on television one night. Remember? They were scary! "Joe said, "Yes, I still remember that! I thought they were going to jump off the television screen any minute." By this time they had reached the Pickwell Apartment Complex and went inside. They told Mrs. Pickwell in her office what happened and she in turn called the St. Louis Police Department saying, "A group of zombies are headed this way from the St. Louis Cemetery. You will need lots of patrol cars." Officer Shelton thanked Mrs. Pickwell for the information and said, "We will get right on it and thank you for the call." The policemen searched for the zombies but they were nowhere to be found. Where do you suppose they went? How did they find their way around? Somehow, it just seems like I recognized some of their faces. Maybe they lived in the complex at one time. Are they the small group of people that got killed a couple of years ago? You know, there were three that got killed in the elevator, three were chopped up and lying under the cement in the basement, three women died because of what they ate, Mrs. Sylvia Bond was killed and Marcus Reil was killed in Rockwood, Illinois. There might have been a few more. Like I said before, half of the people looked very familiar to me. Now I know, I've seen them here at the complex at meetings, Bingo, pot luck suppers and other events. I'm positive.

Now that Joe and Marla were back visiting at the complex, Joe decided to call Bob and explain to him what he saw when they left their house earlier this evening. Joe started enumerating the odd things he and Marla noticed about them. Joe said, "One of the zombies took a club and beat the hood of my car making a huge dent. I hope my insurance company will pay to have my hood repaired after they hear my story."

Bob remarked, "Well, after you left we turned the television on to get the 10:00PM news and that was the first news release they announced. The police are looking for them but so far they haven't had any luck. Did it ever occur to you, Joe, they could've walked back to the cemetery and crawled back in their caskets? That's not impossible, is it?"Joe said, "No, not really. Anything's possible nowadays anymore. The only way to check this out is to go to the cemetery in broad daylight so we can see how the ground has cracked open and we'll be able to tell more." Joe said, "I think I'll explain everything to the caretaker, Mr. Lorenson, and see if he'll meet us there at 5:00PM. The caretaker definitely needs to know what's going on at the St. Louis Cemetery." Bob agreed to meet them at the cemetery at 5:00PM tomorrow night and settle this once and for all.

Tomorrow night came faster than the men thought it would as they all headed to the St. Louis Cemetery in their own cars. When they walked in they noticed there were large, gaping holes on top of the mounds of dirt. Bob flashed into the holes with a flashlight and said, "All the lids of the caskets are open and empty. Where have they gone tonight?" Joe said, "Who knows? What are we supposed to do? This is the police department's job. I will call them when we get back into the city."

Just as they were getting ready to leave three zombies entered the cemetery and came up behind Joe beating him on the back of the skull. Joe immediately collapsed with blood gushing from his head. Bob and Mr. Lorenson screamed and chased them but the zombies eluded them running into the thicket for cover. Mr. Lorenson and Bob picked Joe up, laid him in the car and transported him to the St. Louis Memorial Hospital. They immediately wheeled him into the emergency room and called his wife, Marla. She answered the phone amidst tears telling them, "I will be at the hospital soon." When she arrived in the emergency room she took one look at Joe and the situation was not good. He had a severe hemorrhage on his head and the emergency room staff had a hard time stopping the bleeding. He was bleeding profusely and had slipped into a coma. At this point in time nothing could rouse him. No talking, prayers, laughter, or music because Joe didn't respond to any stimulus. He is being taken to the intensive care unit at the hospital because of his comatose state. Everybody left the hospital except Marla and she would probably spend the night at the hospital because of Joe's condition. Marla stayed in the intensive care unit hoping he might revive from his comatose state. When that didn't happen Marla stayed at Joe's bedside till 10:00PM, then went to a bed that was reserved for her in a private part of the hospital.

Marla was awakened by Nurse Liann at midnight telling her the sad news saying, "Joe passed away while he was in the coma. I had made my rounds, Joe being my last patient. When I came into the intensive care unit I went to Joe's bedside noticing that his breathing and pulse had stopped. I immediately lifted his eyelids and he had a blank stare with no eye movement which usually indicates the cessation of life. I'm sorry, Marla." Marla wept uncontrollably and said, "Poor Joe, he was only sixty eight years old and had so many things he wanted to accomplish while he was still living. Our three children will be devastated without their father and so will I. I don't know what I'll do without Joe to pass the time away." Marla was overcome with grief that the attending physician had to give her an injection to bear the brunt of this tragedy. Oh dear! Isn't this awful? Joe's life was snatched away at the hands of a zombie! Can you imagine that?

Joe's Funeral

Joe Hines funeral was well attended with hundreds of mourners present for the 10:00AM service at the Jerusalem Baptist Church and burial at the St. Louis Cemetery. There were many residents from the Pickwell Apartment Complex in attendance because Joe and Marla had many friends there. They had a wide circle of friends, neighbors and relatives to fill in the void everywhere.

Marla, her three children and six grandchildren sat in mourners' row staring at Papa and Grandpa Joe lying so peacefully with a smile on his face as if to say, "I'm at peace with the Lord." Joe's neatly manicured nails, thick, brown, stylish hair and exquisite dark brown suit complimented his appearance.

Pastor Brown gave the eulogy amidst tears, sniffles and heaving sighs of sadness. Before the close of the service everyone filed past the casket for one more last look at their friend, neighbor and relative Joe. Everybody followed the hearse and procession to the St. Louis Cemetery for the last rites of Joe Hines. Pastor Brown said some prayers and then everybody walked past the beautiful, brown, wooden casket paying their final respects to Joe Hines and his family.

A heavy luncheon followed the services in the basement of the Jerusalem Baptist Church which was also in well attendance. The luncheon closed at 2:00PM after everybody had eaten and visited with one another. There were people that came from afar that hadn't seen each other for years. Yes, it's too bad they had to get together under these circumstances.

Where Are the Walking Dead?

Officer Shelton and Officer Gramel are on the night patrol shift from 8:00PM this evening until 8:00AM tomorrow morning, not experiencing anything different than the usual robberies domestic abuse, speeding tickets etc... But they were not prepared for the following:

As they were patrolling Blakely Boulevard on the eastern side of St. Louis, Officer Gramel asked Officer Shelton, "Heh! Who is that group of people walking in the middle of the boulevard? I've never seen anything like that before, have you?" Officer Shelton said, "No, I'm going to pull over and question them. What do you think?" Officer Gramel said, "OK! Let's go for it!" The police officers pulled the patrol car to the side of Blakely Boulevard and the zombies, basically The Walking Dead, stopped walking instantly and stared at the police officers.

Officer Gramel said, "What are you doing out here on this bitterly, cold night and where are you going?" They looked at Officer Shelton and Officer Gramel with bulging eyes, distorted faces and saliva drooling from their lips. They looked like caged animals with a white, filmy like mold hanging from their clothes and hair. The only thing they could say was "Arg! Arg! Arg! "Nothing else! One of the zombies took his club and beat on the patrol car actually smashing a hole in the hood. The police officers got angry and called several more patrol cars to take eleven zombies and book them into jail for the night against their will. They would decide what to do with them in the morning after they talked to the police chief.

The next morning after they conferred with Mr. Rhine they decided to take them to the hospital and have them injected with medication to put them to sleep permanently. They did this and they all died immediately. They used a Police Bus and transported them to the St. Louis Cemetery where Mr. Lorenson, the caretaker, and his assistant, Mr Lake, reburied them again. Well, that takes care of The Walking Dead. I'm sure that's the last we'll see of them!

Back to the Complex 2007

Valentine's Day is fast approaching and the residents are anxiously awaiting the Valentine's Day festivities, which include a pot luck supper, an exchange of Valentine cards and a dance. The pot luck supper starts at 5:00PM with ladies bringing their heated casserole dishes, savory roast beef and other meats in crock pots, a variety of vegetables, breads and desserts. After they were finished eating they exchanged Valentine cards and proceeded to dance with each other until 10:00PM. After that they went back to their apartments for the evening.

Another Elevator Murder

A group of residents are reading the events on the bulletin board coming up for the month of March, namely St. Patricks's Day, an Irish celebration. There will be an Irish pot luck supper at 5:30PM on March 17th and Bingo for the evening. After the pot luck supper Mrs. Pickwell will conduct a short meeting and then back to Bingo. It will be a fun time for all.

The night of St. Patrick's Day was clear and bitterly cold but the All Purpose Room was warm and cozy. The fragrance of Irish stew, corned beef and cabbage, their favorite Irish chocolate pudding cake, salads and a wide variety of other Irish delicacies wafted through the air. The aroma was floating up and down the hall drawing the residents to the Barlow Dining Room sooner than usual.

As the first group entered the new elevator which was just installed last week, blood curdling screams could be heard throughout the whole Pickwell Apartment Complex. The police report stated, "In one corner of the elevator lay Mrs. Gladys Mission's body with her insides cut out. Her intestines were hanging from the edge of the ceiling in a scalloped fashion. Her organs such as the gall bladder, liver, stomach, etc… were hanging from the actual ceiling itself. Mrs. Mission's legs were amputated at the groin as well as her arms at the armpits. Her head was intact but her eyes were dug out. Her tongue was also sliced out of her mouth. Her ears were cut off and her mouth had the barrel of a gun sticking in it."

Several of the residents fainted when they witnessed the scene in the elevator and had to be revived in their apartments keeping the paramedics busy for hours. The next group that was to take the elevator to the main floor was appalled at the sight and started crying for fear. Mr. and Mrs. Pickwell were also crying because of what transpired, plus the fact they knew some more residents would be moving out. In fact, Mrs. Marla Hines, whose husband Joe had been buried several weeks ago, had been planning on moving into the complex until she heard from the tenants about all the killings. Marla said, "No, I don't want to live in the Pickwell Apartment Complex since all those murders are going on. I want to move into St. Louis from the edge of town because I'm by myself now. I don't consider that part safe anymore, even though the zombies that killed Joe are dead and reburied. I'm scared out there now living all by myself. My three children want me to move into an apartment complex here in town but not the Pickwell Apartment Complex. My daughter in St. Louis wants me to move in with her and the family until I am established here in the city. I guess that's what I'll have to do. Does anybody have any other suggestions?" Nobody had any response so the matter wasn't pursued.

The Irish pot luck supper was cancelled with everybody coming into the dining room to get their dish muttering to themselves, "This is preposterous! I wonder who is doing all these killings?" Another male resident, Mr. Norton said, "I'm by myself since my wife died so I'm planning on moving into another high rise apartment building because this living situation is too dangerous for me. Nobody is doing anything about these killings which have been going on for several years now. Even the police department hasn't been able to come with anything, not even a "person of interest. It's just unbelievable what's happening here." Mrs. Brown voiced her opinion, "I know what you mean by that! I'm thoroughly disgusted with this place. I should've never moved in here because someone warned me about the different things that were going on here. I ignored the warning and moved in because the rent was cheap. It wasn't worth it. What do the rest of you think?" By this time a group of residents had gathered around to participate in the conversation. Mr. White stepped forward saying, "I'm fed up with this damned, ugly place and I'm getting the hell outa here. My wife, Yolanda, and I are scared spitless day and night. Yolanda cries herself to sleep most nights and I try to console her but it doesn't do any good. We've been here a year now thinking things would get better but they haven't so it's time to move on. Anybody want to go apartment hunting with us?" A few people spoke up saying, "Yes, we'll go along. Just tell us what time and where to meet you." Mr. White said, "How about tomorrow morning at 10:00AM. My wife and I will meet you in the Community Room and we can take my car. I'll also bring the St. Louis Gazette with a list of apartments for rent in the St. Louis area." Mr. White bid everyone "Good evening" and retired to his room.

Albert Fleming also spoke up saying, "If anybody cares to go apartment hunting with me let me know because I'm also planning on going tomorrow afternoon. I told one of my friends the other day I'm getting sick and tired of this place. Awhile back I was one of the unfortunate tenants that had their door banged on at all hours of the night and I was also the recipient of some late night phone calls. I'll tell you one thing, this crappy place is giving me the creeps. That elevator murder and carving put the icing on the cake for me. I have a hard time sleeping these times. Has anybody else experienced the same trauma?"Several residents said, "Yes, we've all experienced the same emotions and we're anxious to get the hell out of here. Mr. and Mrs. Arnold Jones and Ann Gorde spoke up saying, "We're ready to go along tomorrow afternoon. Where do you want to meet us and what time?" Albert Fleming said, "I'll meet you in the All Purpose Room at 1:00PM with the newspaper and we'll go from there."

The next morning Mr. and Mrs. Louis Jackson and Ann Shields went apartment hunting with Mr. White and they all secured an apartment in the same building several miles north of the Pickwell Apartment Complex. The name of this rental is the Brown Apartment Building and they paid their first month's rent which is cheaper than Mrs. Pickwell's price. They'll be moving into their apartment in two weeks because they have to give the existing tenants two weeks notice to pack their belongings and vacate the apartment because they are moving out of the state.

Albert Fleming, Mr. and Mrs. Jones and Jane Gorde also left the next afternoon to go apartment hunting in the St. Louis area downtown. They found an ad in the paper that they answered and were ushered into a beautiful apartment building on Crosby Street, a mile south of the downtown area. The price was a little more expensive than Mrs. Pickwell's complex but they decided it was well worth it. They paid their first month's rent and decided to move into their apartments in about three weeks. Naturally, they are looking forward to the move. Wouldn't you be? I would.

Announcement at the Dinner Table

Today Mrs. Pickwell made an announcement at the dinner table saying, "Once again, I'm sorry about the gruesome violence in the elevator on St. Patrick's Day that caused the death of June Mission. I received a telephone call from the State Building Inspector Department requesting more information about all the killings that have taken place in the past. One of our inspectors will be paying us a visit to monitor the incidents that have transpired at the complex. They will be coming Monday morning at 10:00AM. Remember, this meeting is open to the public and anyone is welcome to attend.

In the meantime Mr. John White, Mr. and Mrs. Louis Jackson, Ann Sheilds, Mr. Albert Fleming, Mr. and Mrs. Arnold Jones and Jane Garde notified me stating, "We will be moving out of the complex in the next two or three weeks because of the existing conditions. These killings and mutilations have gone on way too long with nothing being resolved by the police or otherwise. We think this apartment complex should be condemned and another apartment building should be provided for everyone that still lives here. We are glad we are leaving here and we wished the rest of th7e tenants were going with us."

Mrs. Pickwell said, "In all sincerity I think you eight are not the only tenants moving out the way I have heard. If this apartment building gets condemned, my husband and I have another building in mind downtown.

Please continue with your dinner as these are the extent of my announcements for today."

Monday morning arrived with Mr. and Mrs. Pickwell sitting at a table in the Community Room at 10:00AM awaiting the arrival of the two State Department Building Inspectors at 10:00AM. So far none of the residents have shown any interest in attending the meeting. Mr. and Mrs. Pickwell studied the documents on the table and conversed among themselves in regards to the matter at hand. Suddenly there was a knock on the door and Mrs. Pickwell said, "Come in, please." Two State Department Building Inspectors entered the room greeting them, "Good morning, Mr. and Mrs. Pickwell. I am Lloyd Bark, the State Department Building Inspector for Missouri and this is my associate Gerald Kone. Mrs. Pickwell, can you refresh our memory on the different incidents that occurred while living here at the complex?" Mrs. Pickwell said, "Very well. We'll show you the elevator where all the actions been taking place. Here we are, on your left." Mr. Pickwell said, "We've been living in this apartment building five years this summer. It all started with three of the residents getting killed, chopped to pieces and buried under broken cement in the basement. Another incident that occurred not too long ago when three women ate turkey vegetable broth, immediately became violently ill and were taken to the St. Louis Memorial Hospital where they died within a very short time." Mr. Pickwell continued, "One night before another pot luck supper the elevator door swung open and Mrs. Mission's body was lying on the elevator floor, split open with all her organs hanging on the walls and ceiling for decorations while her intestines were draped around the edges of the ceiling. There were also other things too numerous to count."

Mrs. Pickwell said, "Everything was cleaned up the same night the funeral home picked the body and organs up while the police started their investigation which was inconclusive. Also, several men were found by the residents hanging from the ceiling and walls with their arms and legs dismembered, tongues cut out, etc.… The killings just went on and on and on!" The two State Department Building Inspectors recorded everything as they went back to the Community Room for further discussion. Mr. Bark made the comment, "After viewing and hearing all the different killings that took place here at the complex, I have decided to condemn this building from further use. My associate, Mr. Kone, is in agreement with this decision. Please post a notice immediately stating, Everybody needs to make further arrangements to vacate the premises soon because after the last resident is gone we will hang a "Condemned "sign on the building. Mrs. Pickwell and her husband had tears well up in their eyes but they said, "We figured everything would turn out this way because people lost their lives at an alarming rate and nothing was done about it. The police investigated every killing but to no avail. They didn't ever come up with "a person of interest" or anything else for that matter."

Mrs. Pickwell told the State Department Building Inspectors, "We have another building downtown that we are interested in buying to renovate for people that need a place to live similar to the Pickwell Apartment Complex that's going to be condemned." Mr. Bark said, "That's wonderful, Mrs. Pickwell. Please call us when you are ready to have it inspected. Thank you! Oh, here's my business card with my phone number." Mr. and Mrs. Pickwell said, "Thank you" and bid them farewell.

As soon as they left Mrs. Pickwell posted a sign on the bulletin board and word spread like wildfire. Some of the residents looked like they had been crying while others actually were crying at the thought of leaving. Everybody was wondering where they were going to go on such "short notice." Where would you go?

Apartment hunting

The next day everybody was in the All Purpose Room with their cell phones and newspaper Want Ads. Most of them are going apartment hunting with someone that has a car. Some might take a bus and others might wait a few days because it looks like rain. That's okay because St. Louis is experiencing a drought with the soil dry, parched and cracked.

Eight residents have moved out a week ago and more will be leaving soon. Mrs. Pickwell told everybody at another meeting the other night, "My husband and I are going to buy another building and want to know if you would be willing to relocate when we open up?" Most of the residents said, "No." A few said, "They might reconsider." Nobody knew for sure what they would do if they were confronted with a situation like that. What would you do? I would move out and never set foot in another apartment building Mrs. Pickwell has for rent. But then were not all the same, are we?

Within the next month seventy two people moved to other apartment buildings in different areas of St. Louis. Nineteen people still remain at the Pickwell Apartment Complex undecided what to do. As soon as Mrs. Pickwell and her husband are finished renovating their new apartment building it will be in the "Apartments for Rent" section of the St. Louis Gazette. Surely they will be able to rent all the apartments to other people without any problems since they have put the past behind them.

Finally the day has arrived for the other nineteen residents to move into the new apartment building and vacate the existing one they live in now. A "Condemned" sign was posted by the State of Missouri Building Inspectors. The building is sealed off with yellow police tape and all doors are locked. Mr. and Mrs. Pickwell and the city of St. Louis will have to decide whether they will have the building torn down and sell the lot for what it's worth.

The new apartment building is centrally located in downtown St. Louis on Finley Street #579. The forty eight residents have relocated into the new building and are going about their business. It is six stories tall with eight apartments on every floor which consists of a total of forty eight apartments. The main floor houses the Barker Dining Room, an Exercising Room, a Community Room, kitchen, three elevators and a public bathroom on every floor plus a basement for storage. The name of the building will be "The Pickwell Apartment Complex" same as before.

Sue Visits Jane

Sue hasn't been to visit Jane at the prison for several months because there have been too many incidents occurring in Sue's life. Actually she was confined to the Nevada Commune for three months out of her life. Jane is aware of everything that went on with Sue yet she is extremely happy that she is back among the people at the apartment complex.

Jane met Sue in the visitation room and they each picked up a phone with a glass shield between them and started to carry on a conversation with Jane saying, "Oh Sue, I'm so glad to see you. It's been months since you've been here to see me. I always enjoy your visits more than I can say. How about you, Sue? How do you feel about that?" Sue said, "Of course, mother, I always enjoy our visits whenever I come." Jane said, "What's been happening at the complex, Sue? Any news?" Sue said, "Mother, remember Harold Rane?" Jane said, "Yes, just vaguely. Why?" Sue made the remark, "Harold was sliced to death one night by the so called "slasher" while he was in bed at 3:00AM in the morning. Mrs. Rane was lucky and escaped unscathed. We all went to the funeral service to pay our respects and luncheon at the Barlow Dining Room which was well attended. Mrs. Rane will be relocating to Indianapolis, Indiana to be closer to her daughter. Everything is getting too scary and creepy to continue living at the complex anymore. That's why I told you I moved to the Pickwell Apartment Complex downtown." Jane said, "I remember that, Sue. How do you like your other apartment now?" Sue said, I love my new apartment, mother, because it's so airy, spacious and light compared to my old apartment. It was kind of dreary, dark and dingy. Mother, do you remember Mrs. Cane from the complex? She was also murdered by the "slasher" and then both of her legs were cut off at the groin and disappeared which seemed so strange." Jane said, "Yes, I remember Mrs. Cane. I visited with her when I ate lunch with you one day. Did they finally find her legs?"asked Jane. Sue said, "Yes, in a very grisly way. I remember telling you about Mrs. Peebles, Mrs. Cole and Mrs. Skill. Well, their Thanksgiving dinner started out with some turkey vegetable broth as an appetizer with the remainder of the meal to follow. They immediately got deadly sick and had to be transported to the St. Louis Memorial Hospital for treatment. They couldn't breathe besides having terrible stomach pains and passed away within minutes of each other. An autopsy was taken of the stomach contents and it was disclosed indicating the three women had eaten chunks of human flesh, blood and particles cooked together, hidden in the form of a soupy broth. Their sensitive stomachs couldn't withstand the form of ingestion which ended their lives. The human flesh was the two legs of Mrs. Cane that had been cut off. The laboratory tests confirmed the results of the autopsy.

Jane said, "Oh, I feel sorry for the families of the three women that died. How are they coping with everything?" Sue made the remark, "Very well, considering."

Sue also explained to Jane how they had to go to the St. Louis Police Station for a fingerprinting procedure to insure that no one at the complex was guilty of these murders. After all you never know for sure. Sue also told Jane how Germane Lipman, Martha Minton and herself had been falsely declared "persons of interest" by the police department. They all had to retake the tests and were cleared of any wrong doing. The lie detector machine's power was lower than it should've been and that caused the misinterpretation of the tests of Germane, Martha and herself.

As Sue was saying, "Mother, I'm sorry we couldn't get together at Christmas because of the weather so we exchanged gifts through the mail." Jane said, "Yes, I'm glad we sent our packages back and forth. That's the next best thing to getting together in person."

Friends of the Complex

Sue said, "Mother, did you see that article in the St. Louis Gazette about the walking zombies?" Jane said, "No, I didn't see that article because sometimes all the St. Louis newspapers are picked up by readers. By the time their done reading it's 10:00PM and time to go to bed for the night. What did it say?" Sue made the remark, "Well, some friends of people at the Pickwell Apartment Complex were visiting friends east of St. Louis when they encountered a group of zombies walking along the highway headed toward St. Louis. The couple thought they recognized them from the apartment complex meetings, pot luck suppers, Bingo, etc… The next night two men and the cemetery caretaker were checking the graves when one of the zombies bashed Joe on the head, sending him into a coma in the St. Louis Memorial Hospital where he died. The St. Louis Police Department rounded the other eleven zombies up and took them to the St. Louis Memorial Hospital where they were injected with some medication that put them to sleep permanently." Jane said, "No, I haven't heard about that, not even on television. What a gruesome, weird tale. I hope I never encounter those zombies around here."

Another Elevator Murder

Sue also brought up the following, "Mother, did you hear about Gladys Mission getting killed in the elevator last month? It was in the paper, radio and television. You played cards with her one afternoon. Remember? She wasn't very tall, quite thin with brunette hair sprinkled with gray. She had a jovial laugh and very friendly." Jane said, "Yes, I remember Mrs. Mission and I enjoyed her company. She was a very good card player. That's too bad."

Sue proceeded to explain what happened because her body was mutilated beyond recognition. Her insides were completely carved out of her body. Her intestines and all her other organs were hanging from the edge of the ceiling in a scalloped form like a decoration. Her legs were amputated at the groin and her arms at the armpits. Her eyes were gouged out, her tongue sliced out and her ears cut off. Her mouth had a barrel of a gun sticking in it.

Gladys Mission's body was cremated and inurnment followed at the St Louis Cemetery. There was a free luncheon at the apartment complex where everybody got a chance to meet Gladys Mission's two daughters, Glenda Parks and Bertha Lears." Jane said, "Yes, I did hear about Gladys Mission and I was shocked beyond belief. What a pity!" Have they no clue as to who's committing these murders?"Sue said, "No mother, so far they don't even have a "person of interest." I know it's unusual but that s the way it is."

All of a sudden Sue glanced at her watch and said, "Mother, it's almost time for me to leave. The bus will be at the entrance in fifteen minutes. Goodbye and I'll be back sooner the next time because the weather is beginning to get nicer now." Jane said, "Okay Sue, I'll be looking forward to your next visit. Goodbye!" Sue crawled into the bus and the driver sped away. Jane looked after Sue with misty eyes as usual recalling times past before the twelve killings at the Rockwood Apartment Complex. Prior to that she killed three other people because she was mentally incompetent. Jane thinks about her life and has her regrets but it's too late. What do you think?

Life in the New Complex

Life is basically the same in the new apartments as it was in the older building. Nothing really any different except the exercising which can be done on the equipment in the Community Room. There are also extra elevators to accommodate the residents and the rooms are spacious, much lighter and airy. She was convinced of that because her apartment was considerably larger than the one that she had lived in for a few years. Meals will be the same as always, 7:30AM for breakfast, 11:30AM for noon lunch and no evening meal. The bulletin board posts all the activities and any special events that are forthcoming.

First Meeting in the New Complex

This Monday evening will be the first meeting in the new apartment complex. It was well attended with everybody in the complex represented. Mrs. Pickwell asked everybody to stand up and identify themselves which they did. There are forty eight people living in the new apartment building. Mrs. Pickwell brought different issues up regarding the time and price of the meals in which there was an increase, plus an increase in the rent. Everybody has to pay their own water bill just like they did at the old apartment building. She also explained the rules regarding those tenants that come home after 10:00PM. They definitely have to have their key with them to unlock the door. If they don't have their key they can go to a convenience store, The Coastal Mart, one half block down the street to make a telephone call to the complex to have the door unlocked. These were the most important issues on the agenda that had to be addressed at this point. Smaller "discussions of interest" will follow at a later date. Mrs. Pickwell asked, "Does anyone have any questions regarding anything? Please raise your hand."Mrs. Crane raised her hand and asked, "Will the hallway light be on all night or will it be dark like it was at the other building? It was so creepy and scary at the other complex the few times I looked out into the hall during the night."Mrs. Pickwell answered, "No, the hallway light will be on all night until morning so that you don't have to be scared anymore. Does anybody else have any question?"Mrs. Blake raised her hand and asked, "On what day of the month will our rent and water bill be due? I came in late when this was mentioned."Mrs. Pickwell said, "The rent and water bill will be due on the first of every month. Please come to the office in person when these bills are being paid. Any more questions? Very well. This concludes our meeting for this evening. If you have any further questions please contact me in my office. Thank you and Goodnight." All forty eight tenants left the All Purpose Room with the exception of a few that were surrounding Mrs. Pickwell trying to get some last minute details they might have forgotten.

Memorial Day

Today is Memorial Day and the residents hosted their first pot luck supper in the complex since it has been opened. Everybody brought their covered dish to the Community Room at 12:00 noon for a meal and program consisting of several poetry readings by one of the residents written by herself. There was also a variety of patriotic music and a speaker to elaborate on the founding of Memorial Day. Mrs. Blake, one of the residents, has been writing a variety of poetry for years which she reads to the residents at different social functions throughout the year. She also has three poetry books published under her name. Several of the male residents are musically inclined and stage a performance periodically for the benefit and enjoyment of the other tenants. Mr. Teer from the St. Louis Chamber of Commerce gave the keynote address about the origin of Memorial Day with open discussion to follow. The pot luck supper was well attended by everyone but as the evening wore on many of the residents were yawning, slow to respond and acting very tired in general. All the activities came to an end sooner than usual and everyone retired to their rooms.

Chapter 12
Return of the Zombies

During the night the residents were awakened by the same zombies that infiltrated the streets of St. Louis, killing Joe Hines at the cemetery with a club to his head and the hood of his car. Mr. Bob Cover and Mr. Fred Lorenson, the caretaker of the cemetery, escaped with their lives. The St. Louis Police Department captured the walking zombies and carted them to the St. Louis Memorial Hospital to have them re-injected with fatal medication to end their lives. They took them back to the cemetery and reburied them, heaping mounds of dirt on their caskets, sealing the ground as if nothing had ever happened. Their bodies were sealed in the caskets for several months when all of a sudden they are back stalking the people of St. Louis at night on the streets.

The St. Louis Police Department was called to the Pickwell Apartment Complex in response to the disappearance of six residents, four men and two women. Missing are Jane Parrot, Nellie Forbs, Charla Blant, Betty Slin, Mike Slane and Steve Archer. Officer Shelton is interviewing the remainder of the residents asking them, "Did you hear or see anything unusual before you went to bed last night? Did you see anybody lurking around in the foyer, Community or all Purpose Room? Have you encountered any strange characters prowling around in your hallways at night?" They all emphatically said, "No!" Officer Shelton said, "Very well. We will continue our city wide, county and state wide search for the perpetrator of these terroristic acts. Six people are a lot of people to disappear at one time." The residents agreed saying, "Yes, and we're scared here at this new complex just like we were at the old one. Can we have police protection during this stressful time?" Officer Shelton said, "Yes, we have ordered extra security to be posted at your doors until this problem is cleared up." The residents said "thank you" and went back to their rooms.

The next morning at breakfast the residents were discussing the whereabouts of the six complex tenants that disappeared. Mrs. Barnes made the remark, "Let us all bow our heads in reverence to our Almighty God and pray for the safe return of the six victims that are at the mercy of unknown people. Amen." As they all lifted their heads back up some of the residents had tears in their eyes and others were crying openly.

In the meantime the zombies have walked the six tenants back to the cemetery, forced them into the caskets with the tenants screaming and saying, "Who are you? Leave us alone! Please go away, please! Why are you doing this to us?" The zombies in return kept making funny noises such as, "Arg! Arg! Arg!" After they sealed the lids on the caskets they shoveled mounds of dirt into the graves for final closure. The tenants could be heard kicking, screaming and clawing at the upholstery in the inside of the casket to get out but to no avail. The zombies have returned to a small, privately owned mausoleum where they are sleeping at night. The next morning the St. Louis Police Department received an anonymous call from someone in regards to checking the cemetery for fresh mounds of dirt which they immediately did. What they found was six decapitated bodies suffocated with snakes, rodents and insects already infiltrating the caskets. They exhumed the six bodies, brought them back to the hospital for clarification and transported them to the Brown Mortuary for final preparations and internment.

The six bodies were open for viewing in the large All Purpose Room at the Pickwell Apartment Complex. Huge crowds of mourners besides family and friends were gathered to pay their last respects to six souls that didn't deserve this. Right?

The funeral was the following morning at the All Assembly Church of God in downtown St. Louis with burial at the Woodland Cemetery two miles north of St. Louis. Hundreds of people attended the viewing and church burial service. After the burial a large luncheon was held at the Barker Dining Hall and the All Purpose and Community Rooms which were filled to overflowing. The Pickwell Apartment Complex could not accommodate the overflow of people so some of them had to be turned away or wait their turn in line.

In the meantime the zombies are still at large in St. Louis but not too conspicuous because they just come out at night like a nocturnal animal. They prowl around in the evenings, lurking in the dark shadows of tall buildings, cars and doorways where they cannot readily be seen by anybody. Before dawn they trek back to the cemetery and sleep in the mausoleum. Do you see why it's harder for the police to catch them? At this point in time the St. Louis Police Department is going to recruit more policemen because of the influx of murders that is rampant in the St. Louis area. Last night another anonymous caller contacted the police department saying, "I'd like to report a strange, white, filmy group of people standing on the side of the big, red, brick building on Morling Street. There are about ten people gathered and they look rather filthy, scaly and scary with three inch fingernails similar to a monster. They are carrying something in their hands but I couldn't tell what it was, maybe some kind of weapon. I'm not sure. My car windows were down when I passed them and they made a funny kind of noise like Arg! Arg! Arg! Like an animal. I hope you check this out. I'm sorry I couldn't give a better description. Thank you. Goodbye!" The police said, "Goodbye" and went on their way but by the time they got to Morling Street the zombies were gone. They were probably on their way back to the mausoleum for the rest of the night. The police department decided to enlist the help of other security officers outside the St. Louis area in their search of the zombies. There has been an APB(all points bulletin) out for their arrest on television, radio and the St. Louis newspapers.

There have been numerous sightings of the zombies but by the time the police get there they are gone. They've also been known to hide in parks because they have been reported to the police. When they are seen by local people they are usually chasing small children through the park.

What are the zombies eating and how are they staying alive? There is only one way they can be eating and that is out of the trash cans which was also reported. They've been seen digging through the trash cans and even crawling out of them. What did they used to call that? Dumpster Diving?

A man was murdered by the zombies in a back alley off the main thoroughfare in downtown St. Louis before dawn yesterday morning. The zombies were seen sitting in a group behind a building warming themselves by the fire. As soon as this was reported the police left immediately, arriving at the designated location only to find the zombies had re-located. They move very quickly. The only building they have ever kidnapped anybody is the Pickwell Apartment Complex. Does anybody know why? Take a guess. It's easy to figure that out.

Barnum and Bailey Circus

It's time for the Barnum and Bailey Circus to come to St. Louis which they did last night. There are lots of people in attendance at the circus which will be in St. Louis till next Saturday. The circus is open from 10:00AM in the morning until 12:00 midnight. On a recent evening the groundskeeper came out of his trailer after midnight when the carnival grounds were empty and decided to do a quick check on everything before he retired for the evening. As he was strolling between the carnival rides he heard a noise noticing that the ferris wheel was going full speed ahead. He yelled at the occupants, "Heh you, how did you get up there? Get off of there or I'll report you to the manager. Come down here right this minute, did you hear me?"Suddenly he turned his head for a minute and the zombies jumped off the ferris wheel wearing black masks and screaming, "Arg! Arg! Arg!" and ran into an adjoining field off the carnival grounds. This isn't the only night they've been on the ferris wheel or on the other rides because they've been noticed by other late night attendants but they always manage to elude the people in charge somehow. One of these days they'll get caught! Just wait and see!

Zombies at the Zoo

One morning as the zoo attendant was strolling through the zoo he noticed something unusual in one of the empty cages. He went closer and peered into the cage and six zombies were sleeping on some hay. He said, "What kind of people are you? Get out of here this minute or I'll call the person in charge of this zoo and have you thrown out! Out! Don't ever come back! You filthy, slimy mongrels!" The six zombies scrambled to their feet muttering, "Arg! Arg! Arg!" and off they went.

The St. Louis Police Department had a warrant out for the zombies arrest and a reward of $10,000.00 if anybody can capture them and bring them to the local police department. Different people can be seen during the night out on the streets walking and driving. The police ask them, "Why are you out so late at night in this dark alley or street and the answer is always, "I'd like to capture those zombies and I've come prepared. The reward is a good incentive." The officer says, "Keep looking. You've got the right idea." And drove off.

Yesterday someone reported to the police that the zombies were seen walking in a group of about eleven east of St. Louis about three miles toward the cemetery. Since then they have not been seen in the city of St. Louis, Missouri.

Sue visits Jane

This Sunday Sue decided to visit her mother, Jane, at the St. Louis Prison for Women because it's been awhile since she's been to see her mother. Jane is aware that Sue is coming today and is very anxious and happy to see her. As we speak Sue and Jane enter the Visitation Room and each picks up a phone with Sue saying, "Oh mother, it's so good to see you again. How have you been?" Jane said, "Oh Sue, I could hardly wait till you came today because it's been awhile since I've seen you. I've missed you but I've been fine. It's the same old drudgery day in and day out. It'll be like that until I die. You know what I mean, Sue" Sue nodded her head and said, "Yes, I know what you mean. Mother, have you heard about the zombies that have been walking into St. Louis from the cemetery east of the city?" Jane said, "Yes, Sue. I saw it on television, heard it on the radio and it's been all over the St. Louis Gazette. Those six people they killed were from your apartment complex. Aren't you scared to live in that new complex now?" Sue remarked, "Not really, mother, because since the night it happened we've had one policeman posted in every hallway in the complex and everything's been fine. Beside's I know who the zombies are, mother." Jane said, "Sue, how could you possibly know who those zombies are?" Sue made the comment, "Mother, those zombies that killed those six residents at the complex used to live there. I recognized their faces from the picture in the paper. Somehow after they died they revived back to life naturally. They were taken back to St. Louis Memorial Hospital where they were injected with some fatal medication and were pronounced dead supposedly and buried. They again revived back to life making it difficult to capture them by the police department or the local citizens because they can swiftly avoid anybody. Mother, I honestly don't think anybody can kill them, not the police or a local citizen or anybody else because they are indestructible. I don't know what happens in a case like that."

Jane said, "Yes, it's a sad state of affairs. Sue, just promise me you'll be extra careful while you live there." Sue said, "Oh, I promise, mother." Jane said, "Okay."

Sue said, "Any news here at the prison, mother?" Jane said, "No, I'm still helping as a craft assistant like I showed you one evening while I was in class. I enjoy helping other people, Sue. It gives me something to do besides sitting and brooding over all the mistakes I've made in my life. It won't be long and I'll be sending some leather craft articles home with you that I made. I'm working on a different project at this time. I still attend nondenominational church services every Sunday on the next floor. I also help the pastor with various duties when he is extra busy." Sue said, "It sounds like your keeping busier than you were the last time I was here, mother, and that's good."

Jane and Sue visited for awhile and then Sue said, "Mother, it's time for me to go because the city bus will be coming along shortly. Goodbye and I'll be back soon." Sue walked toward the bus and waved goodbye. Jane waved once more with tears welling up in her eyes and running down her cheeks as usual. After she couldn't see the bus any more, she turned around and went about her business.

Bingo and Monthly Meeting —June 2007

A short meeting will be conducted this evening with a guest speaker Officer Peale from the St. Louis Police Department in regards to the numerous murders that have been committed in the old Pickwell Apartment Complex and have shifted to the new building.

Mrs. Pickwell brought up several issues regarding rules and regulations, delinquent rent and water fees, their attendance at mealtime, keeping your key with you at all times since some keys have been found on the dining room table, elevator floor, hallways etc… After these issues were addressed Mrs. Pickwell asked, "Does anybody have any questions before we proceed on to the next phase of the meeting? Raise your hand, please. What is your question, Mrs. Carl?"Mrs. Carl asked, "If we don't feel well enough to come down to the dining room for our meal are we expected to call the office and report this because I had this happen to me yesterday and I wasn't sure what to do?"Mrs. Pickwell said, "Yes, if you don't feel well enough to come down to the dining room for your meals please call the office and report this to me so it can be marked on your chart. Any other questions? Very well. We will move on to Officer Peale's speech." Officer Peale stepped up to the podium and addressed the residents announcing, "Good afternoon, I am Officer and Detective Tom Peale from the St. Louis Police Department here today to update you and to address the different issues regarding the strange murders and circumstances involving both Pickwell Apartment Complexes. In regards to the grisly elevator murders with mutilated bodies and organs displayed all over the ceiling and floor, we have interviewed numerous tenants, local people, inmates and potential criminals to no avail. We even had the residents from the old complex fingerprinted in regards to the deaths of Mrs. June Coyle, Alice Peebles and Mrs. Eunice Skill and everything turned out fine. These three women died because of ingesting turkey, vegetable broth that was laced with the flesh from the legs of a dead woman that had been murdered at the complex. There were other dishes brought to the pot luck supper so possibly none of the other residents tasted the turkey, vegetable broth. Do any of you recall tasting the broth?" Please raise your hand?" No hands were raised so Officer Peale drew his conclusion.

He continued, "Now, in regards to the zombies we have also come to a dead standstill in their capture. They suffocated six residents from the complex by burying them alive at the cemetery. The police brought the bodies back to the Brown Mortuary for the final preparations and internment. We also captured the zombies taking them to the St. Louis Memorial Hospital to have them reinjected with some fatal medicine that would put them back into the lifeless state they came from. But after awhile their bodies rebelled against the lifeless state and they wound up in the "land of the living." At present they are walking the streets of St. Louis preying on people so please be on your guard. They have been seen riding the Ferris Wheel after the circus was closed to the public in the evenings. They have also been caught sleeping in one of the big, empty cages at the zoo where they were chased out. They have also been known to hang out in back alleys where they were responsible for the death of one man. The police received an anonymous call from the park that there were strange, animal like creatures chasing small children around the park. By the time police arrived they had already eluded them. There is a $10,000.00 reward out for their arrest and capture but I wouldn't advise anybody here this afternoon to try this. Even younger people than yourselves are having a hard time. If the police can't capture them how can anybody else? We have gone so far as to seek help from other out of state police officers, security firms and extra detectives but so far we have no leads, clues or anything that will help us in their capture because they avoid the police every chance they get. We have gone to the cemetery where they are supposedly staying in the mausoleum but it is empty and dark inside. No occupants.

So far the killer or killers is still on the loose. My advice to the residents today is to be in your apartments when it gets dark because that's when they prowl the streets and you don't want to be out there. Another suggestion is if you leave in the light and come home in the dark, please leave and come back in a group by bus because it is that dangerous. You never know when the zombies are just around the corner.

Any questions from anybody? I'll be glad to answer as much as I can. Please raise your hand. What is your question, Ma'am?" Mrs. Linn asked, "Will there be any extra lighting in front of the complex if we happen to get caught in the dark coming home?" Officer Peale answered, "I can't answer that because you'll have to take that up with your landlady, Mrs. Pickwell, because she is in charge of that. Thank you for your question though." Officer Peale said, "What was your question Mrs. Fohr?" Mrs. Fohr asked, "What should we do if we accidentally get attacked?" Officer Peale said, "If you accidentally get attacked scream as loud as you can, try to fight them off, or slap them with your purse, anything you can think of. But the main thing is to scream into their ears as loud as you can because the shrill noise bothers them and they usually drop everything and run. That could be your getaway. Anymore questions anybody?" No one raised their hand so this concluded the meeting. Mrs. Pickwell said, "Thank you all for coming and now we will proceed with Sue Benson calling the numbers for the first Bingo game of the evening." After the first fifteen games the residents take a break for refreshments and then resume the last fifteen games for cash prizes. After Bingo was over most of the residents went to their apartments while a few of them went to the All Purpose Room for a cup of coffee, light conversation and the 10:00PM news. Mrs. Linn, Mrs. Flohr and Mrs. Cale were watching television while sipping their coffee when all of a sudden another announcer broke into the news report with an APB(all points bulletin) regarding the zombies in the vicinity of Finley Street where the Pickwell Apartment Complex is located. The complex building number is 579 and the announcer said the zombies broke into a building at 577 Finley Street which would be right next door. Mrs. Linn said, "Should we call Mrs. Pickwell and her husband to see if they know what's happening?"Mrs.

Flohr and Mrs. Cale immediately said, "Yes, let's call them quickly from that phone on the wall over there." Mrs. Linn called and Mrs. Pickwell picked up the receiver and said, "Hello." Mrs. Linn introduced herself telling Mrs. Pickwell, "This is Mrs. Linn from the complex. I, Mrs. Flohr and Mrs. Cale stepped into the All Purpose Room to watch the 10:00PM news after Bingo. All of a sudden another announcer broke into the news reporting the zombies breakin at 577 Finley Street, right next door to the apartment complex." When Mrs. Pickwell heard this she said, "I and my husband will be right down to the All Purpose Room. We'll see you in a few minutes. Thank you!" Mrs. Linn barely hung the receiver up and Mrs. Pickwell and her husband walked into the room very upset, concerned and scared. Mrs. Pickwell opened the front door noticing that the police were next door and a crowd of people had already gathered outside. Mr. Pickwell made the remark, "I am glad we live here in our apartment complex because I would hate to think of walking to my car outside tonight with these zombies prowling around."

The next morning at the breakfast table everybody was looking at the picture in the St. Louis Gazette newspaper of the building next door, while Mrs. Linn, Mrs. Flohr and Mrs. Cale briefed them on the details of the night before. According to the newspaper the zombies ransacked the warehouse building and stole some articles. The police had a person that witnessed the scene as he slowed down his car and drove by. The witness said, "I myself have been trying to catch these zombies because of the $10,000.00 reward money. I could use that cash. I'm not the only person that's on their trail. There are a lot of people in St. Louis looking for them. The only problem is they are hard to catch because they always avoid human beings." After the police interviewed him on the street they took him downtown to the police station for a formal interview caught on tape and then released him on his own recognizance.

Whispering Ghosts in the Complex?

In the evenings when there's nothing to do some of the residents are beginning to play cards in the All Purpose Room. The men like to play billiards, some of the residents like to watch television or just plain visit and drink coffee. Such was the case tonight. After a couple of hours of this everybody was yawning and declaring, "Well, goodnight everybody. I'm tired. I'll see you tomorrow." Consequently everybody followed suit until the All Purpose Room was completely empty.

Sue went to her apartment to get ready for bed because she was very tired from the office and tomorrow wouldn't be any better. She ate an apple before she went to bed, watched a little television and then retired for the evening. For some reason Sue couldn't sleep so she just lay there and started thinking about different things. All of a sudden a white, bright light shown in a corner of the bedroom up high. There was something in the light because it was blurry. After awhile the brightness of the light subsided and in the center was the scary face of a ghost, all white with red, fiery eyes and long, white hair. Her body stopped at the neck in the glowing light of the night. The white ghost whispered, "If you do something I don't like I will kill you!" Sue said, "Why, I don't even know you. What right do you have to kill me? Get away from me because I'm going to report this to Mrs. Pickwell tomorrow morning so you'd better leave. "

The ghost whispered again, "If you report this incident to anybody you won't live to tell about it. I can guarantee you that much. I can see you know very little about ghosts, Sue." Sue said, "No, I don't know anything about ghosts. I don't even know enough to be scared."

The ghost whispered again, "I have the mental telepathy to create unbearable pain in your body. I can alienate you from your friends and family and cause destruction and death to your body! Please don't push me to the brink of reality. I am leaving you now, Sue, but I'll be back. In the meantime, Sue has burst into tears upon hearing the words, "death and destruction, pain, alienation from her friends and family etc." After Sue practically cried her heart out she went on to bed but couldn't sleep because of the fear that gripped her all night long. She forgot to set her alarm clock because of being anxious and upset the night before. So consequently she overslept and called in sick for the day. If she would've showed up late for work she could have lost her job. She also skipped breakfast because of getting up too late. Sue's mind is preoccupied with the appearance of the "whispering ghost" and the fear that has been instilled in her since last night. Sue thought to herself, "What will happen tonight? Will the ghost reappear? Should I tell Mrs. Pickwell? No, I can't tell anyone because my life might be at stake. I can't even tell my own mother. Oh Lord, what should I do?" Sue is at her wits end. What should she do? Should she take the chance and spread the word? Think about it and read on!

The next morning Sue left quickly to catch the 7:30AM bus since she doesn't eat breakfast with the residents. She could hear different conversations among the tenants but nothing was mentioned about "ghosts." But then Sue thought, "If other tenants had experienced the same thing she had they wouldn't be mentioning it either." So she continued on to the bus stop for her ride downtown to the Green Financial Office. It was a slow day at the office, with different people asking her, "Sue, do you feel okay?" She told them, "Yes" and went about her work. She knows she looks pale, worried and all stressed out. She was glad when 5:00PM rolled around and she was headed back to her apartment. When she opened the door she could hear the water running in the kitchen sink. She thought to herself, "The water was turned off when I left this morning. I'd better check with Mrs. Pickwell and see what happened."

Mrs. Pickwell immediately informed Sue there were no plumbers in anybody's apartments and everything was normal as far as she knew. Sue will probably have a big water bill to pay depending on how long the water was turned on. Did the ghost turn the water on?

Sue ate supper and watched television for several hours before going to bed. About 3:00AM she was awakened by a strange noise, so she got up and switched on the light in the front room. She found her old fashioned rocking chair rocking back and forth, in spite of no one sitting in it. Sue extended her hand to stop the rocking and it stopped. In a few minutes it started rocking again and Sue heard a strange laugh. All of a sudden a white image of a head and face appeared, that of a ghost, hanging in midair above the rocking chair. The ghost whispered softly to Sue saying, "Sue, did you tell anybody about your encounter with me last night? There were other residents that had ghosts invade their apartments last night. Ghosts were haunting the new Pickwell Apartment Complex all night long."

Sue said, "No, I didn't tell anybody and I don't think anybody else did. But I'm going to tell our landlady, Mrs. Pickwell, tomorrow about this because I think the other residents are scared to say anything." The ghost whispered,"Remember what I told you last night would happen if you told anybody about this?" Sue said, "Yes, I remember but I guess I'll just have to take that chance. Won't I?" Sue turned and looked above the chair and the ghost made a quick departure. Before Sue went to bed she called Mrs. Pickwell and made an appointment for tomorrow afternoon which would be Saturday at 2:00PM. The next day Sue explained to Mrs. Pickwell saying, "A lot of ghosts have been haunting and plaguing the residents the last two nights. The residents are scared they will get killed if the ghosts find out that everybody knows." Mrs. Pickwell made the remark, "We will call the police department tomorrow demanding police protection and help with the infestation of ghosts. Also, I want every resident to sleep with their lights on all night long because we are going room to room checking on the welfare of every resident that lives here. Those of you that want to spend the night in the Community and All Purpose Rooms, bring your bedding around 10:00PM. You can sleep on the three divans or the mattresses that we'll put on the floor. There are also recliners that people can relax and even sleep in. My husband and I will be sleeping down there likewise."

The "sleep in" is tonight at the Pickwell Apartment Complex Community and All Purpose Rooms at 10:00PM. Fifteen residents showed up earlier, before the 10:00PM news, had their coffee and bedded down for the night. Half of the residents were snoring uncontrollably, so the other half couldn't sleep a wink. In spite of the snoring it was still a peaceful evening, nothing out of the ordinary. No ghosts or anything! Maybe they are gone for good! We hope!

At breakfast the next morning everyone discussed the "sleep in" openly and they were going to try it again tonight. Fine! At least the ghosts aren't approaching! Ever since the "whispering ghost" told Sue, "We have the mental telepathy to annihilate people with our thoughts and I wouldn't hesitate to do so."

After a "sleep in" for several nights in the Community and All Purpose Rooms and one policeman patrolling each floor every night, the ghosts have eased up.

Mr. and Mrs. Pickwell checked each apartment in the complex from the first to the sixth floor and everything was in order. Mrs. Pickwell said, "I think the ghosts have given up on the new complex because they know we have outsmarted them nor are we scared of them. I don't think they'll be back anymore! THEY HAVE NEVER COME BACK!!!

Chapter 13—Zombies Again?
July4, 2007

Now that the residents of the apartment complex have weathered another storm, namely the ghosts, everything is back to normal again.

July 4th is just around the corner and a pot luck supper is planned at the apartment complex plus a public display of fireworks within the city of St. Louis for the enjoyment of the people. Everybody is bringing their covered dish of either meat or potatoes, a vegetable, a casserole, salad or dessert etc…. Cold drinks are furnished by the owners of the complex. The pot luck supper is scheduled for 5:30PM with some of the residents sitting at the tables visiting and getting ready to eat.

By now everybody was seated at the table while Mrs. Pickwell said grace and proceeded to eat until Sue inquired, "Where is Mrs. Faye Lark? I just talked to her this morning and she said she was looking forward to the pot luck supper this evening. I would think she would've been the first one here tonight the way she expresses interest in being here." When Mrs. Pickwell heard this she said, "Sue, would you go to her apartment and check on Faye and see if she is okay? I sure don't want anything to happen to her. After all, she is ninety one years old and couldn't protect herself if someone approached her." Everyone agreed on that and started eating while Sue went to check on Faye. Time lapsed and Sue never came back. Where was she? She was supposed to check up on Faye Lark but why did it take so long? She just lives on the 3rd floor around the corner in apartment 304. Just as the residents were discussing Sue's whereabouts, she came stumbling in with tears streaming down her face, her eyes red and swollen, her clothes tattered and torn, her hands bloody and scratched screaming, "Faye is dead! Faye is dead!" The tenants exclaimed in horror, "Oh no! Poor Faye, what happened?" Sue proceeded to explain, "I started towards the elevator but the door was closed, so I started yanking on it and the door sprung open all of a sudden like someone had pulled on it from the inside. I immediately had to step back for fear of falling, like there was some force from the inside the elevator that I wasn't aware of. When I looked at the sight it was ghastly and gruesome. Faye Lark was sitting on the elevator floor with the blade of a knife stuck down her throat, her abdomen was sliced open and several snakes, one by one, were crawling out of her stomach drenched with blood. The zombie sitting beside Faye was eating each snake as fast as they crawled out of her body. Faye's head was hanging by a nail on the elevator wall and spiders and insects were crawling out of her wide opened mouth and ears. Her eyes were cut to bits and stuck in their sockets while her hair had started a slow burning fire. Faye's arms and legs were thrown in a corner like a heap of trash. I screamed at the zombie but he just kept eating one snake after the other as it crawled out of her stomach. His mouth was drooling with pleasure at the thought of the reptiles he was devouring. The more I screamed the more he said, "Arg! Arg! Arg! I tackled him with my hands but he got the best of me, ran out of the elevator and out the side door. I started running after him down the street but he was too fast for me, so I gave up, came back and called the police to give a report of what happened to Faye. The police came immediately, gathered the body parts in a container for final preparations, notification of next of kin and the funeral." The residents were shocked at what Sue told them, to the point of some residents crying out loud, some were whimpering to themselves and others were dismissing themselves because they were getting physically sick. Mrs. Pickwell was shocked beyond words and retreated to her office to call the police department to see if she could get any other details.

Officer Sheldon answered saying, "The description that your tenant, Sue Benson, gave you of what she saw and her encounter with the zombie is basically correct. No, we didn't apprehend the zombie because they have a mode of eluding the police every chance they get. By the time we got to the complex the zombie was long gone. What beats us is when one zombie is in an elevator, where are the other zombies?" Mrs.Pickwell said, "I wish I knew. I wasn't aware this happened until Sue came into the pot luck supper and revealed everything that transpired. We were all shocked to the point of getting physically sick as to the mutilation of Faye Lark's body. Well, thank you officer and if we can be of any assistance, please don't hesitate to call." Officer Sheldon said, "Yes, we were planning on coming by sometime tomorrow to talk to some of the residents, ask a few questions, check the elevator etc"…. Mrs. Pickwell said, "That will be fine and no appointment is required. Thank you!"

Officer Sheldon and Officer Peale visited the complex today for routine questioning and to check the elevator for fingerprints. It was a standard police investigation that is always required.

At this point, nothing was gained from the police investigation because everybody was at the pot luck supper, so they wouldn't have seen anybody even if there was somebody in the building. Also, there were no fingerprints to be found in the elevator because the zombie was too smart to let that happen. How did the zombie cover his tracks? Sue did tell the police one thing that, "I think the zombie that killed Faye Lark was one of the tenants from the complex that died several years ago with five others. They were buried alive and later all six tenants were revived by some unknown force. I recognized his face, except now it's gross and disfigured almost beyond recognition. Even his voice has a certain ring to it when says, "Arg! Arg! Arg!" I kinda remember what his voice sounded like when he was living. I still think I'm correct in my speculation. What do you think Officer Peale? Do you think I'm correct?" Officer Peale made the remark, "Yes Sue, I think you might have a good speculation there like you said but we can't base this whole case on one person's opinion. No offense, of course! The police are going to have to investigate above and beyond this case to come up with some concrete evidence of things that have transpired with these zombies through this past year. We have a lot of incoming calls from the public because of the large reward but we can't seem to corral them."

A Hunting Expedition—August—2007

At this month's meeting Mrs. Pickwell announced there would be a hunting expedition in St. Louis Park itself and around St. Louis Lake. Everybody is to bring a brown bag lunch and drink for their noon meal. It will be followed by something similar to a scavenger hunt in the surrounding area to see if anyone can uncover anything personal that may have been dropped or lost by a killer or killers related to the mysterious deaths over the past several years.

Everybody is up bright and early at the complex this morning preparing their brown bag lunch and drink for the hunting expedition. The bus picked everyone up at 10:00AM for the trip to St. Louis Park and Lake on the north edge of the city. They pulled into the park at 11:00AM just in time to eat their brown bag lunch, drink and congregate at the shelter house for their hunting expedition directions. Mr. and Mrs. Pickwell designated two people for every area and told them to be back at the shelter house by 4:00PM. Mrs. Pickwell also said, "Do not approach or tease any wild animals but use your cell phone and call the shelter house for help. Mr. Pickwell and I will be here the whole time. Our number is 470—9249. Please write this number down. Okay everybody, go to your designated areas two by two and we'll see you back here by 4:00PM. Please don't be late because it is a long drive back to St. Louis and it looks like it might rain."

Everybody was back at the shelter house at 4:00PM with details of their hunting expedition. Nobody encountered any wild animals but a few residents found several articles that will be turned over to the St. Louis Police Department for possible investigation. Mrs. Teal found a lady's silk scarf while Mr. Grole found a pocket knife with the initials R. B. engraved on it. Mr. Poole found a men's wallet with no identification or money, just a few papers. Everyone boarded the bus at 4:00PM and arrived at the complex at exactly 5:00PM just in time for supper. Everybody retired to their apartment for the evening after the long bus ride to the park and lake, plus the "hunting expedition" Even the All Purpose Room was empty this evening for a change. Sue ate supper and started watching television when the movie was interrupted with a news flash from a local station. The announcer said, "I have just been handed a report from my colleague about an infestation of zombies this afternoon at the St. Louis Park and Lake. The zombies were reported to have approached families and their children while they were trying to enjoy a summer afternoon at the park and lake. Several of the zombies grabbed the smaller children and bit them in the arms and legs as they ran by. They were bitten to the point where they were taken to the St. Louis Memorial Hospital Emergency Room for treatment. One of the families called the police department indicating what type of a problem the zombies had created among the public at the park and lake. Several people had their boats anchored at the St. Louis Lake when the zombies came by, unanchored them, letting them drift out into the lake.

A few of the smaller children ran to their parents crying as the zombies infiltrated the slipper slide with their slimy, filthy, moldy bodies leaving a foul stench on the slide.

In the distance one could hear the police sirens blaring as they were headed toward St. Louis Park and Lake to try and capture the zombies. As soon as the zombies heard the police sirens they dispersed into four directions so that the police department could not locate them which they didn't. This concludes our broadcast for this evening."

The residents of the Pickwell Apartment Complex nor Mr. and Mrs. Pickwell had any idea the zombies were infesting the St. Louis Park and Lake. Evidently, they were on the other side of the park because they didn't hear any screaming or commotion of any sort. Everything was relatively quiet in their area as they ate their lunch and went on their hunting expedition. Why can't the police department set a trap for the zombies? Actually, they don't know where they will be at any given time.

Storm Clouds Rolling In—August 12—2007

It is blistering hot today with a 108 degree heat smothering the city of St. Louis. The public is warned by radio, television and newspaper "that the intense heat wave could cause a variety of medical problems, even death if one did not use proper precautions when exposed to such conditions."

Sue Benson was the only resident that left the complex to go to work downtown at Green Financial Services. It will be a slow day today because of the extreme heat, so she can catch up on her other office work where she is lagging behind. Sue took the 7:30AM bus downtown and the temperature was 87 degrees. Supposedly this heat wave is coming from the southern part of the United States accompanied by occasional large gusts of wind.

When Sue boarded the bus for her trip back to the apartment complex the temperature had reached 113 degrees. It was an older bus with limited air conditioning, so Sue was happy when they reached the corner where the apartment complex is located. Sue and another lady, Lila, that she became friends with on the bus trips got out at the same corner. Sue and Lila bid each other goodbye as they each headed in the opposite direction. Lila lives in another apartment complex two blocks east of Sue on Winley Street. Sue enjoyed the blast of cold air as she opened the door of the complex. She went into the All Purpose Room for a glass of iced tea as she sat down to rest her weary, perspiration soaked body and sore feet from the ravages of the heat. Mrs. Pickwell was visiting with the group and said, "Sue, how hot was it when you left the office? It doesn't seem very cool in here anymore." Sue said, "It was 113 degrees when I boarded the bus downtown. Actually, we weren't busy at all today and there were only a limited amount of people on the streets. The ones that were walking were enjoying a cool drink. I'm glad I didn't have to be outside very long today. Were any of you running errands today?" A few of the tenants said, "yes" they were when it was cooler this morning but this afternoon everybody was back in their apartments again. After a little more discussion Sue finally arose saying, "Excuse me but I'm going to my apartment now. See you tomorrow!" Everybody bid Sue "good evening" and left also.

When Sue walked into her apartment she looked outside and noticed dark, storm clouds on the horizon, so she immediately turned her television on to catch the most recent weather report.

The announcer was just giving the weather report for the St. Louis area saying, "There will be increasing clouds and thunderstorms with large hail and damaging winds but no tornadoes at this time. Kansas has had numerous sightings of tornadoes this afternoon and this evening, but as of now none have materialized. Please stay tuned to this station for further reports as they come in. If you have access to a lower area of your home, preferably a basement, please seek shelter immediately until the brunt of the storm subsides"

In a matter of minutes Sue heard Mrs. Pickwell announcing on the intercom, "Everybody please report to the All Purpose Room because of the severity of the storm and we will proceed to the basement for safety. Please come immediately because the thunderstorm is getting more intense. Thank you."

The residents hurriedly met in the All Purpose Room, some with their nightgowns, dusters and house slippers on prepared for bed. They went to the basement and waited while the storm raged on. Mrs. Pickwell and several other tenants brought their radios along so they could be updated After about one and half hours of listening to the storm battering the outside of the complex Mrs. Pickwell said, "I hope we don't have any damage on the complex because we haven't been open that long. Yes, the complex and the contents inside are insured so there is no need for concern. I also think it's safe to go back upstairs now, so let's gather your personal belongings together that were brought along down and we will go back to the main floor."

When they were on the main floor Mr. Pickwell looked outside and said, "It's only raining lightly now, but I can tell there's a lot of damage."When the rain completely subsided, Mr. Pickwell went outside with a flashlight and surveyed the damage to the complex. He came back in and said, "A huge amount of shingles are ripped from the roof while siding is torn off the complex and several windows are broken. I think tree branches and hail hit the complex with a strong force." Everybody had congregated in the All Purpose Room to watch television for the assessment of the damage and the weather forecast for the remainder of the night. The announcer said, "There has been devastating damage in the city of St. Louis with a severe thunderstorm containing large hail and a wind velocity up to 85 miles an hour. At this point there is no indication that St. Louis experienced a tornado, but not all reports are in yet. For the rest of the night there will be rain, but nothing severe as of now." After the weather discussion everybody decided to go back to their own apartments, keep an eye on the weather intermittently and retire for the night.

An Early Grave?

Sue went to work as usual at Green Financial Services with everyone discussing the weather from the night before on their break. Sue's co-worker said, "I live in an apartment house and everybody went down in the basement for fear of a tornado. I guess there were many tornado sightings in Kansas, west of Missouri but none around here. I'm glad of that!" Sue's other co-worker, Molly, said, "I quickly jumped in my car and drove to my parents home for safety because I don't have a basement. It was very hard to drive in a thunderstorm because of the pouring rain in spite of the windshield wipers doing their job." Sue proceeded to say, "All forty eight of us at the Pickwell Apartment Complex where I live went to the basement at the request of our landlord for about two and half hours till the bad weather was over. Our landlord went outside to assess the damage and he reported siding and shingles ripped off the complex and several broken windows. I guess that was mild compared to what some businesses and private homes sustained. Coming to work this morning I saw numerous store fronts with their picture windows completely smashed." Everyone on break marveled that the damage wasn't worse than it was because of the sheets of rain, hail and high velocity of the wind. Everybody agreed to that and went back to their desks to work. Today Sue was tired because they were unusually busy for a Tuesday so she welcomed the ride back to the complex with limited air conditioning because she had no choice. She was glad to get to her apartment because of the muggy air that clung to everything. It looked like thunderstorms again but they were not in the forecast. That's good! Sue decided to retire early since there wasn't anything in particular she wanted to watch and most movies she had already seen. For some unknown reason Sue opened the door and looked in the hallway to see if there was any activity, ambling to the elevator for curiosity. When her curiosity was satisfied she went back to her apartment and to bed. At 2:00AM she was awakened by a loud knock on the door and a harsh, grating sound! Sue asked, "Who is it? Who is it?" No answer. Just a harsh, grating sound! Sue opened the door, only to be confronted by the same zombie that ate Faye Lark's snakes as they came crawling out of her opened stomach. The zombie had a rope that he immediately tied Sue's hands with behind her back and stuffed a handkerchief in her mouth so that anything Sue tried to say would be muffled. The zombie forced Sue to climb through the window from the 3rd floor on to the fire escape and down to the first floor which she did. They left the complex by the way of a dark alley, walking east towards the highway for several miles until they arrived at Potter's Field Cemetery.

Now Sue thought to herself, "Here's my chance to get away. I'd better take it while I can." She quickly darted past the zombie and headed down a side road with the zombie in tow. He used his rope for a lasso and drew closer to Sue, threw the lasso but it missed her neck. She kept on running and the zombie tried to lasso her again but he failed. She is getting tired but she continues to run with the zombie running after her. All of a sudden the zombie threw the lasso again and it wrapped around Sue's neck causing her to fall. She got back on her feet and they walked back to Potter's Field Cemetery where the pauper's graves are erected. The zombie led Sue to a grave that had been occupied by people from the past. Sue noticed the grave was dug open with mounds of insects crawling in and out of the opening. The zombie tried to force Sue down into the hole but she wouldn't budge. She fought the zombie with her hands, kicked him with her feet, biting him in the arms and hitting him with a shovel, anything she could get her hands on. Finally the zombie got the best of her and forced Susan down the hole where there was a casket at the base of her feet. It had been pre-occupied at one time but now the zombie saved it for Sue Benson. The zombie slid down on a rope right after Sue, forcing her into a casket that he closed with small clasps that fit into certain locks. He was thinking about suffocating Sue and leaving her dead while he banters around the cemetery. Let's wait and see what happens this morning!

Finally the zombie approaches Sue's grave knowing full well that she is in the blue casket maybe already dead. He doesn't like her, that's why he's trying to kill her. He remembers her as the person who tried to stop him when he was eating the snakes as they were coming out of Faye Lark's opened stomach but she was unable to stop him. The zombie was too quick for her because they are too quick for the police or anybody else. They are just a fast breed of mutants. As he gets closer to where Sue is buried he's positive Sue is dead so he bypasses the grave and heads toward the mausoleum where he sleeps with the other zombies for the night.

Scratching and Clawing

As far as Sue is concerned let's check up on her. She is on her back, face up in the casket, kicking, scratching and clawing the interior of the lid and casket itself but it doesn't budge. How is she going to get out? Also, there are mounds and mounds of dirt piled six feet high to contend with. Sue was thinking, "I cannot turn on my side to help myself, or do I have any tool to use to get out of here. Dear Lord, please help me! What can I do? If I yell and scream no one will hear me unless there are people at the cemetery and there usually aren't. Maybe I'll try again. Bang! Bang! Boom! Boom!" Sue noticed it was getting rather stuffy as she continued pushing the lid, scratching, clawing and screaming making as much noise as she could to be heard. But to no avail. Thoroughly disgusted Sue fell asleep much to her surprise, waking up several hours later to continue her futile attempt to escape from this pauper's grave. Sue prayed again, "Dear God, please give me the strength to be able to lift this lid in order to escape from my confinement." Sue started pushing and pushing on the lid till she was out of breath and had to rest for awhile. All of a sudden she started kicking as loud and as hard as she could thinking someone might hear her but no luck. Sue has been in this casket since dawn this morning so she knows it is nightfall by now because she's wearing her watch. Sue started kicking again against the inside of the lid and thought she heard a slight crack. She gave the lid several more shoves and it slowly creaked open with dirt pressing in from all sides. She slowly crawled out of the casket and started grappling and clawing her way out of the grave.

She could hardly wait to reach the outside for her first breath of fresh air. As she was coming closer to the opening of the grave, she could feel the cool, moist earth from the recent onslaught of the devastating storm the city of St. Louis experienced. When Sue reached the top of the grave and crawled out it was almost dark and slightly cool. She hurriedly started walking back to the complex by the same route she and the zombie took out to Potter's Field Cemetery. Sue finally reached the Pickwell Apartment Complex and went inside to the All Purpose Room to be greeted by her fellow residents. Everybody asked, "Sue, where have you been? We've been worried about you. Did someone kidnap you again? Why are your clothes all muddy and your hair full of dirt? Sue, where on earth were you?" Mrs. Toole exclaimed, "You look like you've walked miles." Sue answered, proceeding to explain how the zombie kidnapped her and made her walk out to Potter's Field Cemetery. There he forced her into a casket which he locked and shoveled tons of dirt on top so that she couldn't crawl out. Mrs. Spiel asked Sue, "How did you finally manage to get out of the casket with six feet of dirt on top of you? I can't even imagine anybody clawing their way out of something like that!" Sue answered amidst gulps of warm tea since it was still cool in the evenings after the storm and a sandwich someone brought to the All Purpose Room since she hadn't eaten all day. Sue said, "I managed to get out of the casket by kicking on the inside of the lid repeatedly and finally the lid gave way, cracked and I was able to crawl out. I can see why the six residents from the complex suffocated to death because they should have tried to get out of the casket somehow the first day they were put in. It probably never entered their minds that they could've had a means of escape. It's too late now!" Mrs. Burns asked Sue, "I wonder why he singled you out as his victim, Sue?" Sue answered, "He singled me out, Mrs. Burns, because I was the first person that caught him in the elevator after he killed Mrs. Faye Lark and mutilated her body to the point of no recognition. I fought him when he was eating every snake that came out of Faye's opened body. Evidently he kept me in his mind."

Mrs. Burns made a remark again, "Yes, I vaguely remember that you were the person that approached the zombie after he had killed Faye. At ninety three your memory is going to lapse once in awhile." Mrs. Pruitt spoke up, "Sue, it's too bad you couldn't get a ride back to town with some respectable couple that you could trust, instead of walking three miles back to the complex by yourself." Sue answered, "Yes, I thought of that also but sometimes people are hesitant and not inclined to give a person a ride because of the fear instilled in them. I didn't present a pretty picture with my hair, body and clothing caked with dirt and mud. If I would've seen a person like myself walking I probably wouldn't have picked them up either." Mrs. Pruitt said, "Well that's a satisfactory answer, Sue. I never thought of it that way."

After the question and answer period was over Mrs. Pickwell gave Sue a key to the room and accompanied her to the third floor by way of the elevator. Mrs. Pickwell said, "I'm glad your back, Sue, and I am sorry this happened to you. If I can help you with something please call the office. Goodnight." Sue said, "Thank you and Goodnight" going to her apartment and to bed.

Back to Work

Immediately upon arising this morning Sue reported the kidnapping and escape to the St. Louis Police Department and they said they will be by later to question her at length. After that was taken care of Sue showered, ate breakfast and walked to the bus stop for her 7:30AM ride downtown.

Sue explained her absence to her boss, Mr. Green in this manner, "I'm sorry I forgot to call in sick yesterday but I was in bed all day not feeling well. It totally slipped my mind."Mr. Green said, "That's all right, Sue. I understand." Once in awhile Mr. Green makes an allowance for an absence. She didn't like to lie to Mr. Green but she didn't want to be embarrassed in front of her coworkers about the zombie story. Sue went to Barb's Café across the street for dinner and then back to the office. At 5:00PM she wrapped up her work and took the evening bus back to the apartment complex.

Chapter 14
Buried by a Zombie

It's a Sunday afternoon in September and Sue hasn't seen her mother, Jane, for about a month so she decided to take the city bus to the St. Louis Prison for Women for a visit. When she arrived the prison inmates were out in the prison yard for exercise, some are visiting with each other while others are leaning against the prison building and staring into space oblivious of everything around them. Sue immediately sees Jane slumped against the building by herself looking sick and forlorn. She contacts a prison warden for permission to meet with her mother in the visitation room. They each pick up a phone and Jane immediately started crying and saying, "Oh Sue, I've been so deeply depressed lately almost to the point of suicide but they have been keeping a close watch on me. They have someone posted at my door every night for safety's sake." Sue said, "Mother, why are you so depressed all the time?" Jane said, "You would be too, Sue, if you would have killed fifteen people like I did. It's all coming back to me now to haunt and depress me. I feel so guilty because of the murders I committed." Sue made the remark, "Mother, where do you come up with fifteen people?" Jane said, "Sue, remember I murdered twelve people at the Rockwood Apartment Complex at Rockwood,

Illinois and that's why I'm in prison for life. Prior to that years ago when you were younger I murdered three women and I was declared mentally incompetent to stand trial at a later date. Once my case went to court I was acquitted because of my mental incompetence. It's a sad, sad story and I wish I could take everything back but I can't. It's too late now. What do you think, Sue?" Sue answered, "I agree with you, Mother. You'll just have to come to grips with everything and go on from there. Maybe you need to pray more, Mother, so that God will help you cope with your problems. Mother, I guess you didn't hear what happened to me last week. It was horrible." Jane said, "What happened, Sue? Were you sick?" Sue said, "No, I was kidnapped by a zombie and forced to walk with him to the Potter's Field Cemetery three miles east of St. Louis at night where he buried me alive in a pauper's grave and shoveled mounds of dirt on top of the casket." Jane said amidst tears, "Oh dear, Sue, how did you get out of the grave? Did someone dig you out?"Sue said, "No, I kept kicking my feet against the lid of the casket, finally kicking one of the locks open with the lid coming undone which allowed me to crawl out." Jane said, "But how were you able to get to the top of the grave?" Sue told her, "Well, it isn't a pretty picture, Mother, but I kept grappling and clawing with my hands through the dirt until I reached the top and crawled out. I walked back to town with my hair and clothes filled with dirt but I had no choice so I just kept on walking. People passed me but no one offered a ride. I guess they were scared of me because I looked like a zombie myself." Jane and Sue shared a little chuckle at this point but it was short lived. Sue was checking the time as she said, "I guess it's time to leave, Mother. I hope you get better." Jane said, I do too, Sue, and I think I'll take your advice. I hope you can come a little sooner the next time. Don't wait so long, Sue." Sue yelled back, "I won't, mother" and boarded the bus with Jane watching from the Visitation Room waving goodbye with tears glistening in her eyes.

The Park and Petting Zoo

This Sunday while the weather is still accommodating the residents of the Pickwell Apartment Complex are going on an outing to the McLellan

Park and Petting Zoo. Mrs. Pickwell told them at the meeting the other night, "Please pack a brown bag lunch, drink and an umbrella in case it rains. I will accompany you on the outing. The bus will leave Sunday at 9:00AM."

At 9:00AM all the residents had eaten breakfast and were ready to board the bus for the outing at McLellan Park and Petting Zoo. Mr. Pickwell was driving the bus as the residents were saying, "I wish we could pet the animals here at the zoo. We've never been here before." Somebody else made the same remark so Mr. Pickwell decided to stop at the petting zoo for a little fun with the animals. After they were done petting the zoo animals they took the bus back to the park where they ate their brown bag lunch, cold drink and visited with one another while a few others started to play cards in a shelter house not far away. Everybody was occupied with something. Mrs. Pickwell announced, "If you want to go in groups to explore the different areas of the park you are welcome to do so at your leisure today. Please be back by 4:00PM because that's when the bus will depart." All the residents dispersed to different areas of the park and beyond in groups of three or four. The remainder of the residents continued to visit with each other while the others are content to play cards in an enclosed shelter house in the area. A few of the residents enjoyed playing some games of horse shoe to pass the time. Mr. Pickwell left with the bus while Mrs. Pickwell stayed with the residents.

After the residents were gone about an hour Mrs. Pickwell made a remark to Mrs. Cole, "Listen, do you hear that noise? There must be some children playing and screaming for fun in the park this afternoon. That's strange! I don't see any children though, do you?" Mrs. Cole said, "No, but I sure hear them screaming and yelling. I can remember when I was a child playing, that's all I would do, yell and scream." Mrs. Cole gave a chuckle and smiled to herself as Mrs. Pickwell said, "I know what you mean. I remember those days like they were yesterday. There's no way we'll ever forget those times."

In the midst of Mrs. Pickwell and Mrs. Cole's conversation, off in the distance to the west, they could see people running and screaming towards them some even crying, stumbling and falling as they edged their way closer to Mrs. Pickwell and Mrs. Cole. They were screaming, "Help us! Help us! The zombies are after us! They are coming!" Mrs. Pickwell and Mrs. Cole could see the zombies chasing them at breakneck speed, only to retreat as the residents reached Mrs. Pickwell and Mrs. Cole. Immediately the residents related what happened, "We were exploring the different areas of the park west of here when a band of zombies came out of nowhere, grabbed us, pulling our hair, biting and scratching us yelling, "Arg! Arg! Arg!" We fought them off as best we could and then started running when we had the chance. We were scared they would take us with them to the cemetery like they did Sue. Mrs. Pickwell, none of the residents are interested in going for outings in the parks anymore because of the fear of zombies attacking us like they did today. This needs to be reported to the police." Mrs. Pickwell said, "I agree. As soon as we get back to the complex I will call the police department and tell them what happened. I'm sure they'll come to the complex to question those of you that went exploring. Please give me your name before you get off the bus so the police can contact you personally."

The bus arrived at the apartment complex at 5:00PM, just in time for the residents to eat their supper in their apartments. In the meantime Mrs. Pickwell called the police department and reported the following: "The residents of the Pickwell Apartment Complex were attacked by zombies while on an outing in McLellan Park and Zoo. They were scratched and bitten as they tried to fight them off. Eventually they started chasing the residents and when the zombies saw us they retreated. Please send an officer to the complex to question the residents because they might have vital information to this case." Officer Sheldon assured Mrs. Pickwell, "An officer will be out sometime tomorrow to interview the residents and file a report on the incident."

Monday Morning

After the residents ate their breakfast this morning the ones that were approached by the zombies at Mc Lellan Park and Zoo congregated in the All Purpose Room. They will be interrogated individually and as a group. Officer Sheldon asked the group, "Can the zombies say any words at all?" The group said, "No, the only thing they say is "Arg! Arg! Arg!" Officer

Sheldon continued on, "Do any of you recognize any of the individuals as having lived here at the complex before?" Mr. Ames raised his hand and said, "Yes, it seems like I recognized one of the men as Mr. Lake that used to live on the sixth floor. In fact, I asked him if he was Mr. Lake and he looked at me in a strange manner, his eyes glazed over while one eye started twitching uncontrollably and he said, "Arg! Arg! Arg! As if he knew what I was saying. The zombies up close are very filthy, with dirt particles falling off of their clothing, a white, thin, stringy film covering their whole body and a foul stench about them. They have a very strong grip about them that is hard to break away from but somehow we managed." Officer Sheldon interviewed a few more residents then went back to the police department to file a report.

So far the six zombies have been apprehended once, taken to the hospital to be re-injected with a fatal vaccine that killed them and then to Potter's Field Cemetery to be buried. Later they re-emerged and since then have been terrorizing the city of St. Louis with their scary antics to the point of burying people alive such as Sue Benson. The police department has followed numerous leads to apprehend them but to no avail. The zombies are very good at eluding the police, they always have been. The National Guard and other security forces from other states have been brought in but nothing ever materialized.

Ghosts Again

The ghosts have never reappeared at the Pickwell Apartment Complex until something strange happened last night. Mrs. Cole was standing at the top of the stairs by herself ready to walk down when she felt a pair of hands give her a shove as she fell down the flight of stairs to the first floor where she was going to eat supper. She knew immediately that nobody from the complex would shove her down the stairs so it had to come from a different source. But where?

Mrs. Pickwell and several other residents came running as soon as they heard the noise. Mrs. Pickwell exclaimed, "My goodness, Mrs. Cole, are you all right?" Mrs. Cole said, "I didn't lose my footing, slip or anything of the sort. I felt a pair of hands shove me before I started falling. Now my head is pounding and I have a lot of pain." Mrs. Pickwell said, "I called an ambulance and it's on the way. I'll accompany you to the hospital and wait for the doctor to examine you."

When they arrived at the hospital Dr. Stevens examined Mrs. Cole and said, "Mrs. Cole, you have a concussion from the fall and we'd like to keep you in the hospital overnight for observation if that's okay with you." Mrs. Cole said, "Yes, that'll be fine." Mrs. Pickwell waited until she was transported to her room and then she also left. Before she walked out the door she said, "I'll be up to see you tomorrow just in case you get dismissed." Mrs. Cole said, "Thank you" and closed her eyes hoping to get a little rest. She was glad she was on the third floor and had a private room because it was nice and quiet. Mrs. Pickwell came to visit Mrs. Cole the next day asking her, "How do you feel today, Mrs. Cole?" She replied, "My pain in my head has eased up quite a bit and I feel much better now." At this point a nurse entered the room and said, "Mrs. Cole, the doctor will dismiss you in about an hour if your friend cares to wait. Mrs. Pickwell waited and took Mrs. Cole along back to the complex.

Monthly Meeting-October-2007

After supper in their apartments the residents proceeded to the All Purpose Room to visit and watch television before the meeting began at 7:00PM. Mrs. Pickwell lit the fireplace so it would be nice and warm because it had been a cold, blustery fall day. At this point Mr. Pickwell's also glad he had the shingles, siding and several windows replaced after the storm back in August because of fall and winter coming on.

Mrs. Pickwell is ready to start the meeting with the residents filing in and taking their place. Mrs. Pickwell called the meeting to order and said, "I have a few issues I would like to present to you this evening and hope I can get a full response. The first issue on the agenda is Mrs. Cole's accident and current condition. Mrs. Cole is with us this evening as you can all see. Would you stand up Mrs. Cole and tell us what you experienced and how you're feeling? Mrs. Cole got up slowly saying, "Well, I was coming down for supper the other night by myself when I felt a pair of hands shove me on my back as I fell down the flight of stairs. No, there wasn't anybody with me, behind me, anywhere. I was standing by myself when this happened. Mrs. Pickwell came to my rescue and called the ambulance. I was taken to the hospital where I was diagnosed with a concussion and kept overnight for observation. Mrs. Pickwell was kind enough to bring me home yesterday afternoon. I am grateful to her for her help. At present I am feeling much better with only an occasional headache. Any questions?"

Mrs. Brooks asked her, "Mrs. Cole, when you fell did you cut yourself or bleed anywhere?" Mrs. Cole said, "No, the only thing I received was a concussion on my head."

Mrs. Pickwell continued the meeting saying, "Since we've had these encounters with the zombies Mr. Pickwell and I would like to warn you about going out at night by yourself or even in a group because it is very dangerous. Everybody knows what happened a couple of weeks ago when we went to McLellan Park and Zoo. Some of you were approached, bitten, scratched and chased by the zombies in broad daylight. There are those of you that still bear the marks. At this point we are not planning on going to anymore outings at McLellan Park and Zoo. Mr. Pickwell and my main concern is that if you insist on leaving and coming back after dark please be sure that you have your key with you. Any questions? Mrs. Chase, what is your question?" Mrs. Chase asked, "Wouldn't it be safer to leave in a taxi instead of walking downtown, especially in inclement weather?"Mrs. Pickwell said, "Yes, but still be on your guard when strange people approach you. Anymore questions? Now's the time to speak up." No one spoke up so Mrs. Pickwell said, "I have another warning to issue . I noticed that a lot of you are exceptionally friendly with people you don't know. Please exercise caution in this respect because many people will take advantage of circumstances such as this. Please don't approach strange people in conversation if you're unfamiliar with them. It's just a good practice. This concludes this evening's meeting. Goodnight. Any other unanswered questions that you might've thought of can be asked in my office tomorrow." It was close to 9:00PM at the conclusion of the meeting so everyone decided to skip visiting and television, retiring for the night.

Zombies Re-buried

After the meeting Sue went to her apartment to watch television, eat a snack and then to bed because tomorrow was the beginning of another work week. While she was watching a movie the news department broke in with the following, "Today the St. Louis Police Department apprehended seventeen zombies in Richmond Park as they were approaching and trying to kidnap men, women and children while they were at play. This time the zombies couldn't elude the police so they were captured by force as the result of a telephone call from the park. They were taken by bus once more to the St. Louis Memorial Hospital and re-injected with a deadly virus that killed them immediately. The police contacted the caretaker, Mr. Lorenson, for assistance in burying the seventeen zombies at Potter's Field Cemetery where they originated. Mr. Lorenson knew immediately saying, "I know which grave each zombie came out of because each zombie has a small identification number on their forehead that coincides with a number on the tombstone. Mr. Lorenson and several other caretakers buried the seventeen zombies saying, "We hope this is the last time they get buried."As the caretakers left the Potter's Field Cemetery close to dark a light mist fell on the already dampened graves.

What's in the Elevator Now? October 31, 2007

Its Halloween night and everybody is gathered in the All Purpose Room for the annual Halloween party of the year. Mrs. Pickwell allows the ghosts and goblins from outside to enter the complex for some "trick or treat" candy and a display of their costumes for the residents to see. The residents and Mrs. Pickwell have furnished the Halloween cupcakes, a variety of trick or treat candy, balloons, a Halloween cake and an apple cider drink. The residents are also dressed in their Halloween costumes ready for the party with one exception. Ninety year old Mr. Rimm said last week with a laugh, "I'll be one of the first trick or treaters down there. You might not even know me in my costume." Where is he tonight? He never came! While the party was in progress Mrs. Crane said something to Sue, "Sue, did you see Mr. Rimm at the party tonight?" Sue said, "Now that you mention it, no I didn't. Actually, I haven't seen him for several days." Mrs. Crane said again, "Sue, do you hear a piercing, shrill noise?" Sue said, "No, but then I have a slight hearing loss in my left ear which might account for the fact that I didn't hear that noise." Mrs. Crane said, "Oh, I was probably imagining things like I sometimes do."

In the meantime, while everybody was enjoying the party Mr. Rimm was running late. He decided to take the elevator like he always does. Mr. Rimm is nearly blind but nevertheless he stepped into the elevator unbeknown what lay in the corner. In a box behind Mr. Rimm's feet lay a smaller than average, mean spirited, very dangerous alligator with its jaws wide open to bite Mr. Rimm which it did. The alligator kept biting, chomping and eating continuously until it had devoured most of Mr. Rimm's body. The only thing left of Mr. Rimm was his bedraggled Halloween costume lying on the elevator floor. No wonder Mr. Rimm fought and screamed while he was being eaten alive. Is that what Mrs. Crane heard? By now Mr. Rimm had been completely forgotten because of the excitement of the party.

During the course of the party Mrs. Crane mentioned to Sue again saying, "The absence of Mr. Rimm from the Halloween party is unusual. Especially the way Mr. Rimm was looking forward to being the first trick or treater at the party. He even said we might not know him. Something seems strange, Sue, would you go and check up on Mr.Rimm?" Sue said, "Of course, I'll be right back." It was an anguished wait but Mrs. Crane's supposition was correct. Her suspicions had been confirmed. She knew immediately by the expression on Sue's face that something terrible had happened to Mr. Rimm. Mrs. Crane said, "Sue, what's the matter? Why are you crying?" Sue said, "I went to Mr. Rimm's door, knocked and no one answered.

As I was heading towards the elevator one of the residents that wasn't at the party noticed that the elevator door was open a little bit so she peered in and was horrified at what she saw. There was a 4 foot man eating alligator in a box that someone had pulled into the elevator. Its mouth was wide open and part of a shoe was stuck in it. She said she didn't see Mr. Rimm except she did see his Halloween costume lying on the elevator floor and his head and part of his chest in a corner." Sue went on to say, "Mrs. Gale reported this to Mrs. Pickwell and she reported the incident to the police department. They are on their way out here as we speak."

By now Mrs. Gale and the other residents were whispering amongst themselves and crying for Mr. Rimm and the fear this would instill in themselves. They were thinking, "This complex is as bad as the one we moved out of. What are we going to do? God, help us." The police department arrived and went to the elevator immediately with the help of Mrs. Pickwell. The elevator had to be locked because the alligator was still inside with no means of escape. When the elevator door opened up the alligator was slithering around on the floor making strange noises. The police captured it putting it in a cage for transportation to the local zoo for an evaluation. The medical zoo-ologist had the alligator x-rayed for the consumption of human body parts.

Mr. Rimm was small in stature and body weight barely weighing 85 pounds. The x-rays turned out positive because they could actually see chunks of Mr. Rimm's legs and other body parts inside the alligator's body. The 4-foot alligator had eaten part of Mr. Rimm alive unbeknown to the residents at the Halloween party having a good time. Who could have managed to transport an alligator in an enclosed cage with a lid on top into the complex and then an elevator without being seen? It would've been done during the night and then on the other hand it could've been done during the day. Right? Read on and see what happens!

The police transferred the remainder of Mr. Rimm's body parts to Gilbey's Funeral Home for cremation, a memorial service and inurement at the cemetery. The memorial service was attended by everybody at the apartment complex, numerous friends, relatives and his immediate family. Mr. Rimm's wife, Ada, passed away seven years ago and he is survived by his son, Bob, wife Joan and two children Alex and Grace, his other son, Joe, wife Betty, and daughter Melissa. He is also survived by a daughter Dixie, her husband, David and son Danny. They all live in St. Louis, Missouri.

Lunch was served in the Barker Dining Hall at the Pickwell Apartment Complex for family and friends. Mr. Rimm's family is contemplating a lawsuit for the wrongful death of their father Mr. Joe Rimm. The family said, "This is unbelievable and should never have happened! How could the landlady have been so negligent as to have something like this happen? A boxed alligator in an elevator! We've never heard of anything like that!" Mr. Rimm's children's attorney will be in contact with Mrs. Pickwell's attorney in the near future. Mrs. Pickwell isn't aware of this so it might come as a surprise to her. She hasn't got an inkling of what's going on.

Sunday Services

Mrs. Pickwell was posting new notices on the bulletin board while everybody craned their necks to read what they were all about. One notice they were reading was about the Sunday morning bus that will take everybody to a nondenominational church, basically The New Baptist Church on Morley St. in downtown St. Louis. The bus leaves at 9:15AM and after church the bus will be there to pick you up to go to a local restaurant for dinner and then back to the complex. About half of the residents expressed interest in going to The New Baptist Church for services and dinner with everybody saying, "We'll be down Sunday morning at 9:15AM to meet the bus."

Sunday morning rolled around quite soon with everybody meeting in the lobby of the complex for their ride downtown to church services and dinner. When the bus pulled up all the residents climbed in sitting with their favorite friend or partner.

The bus parked in front of the The New Baptist Church to drop the residents off and will wait till services are over to take them to the restaurant of their choice which is usually Pedro's, a Spanish restaurant they've all come to like. The bus driver, Mr. Stone, usually goes along in with them for his noon meal and drives them back to the complex. Everyone enjoyed themselves immensely and were already looking forward to next week's Sunday trip to church services and dinner. They all climbed out of the bus, bid Mr. Stone goodnight, entered the complex and went to bed.

Thanksgiving Day—Nov. 23, 2007

The residents of the apartment complex are hosting a pot luck supper tonight at 5:30PM with Bingo to follow. Some brought baked turkey, mashed potatoes and gravy, dressing, savory vegetables, salads, hot rolls, cranberry sauce, pumpkin pie or cake. The complex provided the drinks. All the residents attended including Mr. and Mrs. Pickwell.

After supper everybody that was interested in playing Bingo went to the All Purpose Room for a couple of hours of their favorite game. This evening there were money prizes and also donated items. Sue was the Bingo caller for the evening with a short intermission. After intermission Bingo resumed until all the prizes and money were given away. After Bingo the residents picked up their prizes and went back to their apartments.

Where's Mr. Pickwell? Dec 1, 2007

Mrs. Pickwell arose this morning at 6:00AM to discover Mr. Pickwell had already risen for the day. He was probably out for his morning walk as usual to a small neighborhood café nearby on Binny Street. He frequents the local café every morning to share a cup of coffee with his old friends and catch up on the local gossip that he might've missed out on the day before. So Mrs. Pickwell wasn't concerned about the whereabouts of Mr. Pickwell because this has been his morning ritual for years. Nothing new. The "old cronies" he has coffee with are Joe Williams, ex President of a St. Louis Bank, Bob Miller, a retired physician from St Louis Memorial Hospital, Glenn Stroll, a musician with the St. Louis Municipal Band, Don Solan, a retired policeman from the St. Louis Police Department and Arnold Dillman a retired Red Cross volunteer. Mr. Pickwell and his cronies share their coffee, rehash the local gossip, plus swap stories from their childhood years gone by to the present days. They all disperse at 9:00AM after their morning entertainment to start the day. A light mist falls as they leave the café and Mr. Pickwell walks north towards the Pickwell Apartment Complex. Well, it's December and it's supposed to snow today. What else can you expect for December?

Everybody is seated for dinner at the complex with everyone chatting and visiting as usual and a healthy appetite to go with it. One of the residents asked several of her friends at the table, "Have you seen Mrs. Pickwell already today?" and they said, "No, we haven't paid any attention to her today. Why? Is there something wrong? We can see her sitting in her office right now." The other resident remarked, "When you are up close to her like I was this morning she has a worried, perplexed look on her face like she is ready to burst into tears. I only said what I had to and moved on." At this point the subject was changed and they began eating their dinner before it turned cold.

After everyone finished eating some of the residents chose to go to the All Purpose Room for a game of cards, television or a gab fest to pass the time. Two groups of women decided to play pinochle while two men played on the new billiard table and the rest caught up on the latest news. Mrs.Pickwell walked through the All Purpose Room on her way to the Community Room usually speaking and sharing a laugh but today was different. Nothing was said as she walked through the All Purpose Room rather hurriedly with a harried look on her face going back into her office. Mrs. Pickwell could be seen from her office making telephone calls periodically and then closing the door which was unusual for her in the middle of the day. Later Mrs. Pickwell came through the Community

Room again and made an announcement. "Good evening. Ordinarily I don't make announcements like this but tonight is an exception to the rule. I've been emotionally upset all day, as I'm sure most of you noticed, because Mr. Pickwell has been missing since I arose at 6:00AM this morning. I will wait through the supper hour this evening and if he doesn't come back I will have no choice but to report him as a missing person to the St. Louis Police Department. By the way have any of you seen Mr. Pickwell today?" Everybody shook their head and said, "No." Mrs. Pickwell made the remark, "The police will be sending someone out to the complex for more information so they can file a missing person report on Mr. Pickwell." After the announcement Mrs. Pickwell went to her office and the residents went back to their apartments. Later on in the evening residents saw two policemen talking to Mrs. Pickwell in her private office and then leaving by way of the front entrance. Later that evening several women were gathered around the television in the Community Room watching the local news on Channel KIBX when the announcer was handed a news report. It stated, "A local St. Louis, Missouri resident, Arthur Pickwell, part landlord of Pickwell Apartment Complex, has been reported missing since 6:00AM this morning, Tuesday December 1, 2007. Arthur is 6ft. 1, steel gray hair and weighs 215 pounds. He was last seen at 9:00AM leaving George's Café on Binny St. headed north towards the Pickwell Apartment Complex. If anybody has seen or knows of Arthur Pickwell's whereabouts please call 742-681-2927. Thank you!" The residents were not surprised at this announcement since Mrs. Pickwell had informed everyone in the Community Room this evening. What happened to Arthur Pickwell? Did someone kidnap him? Read on!

A week has passed by with no report of Arthur Pickwell coming back to the Pickwell Apartment Complex, being seen in St. Louis proper or in outlying areas. Nightly news reporters are still announcing his disappearance but nothing has materialized. Several anonymous telephone calls have come to the police department regarding sightings of Arthur Pickwell which were investigated but nothing was confirmed. Mrs. Pickwell has received numerous calls from friends and relatives about the disappearance of Arthur Pickwell as he was leaving George's on Binny Street heading north to the Pickwell Apartment complex. Mrs. Pickwell is beside herself with fear for Arthur and herself as she continues to be the main landlord at the complex since Mr. Pickwell is out of commission. Mrs. Pickwell is scared to walk anywhere for fear the same thing will happen to her and then they'll both be missing.

A month has passed and still no sightings or information about Arthur Pickwell. The television and radio station still continue to announce the disappearance of Arthur Pickwell periodically with no leads. Yesterday an anonymous caller telephoned the police department saying, "I think I saw the Arthur Pickwell you're looking for. At present I am calling from my car, following him coming out of Shard's Hardware Store walking down Bailey Street headed west." The description that the news announcer on television gave did not coincide with the description of the anonymous caller. The police immediately followed the lead but it was a false alarm. The person that was sighted was a local resident with a different description and name residing with his family on Bailey Street. Actually he worked in Shard's Hardware Store part time as a sales clerk and had just gotten off work for the day. Just a case of mistaken identity.

Chapter 15
Will They Find Arthur Pickwell?

In spite of being mid December Sunday is supposed to be a mild, warm day so Mrs. Pickwell is organizing a search party for the residents in McLellan Park. Not ever wanting to go to McLellan Park and Zoo again because of the zombies that the residents encountered, Mrs. Pickwell decided to get police protection while they were at the park. Mr. Pickwell enjoyed McLellan Park and Zoo the best of any park and zoo in the St. Louis area. Sunday morning after the 10:00AM services at the New Baptist Church and dinner at Pedro's Restaurant downtown the residents were taken to McLellan Park and Zoo to search for the whereabouts of Arthur Pickwell. Mrs. Pickwell is accompanying the residents and will be searching herself.

After a futile three hour search in the park and wooded area nothing was accomplished because nobody found anything of any significance except a resident, Mr. Mark. He handed Mrs. Pickwell a work shoe and said, "I found this in that wooded area over there." She asked, "Did you only find one shoe?" and he said, "Yes." She said it was one of Mr. Pickwell's work shoes because he had a pair like that but then they could've belonged to someone else too. So she thanked Mr. Mark, took the shoe into the bus and would turn it into the police department tomorrow.

This morning Mrs. Pickwell had the police pick up the shoe to see if they could tie it in with anything regarding the investigation as to the whereabouts of Mr. Pickwell. It is two weeks since Mr. Pickwell's disappearance and the leads the police received were all false alarms. The police aren't any closer to solving the case than they were the first day he disappeared. Mrs. Pickwell has not given up on Mr. Pickwell because she still checks with the hospital and the police department and has organized searches every once in awhile in other parks also to no avail. As far as the shoe investigation is concerned the police decided the shoe can't be associated with Mr. Pickwell because there's also a chance it isn't even Mr. Pickwell's shoe. If he was in the park at one time he isn't there anymore.

Mrs. Pickwell again decided to organize another resident search party at Filman Park in south St. Louis where she and Mr. Pickwell took their children years ago for an outing. After Mrs. Pickwell made the announcement saying, "The bus will leave this Sunday afternoon going to Filman Park for an organized search for the whereabouts of Mr. Pickwell. This Sunday the weather is supposed to be beautiful, 65 degrees, even though it's only two weeks before Christmas. When the snowy season begins we will discontinue our search for Mr. Pickwell. Even if there was a personal belonging of my husband's lying on the ground it would be covered with snow and would never be found."

Sunday afternoon at 12:30PM twenty five residents were headed by bus to Filman Park in the southern part of St. Louis at the request of Mrs. Pickwell for an organized search for her husband. After they reached the park they all dispersed in groups of three to different outlying areas in hope of finding something personal that could relate to Mr. Pickwell. At 4:00PM everybody was to return to the shelter house where the search originated. The residents all came back empty handed except for Mrs. Shale. She handed Mrs. Pickwell a men's chain with a gold cross on it.

Also a small piece of silver was attached with Arthur Pickwell's initials (AP) engraved on it. Mrs. Shale said, "I found this chain by the water fountain with Mr. Pickwell's initials on it. There's a good chance this belongs to your husband." Upon receiving the chain Mrs. Pickwell was overcome with emotion and burst into tears saying, "Yes, this is Arthur's chain he wore around his neck ever since the day we were married. He had his initials engraved on the silver piece the day he bought the chain saying, "I'd better have my initials engraved on here just in case I ever lose it. He was a very devout and religious man. I"ll be calling the police department when we get back today." Mrs. Pickwell thanked Mrs. Shale and they boarded the bus for the ride back to the apartment complex.

Christmas Preparations—2007

Everybody arose bright and early Monday morning for breakfast at 7:30AM and to help decorate the main floor and hallways of the complex. They were late with the Christmas decorations because of what had transpired with Mr. Pickwell. Boxes of Christmas decorations were brought out as the residents proceeded to put them in their respective place. A large fir Christmas tree was erected in the lobby of the complex with the residents taking charge of decorating that also. The atmosphere was jovial and festive while the residents were busy decorating but as soon as Mrs. Pickwell entered the scene the atmosphere turned gloomy. She was very distraught at the thought of the possibility that her husband might have been killed.

Christmas came and went with church services, a Christmas meal and gift exchange, plus some shared laughter and music coming out of the Community Room.

New Years Day—Jan, 2008

It is a month today since Mr. Pickwell disappeared after he left George's Café on Binny Street for the walk back to the Pickwell Apartment Complex. Mrs. Pickwell's thoughts run rampant, "If only

Arthur would not have gone for coffee that morning! Was someone stalking Arthur for days or was he just picked up on a sudden impulse, maybe at random? Did someone follow him out of George's Café that morning?" Mrs. Pickwell went into the café the next day and inquired after Arthur never came back. George and his help said, "No, in fact that group of men that Arthur met with every morning were the only customers in the café at that time."

Mrs. Pickwell has done some private research on the disappearance of Mr. Pickwell on her own but has come up with nothing. She turned the chain over to the police department and let them handle the investigative process. Several days later the Chief of Police, Mr. Rhine, called Mrs. Pickwell saying, "The chain that we received from you, Mrs. Pickwell, was definitely your husbands, there's no doubt of that. At some point in time your husband was abducted, possibly at gunpoint and taken to several parks here in city of St. Louis. Why, we don't know. As you told us your husband owned a pair of shoes just like the shoe we have in our possession now. Well, it's also a possibility that whoever abducted him took him to McLellan Park and Zoo and definitely to Filman Park because his chain was found there at the water fountain. We've already interviewed a list of potential suspects, coming up with nothing so far."

The New Year's Day celebration today consisted of church services, a pot luck dinner and meeting, plus Bingo in the All Purpose Room. "White Elephant" prizes were given away at the Bingo games. Mrs. Pickwell retired to her room after the meeting because she is suffering from a bad case of depression due to the disappearance of her husband. She is also experiencing recurring stomach pains that have her up almost every night vomiting. She is to the point of seeing a physician and getting admitted to the hospital for further testing of her stomach and otherwise.

What's in the Box?

The month of January wears on as the atmosphere is even drearier at the complex with Mrs. Pickwell not being able to get out of bed for days due to stomach problems and depression. An assistant landlord Mrs. Amble has been hired for the duration of Mrs. Pickwell's illness to do the office work, phone calls and conduct meetings if need be. Mrs. Amble will generally oversee the operation of the Pickwell Apartment Complex while Mrs. Pickwell hopefully will be recuperating.

Well, we are now reaching the middle of January and Mrs. Pickwell has not improved at all. Her last resort is to call her physician, Dr. Byrd, for an appointment which she does. His diagnosis is a deep, deep depression with suicidal tendencies plus recurring stomach problems due to her nerves, acid reflux and intestinal problems. Mrs. Amble had Mrs. Pickwell admitted to St. Louis Memorial Hospital for several days upon Dr. Byrd's request for observation and treatment. When Mrs. Amble came back to the complex she announced at the dinner table, "We will have an emergency meeting at 7:30PM tonight in the All Purpose Room. I would like everybody if possible to be present."

At 7:00PM all the residents that lived in the complex started filing into the All Purpose Room for the meeting which will be conducted by Mrs. Amble. When they were all seated Mrs. Amble said, "Dr. Byrd, Mrs. Pickwell's physician, admitted her into the St. Louis Memorial Hospital for several days for observation and treatment. He diagnosed her with a deep, deep depression, a bad case of nerves, acid reflux and intestinal problems. If any of the residents wish to visit Mrs. Pickwell her room number is 314. Please limit the time of your visitation no longer than 30 minutes as she is in dire need of rest. Are there any questions? Please raise your hand. Mrs. Ardell, what is your question?" Mrs. Ardell asked, "Does Mrs. Pickwell need a ride home the day she is dismissed from the hospital because I am visiting my brother—in—law everyday and I'll be glad to bring her back to the complex?" Mrs. Amble said, "No, thank you for the offer but I'll be bringing her home the same day she gets dismissed. Any other questions?" The residents shook their heads no so Mrs. Amble dismissed everyone for the evening. A few residents approached Mrs. Amble after the conclusion of the short meeting with a few private questions and discussion while the remainder of the residents went to their apartments.

The next day three residents, Sue Benson, Alice Shale and Lela Burrs shared a taxi to the St. Louis Memorial Hospital to visit Mrs. Pickwell. They called in advance and asked, "Is Mrs. Pickwell feeling well enough for company this afternoon and they were told that she was." Mrs. Pickwell was happy to see them saying, "I'm so happy to see all of you today. I feel much better now because my pain has subsided with the medication they've given me. I am also getting antidepressant medicine which doesn't take effect for about a month. Has there been any news on the radio or television that I might've missed about my husband, Arthur?" Sue and her lady friends said, "No, there hasn't been anything on the radio or television the past few days to our knowledge. I guess it's time for us to go, Mrs. Pickwell, because our visitation limit has exceeded. We hope and pray that you will get well and we will see you back at the complex." Mrs. Pickwell said, "Goodbye and thank you for coming. I'm sure I'll see you at the complex in a few days."

With that the three ladies shared a taxi again back to the complex. Other residents visited Mrs. Pickwell at the hospital during her stay. Several days later, on Saturday, she was dismissed with her medication and Mrs. Amble brought her back to the apartment complex.

Happy Homecoming—January—2008

Everyone welcomed Mrs. Pickwell back to the complex and hosted a social gathering for her in the Community Room. Mrs. Pickwell was overcome with joy to see the entire complex represented for her benefit. She said, "I would like to thank everybody from the bottom of my heart for the welcoming party you organized in my honor this evening. This alone brings my spirits back to normal besides my medication."

Dr. Byrd recommended a few days of bed rest and then Mrs. Pickwell will be able to resume her regular duties at the complex, in the office and otherwise.

A month has now passed and Mrs. Pickwell's depression is not recognizable anymore. She has dismissed Mrs. Amble of her duties and manages the complex on her own without any help. She still contacts the police periodically about her husband, Arthur, but the news is always the same. They tell her, "I'm sorry, Mrs. Pickwell, but there have been no new leads for quite awhile. We even solicited outside detectives and security personnel from other states to assist us in the search for your husband but so far we have reached a dead end. We have nothing else to tell you. As soon as we get anything new on your husband's case we will call you. Okay?" Mrs. Pickwell said, "Okay" and hung up the phone.

A Valentine's Day Party —Feb. 2008

Mrs. Pickwell scheduled a Valentine party for the residents of the complex tomorrow night in the Community Room. The residents will be serving the drinks and cookies, an exchange of cards and a dance in the evening. Sounds like fun, doesn't it? Read on!

On Valentine's Day Mrs. Pickwell received a phone call from the postal department telling her, "There is a big box for you, Mrs. Pickwell. Do you want to come to the main office in downtown St. Louis to pick it up or do you want it delivered to your door tomorrow?" Mrs. Pickwell said, "I'll just have it delivered tomorrow. I wonder where it's from? I haven't ordered anything lately." The postmaster said, "It was sent from St. Louis. That perplexed her even more so she said, "Well, I'll just wait until tomorrow. Maybe someone sent me a Valentine gift."

The next morning Mrs. Pickwell arose extra early anxiously awaiting the arrival of the big box today which is Valentine's Day. Around 11:00AM two postal deliverymen from the postal department carried the big box up the steps to the front door of the complex and rang the doorbell. Mrs. Pickwell answered and said, "Thank you for delivering this box because I didn't have time to pick it up yestrday. I appreciate that." The postal deliverymen said, "thank you" and left. Mrs. Pickwell pulled the big box into the lobby and went to get the box cutter. When she came back she noticed that the box was actually packed in another box. Now why would a person do that, do you suppose? All of a sudden as she got closer to pulling the cardboard back she noticed a strange, rancid odor coming from the box itself. Mrs. Pickwell thought to herself, "Don't tell me someone sent me some food and it spoiled?" She continued peeling the cardboard back to discover piles and piles of human, rotted, flesh chopped up and in the middle of the whole mess lay Mr. Pickwell's severed head with his eyes wide open. Mrs. Pickwell screamed out loud and cried saying, "Oh no! My poor Arthur! Look what someone did to him! Look at that!" By this time the residents had gathered around the box to see what all the commotion was about. Everybody was shocked at what they saw before them. Some residents chose not to look into the box but most of them did. They could hardly believe what they saw in the box. Mrs. Pickwell went to her office and called William's Mortuary and had them pick up the box for cremation. She told them, "I would like to have the memorial service as soon as possible so I can put some closure to my husband's death. Please call me when the first available memorial service and inurement will be. Thank you!"

Oh! By the way, the Valentine party was cancelled because of all the commotion about the box. Several residents went to Mrs. Pickwell's apartment to comfort her as she is in the grieving process once more. They prepared something to eat for her and tried to soothe her frayed nerves. By now it was getting late and Mrs. Pickwell said she would be all right by herself at night so the residents left and went to their own apartments. Besides if Mrs. Pickwell has any problems during the night all she has to do is knock on Sue's door because Sue's apartment is just down the hall.

The next day William's Funeral Home called Mrs. Pickwell telling her, "The soonest memorial service would be this Saturday morning at 10:00AM with inurement to follow at 11:00AM at the St. Louis Cemetery." A luncheon will follow at the Barker Dining Hall for friends and relatives. Mr. Pickwell was well known in St. Louis because he served as mayor for two years, plus he was a city commissioner for several years besides serving on other various boards. Mr. and Mrs. Pickwell were always accepted in various social circles around the city.

Saturday brought hundreds of people to the memorial service and inurement at the St. Louis Cemetery, plus the free luncheon at the Barker Dining Room. There was such a large crowd of people that they had to wait outside till they could get in to eat. Everybody approached Mrs. Pickwell where she was sitting to express their condolences upon the death of Mr. Pickwell under such unusual circumstances. Mr. Pickwell is survived by his wife, Mrs. Pickwell, a son, Norbert, wife, Clara, and two grandson's Felix and Simon. He is also survived by a daughter, Marla, husband, George and one granddaughter Nadine. After everyone left the kitchen staff cleaned the Barker Dining Hall and went home because it had been a long day.

An Investigation—March, 2008

Since Mr. Pickwell's life is now in the past tense Mrs. Pickwell remembers there was no name of the sender on the box which leads her to the postal department in downtown St. Louis. She inquired about the senders name and was told they do not keep track of who sends packages when their name is not in the left hand corner on top of the package. She told them what the box contained and they said, "We're well aware of that from the media information. We extend our personal condolences to you, Mrs. Pickwell. I'm sorry we can't be of any further help to you. If we can be of any assistance to you in the future please let us know." Mrs. Pickwell said, "Thank you" and left. She went to the St. Louis Police Department the same day to report the incident at the postal department. She was ushered into the Chief of Police, James Rhine's, private office for an update on the case. Mr. Rhine said, "I'm sorry, Mrs. Pickwell, but at this point we have no leads on this case. We have sent our out of town detectives and state security personnel back home because as I said once before, "We have reached a dead end. We have interviewed our inmates to see if they have friends and fellow inmates who would be capable of doing this and the answer was no. We also questioned suspects that are not jailed but have a history of violent crimes of this nature and the answers were also no. In fact, all inmates and suspects were subject to a lie detector test which turned out negative for everyone. The anonymous calls and leads that we followed did not materialize either. There's nothing else conceivable that we can do. At this point our hands are tied unless something new surfaces that we are unaware of. Feel free to call us periodically for an update on your husband's case. Do you have any other questions or issues, Mrs. Pickwell?" She said, "No, not at this time," bid Chief of Police, Mr. Rhine, goodbye and left his office. A light snow was beginning to fall so she hurriedly drove back to the apartment complex.

Different Activities

This Monday morning at 9:00AM the residents will board the bus for an excursion to the St. Louis Public Library in downtown St. Louis. It's been several months since the residents have been to the library. They used to frequent the library oftener when they lived at the old apartment complex that Mrs. Styles used to manage before she passed away. Today is a perfect day to visit the library with the snow melted and the temperature a balmy 65 degrees and jacket weather. Many people are at the library today to return books, check out other books, work on the computers, surf the internet etc.…. Some of the residents sit in groups of five at the library tables to browse through a variety of books and compare notes on certain issues. Many of the residents do not have access to the computer or internet at the complex, so this is why they like to come to the library. They use the internet where there are volumes of information about everything. Mrs. Pickwell has three computers and internets in the Community Room but they are always in use.

Several of the residents signed up for free computer and internet classes while the remainder of the residents are pretty well adapted to the world of computers and internets. A few of the other residents went to the technology department to sign up for genealogy classes at a later date. They like to trace their ancestry as far back as they can go and then share it with their family and friends.

The bus came at 11:00AM to pick the residents up and take them back to the apartment complex. Most of them are tired and ready to eat their dinner and take a nap.

This evening is the annual St. Patrick's Day pot-luck supper at 5:30PM in the Barker Dining Hall. Most of the residents prepared their favorite Irish stew, casserole, potatoes, dessert etc. yesterday because they knew they would be going to the library this morning and wouldn't have as much time. Everybody brought their hot dish to the Barker Dining Hall promptly at 5:30PM and proceeded to pick up their favorite Irish foods in the receiving line. Sue brought her scrumptious Irish stew while Mrs. Tyler brought a pie for dessert and Mrs. Speer brought a potato casserole. Mrs. Pickwell furnished the drinks and different types of bread. Everybody enjoyed the meal and to highlight the evening Mrs. Pickwell invited the residents to the Community Room for an evening of movie entertainment for the benefit of those who were of Irish descent which were quite a number. The O'Hara's, the O'Malley's and the O'Riley's just to mention a few. The movie was based on the scenery and lifestyle of the people of Ireland and beyond. After the movie was over several of the residents arose and told of their experiences when they went to visit their homeland of Ireland. After the question and answer period was finished the residents picked up the remainder of their food and went back to their apartments remarking among themselves, "We all had such an enjoyable time this evening. The meal was delicious and the movie was very entertaining" they all agreed.

Who Made that Call?

Things have been going pretty smooth since Mr. Pickwell's death in the middle of February. No killings, no murders, no attacks, no scares of any sort. Maybe that part of life at the Pickwell Apartment Complex is over. We hope so! Right?

Mrs. Pickwell was working in her office this afternoon when the phone rang and she answered, "Hello...Hello...Hello, Who's calling, please?" The voice on the other end of the line said, "A bomb is set to go off in the apartment complex this afternoon." Click! Mrs. Pickwell said again, "Hello…Hello…Hello, Who is this?" Other than the dial tone there was dead silence. Mrs. Pickwell laid the receiver on the hook not knowing what to think. She was overcome with emotion and scared for herself and the residents. She quickly got on the intercom and made the following announcement: "All residents please listen carefully: I received a bomb threat by phone a few minutes ago, saying a bomb is set to go off sometime this afternoon. Please evacuate the building immediately. Take any personal items that you wish with you, walk single file out the front lobby door, cross the street and wait. Please hurry! I have already called the police and they in turn have called an army base close by to detonate the bomb if one is found. Go now!" The residents quickly grabbed personal belongings, lined up single file, headed out the door and across the street. Most of them were scared and a few were crying as usual. The police and fire department arrived, entering the complex before anybody else, hoping the residents have all evacuated. By now onlookers have congregated in front of the complex and were told by the police, "Please stand across the street where it is safer. You're never to stand in front of a building in a situation like this because it is dangerous." The onlookers were mad because they wanted to get a firsthand look but continued to go across the street. The police surrounded the complex with yellow crime tape and a No Trespassing sign. After awhile the police and firemen came out of the complex and handed a small box to a soldier from an army base close by. He left immediately with a small group of soldiers to detonate the bomb in an open area outside of St. Louis. They called back to the police at the complex and told everyone, "We just received word from the soldiers that were here from a nearby army base that they detonated the bomb in an open area outside of St. Louis and everything is fine. The residents can go back into their apartments now. Thank you!" The residents were just entering the complex again when Sue walked up and said, "What happened here this afternoon? I just got off the bus from my job downtown." Mrs. O'Hara said, "Someone called in a bomb threat to Mrs. Pickwell's office this afternoon and we all had to evacuate. The police and fire department found the bomb and some soldiers from an army base close by detonated it in an open area outside of St. Louis. We can go back in now because we were told everything's fine. So that's where we're headed." Sue said, "Oh, my goodness! I wonder if it was announced on the radio this afternoon but then we probably didn't have the radio turned up loud enough. The nerve of some people!"

The next day Mrs. Pickwell contacted the phone company in hopes of finding out who made the bomb threat telephone call to the apartment complex. They told her it couldn't be traced because it was a blocked call from a cell phone. So there was no way of telling who it was.

Monthly Meeting—April, 2008

Everybody filed into the All Purpose Room this evening for the 7:00PM monthly meeting. Mrs. Pickwell is starting the meeting from now on with a nondenominational prayer because of all the fearful events that have taken place lately. The meeting was started by addressing the first issue on the agenda which is the investigation at the postal department and her visit with Chief of Police, Mr. Rhine. Mrs. Pickwell stated, "The postal department told me there's no way the sender of Mr. Pickwell's box can be traced because there was no name in the left hand corner of the box. I also realize they cannot remember every person that comes into the post office every day and I don't expect them to. So that's a dead end. Next I visited with Chief of Police, Mr. Rhine, in his private office at the police station. He said they have explored all avenues in regards to Mr. Pickwell's case and they have also reached a dead end. If something new comes up in regards to my husband's case they will notify me immediately. I just thought I'd brief everybody on my husband's case so you know what's taking place.

The second issue on the agenda is the bomb threat that took place last week. I personally called the phone company to see if the call could be traced and they said no because it was a blocked call coming from a cell phone. So there's no way of knowing who made that call. By the way, did anybody see a strange character in the complex at any time lately? Please raise your hand." No hands went up so Mrs. Pickwell said, "Very well then." She did make a remark, "That's strange though. How would the bomb have gotten into the apartment complex then? Someone had to bring it in. There's no other way. I hope this doesn't happen again. What a scare! If any of you get a bomb threat call at your apartment please call me immediately. Don't waste a minute's time.

The third issue on the agenda this evening has to do with the rent and water bill. There are some of you here tonight that have not paid your rent or water bill for the month of April. Today is April 21 and your rent and water bill were due on April 1 because you always pay one month in advance. Those of you and you know who you are that have an overdue payment please take care of it immediately. From now on resolve to make your payment by the first of the month.

The fourth issue on the agenda tonight has to do with your mealtimes. I have mentioned numerous times that some of you are as late as fifteen minutes for your breakfast and dinner meal. That causes you to sit longer than expected after your mealtime is over and the kitchen staff is ready to clear the tables.

Also the other day from my office I heard exceptionally loud screaming coming from the tables. I cannot accept that kind of behavior in this apartment complex because periodically we have state inspectors visit our retirement center. I wouldn't want my business to get a poor rating because of several loud residents. Are there any questions or comments this evening?"Mrs. Gray raised her hand. Mrs. Pickwell said, "Yes, Mrs. Gray, what is your question?" Mrs. Gray said, "Is our water bill always due the same day as our rent?" Mrs. Pickwell said, "Yes, your water bill is always due the same day as your rent, the first of every month. Any other questions?" Mrs. Nole raised her hand and asked, "Will we ever be allowed to have pets in our apartments?" Mrs. Pickwell said, "No pets will ever be permitted in the apartments as long as I'm the owner. This concludes our monthly meeting for April. Thank you and Good evening."

As the residents were leaving the All Purpose Room some of them were mumbling and grumbling between themselves. The issues that Mrs. Pickwell referred to were met with dissatisfaction among the residents. Sue made the comment, "I can't pay my rent and water bill by the first of every month because I don't get my paycheck until the seventh of the month. I thought I told Mrs. Pickwell this but maybe I'd better remind her again." Mrs. Nole also made a comment, "Please don't repeat this but as soon as I can get a different apartment where I can have a pet I'll be leaving. When I lived in my own home I, my husband and family had a pet for as long as I can remember. There such a joy to have around besides the companionship." Mr. Eber was walking behind Sue and her friends and he made the remark, "Did anybody notice how firm Mrs. Pickwell was about every issue, almost to the point of being angry at the residents?" Sue and her friends nodded yes and Mr. Eber said, "Mrs. Pickwell's personality has changed since her husband passed away. Her depression has improved but her mood swings leave a lot to be desired." Sue and her friends agreed wholeheartedly. By this time they had all reached their apartments to retire for the evening.

Sunday Services and Festival—April 2008

The bus picked up the residents for the New Baptist Church services at 10:00AM on Morley Street in downtown St. Louis. It's a beautiful day with temperatures to exceed 75 degrees plus a slight breeze. The residents brought along a covered dish for the pot luck dinner they would be attending at the church festival as soon as services are over. When the bus reached the festival grounds the residents immediately took their covered dish to the pot luck dinner area and back into the church. After services were over Pastor Renton invited the congregation to the festival for an afternoon consisting of a pot luck dinner, booths with various games and prizes, Bingo, a chance to purchase raffle tickets for large prizes, etc.

The residents enjoyed the pot luck dinner mingling with new acquaintances they met since their attendance at the New Baptist Church. They also meandered around the festival grounds playing games, eating ice cream cones and playing Bingo while others bought raffle tickets for the 4:00PM drawing. Mrs. Blake got lucky and won the third prize of $100.00 in cash at the drawing a few minutes before the bus arrived to take them back to the complex. On their way back Sue said, "I really enjoyed going to the festival this afternoon. The weather was very accommodating, the food was delicious and the booths, games, Bingo and the local singers were very entertaining. Don't you all agree?" Everybody in the bus nodded in agreement, especially Mrs. Blake laughed saying, "I enjoyed the festival today because of the third prize of $100.00 in cash that I won at the drawing." Everybody laughed and agreed telling her how lucky she was that she won. It's not that easy to win with so many tickets being sold. "The proceeds from the festival will be used to refurbish the New Baptist Church on the outside this summer," according to Pastor Renten's announcement from the pulpit this morning.

After supper in their apartments the residents went to the All Purpose Room to watch the news on KIBX television. After the local news was over the weather report followed with heavy rain most of the week and localized flooding in the area of the Pickwell Apartment Complex. Day time temperatures will be in the seventies.

Chapter 16
Earthquake and Flooding
May, 2008

Sue was awakened during the night with the heavy rain so she got up extra early because of this. She quickly turned television on to get the local weather report. The announcer said, "At present St. Louis is experiencing a torrential downpour and the downtown area is flooding fast. Anybody that works between Dickerson and Farley Streets or in that area will be advised not to enter until further notice. Also, please refrain from calling a taxi since they are unable to enter the flooded area. Downtown traffic is discouraged and streets are cordoned as policemen are directing traffic out of the flooded area. Sue knew she would not be able to get to work because Green Financial Services where she is employed is right off of Dickerson Street. Sue thinks, "What a mess! How long will this last? When will I be able to go back to work? This could go on for a week or more if it doesn't stop raining. I will surely notice this on my next paycheck because I can't afford to miss any days of work anymore. I'm sure I'll be in a bind again. What shall I do? I'm just living paycheck to paycheck because of my medication and other expenses." Thoughts run rampant in Sue's mind as she looks out her front room window. The curb is beginning to fill up in front of the complex as the skies are unleashing torrents of rain on a city that is already inundated with flood waters beyond belief. The sky is beginning to darken as the raging waters keep pouring down.

Sue hurriedly eats breakfast in her apartment, calls Mr. Green at his residence since he is unable to get to work saying, "Mr. Green, this is Sue calling to tell you that I'm unable to come to work today because of the flooding situation. I'm sorry." Mr. Green said, "That's fine, Sue. Everybody from the office called in today and excused themselves from work because it is weather related. As soon as the flood waters recede around our office downtown we will be able to go back to work again. Thank you for calling." They said "goodbye" and hung up. Sue continued on down to the All Purpose Room where more residents than usual were gathered in front of the television watching the news and weather report. Various residents said they had to cancel their doctor and dentist appointments. Several residents also had to cancel appointments with their attorneys while others had to make a trip to the supermarket etc…Some of the residents at the Pickwell Apartment Complex still drive their own car so they are all stranded. The lakes and rivers were overflowing with water causing major flooding in the city of St. Louis. The water downtown has receded to the point of allowing traffic to move and businesses to reopen their stores and offices. Sue has gone back to work and everything in the city is back to normal.

Sue Visits Jane—May, 2008

Sue decided that it's been a long time because of all the things that have transpired since she's seen or talked to her mother, Jane, so it's time to pay her a visit. She hopes her mother is in better spirits than she was the last time she visited her. Jane is always very despondent when Sue is there. Why? Because she has no one personal to confide in besides Sue and she gives Jane the hope and encouragement she needs to cope with her life in prison. Sunday Sue takes the 1:00PM bus to the St. Louis Prison for Women arriving at 1:30PM and departing at 2:30PM. Sue met Jane in the Visitation Room and both of them talked by phone. Jane asked her mother, "How have you been, Mother? It's been quite a long time since I've been here last. Anything new?" Jane replied, "Well, I've been very depressed as usual and I was told that if I don't get any better they will be giving me shock treatments to my head which is supposed to help me forget some of the things that are bothering me so much. They also told me that shock treatments have been around for years. Do you know any news, Sue?" Sue said, "Yes, as a matter of fact, a lot of news. Mrs. Cole was pushed down the stairs at the complex by some strange force and received a concussion on her head but she is fine now. None of the residents would do such a thing even though she felt two hands push on her back as she fell forward. We think it's the ghosts that infiltrated the apartments again. Remember I told you that one of the ghosts appeared to me and said, "I'd better not report this or I will die for sure. It was awful." Jane said, "Oh Sue, I've never heard about the ghosts before. I'm sorry to hear about that." Sue continued, "Also, since I've last seen you, mother, seventeen of the zombies were captured in Richmond Park trying to kidnap families. The police transported them to St. Louis Memorial Hospital and re-injected them with a deadly virus and reburied them in Potter's Field Cemetery.

Now listen to this, mother, on Halloween night ninety year old Mr. Rimm got eaten by an alligator in the elevator. One half of his body was eaten while the other half, his head and chest, lay in a corner." Jane said, "Oh no! How awful! Have the police been investigating the case?" Sue said, "Yes, but they haven't been able to come up with anything. Only a crazy person would bring an alligator into an elevator. Something equally bad happened two weeks before Christmas to Mr. Pickwell, my landlord's husband. Evidently he was kidnapped while walking home from a local café on Binny Street where he went every morning for coffee with his friends. He was missing for quite awhile when a box was delivered one day by the postal department to the complex. Guess what was in it?" Jane said, "I have no idea." Sue said, "Mr. Pickwell's body all chopped in small cubes and his head with his eyes open was placed in the center of everything." Jane had tears in her eyes as she said, "Sue, that's terrible. Poor Mrs. Pickwell!" Sue said, "That's correct, mother. Poor Mrs. Pickwell wound up in the hospital with stomach problems and a bad depression. She is back at the complex now but she's not the same as before. Her stomach problems are over and her depression is greatly improved but she is suffering from a case of difficult mood swings. Everybody at the complex has noticed this." Jane said, "Sue, one thing you're telling me is worse than the next. How awful! I had no idea all this was going on." Sue said, "We also had a bomb threat while I was at work one day. Everybody is fine because they found the bomb and some out of state soldiers detonated it in an open field outside of St. Louis. The police investigated the case and it was a "blocked call" that was placed to Mrs. Pickwell's office in regard to the bomb. So there's no way it can be traced as to who made the call. Some people are very smart at those things." Jane made the remark, "I can't believe all that's happened since I've seen you last, Sue. I'm getting scared for you. Aren't you scared, Sue?" Sue said, "Well, I'm a little apprehensive but I'm also very careful." I guess I'd better be leaving, mother, because the bus comes at 2:30PM and I don't want to be late." Sue left with her mother watching, tears glistening in her eyes as usual. Jane thought to herself, "If only I could see Sue oftener. It's such a long wait between visits. But this is the price I have to pay for my wrongdoing. Prison for the rest of my life with no chance for parole. What a life!"

Wrongful Death?—June 2008

Mrs. Pickwell received a letter in the mail today from the attorney of Mr. Joe Rimm's two children from Kansas City, Missouri. Mr. Arnold Pile and Mrs. Heather Day have filed a consecutive lawsuit against Mrs. Pickwell in the wrongful death of their father Mr. Joe Rimm. Mr. Rimm was eaten alive in the elevator by a smaller than average man eating alligator while no one came to his rescue until it was too late. Mr. Rimm's two children cited negligence on Mrs. Pickwell's part to have something like this happen. Since so many different violent crimes of kidnapping, murder, etc…. have been committed a policeman should be posted at the elevator, plus all six floors of the complex because people's lives are at stake. Various people have been snatched at an alarming rate because of the inconsideration of the landlord, Mrs. Joan Pickwell. The family of Mr. Joe Rimm, Mr. Arnold Pile and Mrs. Heather Day are filing a lawsuit against Mrs. Joan Pickwell in the sum of $3,000,000.00 for the wrongful death of their father, Mr. Joe Rimm. If the defendant is not in agreement with the following terms, the plaintiff has no recourse except a trial on an appointed court date yet to be determined. Mrs. Pickwell was very upset when she read the letter because she does not have that kind of money. Should she go to the bank and borrow the money because their credit has always been good? What do you think? That's a lot of money, isn't it? I don't know what I would do. Mrs. Pickwell has a few days to decide before the appointed court date. Tomorrow morning she will make an appointment with her own personal attorney for some financial advice as to go to the bank and borrow the money or to appeal the case in court.

The next morning Mrs. Pickwell was scheduled for an appointment in the afternoon because of another client's cancellation at 2:00PM, which suited her just fine. She wants to put everything behind her and go on with her life. Mrs. Pickwell met with her attorney, Mr. Slide, and he suggested, "Mrs. Pickwell, I strongly suggest that you borrow three million dollars from the bank as compensation for the wrongful death of Mr. Rimm. If a court case proceeds your recompense might very well exceed the written amount. I'm very sorry this happened to you but that is my legal suggestion. Naturally, Mrs. Pickwell decided to take his advice and said, "Mr. Slide, I guess I have no other choice like you mentioned but to borrow the money from my bank, make the payments and close the case. Thank you for your legal advice." Mrs. Pickwell left her attorney's office to go to the bank to make the transaction and then back to the apartment complex. What a day! She should've been more careful! After all a life was lost! How about that?"

As if things weren't bad enough for Mrs. Pickwell, in the next day's newspaper, the St. Louis Gazette, was a large article about Mrs. Pickwell's lawsuit in the amount of three million dollars. It was for the wrongful death of Mr. Joe Grimm filed by his two children, Mr. Arnold Pile and Mrs. Heather Day. In addition to being in the newspaper it was on the radio and national television because of the amount of the lawsuit. It was a cause for embarrassment and shame to Mrs. Pickwell because the residents are well aware of what happened. Nobody mentioned anything but how could they miss it? Her depression has gotten worse and her stomach pains have started back up again. Since this happened her medication isn't working anymore and her symptoms are worse than ever. She went back to Dr. Byrd, her physician, for an appointment and he immediately admitted her to St. Louis Memorial Hospital for observation and treatment. Mrs. Amble is in charge of the apartment complex while Mrs. Pickwell is in the hospital.

Mrs. Amble called an emergency meeting to order after she heard the news about Mrs. Pickwell being in the hospital. After the residents were seated Mrs. Amble said, "This is an emergency meeting this evening because of what happened today." Everybody looked startled wondering, "What happened today that we weren't aware of?" Mrs. Amble continued, "Mrs. Pickwell was admitted to St. Louis Memorial Hospital this afternoon because of her depression and stomach pains. Her medication hasn't been working anymore therefore Dr. Byrd thought it best to admit her to the hospital for further testing. I will update you on her condition as time progresses. If anybody wishes to visit Mrs. Pickwell do so at your own discretion. Her room number is 302. My advice is to call the nurse's station and inquire about her condition. Thank you. Good evening."

The next several days brought dire results in regards to her depression. Mrs. Pickwell will receive a series of shock treatments to her head to rid her of the thoughts and worries that are plaguing her at this time. They have been known to work on a wide variety of patients. Mrs. Pickwell will receive stronger medication for her stomach pain which is related to heartburn and she will be dismissed in several days. Since she will be back in a short time it really doesn't pay for the residents to visit her because she needs all the rest she can get. This time she was in worse shape at the hospital than the time before.

Several days have lapsed and Mrs. Pickwell is back at the complex again but not back to work. As usual, the residents welcomed her back saying, "We're glad to have you back, Mrs. Pickwell. We missed you!" Mrs. Pickwell said, "And I'm glad to be back among all of you. There's nothing like "Home Sweet Home" as everybody broke into laughter and remarks. Mrs. Pickwell said, "While I was at the hospital I received some treatments for depression and stronger medication for my stomach pain. I plan to be back to work after a few days of bed rest. In the meantime Mrs. Amble will be taking my place as your landlord until I'm able to resume my regular duties. Now I think I will go to my room, if you'll excuse me, for some much needed bed rest. Thank you for everything once again. I deeply appreciated it. Goodnight, everybody." Everybody said, "Goodnight" as Mrs. Pickwell left the All Purpose Room.

Earthquake—June 2008

The next morning at breakfast finds everybody chatting about the coming activities for the week that they would be involved in, in the midst of their bacon, eggs and sweet rolls. In the middle of their conversation plates and silverware are beginning to rattle, cups are falling to the floor while a plate of sweet rolls slides off the table. The residents are yelling, "It's an earthquake! It's an earthquake! Let's watch television." They all jumped up from the breakfast table, their meal unfinished and headed for the All Purpose Room as the rumble continued and dishes kept falling. Some residents went to their apartments to evaluate the damage done to their expensive knick knacks coming back saying, "A lot of my heirlooms are broken to pieces and can't be salvaged anymore. There was no insurance on them and now they're gone. Just broken bits of glass lying all over." There was a repetition of this complaint for the rest of the day as everybody lost their prized knick knacks while watching television for news of the earthquake that rattled St. Louis. The announcer on Channel KIBX broke in the program and gave a full detailed account of the devastation that rocked the city of St. Louis for twenty minutes. Downtown buildings were swaying with motion while people were screaming and fearing for their lives. As the electricity went off in the tall office buildings people that were confined to elevators were screaming, crying and beating on the doors saying, "Help! Help! Let Us Out! Help!" while others are praying amongst themselves for their safety.

The rumbling and rattling have stopped and there is dead silence in the air, ominous dark clouds overhead and a premonition of more to follow.

What happened to Sue? Did she go to work this morning? Did she catch the bus? Someone called to Green Financial Services where she works and Sue answered saying, "The bus picked me up at 7:30 AM this morning and the tremors from the earthquake started after I walked into the office. Some of the downtown buildings are damaged but none of them collapsed. Our building isn't quite as tall as some of the others so it withstood the swaying and tremors from the earthquake. I am going to stay downtown till everything subsides and then I'll come back to the apartment complex. I don't want to be caught in any aftershock."

A couple of hours later St. Louis received a series of aftershocks and tremors that shook small buildings and sent pedestrians scurrying for shelter and safety. Traffic was halted as people crossed streets, oblivious of traffic signals and their counterparts. Sirens were blaring from designated areas of the city to alert everyone of the possibility of more aftershocks to come.

Sue eventually came back to the apartment complex by way of the city transportation bus which drops her off two blocks from the complex. After she entered her apartment she got caught up on the news about the earthquake that shook St. Louis proper. A seismograph used to determine the tremors of the earthquake indicated 5.2 on the Richter scale. At this point everything seems to have subsided for now, as views of the downtown area are reporting everything has returned to normal with the exception of the damage, of course.

This evening many of the residents, plus Mrs. Pickwell, gathered in the All Purpose Room to watch the special report on television about the earthquake that shook the city of St. Louis at a measurement of 5.2 on the Richter scale. Neighboring communities outside of St, Louis also felt the tremors and were affected by wide cracks on country roads and in outlying areas.

Mrs. Blake said, "Sue, weren't you scared in your office downtown this morning? After all you never know what can happen anymore. I don't trust anything!" Sue said, "Yes, we were all scared because of some damage to tall, office buildings several blocks away. We all took precautions like waiting the earthquake out in the basement or the storage room. I myself preferred the storage room on the main floor while others were comfortable with the basement." Mrs. Pickwell made the remark, "This apartment complex is considered in the downtown area but not in the heart of downtown where all the tall, office buildings and businesses are located. We are still north of that so that's why Sue has to take a bus downtown to work every morning." Mrs. Pickwell continued to say, "I hope we don't have anymore aftershocks because I've had enough misery to last me a lifetime. First, my husband suffered a horrible, violent death, then I got sued for three million dollars because Mr. Joe Rimm's death of being eaten alive by an alligator in the elevator. In case you're wondering I might as well tell you what I did. I borrowed three million dollars from my bank and paid the lawsuit the other day. I had to put the apartment complex and other investments up for collateral in case I can't make the payments as they come due. Does anyone want to trade places with me?" Everybody shook their head and said no.

By this time the news special on the St. Louis earthquake had come to an end and regular programming resumed at 8:00PM. Another news update will follow at 10:00PM when more will be available. More news reports of damage are coming in than they expected. Mrs. Pickwell excused herself saying, "Excuse me, but I think I'll retire for the evening. I'm planning on starting back to work tomorrow morning so I'll need all the rest I can get tonight. Goodnight." Everyone said, "Goodnight" and continued watching the 8:00PM movie until 10:00PM when the local news and weather report would come on.

Most of the news and weather was earthquake related and would be for quite awhile. An assessment of the damage will be millions of dollars for lack of a better figure. There were no earthquake related deaths in the city of St. Louis or the outlying communities but lots of damage. After the news and weather were over the residents decided to go to their apartments for the night.

Another Killing—June 2008
Everyone is seated the breakfast table this morning at 7:30AM waiting for the first plate of homemade pancakes and sausage to be served. Here they come hot and steamy with syrup on the side. Scrambled eggs are also on the menu for this morning along with some fruit, coffee and hot chocolate. Sounds delicious, doesn't it? Let's eat breakfast with them!

Mrs. Zell said, "We're missing two people this morning. Mr. and Mrs. Adam Blasell didn't show up for breakfast this morning." Mrs. Zell said, "Oh, I know! Once in awhile they walk downtown for breakfast to their favorite restaurant called "Smiley's." They eat breakfast visit with their friends and then walk all the way back to the apartment complex. They told the other residents, "We really enjoy the walk even though it's quite a jaunt. It does our old bodies a world of good." Everybody agreed and vowed to try it sometime themselves.

Well, that's strange. It's dinnertime now and Mr. and Mr. Adam Blasell didn't come down with the rest of the residents for their noon meal. Mrs. Pickwell asked the residents at the dinner table, "Did anybody see Margaret and Adam Blasell anytime today?" Everybody shook their head and said, "No." Mrs. Pickwell said, "Very well then, I'll just go upstairs and if they don't answer I will enter their apartment with my key. Excuse me." When Mrs. Pickwell came back she said, "They didn't answer so I let myself in. They aren't in their apartment and nothings been disturbed. They might be visiting some of their friends here in St. Louis. They've been known to do that every once in awhile. I'm not going to call the police yet because they have been missing for breakfast and dinner only. We'll have to wait and see what happens in the next couple of days."

Well, guess what? It's suppertime and Mr. and Mrs. Adam Blasell never did come back. Where are they? What happened to them? Did something befall them? Did they meet with bad luck? The next morning the residents are seated at the breakfast table again waiting for the French toast platter to be set before them. Everybody is looking around but nobody sees Mr. and Mrs. Adam Blasell. Could they have come home late last night and left early this morning not saying a word to anyone? I don't think so! Not likely! What do you think?

Mrs. Pickwell asked the residents again, "Did anyone see Mr. and Mrs. Adam Blasell at all today?" Everybody answered, "No." Mrs. Pickwell said, "I'm going to call the police department and report Mr. and Mrs. Blasell missing. The sooner they can get an APB out on them the sooner they can be found. This is getting to be a very serious situation and the police department needs to be notified. I wonder why the Blasell's didn't tell anybody about their absence from the apartment complex so the remainder of the residents wouldn't be worried or scared?"

Mrs. Pickwell went to her office and filled out some papers, signed them and forwarded them on to the St. Louis Police Department. She reported that Mr. and Mrs. Adam Blasell have been missing since yesterday morning. A photographer took some pictures of the apartment complex and Adam and Margaret Blasell. The police came out and did some investigating and talking to the residents in hopes of getting some more information. But nobody knew anymore than what they were telling. The police went back to the police station to file a missing person's report and notify the next of kin.

On the evening news on Channel KIBX the television announcer gave this report: "Mr. and Mrs. Adam Blasell are reported missing from the Pickwell Apartment Complex. They were last seen Sunday evening at the supper table eating and visiting with the other residents. Adam is 75 years old, 6 ft. 2inches tall, and thin with gray hair while Margaret is 73 years old, 5ft. 6inches tall; also thin with dark brown hair. They are both wearing blue jeans and white t-shirts. If anybody knows the whereabouts of these two people please contact the St. Louis Police department immediately at 1-623-294-6726. Organized church members and friends of Mr. and Mrs. Adam Blasell are conducting a search party for them. They will canvass the city of St. Louis area and beyond for anything related to Mr. and Mrs. Adam Blasell. After this announcement the normal television programming resumed.

The next day found the search party covering different areas of the city of St. Louis and the outlying communities in search of Mr. and Mrs. Adam Blasell. Nothing has turned up so far. The police department also conducted an extensive search of the city but everything was negative at this point. They combed the city with different leads they obtained but everything was to no avail. There were several sightings but they didn't materialize. Helicopters have covered the city in search of disturbed areas where Mr. and Mrs. Blasell could've met with violence but nothing was sighted or uncovered much to their dismay. In some cases darkness sets in and search parties are halted then resumed the next day.

Still Searching

A good part of the summer will be spent searching for Mr. and Mrs. Adam Blasell but it looks like everything has reached a dead end. The police department has discontinued their search but the case is not closed. A case of this caliber is never totally closed because of the open leads that can surface at any time.

The family of Mr. and Mrs. Adam Blasell were notified and are very sad and distraught at the thought of losing their parents in such an untimely manner given the circumstances. Surviving are a son, Dale, his wife and three grandsons living in St. Joseph, Missouri, and a daughter, Robin, her husband and one grandson living in Kansas City, Missouri. His other son, Rob, his wife and four granddaughters live in Springfield, Missouri. An APB (all points bulletin) has now been released covering the United States on radio, newspapers and television. Flyers have been distributed with their photographs displayed plus information regarding them. Do you suppose they were kidnapped? Where did they go on such short notice? Let's find out!

A month has passed since the disappearance of Mr. and Mrs. Adam Blasell into thin air. Was it foul play? Time will tell because it always does! The 4th of July came and went with a pot-luck celebration in the All Purpose Room and an outdoor viewing of the fireworks display in the city of St. Louis. An array of brilliant lights flashes across the night sky illuminating the horizon with beautiful colors. As the 4th of July comes to a close I think to myself, "Now back to the world of reality."

On these warm, summer nights a group of residents have been congregating on the patio, visiting and discussing upcoming events among other issues. Mrs. Bloxe made the remark, "This doesn't apply to our ongoing conversation this evening but I would like to draw everybody's attention to something I have been noticing lately. Once in awhile when it's not too hot, I sit out here on the patio in the afternoon. I have been aware of a rancid, foul odor coming from an area behind the apartment complex where we are sitting now. It is over in the far right hand corner not far from Mrs. Pickwell's garden. At present I don't smell anything. I mostly notice it when it is hot and humid like this afternoon. I walked over to the spot where I smelled the odor and saw where someone had used a spade to turn the soil several times. Also a deep crack had begun to form on top of the area. No, I haven't reported this to Mrs. Pickwell but I plan to soon. Has anyone else smelled this odor and are we all in agreement in regards to reporting this to Mrs. Pickwell?" According to the residents none of them have smelled anything unusual but they are all in agreement it would be wise to bring this matter to Mrs. Pickwell's attention soon.

In fact, Mrs. Pickwell just happened to appear on the scene because she stepped out on the patio for a breath of fresh air to encounter the residents in discussion. Mrs. Bloxe brought up the issue saying, "Mrs. Pickwell, once in awhile I have been coming out here in the afternoon when it's not too hot to sit, relax and collect my thoughts. I have been noticing a rancid, foul odor coming from an area over in the far right hand corner not too far from your garden. Have you ever noticed anything the times I have seen you sitting out here?"Mrs. Pickwell said, "No, not really."

At this point Mrs. Bloxe invited Mrs. Pickwell and the residents to come to the area she was referring to. She showed everybody the crack on the surface of the soil where it had been turned over a few times. Mrs. Pickwell said, "When I go back into the complex, I will call the maintenance man, Mr. Pierce, and ask him to come over and assess the situation. Thank you for bringing this to my attention." The residents were happy this was being taken care of because they don't need foul stenches infiltrating the air to make them ill. In fact, several residents have been considering moving out of the Pickwell Apartment Complex because of the horrendous deaths that have occurred inside and outside the elevator. And isn't it strange that the St. Louis Police Department cannot get to the core of the killings?

Mrs. Pickwell called Mr. Pierce and he said, "I'll be over first thing in the morning to start digging the area you are referring to and see what I come up with. It will probably be some rodents and snakes that I dug up months ago. Remember?" Mrs. Pickwell said, "Yes, I remember that strange smell that was permeating the air. A couple passing by brought my attention to it. I'll see you in the morning."

Mr. Pierce starting digging at 8:00AM the next morning only to recover nothing after he dug down several feet. As he started digging down even farther with the spade he hit a soft, spongy surface similar to that of a carcass. Mr. Pierce peered into the dark, gaping hole he had uncovered to see a wide patch of hair peeking out from underneath the soil. He was shocked and shoveled farther into the opening he had dug to uncover the body of Adam Blasell with his back to Mr. Pierce. Beneath Adam Blasell lay his wife, Margaret, with her face turned upwards, eyes wide open like she was staring at Mr. Pierce. Adam and Margaret were both shot in the head execution style at close range. Several small rattlesnakes were devouring parts of their bodies while a black spider was crawling into Margaret's open mouth already full of insects. Adam's eyes were already eaten out and a stench was coming from the grave that was unbelievable. Mr. Pierce took off at a fast pace to the apartment complex to report his findings to Mrs. Pickwell saying, "I uncovered the bodies of Adam and Margaret Blasell in a grave. Come and see!" Mrs. Pickwell was aghast at the sight, her face covered with tears, as she let out a loud scream!

Chapter 17
Blasell's Bodies Recovered

With the recovery of Mr. and Mrs. Adam Blasell from the backyard of the apartment complex, a stream of reporters, police and photographers from the newspaper, radio and television station came out for the story and photographs. All day long the television announcer's voice was blaring away regarding Mr. and Mrs. Adam Blasell's bodies recovered from a grave in the Pickwell Apartment Complex's backyard. Not only was the media having a heyday with the Blasell's murders, hordes of people drove past the apartment complex to see where everything took place. Mrs. Pickwell closed the curtains and told the residents to stay away from the windows. The residents were perplexed at the orders Mrs. Pickwell was giving in regards to "staying away from the windows."

The immediate family arrived and had the bodies cremated and made arrangements for a memorial service to be conducted Friday July 24, 2008 at 10:00AM at the New Baptist Church where Mr. and Mrs. Adam Blasell were lifelong members. There will be an inurement at the St. Louis Cemetery for family, friends and a free luncheon to follow in the Barker

Dining Hall at the Pickwell Apartment Complex. They had a son, Richard, his wife Pat and two sons Jake and Jeb. The family is saddened and distraught at the thought of what his parents had to endure at the hands of a serial killer. How awful! The family hopes that the killer will be apprehended and justice will be served.

Monthly Meeting—July 2008

It's time for the July monthly meeting in the All Purpose Room scheduled at 7:00PM. The residents are filing in to attend the meeting as Mrs. Pickwell waits for everyone to be seated. She addresses each issue individually saying, "First of all I'd like to thank Mrs. Eunice Bloxe for being so observant on the back patio in regards to the odor coming from the farther corner of the backyard. I'm always so busy I guess I never sit there long enough to notice anything like she did. If Mrs. Bloxe hadn't noticed the stench Mr. and Mrs. Blasell's bodies might've never have been uncovered. Thank you once again, Mrs. Bloxe." Mrs. Bloxe acknowledged Mrs. Pickwell with a smile and said, "Thank you."

The second issue Mrs. Pickwell addressed is the rent and water bill. As she was saying, "I don't like to bring this issue up again but there are still some of you at this meeting tonight that are back on your rent as far as two months plus your water bill. None of you have made an attempt to come into my office to clarify this matter. I won't mention any names because you know who you are. I don't like to evict anybody but I will if I have to. I won't have a choice anymore."

Another issue Mrs. Pickwell had to address was their behavior at mealtimes. She said in a rather irritating voice, "I mentioned this at the last meeting and I will mention it again this evening. I will not tolerate coming fifteen or twenty minutes late for meals because this throws the kitchen staff off schedule. Several of you are very loud and I heard someone yelling again at dinner yesterday. Please refrain from this atrocious behavior.

Are there any questions so far?" Mrs. Pickwell asked. Mrs. Gray raised her hand, "Are we still not allowed to have pets in our apartments? I sure miss that part of living in other apartment complexes where we were allowed to have pets. I have even considered moving to another apartment complex for that specific reason." Mrs. Pickwell answered, "Like I said at our April meeting, I will not tolerate pets in the apartments as long as I'm the owner. If any of you wish to leave because of this reason please share your grievances with me to see if any adjustments can be made." Mrs. Pickwell asked, "Has anybody else got a question they would like to ask, please come forward?" Mrs. Biggs asked, "How many days in advance do we need to let you know before we move out?" Mrs. Pickwell said, "I think two weeks would be appropriate because that would give us time to reclean the apartment and advertise it "for rent." Mrs. Biggs said, "Thank you for the information." Mrs. Pickwell concluded the meeting for this month saying, "If you have any further questions please see me in my office in a few minutes. Thank you and good evening." Everybody left the All Purpose Room, a few in discussion with Mrs. Pickwell while the rest went to their apartments for the night.

Sue Visits Jane—July 2008

Today is Sunday and the weather is more accommodating, not quite so hot. It's been quite awhile since Sue visited her mother, Jane, in prison so she decided it's time to see her again. Sue took the transportation bus to the St. Louis Prison for Women getting there just in time to see a baseball game in progress involving the inmates. Her mother was nowhere to be seen, so Sue asked a prison official for assistance in locating her mother. In a few minutes Sue met Jane in the Visitation Room where they each picked up their phone and started a conversation with Jane saying, "Sue, I had no idea you were coming today. I'm so glad you're here because I have something interesting to tell you." Sue said, "What is it, mother?" Jane said, "Remember the shock treatments that I was talking about the last time you were here to visit?" Sue said, "Yes, I remember that. What happened?" Jane made the remark, "Well, I have had several shock treatments to my head to help me forget my problems and it is working. At this point I'm not really sure why I'm in this prison." Sue said, "That's wonderful, mother, I'm glad to hear that. Anything to make you feel better." Jane said, "I'm not depressed anymore and in good spirits. Can you tell?" Sue said, "Yes, mother, I could tell the minute I walked into the Visitation Room because you had such a calm, serene look on your face that I hadn't seen in a long time and a happier tone to your voice. I'm so glad for you, mother!" Jane said, "I am too. How have you been with your depression, Sue?" Sue said, "Oh, I have my good days and bad days. Today I feel pretty good. Some days my medication works better than others. I don't know why." Jane said, "Maybe you should consider these shock treatments I'm getting." Sue replied, "Well, I'm seriously thinking about it. Of course, living in the Pickwell Apartment Complex would depress anybody. I'm not the only person depressed there. Half of the residents at the Pickwell Apartment Complex including Mrs. Pickwell herself are on anti depressant medication. There have been too many murders and horrible scenes for us not to get depressed. We had a couple, Mr. and Mrs. Adam Blasell that were missing for several weeks. Finally one of the residents noticed a strange, rancid odor coming from the backyard of the apartment complex. Mr. Pierce, the maintenance man, started digging with a spade and unearthed the bodies of Mr. and Mrs. Adam Blasell each shot execution style repeatedly in the forehead. The police were notified but so far no one's been apprehended.

We also had our monthly meeting and Mrs. Pickwell announced, "Those of you that don't get your rent and water bill caught up could possibly be evicted." Jane said, "Don't tell me your one of those that might get evicted, Sue?" Sue said, "I'm afraid I am, mother, because I lost so many days of work due to the flooding and earthquake. Also my anti depressant medication is very expensive. Everything combined caused me to get behind on my rent and water bill which really upsets me. I might have to start borrowing money from my bank so that I can pay these bills. I sure don't want to get evicted. That would be embarrassing." Jane said, "Of course, it would be. I'm sorry I don't have any money to lend you, Sue, or I would. I don't have any money of my own and I don't have access to any money either." Sue said, "That's all right, mother, because I understand your situation."

Jane asked Sue, "Sue, what did you do when the earthquake started?" Sue said, "I took the 7:30AM bus downtown as usual and when I entered the office the swaying of the buildings and tremors started. I stayed downtown till everything was over because I didn't want to experience any aftershocks on the way home in the bus." Sue said, "Mother, I thought of you that day wondering if you felt any effects from the earthquake?" Jane said, "No, we hardly felt anything because of the brick and steel structure of the prison buildings and we think it was mostly confined to the downtown area." Jane asked Sue, "Sue, was the flood close to the Pickwell Apartment Complex that day? I, in turn, thought of you that day also." Sue said, "No, we were fine in the area of the complex but my job at Green Financial Services was right in the middle of the flooded area, so I didn't have to report for work for several days. Did you have any flooding out here at the prison, mother?" Jane said, "No, we didn't have any flooding in this area at all.

By this time Sue is watching her wrist watch for her departure time at 2:30PM because her city transport bus picks her up at the prison gates. She said, "Mother, I'll be leaving now because it's almost 2:00PM. I will be back again in about a month for a visit. Keep your spirits up and I will try to do likewise. Bye!" Jane said, "Bye" with tears rolling down her cheeks as the 2:30 bus is already off in the distance.

Now Jane has something else to worry about. Why is she in prison? What did she do that has her confined to prison for the rest of her life? This is what the shock treatments did to her mind. They made her forget what she did to deserve prison. Is that good or bad? What do you think?

Sue reaches the Pickwell Apartment Complex after a short walk from the bus stop. The sun isn't near as hot as it has been as she enters the complex. She gets a reprieve from the sun with the cool, soothing effect of air conditioning on her already parched, dry skin. After supper in their apartments some of the residents are congregating in the All Purpose

Room to partake in a card game. The men will play on the new billiard table, some will watch television, while others will just plain visit. And there are always those that will go back to their apartments.

St. Louis Community Theater—Aug. 2008

This evening the bus will take eleven residents to the St. Louis Community Theater downtown to see a play. The residents have season tickets, including Sue, in spite of her financial problems. This is the last night of the play performance with the title, "My Darling Grace."

Everybody enjoyed the two part performance with an intermission in between plus a concession stand for popcorn and a cold drink. At the end of the play the bus was at the front door of the theater to take them back to the complex amidst ominous, dark clouds ready to release torrents of rain. In Sue's mind she was immediately worried about the threat of flooding similar to awhile back where she lost several days work. When they got back to the complex they watched the KIBX news but it was only a thunderstorm or two.

Prayer Service—Aug. 2008

The residents attend Thursday night prayer service every week weather permitting at the New Baptist Church in downtown St. Louis. There is one pastor and several associate pastors because it is a large church with a seating capacity of 1,200 people. Mrs. Pickwell made a special arrangement with the pastor of the New Baptist Church to officiate at the church prayer service every Thursday night. Prayers are said for the apprehension of the serial killer or killers that is responsible for all the deaths at the Pickwell Apartment Complex. After the prayer service everybody rides the bus back to the apartment complex. The bus was packed this evening with twenty five people attending the prayer service. Maybe God in his infinite power will put an end to the gruesome killings at the apartment complex. We hope and pray.

What Happened to Mrs. Pickwell?

Everything has been running quite smoothly lately at the Pickwell Apartment Complex. In spite of all the murders that have taken place no one has been apprehended as of yet. Mrs. Pickwell still feels she has to have an emergency meeting tonight because of complaints that she has been receiving in her office from certain residents. She posted the meeting for tonight at 7:00PM in the All Purpose Room on the bulletin board in the lobby hallway. At 6:45PM the residents started filing in to the All Purpose Room and took their places. At 7:00PM everybody was waiting for the meeting to begin. Mrs. Millis said, "I guess Mrs. Pickwell's a little late tonight. She must have had an extra busy day today. She's always on the go!" The resident's were also waiting for Sue because she is the presiding secretary at all the meetings. Where's Sue? Well, let's wait awhile. Some of the residents do run late you know! Here comes Sue running late because she just got home from work a few minutes ago. Now it's 7:30PM and the residents are still waiting for Mrs. Pickwell. Where is she? This is not like Mrs. Pickwell not to show up for a meeting especially an emergency meeting.

Mrs. Amble, her assistant, excused herself and said, "I will go and check on Mrs. Pickwell and see if she is in her apartment. Everybody stay seated as I will be back immediately." She left by way of the lobby elevator and was back in a few minutes saying, "Mrs. Pickwell doesn't answer her door, her office is locked for the night and I don't have the right key. I asked the staff and they said they haven't seen her all day. I don't know what to say or do. Does anybody have any suggestions?" Sue said, "Well, we can either go back to our apartments or go to the All Purpose Room. Maybe Mrs. Pickwell will accidentally come in and say she's sorry she forgot about the meeting and had other things to take care of. But I don't think that'll happen because Mrs. Pickwell isn't the type to forget an emergency meeting." Everybody nodded their head in agreement to Sue's suggestion and either went to their apartment or to the All Purpose Room to await Mrs. Pickwell's appearance. When Mrs.

Pickwell didn't appear by the time the 10:00PM news aired everyone gave up hope and went to their apartments.

The Fourth Floor—Aug. 2008

The next morning at 7:30AM everyone was seated for breakfast with the exception of three residents residing on the third floor besides Sue Benson and Mrs. Pickwell. Sue left to catch the 7:30AM bus but where is Mrs. Pickwell again? Mrs. Amble said, "Start eating your breakfast and I'll see what's going on." When Mrs. Amble arrived on the third floor, she noticed a small group of people gathered at the other elevator. She walked over there to discover that Mrs. Pickwell was lying in the elevator all night long beaten to a pulp by, as of yet, an unknown assailant. Mrs. Pickwell's eyes are black and blue with several cuts on her face oozing blood. Several teeth are broken out and lying on the elevator floor. Her arms have gashes on them and her body is fatigued and limp. Volumes of blood are gushing from a small knife wound in her neck. At this point Mrs. Pickwell is unconscious surrounded by the St. Louis Police Department which was called as soon as the elevator door was opened. What actually happened was: Three residents that live on the third floor were ready to take the elevator to the 1st floor for breakfast when they noticed that the elevator door was jammed and wouldn't open. That's strange because it had worked the night before. Finally Mr. Pierce, the maintenance man, just happened to be on the third floor and stopped saying, "What's the matter, ladies?" To which they replied, "The elevator doors won't open up. We'll be late for breakfast and we've already been reprimanded for that from Mrs. Pickwell more than once." Mr. Pierce said, "Let me work on the outside control panel, which he did, and the door opened in a matter of minutes with Mrs. Pickwell lying on the elevator floor barely breathing with a deathly pallor creeping over her face. Mr. Pierce called the police and ambulance as soon as he noticed Mrs. Pickwell's grave condition.

Mrs. Amble wasted no time getting back to the breakfast table to tell everyone what happened. She said, "As I speak, Mrs. Pickwell is being transported to St. Louis Memorial Hospital and will probably be put in the intensive care unit. She will ride along to the hospital and spend the night there on a divan or spare bed. Mr. Pierce and his wife will be in charge of the apartment complex until Mrs. Amble returns and they will converse by phone.

When Mrs. Pickwell was wheeled into the emergency room with Mrs. Amble by her side she was hovering between life and death. In other words her life was hanging by a thread. The hospital will put Mrs. Amble in a private room across the hall from Mrs. Pickwell which accommodates visitors that have loved ones in intensive care. Mrs. Pickwell is on intravenous feedings, oxygen, a monitoring device for her vital signs, etc… Mrs. Amble is sitting by her bed watching her vital signs fluctuate from one extreme to the next especially her blood pressure. Her breathing in spite of her oxygen is labored and shallow. She is still unconscious with doctors and nurses hovering over her all night along. They have notified Mrs. Pickwell's family and they are on their way. Mrs. Pickwell is unable to identify her attacker because her vision was distorted when she received severe blows to her eyes and face. She was already partially unconscious when this all happened.

Mrs. Amble was up early the next morning with no change in Mrs. Pickwell's condition. She called the Pickwell Apartment Complex to update Mr. Pierce on her condition saying, "Mrs. Pickwell is still in the same condition as when she was brought into the hospital last night. There is no change. Please announce this when everybody is eating breakfast at 7:30AM this morning. Please tell the residents to keep Mrs. Pickwell in their prayers."

Mr. Pierce said, "Yes, I'll get the message to the residents in regard to Mrs. Pickwell's condition. And I'll mention that you want everybody to keep her in their prayers." Mrs. Amble said she will be back as soon as Mrs. Pickwell is out of danger. Well, the next several days were no better than the first night she was brought into the emergency room. Mrs. Amble has been eating her meals in the basement cafeteria and spending the remainder of the day at Mrs. Pickwell's bedside. Mrs. Pickwell is slowly regaining consciousness as the days wear on to two weeks since it happened. She is barely able to talk above a whisper as one has to crouch down to understand her.

This afternoon Mrs. Amble tried again to talk to Mrs. Pickwell about what she could remember that night two weeks ago when she was attacked and she said, "I don't remember anything except this person kept beating me and screaming, "I hated my own mother and I hate you. I'm going to beat you within an inch of your life today." I couldn't tell if it was a man or woman because the voice was about the same. This person was dressed very sloppily and wearing a dark turban on his head. I remember he was also wearing a long, dark coat to his knees and dark glasses. All of a sudden everything was quiet, the beating stopped and darkness enveloped me. I was unconscious until Mr. Pierce opened the elevator door. I wonder who would come into the apartment complex and beat me like that? Did they know I was the owner of the Pickwell Apartment Complex? Surely it wasn't one of my residents that beat me? Why would they do that? I've never done anything to any of them. I'm sure the police will never find out who did this to me because if it was someone here at the complex they'll never own up to it. If I ever find out that it was one of my residents they'll get evicted the same day. They don't even know yet who killed my poor husband, Mr. Pickwell. What a pity!" Mrs. Amble asked Mrs. Pickwell, "When do you think you'll get dismissed?" and she said, "I don't have any idea. I'm sure I'll have to get better than I am now. Wouldn't you think so?" Mrs. Amble said, "Yes, I would think so. Starting this evening I'll be going back to the apartment complex to spend my nights there and resume my duties until you are able to come back to work." Mrs. Pickwell said, "Thank you for all you've done, Mrs., Amble. I'm glad I have someone I can rely on in times of distress such as this." Mrs. Amble said, "Thank you. I'm glad to be of assistance. I'll be back in several days. Goodbye!" Mrs. Pickwell also said, "Goodbye."

An Update on Mrs. Pickwell

When Mrs. Amble reached the apartment complex she decided to have a meeting this evening after supper to update the residents on Mrs.

Pickwell. At 7:00PM everybody entered the All Purpose Room and took their place for the meeting. Mrs. Amble immediately got to the point telling them, "Mrs. Pickwell is somewhat improved. Her black and blue marks have faded away and her cuts are healed but her disposition leaves a lot to be desired. Mrs. Pickwell said she doesn't think anybody off the street would enter the apartment complex and beat her unmercifully. She said she's not accusing anybody at the complex but it had to be something of this nature. She can't imagine one of the residents doing this to her. She hates to think that someone here at the complex disliked her that much. Mrs. Amble asked, "Does anybody have any comments or suggestions?" At this point all that attended the meeting were silent. After all who's going to tell on themselves? Right? Mrs. Amble concluded the meeting saying, "If anybody has anything to say to me in private regarding this issue please contact me by phone or make an appointment with me for a visit. I can be reached either in the office or in the complex somewhere. Thank you and good evening."

Mrs. Pickwell's Back in the Complex

Mrs. Pickwell was dismissed this morning and Mrs. Amble is bringing her home from the hospital. The residents have organized a get together in her honor with cards and refreshments. When Mrs. Pickwell entered the All Purpose Room she said, "Oh my! What a pleasant surprise! I'm so happy to be back where I belong! I thought of all of you while I was in the hospital. Thank you for keeping me in your thoughts and prayers as I did you. I am greatly improved and not in any pain. I hope none of you ever have to experience the grief and sorrow that I had to endure while I was in the hospital. The residents were listening intently as Mrs. Pickwell reiterated the painful event. As she was saying, "I got a swift glimpse of the assailant as he entered the elevator, grabbed me, spat some hateful, bitter words towards me and started beating me uncontrollably. I screamed because of the fear and pain but it did no good. No one came and the gruesome beatings continued into the evening. I cried and begged, "Leave me alone, please! Leave me alone! He screamed at me saying, "Shut your damn mouth or I'll beat you black and blue which I already have." He also said, "My mother was a mean, hateful, spiteful, old bitch and I think you're the same way." He then said, "I'm not going to waste anymore time on you" and left the elevator. Mrs. Pickwell continued, "I slowly sank to the elevator floor oblivious of what was going on around me. Darkness overwhelmed me as I tried to stand up to regain my composure but I immediately felt myself slipping away toward the floor once more. I lay in the elevator all night long hoping someone would come to help me but that didn't happen. The assailant jammed the door somehow before he left that it couldn't be opened anymore. Does anybody have any questions they would like to ask me?"Mrs. Jenks asked, "Did you actually fall asleep while you were in the elevator?" Mrs. Pickwell said, "Yes, I probably slept about five or six hours on the floor in spite of the pain. Any other questions?" Mrs. Deal asked, "Didn't you experience any hunger pangs while you were in the elevator for that length of time, after all you would've skipped several meals by then?" Mrs. Pickwell said, "No, I lost all track of mealtimes and I was too overcome with stress and excessive pain to be hungry. Well, I guess I'll go to my room now because I haven't had any rest since I came home from the hospital this morning. I want to "thank" all of you for making this wonderful homecoming possible this evening. Thank you for the cards, refreshments and anything else that was affiliated with my homecoming. I'll be getting lots of bed rest for the next several days before I come back to work. In the meantime Mrs. Amble, my assistant, will resume my duties. Good evening to all of you." The residents said, "Good evening" as Mrs. Pickwell meandered down the hall towards her apartment.

Library Day—Aug. 2008

The residents will take the bus to the St. Louis Public Library at 9:00AM this morning in downtown St. Louis because it's been months since they have been there. Those that had overdue books took care of that problem promptly. Some the residents are working on the computers and surfing the internet while others are e—mailing their friends and will hopefully receive an answer on Mrs. Pickwell's three internets if they are not busy. Some of the residents are sitting at the library tables reading books, leafing through magazines, newspapers, etc… Some are in the technology room working on their ancestry while a few are attending a meeting in the conference room. The bus came at 11:00AM to take the residents back to the Pickwell Apartment Complex for supper in their apartments and a quiet evening to themselves.

Labor Day—Sept. 4, 2008

Labor Day is drawing near as the residents are preparing a covered dish for the pot luck supper at 5:30PM to be held every year in memory of this memorialized day.

After everyone is seated Mrs. Pickwell says grace with all heads bowed. Everybody goes through the pot luck supper line to get a portion of their favorite foods before it is all gone. After everyone has eaten Mrs. Pickwell announced, "Tonight we are going to watch a documentary on the founding of Labor Day in the United States.

The documentary will emphasize who the founding father of Labor Day was and which state implemented the recognition and celebration of Labor Day. Everybody went to the All Purpose Room, took a seat and proceeded to watch "The Beginning of Labor Day" unfold before their eyes. After the two hour documentary was over Mrs. Pickwell asked if anybody had any questions in regard to the documentary and they all said no. Everyone thought it was very interesting and enjoyed watching the facts come to life on the silver screen in the form of a documentary. It was truly the history of Labor Day this evening.

Sue made the remark to Mrs. Pickwell, "The residents and myself really enjoyed these last couple of movies that you have shown for us in the All Purpose Room. We wish we could watch movies on a regular basis. Mrs. Pickwell said, "Well, I'll look into that, Sue, and see if that can be arranged. How does that sound?" Sue said, "Fine." Mrs. Pickwell said, "When I reach some kind of decision I'll let you know." Sue said, "That's fine. Goodnight." Mrs. Pickwell said, "Goodnight" and continued taking down the movie screen.

Live Entertainment Concert in Foley Park—Sept. 2008

One place the residents of Pickwell Apartment Complex have never been to see is the Live Concert Entertainment in Foley Park. The bus picked them up at 6:30PM and transported them to the center of town to see this extravaganza. It consisted of live entertainers in concert from Branson, Missouri, Dave letterman from New York City on tour, a live singing group from Nashville, Tennessee and numerous other entertainment groups. Everybody agreed the price was rather steep at $35.00 a seat but the residents still decided to go or else they might never get the chance to see Dave Letterman again.

Intermission was put on hold for 30 minutes and then the Live Concert Entertainment started again. The entertainers even walked up and down the aisle to the amazement of the audience. Dave Letterman also shook hands with the audience, even some from the Pickwell Apartment Complex.

At approximately 10:00PM the concert concluded and the bus picked the residents up and took them back to the apartment complex after a night of entertainment.

Bingo Night—Sept. 2008

The monthly Bingo game will resume this evening since it was cancelled last month in favor of a new activity that was on the agenda. Sue Benson was the caller, as usual, and many prizes were given away. There was an intermission for about a half an hour and then Sue started calling the Bingo numbers again. There was an equal amount of prizes given away after intermission as well. Prizes were donated from the local restaurants, stores that the residents frequented, local convenience stores, etc…some of the business people have parents and relatives that live at the Pickwell Apartment Complex. Some of the residents won Bingo twice and Mrs. Gray won Bingo three times, winning a crock pot, an electric blanket and a set of bed pillows. Among other prizes that were given away were a set of tires, seat covers, an eight piece set of dishes, two lawn chairs, two tickets to the St. Louis Community Theater, two dinner tickets to Pedro's Restaurant and various other prizes. Tonight there was exceptional amount of prizes because Bingo was omitted last month. The residents played Bingo until 11:00PM due to the large amount of prizes plus intermission. More residents attended the Bingo game tonight than ever before which was fine. "The more the merrier!" Maybe from now on more residents will start coming to monthly Bingo games.

Monthly Meeting—Sept. 2008

Mrs. Pickwell has scheduled the monthly meeting for tonight in the All Purpose Room. She is late with her meeting because of her attack in the elevator and her lengthy stay in the hospital. Mrs. Pickwell addresses the residents, "Good evening. I want to thank everyone formally for the lovely cards, phone calls, prayers and personal visits while I was recuperating at the St. Louis Memorial Hospital. I also kept all of you in my prayers every night before I went to sleep."

I also want to thank those that have updated their rent and water bill. It is greatly appreciated and for the few that are still behind I'm sure you'll get caught up soon.

I'm glad everybody enjoyed the Live Concert Entertainment in Foley Park, Library Day, our Labor Day pot luck supper and movie, the St. Louis Community Theater's performance and the New Baptist Church Prayer Service. If there are some of you that missed out on these performances and outings please keep it in mind for the next time.

This will conclude our meeting for tonight. If anybody has any questions regarding tonight's meeting please consult with me in my office. Thank you and Goodnight."

Chapter 18
Mrs. Pickwell's Missing Again

Everyone was seated at the breakfast table in the Barker Dining Hall this morning waiting to be served. Breakfast consisted of French toast, bacon, cinnamon rolls and coffee or hot chocolate. Since everybody decided to go to bed early last night after the monthly meeting for an extra long night's rest they are exceptionally hungry this morning. Mrs. Pickwell has breakfast with the residents every morning so she's probably running a little late. Sometimes residents talk to her after the meeting about issues that weren't brought up at the meeting itself.

Mrs. Gray remarked to the other residents in the course of eating their breakfast, "Did anybody hear a loud bang or crack in the middle of the night? Around 3:00AM this morning? Someone asked her, "What floor?" Mrs. Gray said, "I live on the fifth floor so it would've been on the fourth floor. That's where Mrs. Pickwell, Sue Benson and some others live. We can't ask Sue because she's left for work already." Everybody shook their head and said, "No, we didn't hear anything. I guess we were all sound asleep." By this time the residents had all finished eating and went their own way. Mrs. Pickwell never did show up for breakfast so everybody assumed she ate in her own apartment this morning since she is constantly busy. Even the breakfast cooks joined in the conversation as they were clearing away the breakfast dishes saying, "We haven't seen Mrs. Pickwell this morning either which is highly unusual. I hope nothing happened to her." One of the other cooks said, "Oh, she'll probably show up at dinner time. After all her car is parked in the apartment complex so that means she's in the building somewhere. Right?" The other two cooks said, "Right!" And let it go at that!

Dinner time arrived and Mrs. Pickwell still was nowhere to be seen. The residents ate their dinner and went about their business as usual. Some sat outside on the backyard patio to visit while others chose to take a ride downtown to go shopping while others played cards and watched television. Later on in the day Mrs. Skinner asked a group of residents, "Has anyone seen Mrs. Pickwell today?" Everybody shook their head and said emphatically No!" Mrs. Skinner asked, "Has anyone inquired, knocked on her door or anything?" Everyone said, "No, because we assumed she would be along directly." Mrs. Skinner asked again, "Has anyone contacted the maintenance man, Mr. Pierce?" Several of the residents said, "No, we haven't seen Mr. Pierce yet today. We think he is busy working in the basement."

Sue said, "Mrs. Pickwell lives down the hall from me and before I go to bed I'll knock on her door and see if she's home or not." Before Sue retired for the night she knocked on Mrs. Pickwell's door several times, even trying the lock, but there was no answer. Sue called, "Mrs. Pickwell! Mrs. Pickwell! Are you in there?" There was dead silence. No answer. Sue vowed, "I had better report this to the cooks, Mr. Pierce, the maintenance man, or Mrs. Amble which she did the next morning. Mrs. Amble had the authority to get the extra key for Mrs. Pickwell's apartment which she did and unlocked the door. Mrs. Pickwell's bed hadn't been uncovered or slept in, was still perfectly made and everything looked untouched. Mrs. Amble sensed something was terribly wrong and consulted the remainder of the staff about contacting the police. The cooks and Mr. Pierce are in agreement in regards to reporting Mrs. Pickwell's disappearance to the St.

Louis Police Department. Mr. Pierce made the call and the police came immediately to record the information and file a report on the incident. No one with Mrs. Pickwell's description is on file as a missing person in the St. Louis area or has been in the past. The KIBX Channel 8 news reporter made an announcement plus the radio station announcer brought it to everybody's attention. Numerous photographs and articles of Mrs. Pickwell were in various local St. Louis newspapers stating, "Anybody that has any idea of Mrs. Pickwell's whereabouts please call the police department at 1-749-262-1270. Thank you!"

Mrs. Amble notified Mrs. Pickwell's three children Ann, her husband George, and three children in St. Joe. Missouri, Joe Pickwell, his wife Sharon and two children in Atlanta, Georgia and Arthur Pickwell and wife Heather and one child in Jefferson City, Missouri. The families were filled with mixed emotions consisting of fear of the unknown, confusion and anxiety, not knowing what happened to their beloved mother. Did she meet with an untimely death like their father, Arthur Pickwell? They will be coming to St. Louis, Missouri in a few days to speak with the authorities about their mother's disappearance. Two weeks have passed since Mrs. Pickwell disappeared, no trace of her whatsoever, not hide nor hair. She just vanished into thin air. What do you think happened? Let's find out! Read on!

Mrs. Pickwell's three families have arrived, tearful and fearful for their mother and anxiously awaiting news from the police department in regards to Mrs. Pickwell's disappearance. The police have checked out different leads and nothing has materialized. They have reached a dead end which infuriates the families at this point in the investigation. The families spent several days in the St. Louis area visiting with the police, staff and residents of the Pickwell Apartment Complex. When they left they told everyone, "Please call us the minute you have any information about our mother's disappearance. Thank you and goodbye!"

The next morning after breakfast, Mrs. Amble opened the front door of the complex to pick up the newspaper when she saw a big, cardboard box on the steps. Mr. Pierce, the maintenance man, pulled it into the lobby because it was very heavy and went to get a box cutter. After he sliced the cardboard open and pulled it apart it revealed hundreds of cubes of rotted, rancid, foul, flesh with Mrs. Pickwell's shaved head lying in the middle, her eyes staring at them with her black tongue hanging out. Mr. Pierce and Mrs. Amble let out a blood curdling scream, "Oh no! It's Mrs. Pickwell! Look what they.ve done to her! Mr. Pickwell met his death in the same way." They both cried and lamented the death of Mrs. Pickwell as did the rest of the residents. Most of them looked at the gory sight in the box and then there were those that couldn't bear the sight of Mrs. Pickwell's mutilation. It was truly a horrible sight. Can you imagine seeing something of that nature? What a bloody mess!

Mrs. Amble immediately called the police department and also Mrs. Pickwell's two sons, a daughter and their families breaking the horrendous news to them. Everyone of the family members were beside themselves with grief saying, "We will pack up tonight and leave in the morning for St. Louis. Thank you for calling. We'll see you when we get there."

Mrs. Pickwell's families authorized Mrs. Amble to call Williams Mortuary and have the remains cremated at their request plus an arrangement for a memorial service and an inurement at the St. Louis Cemetery. The luncheon will be at the Barker Dining Hall for friends and relatives. Mrs. Pickwell was also well known, likewise her husband, Arthur, in the St. Louis area being president of the school board for years, an active member of her church, one of the board of trustees at the St. Louis Memorial Hospital and various other committees.

Thursday, hundreds of friends and relatives attended the memorial service and inurement at the St. Louis Cemetery and the free luncheon at the Barker Dining Hall. There was a very large crowd of people that stood outside and waited before they could go inside to eat. Everybody offered their condolences to Mrs. Pickwell's three children and their families upon the death of Mrs. Pickwell under such grisly circumstances.

After the luncheon Mrs. Pickwell's three children and families said their goodbyes vowing to stay in touch and saying, "If any new information arises regarding our mother's death please don't hesitate to call us. Thank you." Before they left Mrs. Pickwell's family went to the postal department while they were in St. Louis because the sender did not put his name on the box. They asked about the name and were told they don't write down names of who sends packages. They told them what was in the box and they were aware of that from the media. They said, "We extend our personal sympathy to you. We're sorry we can't help you any further. If we can be of any help to you in the future please let us know." They said, "Thank you" and left.

What Will Happen to the Complex?

Now that Mrs. Pickwell is no longer with us her family has offered Mrs. Amble a job as the permanent manager of the Pickwell Apartment Complex. Mrs. Amble accepted the position wholeheartedly since she is the sole breadwinner of the family. Mr. Amble has been incapacitated the past several years due to surgery. This permanent position might cause them to sell their home and move into the Pickwell Apartment Complex in the near future. Mrs. Amble will have to confer with her husband on this issue. At their home he can pass his time working in the garden, walking the dog, watching television, enjoying his privacy in his own home etc... in the complex pets were not allowed according to Mrs. Pickwell. Mrs. Amble forgot to ask Mrs. Pickwell's family about this regulation. She will have to contact them soon because she has a variety of questions that will have to be addressed.

From the beginning Mrs. Amble will be on duty seven days a week, twenty four hours a day, until a substitute manager can be hired. Mr. Amble will help with the duties until the position is filled. Mr. and Mrs. Amble live several miles from the Pickwell Apartment Complex and in inclement weather it can be a real problem. It can also be a problem selling your home because at this time homes are not selling good in the St. Louis area. Not many people are relocating because of this.

Sue Visits Jane—Sept. 2008

Just like the last time it's been two months since Sue came to visit her mother, Jane, at the prison. Sue saw her mother immediately the minute the bus pulled up to the prison yard because the inmates were all outside for their hour of recreation. Jane was by herself leaning against the prison building with a sad, forlorn look on her face. Dark shadows creep across her person as she stood idle watching the others play ball in another area. No one bothered to talk to her because they know that she is confined to the maximum security section of the prison.

Jane met Sue in the Visitation Room and they started talking on their phones with Sue saying, "Mother, how are you?" Jane's face began to light up and she said, "Oh Sue! How nice to see you once again. It's been two months since you were here last. My, how the time flies!" Sue said, "That's correct, mother. I have some news from the apartment complex again." Jane said, "Oh! What is it? My news is always the same drudgery, day in and day out. Yours is always different and interesting."

Sue remarked, "Well, last month a group of us went to the St. Louis Community Theater to see a play called, "My Darling Grace." A lot of us residents, myself included, have season tickets for the whole year. It was a two part performance with an intermission plus a popcorn and cold drink concession stand. There was a thunderstorm in progress when we got back to the complex. It was an enjoyable evening in spite of the weather.

Last month we also attended a prayer service at the New Baptist Church in downtown St. Louis. Prayers are being offered every Thursday night for the apprehension of the killer or killers that is responsible for these outrageous murders at the apartment complex. We all hope that God in his almighty power will put a closure to the grisly deaths at the apartment complex.

Now mother, this next bit of news is not too good. Mrs. Pickwell was beaten mercilessly in the elevator by some unknown assailant that has not been captured as of yet. She was left for dead in the elevator all night long because the door was jammed. Mr. Pierce, the maintenance man, worked on the outside panel of the door and it unlatched automatically. Mrs. Pickwell was beaten almost beyond recognition with her eyes black and blue, cuts over her arms and face, dripping blood. A few of her teeth were broken out and she was unconscious, plus blood was draining from a knife wound in her neck. She was taken to St. Louis Memorial Hospital where she was kept for two weeks to recuperate. After her recuperation period Mrs. Amble brought her back to the apartment complex.

Last month the residents, not myself because I had to work, went to the St. Louis Public Library for the day in downtown St. Louis. Some took care of overdue books and others were working on the computer and the internet. A table of residents were reading books and magazines while others were working on their ancestry in the technology room." Sue said, "How does this all sound, mother?" Jane said, "Oh Sue, the activities sound like fun but Mrs. Pickwell's beating is horrible. I hope they capture the person that tortured her like that." Sue remarked, "Oh mother, that's not all of it. There's more to come.

On Labor Day we had a pot luck supper in the Barker Dining Hall and then we watched a documentary called "The Beginning of Labor Day."

One Sunday night the bus transported us to Foley Park for a Live Concert Entertainment featuring entertainers from Branson, Missouri, Dave Letterman on Tour from New York City, a live singing group from Nashville, Tennessee and other performing groups. Dave Letterman shook hands with the audience including several from the Pickwell Apartment Complex.

The residents played Bingo one night last week and I'm usually the bingo caller. Some of the business people donated prizes because they have family and friends that live at the apartment complex. Mrs. Gray got lucky and won Bingo three times. Her prizes included a crock pot, a nice electric blanket, and a beautiful set of bed pillows. Some of the other prizes were a set of tires, seat covers, an eight piece set of glass dishes, two nice lawn chairs, two free dinner tickets to the St. Louis Community Theater, two dinner tickets to Pedro's Restaurant and other prizes. Sue continued on, "Oh, Mother! The worst is yet to come!" Jane said, "Oh dear, what happened?" Sue said, "Have you been watching television, listening to the radio or reading the newspaper lately?" Jane said, "No, not really because of my fatigue at the end of the day and my depression doesn't allow me to do those things. "Sue said, "Well, Mrs. Pickwell wound up missing for two weeks and she could not be traced by the St. Louis Police Department or otherwise. Finally one day the postal department delivered a large box to the Pickwell Apartment Complex. Mrs. Amble opened the box to find hundreds of pieces of chopped, human, flesh with a rancid, foul, fleshy, odor and Mrs. Pickwell's shaved head lying in the middle of the gory mess. Her eyes were wide open and her black tongue was hanging out. Mrs. Amble and the residents that witnessed everything let out a blood curdling scream and then there were those that couldn't bear the sight of poor Mrs. Pickwell's mutilated body. No, I didn't get to see anything because I was at work. By the time I got home her body was already at William's Mortuary." The residents said, "It was a horrible, bloody mess." Sue continued, "Mrs. Pickwell's family was very upset about their mother's untimely death of the same nature as their father and grieved extensively. Before they left for home they went to the postal department and inquired about the name of the sender. They were told that the postal department does not keep track of the names of people who send packages. They were aware of what was in the box and extended their sympathy to the family as they went on their way. Mother, isn't that awful about Mrs. Pickwell?" Jane said, "Oh Sue, that's terrible. I feel sorry for Mrs. Pickwell's bereaved family. Where are they all from?" Sue said, "Mrs. Pickwell's daughter Ann, Charles and family are from St. Joseph, Missouri, their son Arthur, Sarah and family are from Jefferson City, Missouri and their other son Joe, Marla and family are from Atlanta, Georgia."

Jane asked, "Sue, now that both Mr. and Mrs. Pickwell are both gone who will manage the apartment complex?" Sue said, "Mrs. Pickwell's family has hired Mrs. Amble as the permanent manager of the apartment complex. Both parties will have a business relationship by mail from now on. An assistant manager will also be hired in the very near future. If Mr. Amble gives his consent they will sell their home and move into the Pickwell Apartment Complex so Mrs. Amble can be closer to her work."

Sue looked at her watch and said, "Mother, it's time for me to go because it's almost 2:00PM and the bus comes at 2:30PM sharp." Jane said, "Yes, I realize that Sue. We had such a nice visit today. I enjoyed the good news but the bad news was devastating. I will keep them in my prayers."

Sue boarded the city transportation bus as Jane watched longingly with a tearful look in her eyes as always. Jane thought to herself, "Sue is my only child and it had to end like this. I caused the rift between us because of my killing tendencies that I acquired. And now I have to pay for it by spending the rest of my life in prison." How stupid can you be? PRETTY STUPID! RIGHT!!!

Now Where's Mr. Jack Pierce? Sept. 2008

While the residents were eating their breakfast this morning Mrs. Amble asked them, "Has anybody seen Mr. Pierce today?" The residents looked at each other in a strange manner wondering, "Why would Mrs. Amble ask a question like that? He's around here somewhere. He just hasn't come to the breakfast table yet." Someone said, "No, we haven't seen him yet this morning. I'm sure he'll be by shortly." After this short conversation the residents got up and left thinking nothing of the situation.

Everybody is headed for the Exercise Room where a new class of exercising is starting this morning from 9:00AM to 10:30AM. The exercise class is headed by a young, local, volunteer from the Y. M. C. A. by the name of Sheila Slate. The residents got acquainted with Sheila and exercised with her at a steady gait not missing a step. Twenty four of the residents attended the exercising class while the remainder of the residents busily engaged in other activities. Sheila will be coming to the Pickwell Apartment Complex three times a week to teach the exercise class to the residents. The Exercising Room is also equipped with a variety of exercising machines that the residents use quite frequently. After the class was over a few of the residents remained behind to discuss the different aspects of exercising with Sheila.

Dinner is served at 11:30AM so the residents start entering the dining hall at 11:15AM to take their favorite place at the table. Naturally, the conversation turned to Mr. Pierce as someone asked, "Did anyone see Mr. Pierce today?" Everybody nodded no and someone said, "He probably didn't come to work today because he was sick or something. Maybe he forgot to call Mrs. Amble." No one gave it the slightest thought.

Some of the residents went to the All Purpose Room to play cards while others watched their favorite television programs. Some even went shopping at the malls with someone that had access to a car. In this case there are still residents that drive their own cars and are willing to take their friends along. Tonight Mrs. Amble approached some of the residents and asked the same question she did at the breakfast table saying, "Did anybody see Mr. Pierce at the complex today? I tried to call him several times and the phone always gives a busy signal, yet Mr. Pierce lives by himself. That's what seems so strange. Don't you agree?" The residents nodded their heads because it did seem unusual that Mrs. Amble couldn't reach Mr. Pierce at all today. Mrs. Amble said, "I'm going to wait one more day and if he doesn't show up for work tomorrow I'll call the police. I have no other choice." One of the residents said, "That's a good idea Mrs. Amble. There's been too much happening here at the complex not to check things out." Everybody nodded their head in agreement.

Where Did They Find Mr. Pierce?—Sept. 2008

Everybody gathered at the breakfast table this morning in the Barker Dining Hall but Mr. Pierce. What happened to him? Where is he? As the residents eat their breakfast Mrs. Amble comes by asking, "Has anyone seen Mr. Pierce this morning?" The residents shake their heads as if to say no. Mrs. Amble said, "Very well. If Mr. Pierce doesn't show up by this evening I have no other alternative but to notify the police. Besides Mr. Pierce would've called me if he was unable to show up for work this morning. I hope nothing has happened to him. I am getting scared for my residents and my own personal safety and that of my husband Louis. We are planning on moving into the complex in a couple of weeks and Mr. Pierce was going to help us. I hope everything turns out that way. Continue with your breakfast and I'll check back later in the day."

Since Mr. Pierce did not show up for dinner or later this evening, Mrs. Amble went to the office and called the police department to report a missing person namely Mr. Jack Pierce.

The police came to the Pickwell Apartment Complex and checked Mr. Pierce's office with no response and nothing disturbed. They went to his home, broke the lock and entered to find everything in order except Mr. Pierce wasn't there. His car was also missing from the garage and it was not parked in the parking lot at the Pickwell Apartment Complex either. What happened to Mr. Pierce's car?

Several more days passed since this incident and still no sign of Mr. Pierce. Yesterday one of the cooks said, "Mrs. Amble, would you come with me for a minute?" Mrs. Amble said, "Of course" and followed the cook into the freezer department of the complex, thinking there were problems with the freezer. There were problems with the freezer all right but not the kind you're thinking of. When the cook opened the freezer door hundreds of frozen chunks of foul, human, rotted, flesh with dark, small spiders crawling through the chunks lay before them. Mr. Pierce's head was lying to the side with his eyes wide open staring at them and his dark colored tongue hanging out of his mouth half cut off. When Mrs. Amble saw this she screamed "bloody murder" and started crying. All of a sudden she collapsed in a dead faint and two cooks had to take her to the Community Room and revive her. One of the cooks immediately made an announcement on the intercom: "Can I have your attention please? Mr. Pierce's mutilated, frozen body was discovered in the freezer an hour ago. More details will be released later. Thank you."

Poor Mr. Pierce—Sept. 2008

By this time Mrs. Amble was on her feet again resuming her duties. She called the William's Mortuary and had Mr. Pierce's remains picked up, cremated and a memorial service to be held in a few days. The inurement will be at the St. Louis Cemetery. A free luncheon will be at the Barker Dining Hall following the burial.

It was a small gathering for the memorial service and the inurement because Mr. Pierce had no family and was not well known. He was a nice, quiet man and a "man of few words." No, he didn't deserve to die such a horrendous death. Someone is still lurking out there in the shadows. But where? Let's find him!

The police department has received some anonymous telephone calls on Mr. Pierce's death but none of them have materialized. Once again they've reached a dead end.

Monthly Meeting—Oct. 2008

Mrs. Amble posted a monthly meeting for tonight at 7:00PM in the All Purpose Room. All the tenants attended the meeting with the exception of a few in wheelchairs, walkers, crutches etc...

Mrs. Amble brought the new month's activities for October to order. She said, "No further information has been released on Mr. Jack Pierce's death according to the police department because they have nothing to report." Mrs. Amble also announced, "I am officially the new manager of the Pickwell Apartment Complex. Mrs. Pickwell's family hired me before they departed the day of Mrs. Pickwell's burial. Next week we will be hiring an assistant manager and a new maintenance man. We will have a few new staff members with the exception of the cooks, housekeepers, yard man, gardener etc…My husband, Louis, and I will be moving into the apartment complex next week after the sale of our house is completed. We will be anxious to get settled down once again.

Does anybody have any questions regarding the operation of the Pickwell Apartment Complex?" Sue asked, "Is the policy the same regarding our rent and water bill payment?" Mrs. Amble said, "Yes, the rent and water bill payment is due on the first of every month. If, for some reason, your payment is late I want a logical explanation. I see that a few residents are currently not caught up with their payments. They are behind considerably and if they fail to catch up they will be evicted. I definitely want to be contacted in regards to their payment. Does this answer your question, Sue?" Sue said, "Yes, thank you." Mrs. Gray asked, "Is the policy the same in regards to pets here in the complex?" Mrs. Amble said, "Yes, the policy is the same. No pets are allowed in your apartment. If you sneak a small pet into your apartment unnoticed you will be reported and then evicted. All regulations will remain the same as when Mrs. Pickwell was alive and enforced if necessary. Thank you. This concludes our meeting for this evening. Goodnight."

Chapter 19
Invasion of the Zombies

A group of residents decided to gather in the All Purpose Room to watch an interesting, suspense filled movie. It has been advertised for weeks titled "Three Days to Live" starring Tom Hanks, a well known actor. After that they watched the evening news and then went back to their apartments to go to bed. After sleeping several hours they were awakened by a loud rumble that almost shook them out of bed. Sue could hear knick knacks falling off her night stand, chest of drawers and tables in her front room. She got up and switched the light on to find all of her keepsake knick knacks were broken to pieces. The rumbling continued as Sue turned the television to the KIBX channel for the local news. St. Louis, Missouri was experiencing another earthquake similar to the one several months ago. The announcer was giving a news flash about the swaying and loosening of the brick foundation of some of the higher, older buildings downtown. He announced, "Everybody is to stay in their homes until the rumbling has ceased and it is reasonably safe to leave your home and venture outside." All of a sudden the announcer screamed, "Oh, no! What is that coming down the street? What on earth is that? Oh, no! Those are zombies similar to several months ago!"

The police immediately went to the St. Louis Cemetery only to encounter that hundreds of zombies had grappled their way out of the graves and are invading the city of St. Louis as a result of the earthquake.

They are walking in hordes, their backs stooped over, carrying clubs, knives and dripping blood by the buckets. They have a foul, moldy stench besides sporting three inch fingernails as they walk towards the city. Their faces appear to have a grin and their hair are hanging in their necks. What will they do? How many people will they bludgeon to death? What will the police do? Once they reached the city of St. Louis which is three miles west of the St. Louis Cemetery they invaded as many households in the city as they could manage leaving hundreds dead in their path. Every house they entered they left a trail of blood when they walked out. They beat people with clubs, stabbed them repeatedly with knives and choked them with their hands, a grin on their face repeating, "ARG! ARG! ARG! For the duration of the time they were invading the city they left a horrible wake of destruction in their path.

The St. Louis Police Department enlisted the help of the National Guard nationwide to combat the hundreds of zombies that invaded the city of St. Louis. Together with police and the military they rounded the zombies up and had them cremated at different mortuaries in the city. The mortuaries were inundated with hundreds of bodies, some even being sent to mortuaries outside the city.

The earthquake rumble has now subsided and everything is quiet once again. The next morning will be an assessment of damage over the city of St. Louis and the several hundred lives that were lost because of the zombies.

Chapter 20
Capture of the Serial Killer

It's Sunday evening and that means another good movie on television tonight. A group of residents decided to watch the movie together in the All Purpose Room at 8:00PM. At 7:30PM several of the residents were already sitting around the television patiently waiting for the movie to begin. The name of tonight's movie is "The last Roundup" starring Tom Cruise.

Mrs. Amble was seen stepping into the elevator to go to their fifth floor apartment they had just moved into. While she was in the elevator the door suddenly swung open and a weird looking character also entered the elevator not saying a word to Mrs. Amble. You couldn't tell the difference whether it was a man, woman or beast. He wore a filthy, black coat, sloppy boots, a pointed hat, dark rimmed glasses, stringy hair and a vile odor. He was not recognizable because of the mask he wore to conceal his identity. He reached in his pocket, pulled out a small revolver, pointed it at Mrs. Amble and said in a low, indiscernible voice, "Hand over your money or I'll shoot you immediately." At this point Mrs. Amble was the only resident in the elevator with the killer so she thought to herself, "His voice sure sounds familiar. It's now or never. I'll take my chances." Mrs. Amble reached over and grabbed the revolver from his hand and pointed it at him. With the other hand she yanked the mask from his face with a rip that revealed Sue Benson. Mrs. Amble said, "Sue, what are you doing? Why are you all dressed up in this garb? What is the meaning of this? I don't understand!" Sue was nervous and stuttering saying, "Oh, Mrs. Amble this is all for fun. I was going to reveal myself to you before we both got out of the elevator. You know that, don't you? C'mon now!" Mrs. Amble said, "No, I don't know that and furthermore I don't believe that either! I believe that you are the serial killer that's responsible for all these strange killings that have occurred from the time the new Pickwell Apartment Complex opened up. I remember your mother, Jane Linton, is known as the "Notorious Serial Killer" from Rockwood, Illinois killing twelve people, plus three people prior to that when she was much younger. Isn't your mother incarcerated at the St. Louis Prison for Women?" Sue said, "Yes, she is." Mrs. Amble said, "Sue, you have inherited the killing instincts from your mother. My duty to the residents is to call the police and have you arrested immediately." With a revolver in one hand and a cell phone in the other she called the St. Louis Police Department talking to the Chief of Police, James Rhine, telling him, "I am holding one of the residents captive that is presumably responsible for all the killings that have transpired since the new Pickwell Apartment Complex opened up." Mr. Rhine said, "We will be right out to apprehend her and place her in jail right away. Don't let her get away." Mrs. Amble said, "I have her at gunpoint and will be taking her into my office." Both parties hung up and the police are on their way.

Sue Benson's in Jail—Oct. 2008

The police arrived shortly entering the apartment complex to find Sue sitting in Mrs. Amble's office near tears fearing the worst. She has every reason to fear because of her evil desire and traits. The police approached her asking questions, then handcuffed her for the ride back to the police station. Reporters and a camera crew were on hand inside and outside the apartment complex for photographs of Sue as she left the building. She covered her face with a scarf to shield herself from the staring eyes of onlookers as they passed by.

When they arrived at the police station Sue was ushered inside to the Police Chief, Jim Rhine's, desk for initial questioning. Mr. Rhine got right to the point not wasting any time. He asked her the usual formalities of questioning, advised her of her rights, the lie detector test and standard fingerprinting procedures, especially of the gun that was used to confront Mrs. Amble and other incidentals. They assigned her to Maximum Security Cell No. 14 and told her, "You will be brought out for more detailed questioning later." Sue walked into the cell, all gloom and doom, with no anti depressants with her. She could feel the depression engulf her completely. Sue thinks to herself, "What will happen to me now? Will I go to prison like my mother, Jane. Oh, no! This could've been avoided if only I wouldn't have approached Mrs. Amble the way I did. Everything was fine up until now. My mother, Jane, was caught in an elevator the same way at the Rockwood Apartment Complex in Rockwood, Illinois. I myself caught her in the act of trying to rob me. I'm scared! I don't know what to do! There will be a court trial and I'll go to prison like my own mother." A rattling on her cell disturbs Sue's thoughts as she is taken by a guard back to the Interrogation Room for an evaluation by the Police Chief, Jim Rhine, He asked her, "Sue, how could you possibly have killed a string of people in so many various ways? That's almost humanly impossible. I've never had a case like this since I've been a police chief and that's seventeen years with the force. What caused you to commit these heinous killings with such ease and yet such notoriety?"

Sue said, "I have a simple explanation. As far as I'm concerned I know I inherited this killing tendency from my mother. My mother is in the St. Louis Prison for Women for killing three people when I was seventeen years old. It happened about thirty years ago because she was mentally ill basically criminally insane. She also killed twelve people at the Rockwood Apartment Complex in Rockwood, Illinois." The police chief interrupted Sue asking, "Why didn't your mother take any medicine for her condition?" Sue said, "My mother discontinued her medication because it was too expensive, it made her sick and sometimes she just forgot to take it. The police chief continued with his questioning, "Did you have any personal reasons for killing all these people?" Sue said, "Yes, I had a personal hatred for the people that I killed or else they would still be living today. They were all verbally abusive to me, giving me dirty looks, bumping me deliberately with their carts in the hallway, among a variety of other actions. I knew instantly they hated me and didn't want anything to do with me so I decided to do away with them. And that's what I did. Actually, I have no regrets and would I do it all over again knowing the consequences of prison? The answer is "Yes." At this point the way I feel at times life means nothing to me anymore." Police Chief Rhine continued listening to Sue lamenting her plight and finally said, "Sue, after listening to your story I have no other choice but to keep you incarcerated here in jail until your complete court case is over. That includes your admission of guilt, sentencing and your transfer into a women's prison in another state. My assessment of you is as follows: You will be confined to Maximum Security Cell No. 14, visitation by phone only in the Visitation Room and no personal contact. There will be no outside calls but mail will be allowed to and from this prison. Any questions?" Sue said, "No. "

Police Chief Rhine still has an unanswered question he would like to have clarified. He asked Sue, "Sue, how did you manage to kill and chop up three residents behind everyone's back?" Sue said, "Well, that was difficult to do. First of all, I fatally overdosed the victims and then took a knife and started butchering them piece by piece with the head separate. I piled everything in three different boxes and had them sent to the Pickwell Apartment Complex." Police Chief Jones said, "Well Sue, I guess that answers my question. I was just curious. I should know by tomorrow when your case will be taken to court and I will let you know immediately. Now a guard will escort you to Cell 14 and brief you as to the coming days."

One month has lapsed since Sue's admission into the St. Louis Jail. Her court case will come up Monday Nov. 4, 2008 which she is not looking forward to. In the meantime her family has been notified and are already on their way to St. Louis, Missouri. Sue is a 59 year old divorced woman with two children, Albert, 29 still single and working at the Marriot Hotel in Calgary, Canada. Jean is 31, also single and working at the Mitchell Finance Company in Boston, Massachusetts.

Sue's family arrived this afternoon to be with Sue for the trial Monday morning at 9:00AM. They were all grief stricken beyond belief at the thought of their mother capable of so many heinous killings. Jean and Albert talked to Sue by phone with a glass shield between them.

Jean asked, "Mother, how could you torture and kill all those people? What happened to you since we last saw you? It's been a very long time. I can hardly believe you would do something as evil as that." Sue said in return, "Well, Jean it's like this. I inherited my mother, Jane's, killing tendencies and there's nothing I can do to remedy that. It was instilled in me the day I was born and will probably stay with me unless I'm given medication to counteract that tendency."

Sue's son, Albert, was sitting in the next chair weeping uncontrollably, shunning any advances from his family. Repeatedly Albert screamed into the phone at Sue saying, "Mother, how could you mutilate all those innocent people? Once that is broadcast on national television Jean and I will be embarrassed forever. We will contend with that as long as we live. Incidentally, what did Grandmother Jane have to say about that?"

Sue said, "Grandmother Jane doesn't know about my being in jail. Before you leave St. Louis, please visit her at the prison and tell her everything that happened. I am not allowed to make any outside calls to anyone, not even emergency calls because I am incarcerated in a Maximum Security Cell until my court case comes due."

On Sunday Albert and Jean went to the St. Louis Prison for Women and related Sue's story by phone to Jane. Jane was very upset, overcome with grief and immediately got violently ill and had to be placed in an infirmary. At this point Albert and Jane had no choice but to leave which they did.

Chapter 21
Sue's Court Case—Nov. 2008

Monday morning Albert and Jane are headed for the St. Louis Courthouse in Albert's car with him still ranting and raving. Albert and Jane took their seat in the courtroom, side by side, as their mother came into the room with her orange jump suit on. The orange jump suits are typical of the St. Louis Minimum, Medium and Maximum Security Prison inmates. Sue was seated with her court appointed attorney, Mr. Clyde Simmons, that represents the inmates when they don't have a private attorney.

Mr. Robert Cage is the presiding judge for Sue Benson for the length of this trial in the District Court of St. Louis, Missouri. Mr. Clyde Simmons is the victim's attorney in Sue Benson's case. The twelve jurors are in their jury boxes awaiting court proceedings. Judge Cage is approaching the bench to start interrogating the witnesses in the serial killer murder trial of Sue Benson of St. Louis, Missouri.

Our first witness is Alice Cole. The court reporter, Linda, asked, "Mrs. Cole, do you swear to tell the truth, the whole truth and nothing but the truth so help you, God?" Mrs. Cole said, "Yes, I do" and Attorney Simmons asked, "Mrs. Cole, where was Mr. Cole headed when he was on the elevator?" Mrs. Cole said, "He was on his way to the main floor to pick up the mail and then head back to our apartment for the night. When he didn't show up after being gone about an hour, I ventured out into the hall to hear and see the commotion. I said to someone, "What's going on here today? Why is everybody standing around?" The other lady remarked, "Mr. Cole was found hanging a short while ago. Mrs. Cole broke down weeping in front of the whole court. When she realized what she was doing she quickly dried her eyes and proceeded on. She said, "Yes, I think Sue Benson, the accused, is guilty of Mr. Cole's murder. Attorney Simmons said, "Very well, Mrs. Cole, would you mind stepping down to be seated?"

Judge Cage announced, "Our next witness is Mrs. Platterson. Mrs. Platterson, will you step up to the witness stand please?" The court reporter, Linda, asked, "Do you swear to tell the truth, the whole truth and nothing but the truth so help you, God?" Mrs. Platterson said, "Yes, I do" and the interrogation started. Attorney Simmons asked, "Mrs. Platterson, do you see anybody in court today that you think could've killed Mr. Platterson? Mrs. Platterson said emphatically, "Yes, I do. I think the accused, Sue Benson, is capable of committing these murders. Her mother, Jane Linton, is in the St. Louis Prison for Women for life because she murdered twelve residents at the Rockwood Apartment Complex in Rockwood, Illinois." Attorney Simmons said, "Thank you," Mrs. Platterson. Attorney Snow also questioned Mrs. Platterson asking her, "Mrs. Platterson, did the accused, Sue Benson, ever befriend you or approach you cordially at anytime?" Mrs. Platterson said, "No, not really. Not that I can remember." Attorney Snow said, "Very well, Mrs. Platterson. Step down and be seated."

Judge Cage announced, "Next witness, please. Mr. John Steel step up to the witness stand." Linda, the court reporter said, "Will you swear to tell the truth, the whole truth and nothing but the truth so help you God?" Mr. Steel said, "I do" and Attorney Snow asked him, "Mr. Steel, will you describe to the court what you experienced on Halloween night as you entered the elevator?" Mr. Steel said, "Well, it was a gory sight, I can tell you that. Mr. Brown was hanging from the ceiling dressed as a skeleton with blood dripping from his face. His complete body including his heart, legs, fingers and thighs were cut off and thrown on top of other body parts on the elevator floor. It was a horrible, bloody mess with blood running on the elevator floor and in the hallway. There was so much blood in the hallway that it was very possible that you could slip and fall." Attorney Snow said, "Thank you, Mr. Steel. Step down and be seated."

Judge Cage announced, "Next witness, please. Mrs. John Steel stepped to the witness stand. The court reporter, Linda, asked, "Do you swear to tell the truth, the whole truth and nothing but the truth so help you, God?" Mrs. John Steel said, "I do" and Attorney Simmons proceeded with the questioning, "Mrs. Steel, do you think Sue Benson is capable of performing all of those dastardly deeds she is being accused of?" Mrs. Steel said, "Yes, I think so. Like they say, like mother like daughter. I think Sue has inherited her killing tendencies just like her mother. That's why her mother is in the St. Louis Prison for Women for life." Attorney Simmons said, "Thank you. Step down and be seated."

Judge Cage announced, "Next witness please step up to the witness stand." Mr. Gordon Grebner came forward and the court reporter, Linda, asked, "Will you swear to tell the truth, the whole truth and nothing but the truth so help you, God?" Mr. Grebner said, "I do" and Attorney Simmons asked him, "What is your opinion of Sue Benson, the accused? Have you or your wife ever been in her company at the complex?" Mr. Grebner said, "No, neither I nor my wife have ever been in Sue Benson's company and we wouldn't want to be after we heard about the litany of murders she is being accused of. My opinion of Sue is very low because of her problem keeping a job, shooting herself, slashing her wrists and various other idiosyncrasies." Attorney Simmons said, "Thank you, Mr. Grebner. You can step down and be seated."

Judge Cage announced, "Next witness, please." Mrs. Gordon Grebner stepped to the witness stand. The court reporter, Linda, asked,

"Mrs. Grebner, will you swear to tell the truth, the whole truth and nothing but the truth so help you, God?" Mrs. Grebner said, "I do" and Attorney Snow continued saying, "Mrs. Grebner, do you consider Sue, the accused, very friendly generally speaking?" Mrs. Grebner blurted out, "No! I've heard her speaking very rudely to other residents and screaming at the dinner table to the point of being corrected by Mrs. Amble. Not only that, when I pass her in the hall she rarely gives me the time of day." Attorney Snow said, "Thank you. Please step down and be seated."

Judge Cage announced, "Next witness, please. Arthur Styles, will you step up to the witness stand?"The court reporter, Linda, asked, "Mr. Styles, will you swear to tell the truth, the whole truth and nothing but the truth so help you, God?" Arthur Styles said, "I do." Attorney Snow asked Arthur Styles, "Do you have any idea who played the part of the beast man the day Mrs. Styles was killed?" Mr. Styles said, "Yes, I have an idea who played the part of the beast man. It was Sue Benson, that's who it was because I've seen her at the Halloween party with that beast man costume on." Attorney Snow said, "A lot of people could have a beast man costume like that one. You can't be sure of that." Arthur Styles said, "Yes, I'm sure because so many other incidents indicate she could be the killer. Why is she conveniently gone when something happens?" Attorney Snow said, "Thank you. Step down and be seated."

Judge Cage announced, "Next witness, please. "Will Charles Blane step to the witness stand, please?" The court reporter, Linda, asked, "Will you swear to tell the truth, the whole truth and nothing but the truth so help you, God?" Mr. Blane answered, "I do." Attorney Simmons asked Mr. Blane, "What was your impression of Sue Benson while she and her mother, Jane Linton, lived at the Rockwood Apartment Complex in Rockwood, Illinois?" Mr. Blane said, "I wasn't impressed with her mother, Jane, at all. Sue's mother, Jane, killed my mother with a pit bull in the elevator. Sue was bossy, pushy and sometimes wouldn't even answer you when you spoke to her. I think Sue has the same personality disorder as her mother, killing instincts etc." Attorney Simmons said, "Thank you, Mr. Blane. Step down and be seated."

In the meantime, Sue Benson is sitting next to Attorney Simmons that represents her in this murder trial. Sue has a sad, sorrowful, depressed look on her face as she listens to the witnesses, one by one, criticizing her. They also think she's a number one serial killer like her mother. What do you think? Have any of you formed an opinion of Sue Benson yet? You haven't!!! Get busy!!! Read on!!!

Judge Cage announced, "Next witness, please. Will Bob Dylan step to the witness stand?" The court reporter, Linda, asked, "Will you swear to tell the truth, the whole truth and nothing but the truth so help you, God?" Mr. Dylan said, "I do." Attorney Snow said, "Do you still work for Acme Plumbing Company in Rockwood, Illinois?" Mr. Dylan said, "Yes, I do." Attorney Snow said, "Tell us what you uncovered in the basement of the Pickwell Apartment Complex that day." Mr. Dylan said, "Andrew, another plumber, and I at the request of Mrs. Pickwell drilled and chopped away at the cement until it was loose enough to move around. I moved a big hunk of cement to uncover chunks of rotting, decayed flesh being eaten by large snakes. Also, the severed heads of Stan, Martha and Lois Shohls lay beside the rotting flesh. It was disgusting!" Attorney Snow said, "Thank you. You may step down and be seated."

Judge Cage announced, "Next witness, please. Will Mr. George Bond step to the witness stand, please?" The court reporter, Linda, asked, "Mr. Bond, Will you swear to tell the truth, the whole truth and nothing but the truth so help you, God? Mr. Bond said, "I do" and the interrogation continued. "Mr. Bond, in reference to the court records your mother suffered a horrendous death of being buried alive. She was cruelly beaten, left for dead, taken to St. Louis Memorial Hospital where she was misdiagnosed as being actually dead and consequently buried. In your opinion, Mr. Bond, do you think Sue, the accused, was involved in your mother's death in any way?" Mr. Bond said, "Yes, I feel that if she did all the things that she's being accused of, she probably had a dislike for my mother and tortured and beat her within an inch of her life. I hope she gets the punishment that she has coming to her because she deserves it. My mother didn't deserve what happened to her."

Attorney Simmons continued the interrogation with, "Mr. Bond, do you or the remainder of your family know Sue personally or have ever had any contact with her?" Mr. Bond said, "No, we have not." Attorney Simmons said, "Very well. Thank you and step down to be seated."

Judge Cage announced, "Next witness, please. Will Ann Sikes step to the witness stand?" The court reporter, Linda, asked, "Mrs. Sikes, do you swear to tell the truth, the whole truth and nothing but the truth so help you, God?" Mrs. Sikes said, "I do" and Attorney Snow continued with the questioning. Mrs. Sikes, do you believe Sue Benson, the accused, was involved in your mother's death?" Ann made the remark, "Yes, I do believe Sue was involved in my mother's death because of the beating and torture in her past history of all the other murders she's being accused of. Also, I firmly believe without a single doubt, that she has inherited her mother's killing tendencies. I sincerely hope that she gets the punishment that is due to her." Attorney Snow concluded the interrogation with, "Ann, do you sincerely believe Sue, the accused, tormented and beat your mother, leaving her for dead, prior to being buried alive?" Ann said, "Yes, I do. "Attorney Snow said, "Thank you. Step down and be seated."

Judge Cage announced, "Next witness, please. Will Mrs. Rane step to the witness stand?" Mrs. Rane hobbled to the witness stand supported by a cane and proceeded to sit in the witness stand chair. The court reporter, Linda, asked, "Mrs. Rane, do you swear to tell the truth, the whole truth and nothing but the truth so help you, God?" Mrs. Rane said, "I do," and court proceedings followed. Attorney Simmons asked her, "Mrs. Rane, can you tell the court exactly what you remember the night Mr. Rane was killed? Mrs. Rane said, "Yes, I will to the best of my ability. Mr. Rane and I went to bed about 10:00PM that night and around 3:00AM we were awakened by an intruder dressed in black and wearing a black mask. He was slinging a long bladed knife over us and screaming at us to get out of bed or he will slice us with the knife. Well, I hurriedly got out of bed but poor Harold didn't make it. The intruder chopped Harold's body up but left his head intact to his upper torso. He immediately ran out a side door and out of the building." Attorney Simmons said, "Thank you." Now Attorney Snow resumed the questioning, "Mrs. Rane, when the intruder spoke did you recognize the voice at all?" Mrs. Rane said, "It sounded like it could've been either a man or a woman because it was hard to tell." Attorney Snow said, "That will be all, Mrs. Rane. Thank you and step down to your seat."

Judge Cage announced, "Next witness, please. Mrs. Joyce Blue, step to the witness stand." The court reporter, Linda, asked, "Mrs. Blue, do you swear to tell the truth, the whole truth, and nothing but the truth so help you, God?" Mrs. Blue said, "I do." Attorney Simmons asked her, "Do you believe Sue Benson, the accused, is responsible for the severing of both of your mother's legs and why?" Mrs. Blue said, "Yes, I do. I believe that Sue Benson, the accused, is responsible for the severance of her legs and death of my mother, Mrs. Cane. I believe this because of the accusations against her in court this morning. If she is capable of doing all those other killings then she probably was involved in my mother's killing also." Attorney Simmons said, "Thank you and step down to your seat, please."

Judge Cage announced, "Next witness, please. Will Mr. Bob Carl step to the witness stand?" The court reporter, Linda, asked "Do you swear to tell the truth, the whole truth and nothing but the truth so help you, God?" Mr. Carl said, "I do." Mr. Snow proceeded,"Mr. Carl, according to the testimonies you've heard today, do you feel like Sue, the accused, was criminally involved in your mother's death and how?" Mr. Carl said, "Yes. I believe Sue, the accused, was indeed involved in my mother's death. I actually believe she cooked the turkey soup that had pieces of a leg in the broth that killed my mother and two of her friends according to a laboratory report. Mr. Snow said, "Thank you" and Attorney Simmons resumed with his question. "Mr. Carl, are you or your family familiar with Sue, the accused?" Mr. Carl said, "No, we are not and we surely don't want to be." Attorney Simmons said, "Very well, Mr. Carl. You may step down to be seated."

Judge Cage announced, "Next witness, please. Will Mrs. Jane Peebles step to the witness stand?" The court reporter, Linda, asked "Do you swear to tell the truth, the whole truth and nothing but the truth so help you, God?" Mrs. Peebles said, "I do." Attorney Simmons asked, "Mrs. Peebles, I want you to point to Sue Benson, the accused, and tell me in your own words what you think actually happened to your mother and the other two women." Mrs. Peebles pointed to Sue and said, "I wonder if that woman, Sue Benson, wasn't the person that severed Mrs. Cane's legs, cooking the flesh from the leg into the turkey soup. In other words, there wasn't any turkey in the soup at all, just the flesh from Mrs. Cane's legs. Then my mother, Mrs. Carl and Mrs. Skills ate the soup and died. I firmly believe this is what happened." Attorney Simmons said, "Very well, Mrs. Peebles and thank you. Step down to be seated."

Judge Cage announced, "Next witness, please. Will Nick Skills step to the witness stand?" The court reporter, Linda, asked, "Mr. Skills, will you swear to tell the truth, the whole truth and nothing but the truth so help you, God?" Mr. Skills said, "I do." Attorney Snow asked, "Mr. Skills, how old are you?" Mr. Skills said, "I'm eighty five years old." Attorney Snow said, "Very good. Mr. Skills, was Mrs. Skills ill before she went to the Thanksgiving dinner?" Mr. Skills said, "No, she was fine when she left. Later on I was notified, as were the rest, about their illness and I went to the hospital immediately. Attorney Snow asked, "Mr. Skills, what do you really think happened to Mrs. Skills in regards to her death? Do you think Sue, the accused, had anything to do with it?" Mr. Skills said, "Yes, I believe Sue, the accused, was involved in my wife's death. I hate to accuse a person but I think I'm correct in this case. Her mother, Jane Linton, is in prison for killing twelve residents at the Rockwood Apartment Complex in Rockwood, Illinois. To this day she is still known as the "Notorious Serial Killer of Rockwood, Illinois. Sue, the accused, I'm sure inherited her mother's killing tendencies. Yes, I think she is responsible for every killing that is brought up in this court case." Attorney Snow responded with, "Thank you, Mr. Skills and step down to be seated."

Judge Cage announced, "This concludes our court procedure for today due to the number of witnesses. Court will resume tomorrow morning at 9:00AM. Court is adjourned for today. Thank you." Everybody filed out of the courtroom while Sue Benson is being taken by a police van back to the St. Louis Police Department.

Towards evening Sue lies on her cot engrossed in her thoughts of life in prison without parole for years until her death. Tears well up in her eyes as she thinks about her mother, Jane Linton, in the St. Louis Prison for Women. She also thinks about her family, Albert and Jean, which she won't see much anymore as the years go by. Sue still tells herself, "I'm not sorry for what I did because those residents that I killed were mean, rude and avoided and ignored me whenever they got the chance. I treated these people with respect and this is what I got in return. In fact, I distinctly remember them holding me up for ridicule in front of everybody one day. That day, in particular, I vowed to get even with them one way or another and I did. I'm feeling remorseful,

not for them but for myself, due to the fact that I will have very little contact, probably next to none, with my family after the sentencing. I will be the same as non existent to them and I'll probably wish I was after I get a taste of life in prison."

Sue ate her supper in her Maximum Security cell and watched several hours of television. While she was watching the 10:00PM news KIBX, a local St. Louis Station, she saw herself on television in regards to the twenty two murders she committed. It is the largest killing spree in the history of St. Louis, Missouri in the course of three years. They have already nicknamed her "The Notorious Serial Killer of St. Louis, Missouri." Sue was thoroughly disgusted but not ashamed or sorry when she saw herself on television. Well, it's the news and Sue should've known it would be on television because it was in court today and will be tomorrow. What did she expect?

Chapter 22
Court Case Continues

Judge Cage announced, "Court is back in session this morning for Sue Benson the convicted killer of twenty two people in the Styles and Pickwell Apartment Complexes. "Next witness, please. Will Mrs. Parker step to the witness stand? The court reporter, Linda, asked, "Mrs. Parker, will you swear to tell the truth, the whole truth and nothing but the truth so help you, God?" Mrs. Parker said, "Yes." Attorney Snow said, "Very well then, we'll proceed. Mrs. Parker, your mother, Mrs. Mission met with an untimely and gruesome death at the hands of a serial killer. Can you point to that killer in the court room today?" Mrs. Parker pointed to Sue Benson saying, "There's the killer, Sue Benson. She knows I'm telling the truth. Go ahead and ask her." Sue looked at Mrs. Parker with a spiteful, hateful look, her eyes dark and smouldering with rage.

Mrs. Parker continued, "Everybody knows her mother is in the St. Louis Prison for Women for life for murdering twelve residents at the Rockwood Apartment Complex in Rockwood, Illinois. Sue is headed the same way with the twenty two murders she has already committed. She is following in her mother's footsteps. She has inherited her killing tendency also." Attorney Snow said, "Thank you and step down to be seated."

Judge Cage announced, "Next witness, please. Will Don Rimm step to the witness stand." The court reporter, Linda, asked, "Will you swear to tell the truth, the whole truth and nothing but the truth so help you, God?" Mr. Rimm said, "Yes." Mr. Simmons continued with the questioning, "Don, Mr. Joe Rimm is your father? Is that correct?" Don said, "Yes sir." Attorney Simmons said, "Don, in your perception do you think Sue was capable of sneaking a 4 ft. alligator into the elevator to devour your father? How would she do that? In all my murder cases as an attorney, and there have been a lot of them over the years, I've never, ever heard of anything like that!" Don said, "Yes, I think Sue is capable of doing something like that or even worse. I remember at social functions Sue thought our family was avoiding and ignoring her but we weren't. My father didn't hear well and she must've got that impression. So, I'm sure she didn't like my dad or the rest of our family. I think if she is capable of doing all those other heinous crimes she is being accused of, I'm sure she was able to devise a plan to transport the alligator from one place to the next." Attorney Simmons said, "Very well, Don. Thank you and step down to be seated."

Judge Cage announced, "Next witness, please, Mrs. Clara Brooks. Will you step to the witness stand?" The court reporter, Linda, asked, "Mrs. Brooks, will you swear to tell the truth, the whole truth and nothing but the truth so help you, God?" Mrs. Brooks said, "Yes." Attorney Snow proceeded saying, "Mrs. Brooks, is Joe Rimm your father?" Mrs. Brooks said, "Yes, he is." Attorney Snow said, "How old was Mr. Rimm?" Mrs. Brooks said, "He just turned eighty seven years old a month ago. Attorney Snow remarked, "Mrs. Brooks, do you agree with your brother, Don, on his perception that Sue was capable of sneaking the 4 ft. alligator into the elevator in a box to devour your father, Mr. Rimm?" Mrs. Brooks said, "Yes, I agree with Don most definitely. If Sue, the accused, is capable of doing the horrendous deeds she is being accused of, then it's possible for her to pull a 4 ft. alligator in a box into an elevator. What would stop her from doing that? Nothing! I don't know her personally but I do know she would've had to have been very careful not to been seen." Attorney Snow said, "Thank you and step down to be seated."

Judge Cage announced, "Next witness, please. Ann Brandt, will you step to the witness stand?" The court reporter, Linda, asked, "Mrs. Brandt, do you swear to tell the truth, the whole truth and nothing but the truth so help you, God?" Mrs. Brandt said, "Yes" and Attorney Simmons began the interrogation. "Ann, in reference to your mother, Mrs. Pickwell, did you ever notice any unusual behavior from Sue towards your mother when you were around?" Ann said, "Yes, I can distinctly remember several times when I was in their presence. My mother told a joke and Sue thought my mother was ridiculing her, glared at her and walked off in a huff. I also remember my mother shrugging her shoulders as if to say, "I could care less." Yes, in my opinion I think Sue is very capable of doing anything if she doesn't like someone. I seriously think Sue has a deep seated hatred for certain people that she thinks don't like her, want to avoid her at any length or when she thinks other people are ridiculing her. She acts like she has a psychotic personality. That's all I have to say." Attorney Simmons said, "Thank you. You may step down to be seated."

Judge Cage announced, "Next witness, please. Will Arthur Pickwell step to the witness stand?" The court reporter, Linda, asked, "Do you swear to tell the truth, the whole truth and nothing but the truth so help you, God?" Mr. Pickwell said, "I do" and Attorney Snow proceeded. He started interrogating Mr. Pickwell's son, Arthur. "Arthur, who in this courtroom is the most qualified to perform the grisly acts that we're all aware of?" Arthur didn't hesitate one minute to say, "That ugly bitch over there that's sitting with her attorney. I'd like to step out of the witness stand, walk over there and wring her slimy neck because of what she did to my father. Her own mother, Jane Linton, is the "Notorious Serial Killer of Rockwood, Illinois" which everybody knows about. I know she killed my father because he told me one day that she either looks the other way or tries to pick a fight with him when she sees him." Mr. Snow said, "Thank you and step down to be seated.

Judge Cage announced, "Next witness, please. Will Richard Blasell step to the witness stand?" The court reporter, Linda, asked, "Mr. Blasell, will you swear to tell the truth, the whole truth and nothing but the truth so help you, God? Richard Blasell answered "I do" and the questioning began. Attorney Simmons asked Richard, "When you first heard your parents were missing what did you think of?" Richard answered, "I didn't know what to think. Maybe they were out taking a walk, got kidnapped at gunpoint and were killed. I also thought that maybe they were kidnapped and taken to a commune like Sue, the accused, was up in Nevada. You never know! Never in my wildest dreams did I think they were buried in the backyard of the Pickwell Apartment Complex." Attorney Simmons asked Richard, "Do you think Sue, the accused, had anything to do with your parent's death?" Richard said, "Yes, I do think so because of the different varieties of killings that she committed. Just looking at her sitting with her attorney with that blank, motionless stare on her face, I don't think she feels any remorse for what she did. I really don't. I only hope that the court will give her the punishment that she deserves and I'm sure they will." Attorney Simmons said, "Thank you and step down to be seated."

Judge Cage announced, "Next witness please. Mrs. Lisa Tyler, will you step to the witness stand?" The court reporter, Linda, asked, "Will you swear to tell the truth, the whole truth and nothing but the truth so help you, God?" Mrs. Tyler said, "Yes, I do." Attorney Snow continued, "Mrs. Tyler, your father met with a gruesome and violent death. These are acts of cruelty unheard of in these parts. Do you think the same as the other residents that Sue Benson, the accused, is the perpetrator of these malicious acts?" Mrs. Tyler said, "Yes, I think the same way. I truly believe that Sue Benson, the accused, is the killer of twenty two people and she deserves to be shackled and hauled off to some bigger facility where she will spend the rest of her life. Maybe that will teach her a lesson or two." We hope!!! Right?

Judge Cage announced, "Next witness, please. Will Karen Pierce please step to the witness stand?" The court reporter, Linda, asked, "Will you swear to tell the truth, the whole truth and nothing but the truth so help you, God?" Miss Pierce said, "Yes. I do" and Attorney Simmons proceeded with the questioning, "Miss Pierce, I understand your Mr. Pierce's only daughter. Is that correct?" Miss Pierce said, "Yes, that's correct." Attorney Simmons went on, "Miss Pierce, "Please give the court your honest opinion of everything that's transpired here today. Do you really think Sue, the accused, is the serial killer that put all these people to death?" Miss Pierce said, "Yes, I think Sue Benson is the killer all right because of her relentless desire to pursue her killing tendencies. She is following in the footsteps of her mother, Jane Linton, that is incarcerated in the St. Louis Prison for Women right here in St. Louis, Missouri. I hope she gets punished severely for all the crimes she has committed. Attorney Simmons said, "Thank you and you may step down to be seated."

Judge Cage announced, "Next witness, please. Will Jacob Siller step to the witness stand ?" The court reporter, Linda, asked, "Will you swear to tell the truth, the whole truth and nothing but the truth so help you God?" Mr. Siller said, "Yes, I do" and Attorney Snow interrogated him saying, "Mr. Siller, your sister, Mabel Siller, met with a gruesome, violent death. The mode of death was the same as the other victims were exposed too. Mr. Siller, do you believe that Sue, the accused, is responsible for all these killings and deserves the title, "The Notorious Serial Killer of St. Louis, Missouri?" Mr. Siller said, "Yes, I believe Sue, the accused, is responsible for my sister, Mabel's, death plus all the others. Her mother was the "Notorious Serial Killer of Rockwood, Illinois killing twelve people like all the witnesses have testified under oath, thinking she inherited her mother's killing tendencies. Well, I agree with that because I think the same way." Attorney Snow said, "Thank you and step down to be seated."

This finishes all the testimonies of the witnesses for the twenty two victims that have been killed from 2005—2008. We will now have a recession for fifteen minutes and then resume the testimonies of the accused, Sue Benson's two children, Jean and Albert Benson. Sue whispers to Attorney Simmons seated by her side as they both glance over at Jean and Albert seated in the courtroom. What will Jean and Albert say about her? Sue thinks to herself, "What can they say about her? She has always treated them well and with respect. Surely they won't tell lies about her! It'll be interesting to hear what they tell the court."

Judge Cage is seated on the bench ready to resume with the testimonies of Jean and Albert Benson. Judge Cage announced, "Next witness, please. Will Jean Benson step up to the witness stand?" The court reporter, Linda, asked, "Will you swear to tell the truth, the whole truth and nothing but the truth so help you, God?" Jean said, "I do" and the interrogation began with Attorney Snow asking, "Jean, were you surprised when you received a call from the St. Louis Police Department in regards to your mother being held in a Maximum Security cell at the police station?" Jean said, "Yes, I was shocked because my mother has never had a conviction or a past record of any wrongdoing at anytime. After my parents divorced my mother moved in with her mother and my brother Albert and I, living with us for several years before going on her own. My mother, Sue was always good to Albert and I, mindful of our needs and helpful in so many ways. This is why it is so hard for Albert and I to comprehend what has transpired these past years." Attorney Snow said, "Thank you. Please step down and be seated."

Judge Cage announced, "Next witness, please. Will Albert Benson step to the witness stand?" The court reporter, Linda, asked, "Will you swear to tell the truth, the whole truth and nothing but the truth so help you, God?" Albert said, "I do." Attorney Snow asked Albert, "Albert, were you surprised when you received a call from the St. Louis Police Department in regards to your mother being incarcerated in a Maximum Security cell at the police station?" Albert said, "Yes, I was extremely shocked at the conviction my mother has had to endure these past years especially if they are false. I still find it hard to believe that my mother, Sue, is capable of performing these horrendous accusations. My mother always took good care of us, was very helpful and was always there for us." Attorney Snow said, "Very well, Albert. Please step down and be seated."

Judge Cage made a remark, "We have just finished interrogating the family as to what they witnessed in years past in regards to the accused, Sue Benson. This concludes our court session for today. We will resume the session tomorrow morning at 9:00AM. Court is adjourned for the time being. Thank you."

Chapter 23
Admission of Guilt

When Jean and Albert entered the St. Louis District Court they were shocked when they looked at their mother, Sue Benson. Sue looked like she had aged ten years overnight, her hair were straggly and unkempt and her attire left a lot to be desired. She was sitting next to Attorney Simmons speaking in a hushed tone not to be heard. Every once in awhile a small smile would light up her face only to fade away to a sad, withdrawn, depressed state of mind. At one point Jean and Albert waved at Sue in the courtroom and smiled. Sue waved and smiled back while she was talking to Attorney Simmons.

Judge Cage went to his bench and the twelve jury people entered their jury boxes waiting for Judge Cage to start the court proceedings. Judge Cage said, "Will Sue Benson step to the witness stand, please?" Sue came forward and the court reporter, Linda, asked her. "Sue, will you swear to tell the truth, the whole truth and nothing but the truth so help you, God?" Sue said, "Yes, I do." Attorney Snow continued with the interrogation. He asked Sue if she has intentions of giving an admission of guilt to himself, Attorney Simmons, Judge Cage and the Court and she said, "Yes." Attorney Snow continued further asking Sue, "Did you actually commit these twenty two murders that you are being accused of today?" Sue said, "Yes, I committed all the murders that I'm being accused of today." Attorney Snow said, "Sue, I need clarification on some of these unusual deaths that you are responsible for. Please explain to the Court the reason you took the lives of twenty two people because it hasn't even phased you. You have this nonchalant attitude about you. Why?"

Sue listened intently to what Attorney Snow is expecting her to explain and she is ready with her answers. Attorney Snow asked her, "Sue, how did you manage to kill Marcus Reil in Rockwood, Illinois?" Sue said, "I took the morning bus to Rockwood, Illinois spending the day there waiting till he got back to his apartment that evening. I knocked on his door and when he answered I knifed him in the heart. After that I took a later bus back to St. Louis." Attorney Snow asked her, "Sue, we understand how Marcus Reil's knifing came about but can you explain all the different hangings and mutilations that took place in regards to all those other older people?" Sue said, "Yes, I can explain how that all came about. I usually caught them off guard in the elevator one by one. I approached them with my murderous attire and mask, killing them instantly, knife, gun or whatever it took. I usually carried a knife with me for carving their bodies and draping their innards around the inside of the elevator for everybody to see. When I knew everybody was downstairs eating I transferred some of the bodies into my own apartment till I decided what to do with them."

Attorney Snow had another question to ask. He said, "Sue, can you explain how you got a four foot, small alligator into the elevator unnoticed by the other residents?" Sue said, "It wasn't that hard. I had the alligator in a covered, wire box and pulled him into the elevator about the time I knew there would be some older men and women taking the elevator. I checked the amount of people that would be riding the elevator the day before. It worked out perfect. After the alligator devoured Mr. Grimm I pulled him in the box out of the elevator and returned him that very same night to its rightful owner. Attorney

Simmons asked, "Did the owner ask you what you did with a four foot alligator?" Sue said, "No, and I didn't divulge any information either." Attorney Simmons had another unanswered question, "Sue, how did you get the snakes into the apartments and Mabel into the oven at the Pickwell Apartment Complex?" Sue said, "I stole a skeleton key from Mrs. Pickwell's wall in her office, entered the apartments while they were eating and released a certain amount of snakes into each apartment. I even put some into the toilet stool to give them a good scare. It sure worked! After the cooks were gone I stabbed Mabel in her apartment, cut her body into chunks and placed everything plus her head in the oven and turned it on warm for the night."

"Okay," Attorney Simmons said, "Let's see you explain this one!" How do you describe Mr. and Mrs. Adam Blasell's murders?" Sue made the remark, "I shot Mr. and Mrs. Adam Blasell execution style in the forehead with a gun that had a silencer on it so that it couldn't be heard. I kept their dead bodies in my room and buried them during the night when no would see me. Yes, I buried them in the backyard of the Pickwell Apartment Complex because it was handy."

Attorney Snow had several questions that needed to be answered. He asked, "Sue, how do you explain Stan, Martha and Lois's deaths?" Sue said, "I shot them also with my silencer gun, chopped them up and hid their bodies under the cement in the basement of the Pickwell Apartment Complex. He also asked her, "Sue, weren't you ever concerned that the bodies would be discovered under the cement by workers at some point in time?" Sue said, "No, not really. That thought never occurred to me." Attorney Snow said, "Thank you and you may step down to be seated."

Judge Cage announced, "Court will convene for fifteen minutes and then we will resume the interrogation."

Chapter 24
More Admissions of Guilt

Judge Cage is back on the bench to continue the interrogation of Sue Benson for the killings of twenty two residents of the Styles and Pickwell Apartment Complexes from 2005—2008. He announces, "Will Sue Benson step to the witness stand, please?"

Sue came forward and Attorney Snow continued with the procedure asking her, "Sue, how did you get Mr. Jack Pierce's cut up body into the freezer? Explain that, please." Sue finished the question with an explanation. She said, "First of all I stabbed Mr. Pierce repeatedly when I encountered him in the elevator. Then I transferred him down the hall to my room when all the residents were in the All Purpose Room watching a movie on television. After that I moved his body parts into a box and put them into a freezer when the kitchen staff was gone. It wasn't that hard. I could do it again if I had to." Attorney Snow made the remark, "Sue, the court is interested in how the three women died after eating turkey soup on Thanksgiving?" Sue said, "Well, I went to Mrs. Cane's room, killed her and cut her legs off at the groin leaving her to die. I left the room and went to my own room to cook one of the legs in a large kettle. I made a broth substituting small chunks of her leg instead of regular turkey meat and made soup which I took down to the pot luck supper on Thanksgiving. Mrs. Peebles, Mrs. Carl and Mrs. Skills ingested the soup and died."

Attorney Simmons has another question he would like to have answered. He asks, "Sue, how did you manage to kill Mr. and Mrs. Pickwell and not be seen by any of the residents?" Sue answered, "Well, I stabbed Mrs. Pickwell in the back while I was visiting her in her apartment one night. It was getting late so I carved her body into chunks, took it to my apartment, packed it into a box and mailed it from the post office downtown to the Pickwell Apartment Complex. It was a simple procedure." Attorney Simmons said, "Okay that explains that. Now tell the court how you did away with Mr. Pickwell?" Sue said, "That was probably the most difficult killing of all of them. I rented an older car at the cheapest rental business here in St. Louis and picked Mr. Pickwell up and told him I would give him a ride home from the convenience store. Instead of taking him to the Pickwell Apartment Complex I took him to an undisclosed location and stabbed him to death. I was prepared with a knife and a box for his body contents. After I cut his body into small chunks and packed them and his head into the box, I immediately took it down to the post office and mailed it to the Pickwell Apartment Complex."

Attorney Simmons asked, "How did you manage the killing of Mr. Rane?" Sue remarked, "I broke into Mr. and Mrs. Rane's apartment and stabbed him while he was still in bed. I chopped his body up in large chunks as Mrs. Rane watched in horror and disgust, leaving his head attached to his upper torso. I didn't waste any time running out a side door and down a dark alley."

Judge Cage announced, "We will have a fifteen minute recession and then resume court proceedings." Sue looks downtrodden and low in spirits as she whispers to Attorney Simmons.

Judge Cage walks back to his bench to resume the testimony of Sue Benson. He called Sue Benson to the stand and Attorney Snow continued the questioning. He asked Sue, "Can you explain how you executed the death of Mr. Brown in the elevator?" "Sue said, "I committed the crime just as you saw it in the elevator. I stabbed him, cut his heart out plus his legs, fingers and thighs, throwing the body parts on top of each other. There were volumes of blood on Mr. Brown, his body and the elevator floor."

Attorney Snow asked Sue, "Can you explain Mr. Cole's death?" Sue said, "Yes, that was an easy murder to commit. I robbed Mr. Cole, knocked him unconscious with a sharp blow to his head and tied a bed sheet around his neck which choked him immediately. I left him there to die with his black tongue hanging out of his mouth."

Attorney Simmons also asked, "Sue, did you play the part of the beast man when Mrs. Styles was murdered? We heard you wore that beast man costume to the Halloween party." Sue said, "Yes, I wore that beast man costume to the Halloween party and I wished I wouldn't have because that was a dead giveaway. It's too late now. What I actually did was confront Mrs. Styles in the elevator. She screamed and I started by chopping her head off and subsequently the rest of her body, chunk by chunk." Mr. Snow approached Sue saying, "Sue, this is the last death we need an explanation for and that is Mrs. Gladys Mission." Sue explained, "Oh Boy! That was something else! I stabbed Mrs. Mission repeatedly, then proceeded to cut her vital organs, intestines and all, out of her body and drape them off the ceiling itself. In fact, her intestines were hanging in a scalloped form off the edges of the ceiling. The remainder of her organs were piled in a corner of the elevator. I stuck the barrel of a gun in Mrs. Mission's mouth and I was surprised it stayed there." Mr. Snow made the comment, "Sue, this is the final question. Will you explain to Judge Cage and those present in court today your reason for committing twenty two murders from 2005—2008?" Sue answered, "The reason I committed these twenty two murders is because these were individuals that avoided and ignored me when I talked to them. When the few times they did answer me they were rude and obnoxious. In fact, I vividly remember being the object of ridicule and having everyone laugh and poke fun of me at different times to the point of being in tears. From that day on I decided to get even with them one way or another and I did. I feel like they deserved what they got. After all I treated them with respect and I deserved the same respect back. I am experiencing no remorse for anything. The only remorse I feel is for my sentencing and my life in prison hereafter. I know what that's like when I used to visit my mother, Jane Linton, in the St. Louis Prison for Women.

Judge Cage announced, "Very well, this concludes the remainder of Sue Benson's murder trial. Sue Benson is accused and being tried for the murders of twenty two people from 2005—2008. Court is adjourned until Monday, December 5, 2008 at 9:00AM for the sentencing. Thank you."

Sue was shackled at the wrists, wearing an orange jumpsuit, being led to the police van for her ride back to the St. Louis Police Department. She is being held in Maximum Security for the length of her stay.

Everybody left the courtroom including Sue's children, Albert and Jean. They will visit Sue later on today and speak with her by phone, separated by a screen, after they bring her out of her Maximum Security cell block. Sue is not allowed to talk to her mother, Jane Linton, anymore because she is incarcerated in Maximum Security at the St. Louis Police Department and Jane is incarcerated in Maximum Security at the St. Louis Prison for Women in St. Louis, Missouri.

In the meantime Jean and Albert, Sue's two children, picked up the phone singularly and visited with their mother at length about the court case and upcoming sentencing. By now it was getting close to supper time so Jean and Albert decided to leave saying, "Mother, we will see you in court Monday morning. Goodbye." Sue said, "Okay, goodbye" and looked after them as they walked down the corridor with tears misting up in her eyes as a feeling of depression overwhelmed her. She thought she might never see Albert or Jean again. She walked back to her cell just as supper was being wheeled into her room.

Chapter 25
Sentencing
Dec. 2009

Sue arose this morning with a feeling of foreboding engulfing her body because of the dreaded sentencing she will have to endure today. She has had a strange feeling about this sentencing for quite awhile now. What do you suppose it is? She dons an orange jumpsuit again, eats breakfast and will be transferred by van to the St. Louis District Court where her mother, Jane, was tried. When she walked into the courtroom her children, Jean and Albert, were seated five rows behind her with other people around them. The courtroom was packed as Judge Cage and the twelve jury members took their place. The bailiff and the attorneys got their earlier, shuffling through their papers knowing the outcome of this serial killer murder case in their minds.

After everybody was seated at 9:00AM Judge Cage announced, "Today we are gathered for the sentencing of Sue Benson in the murder trial case of twenty two victims that were killed by her." Judge Cage turned to Sue and said, "Sue, will you please stand up?" As soon as she stood up a member of the jury arose and said, "We, the jury, find the defendant guilty of twenty two accounts of murder in the first degree. The sentence for so many crimes of such an unusual nature is the death penalty at an undisclosed date." Judge Cage announced, "Sue Benson will start serving her sentence immediately in the Indianapolis State Prison for Women in Indianapolis, Indiana."

The courtroom was very quiet as the verdict was read, not expecting it to be the death penalty. When was the last time a person received the death penalty? No one can even remember. As soon as Sue heard the verdict her body began to crumble as two bailiffs ran to steady her and help her into a chair. She was crying uncontrollably and so were Jean and Albert since no one expected such a harsh sentence. People in the courtroom let out a gasp, sniffled and whispered among themselves at the outcome. The judge, jury and attorneys acted like they were not surprised at the outcome of this trial. Sue said her goodbyes to Jean and Albert, got in the car to be transported to the police station to await her trip tomorrow morning to the Indianapolis State Prison for Women in Indianapolis, Indiana. She will be incarcerated in prison until her death penalty is carried out.

Chapter 26
Sue's Arrival in Indianapolis, Indiana Prison for Women
2009

It was snowing when Sue arrived at the Indianapolis, Indiana Prison for Women in the police van from St. Louis, Missouri. A prison guard met them at the gate and escorted her into the prison which was similar to the one Jane is incarcerated. Sue would've liked to talk to her mother but she was not allowed to make any outside calls because she is confined in a Maximum Security cell.

Sue is in the main office of the women's prison waiting for the person in charge to make an assessment of her and assign her accordingly. The assessment included a job placement in the dishwashing part of the kitchen. She will start working in a few days, as soon as she is settled down and used to her new environment. She was handed several navy blue jumpsuits to wear and toiletry articles to use.

Monday, Sue arose at 5:00AM so she could shower, eat breakfast and start her new job in the kitchen at 6:00AM. She will work until 4:00PM with an hour off for lunch.

Sue is not making friends at the prison like she did at the Styles and Pickwell Apartment Complexes. Well, what can she expect with the life she led? Right?

All the inmates get an hour a day to go outside in the afternoon from 4:00—5:00PM. Since Sue is confined to a Maximum Security cell in prison she has to go to a smaller, isolated area not being able to talk to anybody. She stands against the prison building and reminisces about her friends and days gone by, her son and daughter, Jean and Albert. She thinks of her mother, Jane, who knows that she is in prison in Indianapolis, Indiana. Jane knows about Sue's sentencing, was very upset and beside herself with tears. She'll probably have a nervous breakdown once she hears about the electric chair. Sue never a had chance to call her mother because the inmates in Maximum Security cannot accept telephone calls or call out to anyone. Naturally, she was not able to go to the prison in person like she did before. Well, how is she going to notify her mother of her plight? Unless her two children, Jean and Albert, stopped at the St. Louis Prison for Women when they were on their way home to tell their Grandmother, Jane, what happened to Sue? They were planning to do that. What a sad state of affairs! Right?

Prison life is hard work from 5:00AM in the morning when she arises to 10:00PM in the evening when she retires for the night. No friends, very little conversation, boredom, no contact with the outer world and badly depressed. She needs to go to the prison infirmary for medication. She needs to do a lot of things but for what? To go to the electric chair? That's the end result. She should've thought twice before she committed twenty two crimes. "If twenty two people are rude and obnoxious towards you, you don't commit twenty two crimes. You just speak politely and ignore their actions. That's my philosophy."

The Dead of Winter—Mar. 2009

It has been three months since Sue was placed in Maximum Security at Indianapolis State Prison for Women in Indianapolis, Indiana. She has no idea when the date is set for the electric chair procedure to end her life but they will let her know. Yes, she feels bad that her life is finalizing but she feels no remorse for what she did because she still feels twenty two people deserved what they got. She feels sorrow because she won't see her mother, Jane, or her two children, Jean and Albert, anymore. She will continue working in the kitchen, going to the chapel on Sunday's for church services and doing the tasks that are required of her. Eventually she will receive a notice in regards to the day she will be sent to the electric chair.

Today was the day! Sue was called to the prison official's office to be notified of her electrocution date. The prison official said, "Sue, your electrocution date is set for next week Monday, March 10, 2009 at 10:00AM in the morning. If there is anything you have to attend to please let us know. We will notify your family as to the time and date. They have the option to attend but with my experience very few family members attend these procedures. Do you have any questions?" Sue said, "No, not really." The prison official said, "Very well. That will be all. Thank you." Sue arose and left his office more despondent than ever. She thought to herself, "By next week at this time I'll be dead."

March 10 rolled around sooner than she thought when she got up that morning. Instead of working in the kitchen Sue was gathering her few possessions together to either be given to her family or disposed of. At 9:45AM she was escorted by two prison guards to the execution chamber where the electric chair is located. Sue was seated in the electric chair with a blank, motionless stare on her face. A prison guard asked her, "Sue, do you have any last words you wish to say?" She said, "No." The prison guard said, "Very well. Thank you" The prison chaplain stepped forward and said a final prayer. A switch was flipped sending Sue's body into jerking spasms for a few minutes. After that waves of shock went through her body and brain causing her to go limp and fall forward. A groan escaped her lips and her eyes closed in death. At 10:00AM Sue's family wept in the privacy of their environment. Death was pronounced at 10:15AM. A few minutes lapsed and two prison guards removed her body to be sent to the Franklin Mortuary. It is a private funeral parlor the prison patronizes for cremation and burial at the family's request which is the St. Louis Cemetery in St. Louis, Missouri.

Jane, Jean and Albert have accepted Sue's life and death as best they can. If you treated her right she was a warm hearted, loving woman. If she thought you crossed her path she was just the opposite. Don't you agree?